IMMACULATE

IMMACULATE

Katelyn Detweiler

VIKING
An Imprint of Penguin Group (USA)

VIKING
Published by the Penguin Group
Penguin Group (USA) LLC
375 Hudson Street
New York, New York 10014

USA * Canada * UK * Ireland * Australia
New Zealand * India * South Africa * China

penguin.com

A Penguin Random House Company

First published in the United States of America by Viking, an imprint of Penguin Group (USA) LLC, 2015

Copyright © 2015 by Katelyn Detweiler

Penguin supports copyright. Copyright fuels creativity, encourages diverse voices, promotes free speech, and creates a vibrant culture. Thank you for buying an authorized edition of this book and for complying with copyright laws by not reproducing, scanning, or distributing any part of it in any form without permission. You are supporting writers and allowing Penguin to continue to publish books for every reader.

LIBRARY OF CONGRESS CATALOGING-IN-PUBLICATION DATA
Detweiler, Katelyn.
 Immaculate / Katelyn Detweiler.
 pages cm
 Summary: Mina, seventeen, has everything going for her until she discovers she is pregnant and no one, especially her boyfriend and her father, will believe that she is a virgin except for the few who have faith that miracles are possible and that her unborn child could be the greatest miracle of all.
 ISBN 978-0-451-46962-5 (hardback)
 [1. Pregnancy—Fiction. 2. Faith—Fiction. 3. Virginity—Fiction. 4. Family life—Fiction. 5. Friendship—Fiction.] I. Title.
 PZ7.1.D48Imm 2015
 [Fic]—dc23
 2014049410

Printed in the USA

10 9 8 7 6 5 4 3 2 1

Set in ITC Baskerville Std and Sympathique Pro

To Carebear & Denny,

because your faith makes all things possible.

"There are only two ways to live your life.
One is as though nothing is a miracle.
The other is as though everything is a miracle."
—ATTRIBUTED TO ALBERT EINSTEIN

the beginning

Whenever I think back to that night at the restaurant, that night that changed everything—and I do mean absolutely everything—I wonder if I could have done or said anything different, somehow convinced the old woman that she had the wrong girl. That my life was just fine as it was, no life-altering, world-altering miracles necessary, though I appreciated the once-in-a-few-millennia-or-so offer.

Or maybe . . . maybe there'd never been a choice at all, no right or wrong answer.

Maybe the decision had already been made for me from the second my life began.

At the time, she was just one more obstacle standing between me and my freedom, one more slice of wilting pizza to heat up in the oven, one more sticky table to wipe down before I could untie my apron and savor the last precious minutes of my Friday night. It wasn't even just a regular Friday—this Friday had been the last day of junior year, a night to rejoice, to be giddy and high on all the gloriousness of the summer that stretched out ahead. But instead

I was scraping grease off pizza pans and stacking towers of plastic dressing containers in the refrigerator.

I'd never seen her there before, an occurrence which in and of itself was something of note at Frankie and Friends' Pizzeria. Between me, my parents, and my seven-year-old sister, Gracie, we were somehow known or connected to most people in the town one way or another. More often than not I was serving overflowing plates of fettuccini Alfredo to one of my old elementary school teachers or one of my mother's colleagues from the Green Hill Historical Society, someone who would much rather talk about how I'd scored on the SATs or where I was applying to college than about our dinner specials for the night. The same was true for any public place in all of Green Hill, Pennsylvania—not that "all of" means that much in a town that spans about ten miles and has five thousand or so residents, give or take a few recent babies or nursing-home casualties—so, really, Frankie's was no exception. No grocery store, coffee shop, or doctor's office was safe from the threat of discovery and the inevitable and generally unnecessary conversation that followed.

I was staring at the clock by that point in the night, swirling a spoon through the vat of day-old garlic knots and oil, when I heard the bell above the front door jingle. I straightened and glanced back, hoping it was just Frankie or one of the guys from the kitchen coming in after a cigarette break out on the front lot. But instead there was a very short, very wrinkled old woman in a worn patchwork jacket, struggling to keep the front door open as she strained against her tall black cane. After successfully making it across the threshold, she lifted her hunched shoulders and took in the view, bright green eyes scanning the booths and the counter until her gaze met mine. She grinned at me, her lips curling to reveal two scattered rows of broken, yellowed teeth.

"Can I help you, ma'am?" I asked, shifting as best as I could into my perky waitress mode, an automated tone that probably did little to hide the fact that helping her was actually the last thing I wanted to do at 9:55 on a Friday night.

"Yes, dear, I think you can. I know you can, really." She smiled again, her eyes crinkling nearly all the way up to her hairline, a bright white tangle pulled into a loose knob at the top of her head, and started her slow, methodical shuffle to the closest booth.

"Can I start you off with a drink?" I asked, loud and pronounced, as I put a sticky menu down on the table in front of her. "We have Coke, Diet Coke, Sprite—"

"Just a water for now, my dear," she cut in. "With lemon and a little dollop of sugar, if you don't mind."

"Sugar water and lemon, coming right up," I said brightly, as if I got that request all the time, glad for an excuse to turn away and let the edges of my tight smile slip. I grabbed a small paper cup on my way through the kitchen and dragged it along the bottom of the cooler, at that point filled with mostly melted ice water. I sprinkled in a packet of sugar and topped it off with the last wedge of shriveled lemon, and then I started back for the dining room.

I could hear my phone vibrating on the shelf beneath the register, and I looked up at the clock. Ten on the dot. I knew it would be my boyfriend, Nate, checking in to see if I was still coming over to his place, where practically half of the junior class was already gathered, celebrating life and nearly three months of freedom. But I kept walking toward the table, efficiency being my top priority. Older people rarely ate more than half of the food on their plates, so with any luck, this lady would gum a few bites of pizza and be out in less than ten minutes.

"What else can I get for you, ma'am?" I asked, placing the cup between her shaky fingers. Her clasped hands were laced with veins so pronounced and so blue, I almost had to reach out and touch her, had to feel for myself the mark of that much time, that many years of life. I turned my gaze over to her face, the wrinkles etched so deeply into the papery white skin that her other features—her eyes, her nose, her mouth—seemed to poke out defiantly from the folds, as if they were determined not to be swallowed up and erased from existence altogether. She was without a doubt the oldest woman I'd ever seen in person.

"I think the water should be just fine for now," she said, and I snapped back, realizing how closely I'd been staring at her. She smiled again and reached out with one of her hands, patting my wrist as if she had somehow heard my thoughts. I flinched at the leathery cool of her touch.

"A little conversation would be nice, too. Would you sit with me for a bit?"

Frustration flashed across my face before I could check myself, but if the old woman noticed the brief slip, she appeared unfazed, nodding toward the opposite bench of the booth. Guilt settled into my stomach, and I knew I shouldn't reject her. It could have been weeks, months, since she'd had any real human interaction. Maybe she had no family, no kids or grandkids to take care of her. I thought of my own grandmothers, both gone, and missed them with such a sharp, surprising pang that I sat down without even realizing I'd made the decision.

"What a lovely, happy place to work," she said, her wispy voice crackling with effort. "Such wonderful decor, don't you think?"

I glanced around the dining room as if I hadn't seen it thousands of times before, and assumed she must be kidding. Frankie's was a complete pizza joint cliché, tables covered in faded red-and-white-checkered cloths, bunches of plastic grapes clumped along the ceiling, Catholic icons and other biblical paintings squeezed in against landscapes of the homeland and pictures of wine bottles and fancy cheese wheels.

She appeared to be sincere, though, no hint of sarcasm in her twinkling eyes as she looked up at the life-size portrait of the Madonna hanging above our table. It was fairly standard, a poker-faced Mary with a chubby baby Jesus in her arms, halos over their heads. I frowned, noticing the layer of dust coating the painting's thick bronze frame. That would have to be a job for tomorrow's waitress.

"Sure, it's nice enough, I suppose," I said. "I've worked here for so long, I guess I don't really think about it anymore."

"You're a dedicated young lady, working on a Friday night when you could be enjoying yourself instead." She reached out and covered one of my hands with her spindly fingers. "They're lucky to have you."

I blinked, shaking off her strange spell, and shifted my eyes back to the clock. Our kitchen guys, Carl and Johnny, were in the back with Frankie, prepping for tomorrow and no doubt waiting for me on any last plates and utensils that needed to be washed. My hand felt prickly, and I itched to pull it out from under the old woman's grip, but I couldn't bring myself to disappoint her so soon. There was something about her, the hopeful twist of her smile, the soft shine of her eyes, that made me want to please her.

"Do you live in town?" I asked, still curious how a woman like this could exist in Green Hill without me knowing.

"Oh no, no," she gasped, shaking her head. "I'm not from here. This isn't my kind of home."

I laughed out loud. "Yeah, you're not alone. Green Hill certainly isn't for everyone."

She looked puzzled for a second, tilting her head at my response. "I'm not sure I know what you mean, dear, but no bother. I must explain something to you now, something very important. I'm here in your town, in this restaurant, for a special reason." She paused for a few seconds, taking in a deep, rattling breath. "I'm here to see *you*."

A chill spread up through my arm, and I looked down at my hand, numb under the strange, unfamiliar pressure of her palm.

"Why would you be here to see *me*?" I paused, torn between the desire to humor her and the desire to put as much distance between us as possible. My eyes shifted over to the closed kitchen doors. Why hadn't Johnny or Carl come out to harass me about the dirty plates yet? They were usually so dependably cranky at the end of a shift. Why be so patient with me tonight of all nights?

I turned back to her. "We've never met before, ma'am," I said, slow and even, the same tone I would use if I were explaining some serious fact of life to a kindergartner.

"You don't know me. You couldn't possibly be in Green Hill to see me."

"Oh, Mina," she said. "Mina, Mina." She was shaking her head as if *I* were the five-year-old who needed to understand. "Just because we've never met before doesn't mean I don't know you."

I leaned back and jerked my hand free from her grasp. Not disappointing her no longer felt like the most pressing concern. "How do you know my name?"

"I've always known your name, Mina. I've always known everything about you . . ." Her voice trailed off. She bit down on her lower lip and squirmed in her seat, her body squealing against the shiny plastic upholstery.

"Oh, dear, I'm afraid I'm not explaining myself very well, am I?" she said after a few more tense seconds—tense seconds in which I was busy debating the ethics of defending myself in a physical altercation with this obviously very disturbed old lady. That ratty, moth-holed jacket of hers could have easily been hiding a whole treasure trove of potential weapons: a rusty letter opener, knitting needles, the broken shards of a reading glass. It was a balmy June night, after all, and the quilted coat was excessive—maybe it was serving some ulterior purpose beyond just keeping her warm. And her black cane, the cane that had seemed completely innocuous a few minutes ago, suddenly looked so ominous propped against the crook of her arm. Maybe those wrinkles were expertly molded on like a mask, some fancy trick of makeup, and she was actually a spry and powerful warrior who could ninja-kick me over the back of the booth.

Nate had made me watch too many superhero action movies for my own good. My already very creative mind didn't need the additional material.

"I don't want to scare you, Mina. That's really the last thing I want to do. I need you to trust me."

"And I don't want to be rude, but trusting a complete stranger who claims to know everything about me is a little difficult to do. You have to understand that," I responded. "I don't know a single thing about you. I don't even know your name. Who are you?"

"Good idea," she said, looking relieved and more at ease, a small smile back on her face. "Let's take it a little slower, ease into this a bit more." She extended her right hand and let it hover over the middle of the tabletop. "I'm Iris, and it's a pleasure to finally meet you."

I looked down at her hand, hesitating before giving her a few limp, halfhearted shakes. "Okay, Iris, please just tell me why you're here, and then I really have to clean up and close this place down for the night. There are people back in the kitchen waiting for me." *And,* I wanted to add, *I was supposed to be at my boyfriend's house, hanging out with all my friends and actually enjoying one small shred of my Friday* night. But no, I'm sitting here with you, instead. Not quite how I planned on kicking off my summer vacation.

"We've decided that it's time, Mina," she said, her small voice filled with a startling amount of conviction. "It's time. We've decided that you're ready, that everyone's ready. The longer we wait, the more trouble we'll see, and I think that the world has seen enough trouble, don't you?"

"Okay, Iris, I wanted to give you a chance, I really did, but to be completely honest, I'm starting to feel uncomfortable having this conversation. Incredibly uncomfortable, actually." I pushed back from the table and stood up.

"No, Mina, wait. I'm here to warn you . . ."

"Now you're *warning* me?" I asked, snapping at her. I could feel the heat spreading up the back of my neck and flaming out across my cheeks.

Iris drew back. Her face pinched inward, making her wrinkles even sharper and more severe. "No, no," she said, stumbling over her words. "*Warn* wasn't the right word to use. I'm so sorry. I'm making such a mess of this, aren't I? I'm not going to harm you, Mina, of course not. You're so important, so valuable to us. Keeping you and the child safe is all that matters now."

"Child? What child? Gracie? What in God's name are you talking about, Iris?"

Her green eyes, steady and unblinking, pierced me. "No, not your sister. Not Grace. Your child, Mina. *Your* child."

I could feel something in my knees starting to give way, a building tremor that threatened to bring me down to the tile floor. I took a deep breath as I backed away, toward the front counter, propping myself up against the glass pizza display case for support.

"I have no idea what you mean by that, Iris, but I need you to leave."

"But, Mina," she said, putting her cane down and steadying herself as she tried to push up from the booth. "You need to understand—"

"I don't need to understand anything you have to say to me. I just need you to leave."

A bang from the kitchen made us both jump. A very tall, very anxious-looking boy who appeared to be about my age was stumbling through the swinging doors, a big tray of dishes and cups balanced on his forearms. I stared wordlessly at this mystery intruder, sidetracked by his interesting choice in work attire—a bright green newsy cap shoved over messy black curls, and a brown pinstriped blazer rolled up to the elbows under his oil-splattered Frankie's apron.

"Hey. Mina, right?" he said, walking toward me, oblivious of Iris and the tension that hovered over us like a dark gray storm cloud. "I'm Jesse, Carl's nephew. Jesse Spero. Tonight's my first night training in the back." He grinned at me, and his nervousness seemed to fall away, his whole face lighting up in a flash of two precious dimples and a bright white smile that was made all the more perfect by the tiny gap in the middle of his two front teeth. Had I not been tangled up in one of the oddest conversations of my life, I would have been powerless to do anything but grin stupidly back.

I vaguely remembered Frankie saying something to me about the new kid, though I hadn't cared enough at the time to ask any questions. But in this moment, he was my new favorite person, my savior, and relief surged through my body.

"Jesse! It's so nice to meet you," I said, rushing forward to grab one side of the tray. "Let me help you with that."

As soon as I was close enough, I whispered into his ear. "The old woman over there is crazy, seriously crazy. I can't talk to her anymore. I'll explain more later," I added, though I didn't really mean it. For starters I wouldn't even know where to begin in explaining my conversation with Iris to anyone, let alone a stranger. And for some reason, repeating what she said, even if it was complete nonsense, made me feel uneasy. I'd much rather have just forgotten everything about Iris. Pretended the whole meeting had never happened.

"Would you mind covering for me and making sure she leaves while I go back into the kitchen?"

"Uh, sure, yeah, I guess," he said, looking over at Iris

and then back at me as if I were the crazy person in the room. This wasn't the best first impression I'd ever made, but given the circumstances, I could deal with my less than stellar showing.

"Thanks, Jesse, I really owe you," I said, grabbing my phone and my purse from under the counter.

"Mina, *no*! Wait!" Iris called out. "I need your approval, you have to accept . . ."

"*Yes*, Iris, *yes*, whatever you need to hear," I said, without turning back, already trying to erase her face from my memory.

I pushed through the kitchen door and found Frankie in the freezer taking cheese inventory, and told him that I had to leave straightaway—family emergency, no time to clean everything—but I'd make up for it during my next shift. He waved me off, lost in his calculations. I realized as soon as I stepped out into the back lot that I'd forgotten to grab my pile of tip money from the shelf near the register, but there was no way I was going back to the front of the restaurant. I'd just have to pick it up in the morning. The risk of losing a few twenties was greatly preferable to a second round with Iris. I ran to my old silver Jetta, never more beloved than it was in that moment, jammed the key in the ignition, and drove away from Frankie's and Iris as fast as the car would take me.

I debated driving away from Nate's, too, and just heading straight home, where I could hide away under my blankets and wake up tomorrow pretending that this all had been some silly nightmare. But I needed him close to me more than I needed to be alone. Nate was calm and predictable. Nate was solid, always. The world somehow felt much less scary when I was standing next to him, breathing in the same air he touched.

The street in front of his house and the driveway in the back were already packed in with cars, so I parked a few blocks over in an empty lot next to a hair salon. I jumped out and circled my car a few times, hesitating, before grabbing my phone and calling Nate.

"Mina?" he asked, yelling over the loud music and the laughter in the background. "Where are you? Are you still coming?"

"Hey," I said, relief flooding through me at the sound of his voice. "Can you . . . Can you meet me outside quick?"

"Is everything okay?" He paused, the noise around him fading away. "Hold on. I'm already on my way out." The phone clicked off.

I sprinted for three blocks, stopping to catch my breath at the edge of the sidewalk outside his house. The front door swung open. Nate stepped onto the porch and flicked the light on, his worried eyes searching for me in the hazy darkness stretching beyond his front steps. From where I stood he looked entirely lit up, his golden brown hair and fair skin glowing under the small circle of light.

"Mina! What's going on?"

I hurried up to the porch and grabbed his hand, pulling him down with me as I slumped onto the steps. He settled beside me, and I wrapped my arms around him, burying my face in his warm, familiar chest.

"I just . . ." I started, my voice faltering. I could feel the tears spilling out, soaking into his T-shirt. "I just had a long night at work."

"Meen," he said, pulling back to face me. "You're crying. What happened?"

For one crazy irrational second I wanted to tell him. Iris's name almost rolled off my lips. But I bit down and shook my head. Nate was too logical for this, too sure about the world around him—a world that could never include someone like Iris. She would just be a demented old lady to him, nothing more, and I would be demented, too, for letting her get to me. It was easier—safer—to say nothing. "The last day of junior year," I said, seizing whatever excuse I could think of fast enough. "I was lonely at work tonight, and it just made me think about this time next year. Everything will be so different."

"Oh, Mina," he said, his concerned frown lifting into a big little-boy smile, the same smile that still made my cheeks flush and my heart race after nearly two years of being together. Nate's face was strong and angled, "classically handsome," as my mom had always said. But his smile was goofy; it didn't quite match up with the rest of him. His smile made him softer. It made him mine. "Everything will *not* be so different. You'll have Izzy and Hannah no matter what. And you'll have me. Always. You and me, we're not meant to be in Green Hill forever." He squeezed me tighter and rested his chin on top of my head. "This is just the beginning, so no more tears."

I squeezed my eyes shut and nodded against him. I *was* being ridiculous.

My life was on track. I was going places.

We were going places.

And no strange old lady would have the power to change that.

That night I dreamed in bursts of light and explosions of colors like magical fireworks that would put even Disneyworld's most spectacular displays to complete shame. And when I woke up the next morning, Iris somehow felt like more of a dream than those colors, those brilliant colors that I could still see every time I closed my eyes.

the first trimester

chapter one

"Mina, wake up," Nate called out, splashing me from the edge of his round, stone-lined pool. "You look like you're burning, and I have to head out soon for DC, anyway. I'm meeting the rest of the debate team at the high school in an hour."

The cool water dripped down my hot, sticky arms, pulling me out of the hazy almost sleep I'd been slipping into. I peered up at him from behind my dark sunglasses. My eyelids felt so heavy, though, too heavy to hold up as the blazing August sun beat down on me.

"Can't I just lie here a little longer?" I asked, my eyes already closed again as I let my tube drift farther away from him. "You can go finish getting ready and come to get me when you have to leave."

"Are you okay, Mina? Seriously, it seems like you're tired all the time lately. Maybe you should see a doctor or something."

The massive, cloying knot that had been building in my stomach for the past few weeks tightened. "I'm fine," I said quickly, turning to hide my face.

"Are you still upset that I'm going to be away tomorrow for our anniversary?" Nate asked, and my whole body tensed at the edge of frustration in his tone. "I've told you already, Meen, I'm sorry that the schedule worked out this way. I really am. We'll celebrate as soon as I'm back on Monday. Trust me, I'd rather be with you than stuck in a conference room with a bunch of strangers in suits, but I promised the team. I can't let them down. You have to understand that."

But you can let me down, I thought, instantly glad that I hadn't said the words out loud. Nate was right. I had been pouting, and it wasn't fair to him. He'd be back in a few days, and we'd celebrate then. It was just a date on the calendar, and we had plenty of more monumental anniversaries ahead of us. Two years was nothing, really, not when we had the rest of our lives to celebrate milestones.

"I'm not mad. I promise, Nate. Just tired from the sun. Give me five minutes, okay? I'll meet you inside and help you with the rest of your packing."

"Okay," he said, "five more minutes. But then I want to hang out for a little before I have to leave." I could tell from his voice that he wasn't convinced everything was fine. I kept my eyes closed, but I felt him watching me, lingering by the edge for a few more seconds before he started off for the house.

I *had* been tired lately—every day, really, for the last month or two. More than tired, I was completely exhausted, drained of all life, no matter how many hours of sleep I got each night or how many cups of coffee I chugged each day. At first I hadn't tried to hide it from anyone, but the longer it went on, and the more that other . . . *symptoms* started cropping up, the more I'd been keeping most of my observations to myself. My lower back ached for no reason, I'd suddenly been peeing more than I ever had in my entire life, and my boobs were weirdly sore and sensitive. At first I'd been happy about that last one—I was convinced that I was finally going through a much-hoped-for growth spurt. But then I realized that my hormones must have been *seriously* out of whack because I hadn't gotten my period in two months either, and I was usually always regular to the day.

And now, most recently, the nausea. Every morning, like clockwork. I kept the water running, either the shower or the sink, so that my parents or Gracie wouldn't overhear and ask any questions, but the charade was just as exhausting as the actual puking. I'd tried doing some online research, but that only made everything infinitely scarier: diabetes; chronic fatigue syndrome; multiple forms of highly rare, highly untreatable cancers; depression. Nothing fit, not really, but I was still terrified. I wasn't ready to talk about any of it yet, not with Nate, not even with Hannah or Izzy, my two best, closest friends in the universe. To put everything into words out loud for anybody else to hear made it feel too serious, too significant. Too real.

But if Nate was starting to pick up on something, maybe I wasn't as good at hiding everything as I'd hoped. Or maybe Nate just knew me too well.

I was heading to Hannah's house after Nate's for a much-needed sleepover with her and Iz. Maybe it was time to talk about some of this with them. Or . . . no, maybe later would be better. I'd know when the time came, if it came. If it didn't all blow over first.

I sucked in air and slid down through the tube into the icy, tingling water, letting my whole body feel numb and weightless for a few seconds before paddling toward the stairs. I wrapped my towel around me and started slowly up the cobbled walk, trying to make my face look relaxed, carefree.

I was suddenly glad that Nate would be away for the weekend, off to DC with the school debate team for some prestigious national competition, even if it was our anniversary. I had no doubt he'd come home in a few days with a heaping pile of awards. Because that was Nate, always off achieving and succeeding and making his mark on the world. I mostly loved him for it, though a tiny part of me had always resented it, too, even if I had to keep that part to myself. *My boyfriend's just too ambitious and dedicated* didn't seem valid, not when other girls were complaining that their boyfriends smoked too much pot or only cared about video games and beer and baseball. But I still couldn't help wondering sometimes if he cared about his ten—or was it eleven? I'd lost count—extracurricular activities more than he cared about me.

I'd miss him, of course, but I could probably use the time to focus on me. I needed some space to sort out everything happening to my body, everything I was feeling for no clear reason.

I slipped in through his back door and made my way along the familiar path up to his bedroom. Nate's back was to me as he leaned over his keyboard, typing, and I paused in the doorway, admiring him—his perfectly tousled chestnut brown hair, the summer freckles that sprinkled over his warm golden skin, the way the sleeves of his old soccer jersey stretched over his strong, athletic arms.

No matter how long we'd been dating, I still couldn't always believe that *Nate Landis* was actually my boyfriend—probably because I'd had a crush on him since the very first day of kindergarten, a crush that I certainly never thought would come to anything at all. I was the nerdy, chronic overachiever—though nerdy in an *endearing* way, I hoped—the highest ranked in our grade and likely valedictorian next year. But Nate was the wonder boy of both academics and athletics: straight As, captain of the basketball and soccer teams, president of our graduating class, head of a community service group that he had started up during our freshmen year.

Somehow, regardless of any social imbalances, we had become the power couple who everyone assumed would last long past high school and college. I had visions of us going off to some Ivy League school together, maybe Princeton or Brown, and of the late nights studying and having sleepovers in each other's dorm rooms, traveling for our semester abroad in the same city, making new friends who we'd have for the rest of our lives. After graduation, Nate would go to law school, and I'd follow him there. I wanted to be a writer—or an English teacher to start maybe, with novels later down the road—and teachers and writers could live anywhere. Nate and I didn't talk about the plan much, but that was because we didn't have to. That was just how it would be.

I stepped lightly across the room and slid my arms around his waist. "Hey," I whispered, hugging him closer as he jumped, startled. "Sorry for being so spacey lately. It's just thinking about our last year, college, all the applications . . . But I'm fine. Really."

It felt like a lie as soon as it was out of my mouth. But at least Nate seemed satisfied, squeezing me closer to him and pressing us together, hip to hip. And I *was* fine. Probably. Or at least I felt fine then, with his arms around me, and that was what mattered.

He bent down to kiss me, easing me backward until I was on his bed, my legs wrapping around him. His hair tickled my forehead as he dangled over me, and I closed my eyes, letting the total happiness of the moment fill me.

No, I definitely had nothing to worry about.

Nate pulled back, a lazy grin on his face. "Your nose is bright red, Meen. I warned you." He leaned down and kissed the tip of my nose, a soft brush of his lips that then traced up to my forehead, my hairline. "But luckily, it's adorable on you."

The front door slammed, and his mom called from below. Nate sighed, pushing himself up. Our kisses usually ended with him sighing these days—sighing because that was all there ever really was. We'd fooled around a little, of course, but we'd still never even rounded third base. I had been scared to take it any further, scared that if we did, we'd both let it go all the way. Nate didn't pressure me, but I wasn't naive. I knew that he'd be more than *okay* with it if I decided I was ready. But I'd always wanted to wait until at least college to lose my virginity, until I was living on my own and old enough to make the right decision. Now that we had been together for almost two years, though, I was starting to reconsider. I was starting to think that maybe, just maybe, it *could* happen soon. That I actually *wanted* it to happen soon, and waiting for college was a pointless and outdated notion. An arbitrary moral rule created by a much younger, more innocent Mina. But I wasn't ready to tell Nate, not yet, just in case I changed my mind again.

He tugged me up and gave me another quick peck on the nose. "I guess I should finish packing anyway. You shouldn't distract me like that, Meen. I have important things to do."

I laughed. No one could distract Nate. Not really. He was too determined for anything to throw him off track. Ever.

But that didn't mean I would stop trying.

I woke up at Hannah's house the next morning to the smell of bacon and eggs wafting up from the kitchen—and the immediate urge to retch out my insides all over the side of her bed. I was, very unfortunately for all of us, squeezed between Hannah and Izzy, and therefore prevented from any easy access to the floor, let alone a trash can or a toilet. And so I was forced to take the only possible option available—I threw up on myself. All down the front of Hannah's old YMCA T-shirt that I'd borrowed the night before, and all over her bright pastel paisley comforter.

"Jesus, what the hell, Meen?" Izzy said, throwing the covers back and launching herself off the bed. Her already very large, very pronounced brown eyes were wide open and staring at me with horror. "That's so completely nasty. Why in God's name didn't you go to the bathroom?"

"She's obviously sick and couldn't help it, Iz. Don't yell at her," Hannah chimed in from my other side.

I ignored them both and proceeded to puke, once again, right onto my lap.

"Izzy! Get the trash can! Don't just stand there staring at her," Hannah said, her instinctive need to nurture kicking in. She grabbed a wad of tissues from her nightstand and started dabbing at my chin and lips.

Izzy sighed dramatically as she pushed back the hood of her Green Hill High basketball sweatshirt and pulled her stick-straight black hair up into a ponytail. She picked up the trash can as commanded and held it out to me, arms stretched, refusing to get any closer.

Hannah leaned over me and grabbed the trash can with one hand, keeping the other on my shoulders as she rubbed gentle, calming little circles.

"What's wrong, sweetie?" Hannah asked. "Did you just wake up feeling sick?"

I wanted to lie. I'd planned on lying, actually, the words all set to pop from my lips, when suddenly tears burst out and made my decision for me. Not just tears, but the type of heavy, racking sobs that make any sort of intelligible speech impossible.

"Mina? What is it?" Izzy asked, her voice softening, the tough girl from a minute before immediately gone and replaced with the best friend I'd known since second grade. She balled the infected comforter into a heap at the bottom of the bed and sat down next to me.

It was a few minutes before I could slow down, take some deep breaths, and pull myself together, and in the meantime Hannah and Izzy patted my back, pushed my knot of hair behind my ears, and covered me in a fresh, untainted blanket.

"What's going on, Meen? Talk to us," Izzy said, staring straight into my eyes with her trademark blend of concern and impatience.

"I don't know," I whispered, shifting my gaze down to my pale hands, still clasped and shaking around my knees. I focused on the dull, rhythmic hum of the air conditioner, whirring from Hannah's window as it blasted frigid puffs of air into the room. I pulled the blanket tighter around my shoulders, though it wasn't just the cold that was making my body tremble.

"Well, you obviously know something to be crying like that. Right?"

"Isabelle, stop pushing her," Hannah said with an unusual edge to her voice that caught me by surprise. "She'll tell us when she wants to tell us, okay?" I turned to look at Hannah, her soft blue eyes so full of love and worry. She had a stray blonde curl tucked in between her small pink lips, a nervous habit she'd had since the first day I'd met her in preschool.

These are your best friends, I reminded myself. Two people who I knew inside and outside as well as I knew myself. Maybe even better than I knew myself, at least lately. All of a sudden the need to keep it all a secret felt ridiculous. Unnecessary. A waste of precious time, as well as anxiety, that would have been much more manageable divided three ways. We faced everything together. Always.

"I don't know what's wrong with me," I started, still looking down to avoid seeing their distressed faces. "I've been throwing up every morning for the past week—week and half, I guess—but it's more than that. There have been lots of little things, things that I've tried to just ignore, but they keep piling up and I don't know what to do . . ." My voice caught, and I pinched my eyes shut, fighting off more tears. I had to keep going—I needed them to know everything, and I needed them to worry with me. "My back's been weirdly sore and achy. I have terrible headaches, and I can't stop peeing. I get dizzy out of nowhere, my boobs hurt, and I'm just so tired—so tired no matter how much I sleep."

"You have looked a little rough around the edges this

week," Izzy said. "I figured it was just all the manic college stressing, though, so I didn't want to say anything that would upset you. You've had some seriously intense black circles."

"Thanks, Iz," I said, almost smiling. "Blunt as always. Very helpful."

"You know you love me and my gloriously unfiltered mouth." She squeezed my leg and leaned into me, her chin propped against my shoulder. I could feel her eyes on me, processing, evaluating, trying to come up with a rational explanation. Izzy always had answers. Her entire world was built on them.

"So do you have any ideas, Meen?" Hannah asked quietly.

"Not really, no. I've spent unhealthy amounts of time researching online and freaking myself out, but nothing seems to cover all the symptoms. Nothing I could find explains everything. Nothing makes sense."

"What about your parents? Have you told them?"

"No. I mean, I've complained about being tired and my back hurting, but they've just written both off as the stress of senior year coming up and college applications and all the shifts I've had at Frankie's lately. I didn't want to tell them about everything else and get them all worked up, not yet . . . I keep hoping it'll all just go away on its own. And it's probably nothing, just a phase, so why scare them unnecessarily? Right?" I suddenly felt very hopeful. Ridiculous, actually, for ever feeling so worried.

"I don't know, Meen," Hannah said, grabbing my hand, her voice still unnervingly soft and whispery. "I'm no doctor, but it kind of doesn't sound like nothing."

The balloon of hope popped before it had moved even an inch off the ground. I shuddered as I felt another wave of sickness rise in my throat, yelling for Hannah and Izzy to move away. I grabbed the trash can and heaved out every last possible drop until I was convinced that there could be nothing left inside me but blood and veins and organs.

When I finally finished, the girls were still and quiet next to me. I wanted Hannah to wrap her arms around me and say something cheery and optimistic. I wanted Izzy to jump off the bed in disgust, to joke about how completely gross and appalling I looked.

"Mina . . ." Izzy started, and then stopped herself. She seemed nervous and hesitant, which was unsettling. Izzy was rarely nervous or hesitant about anything.

She took a deep breath and looked right at me, her eyes sharper, harder than I would have expected. I tensed, waiting for whatever terrible words were about to come out of her mouth.

"Mina, did you have sex with Nate and not tell us? Because I hate to say it, but everything you're going through sounds pretty damn similar to what you'd be feeling if you were pregnant."

I laughed. Shrieked, more accurately. Hannah flinched from the sound, but Izzy looked unfazed, cold and stiff.

Pregnant?

Ridiculous. Absurd! Entirely and insanely absurd. I kept laughing. I was shaking, crying from laughing so hard, while they both just watched, stunned by my reaction.

And then, with a pang so unexpected and so harsh that I gasped, choking on the last, frozen laugh, I thought of Iris. I thought of that night. And all her words, her strange and terrible words, flooded through my mind, bursting from that little back corner where I'd hidden them so carefully and neatly for the past two months.

"Meen?" Hannah asked slowly, cautious about pushing the question. "Is that a possibility? Because Izzy's right: all the symptoms add up. You know my sister's over eight months in, and this is all the stuff she complained about at the beginning."

"Why didn't you tell us?" Izzy broke in, loud and accusing. She jumped off the bed and stood, glaring, hands on her hips, as if she couldn't bear to be any closer to me. "Seriously, Meen, I thought we told each other everything. Why would you hide having sex with your boyfriend you've been dating for two years? Do you really think we'd judge you? I don't get it. I just really don't get it."

"I didn't have sex with Nate, Izzy. I swear to God. Call him up and ask him right now. I'm a virgin. I promise, I'm still a virgin. I need you guys to believe that."

"So you're not pregnant, then?" Izzy asked, her voice only slightly less damning than before. "You're saying there's absolutely zero possibility that you're pregnant right now?"

I wanted to say no, wanted to promise them that it would be physically impossible for a baby to be growing inside me. But all I could hear was Iris, her words playing on repeat, louder and clearer each time until I was sure my head was actually and literally going to explode all over Hannah's pretty pink and lavender bedroom. *Keeping you and the child safe is all that matters now. Your child, Mina. Your child.* Spinning, twirling, looping, over and over and over: *your child, Mina. Your child. I need your approval.*

Yes, Iris! Yes. I'd said yes. I'd said yes to Iris. What did that mean? What had she been asking?

Why had I said *yes*?

This was crazy. I was crazy. Genuinely, certifiably, without a doubt crazy.

"I mean, no, I don't think so, of course I don't. But . . ." My voice cracked, my brain still resisting saying the words out loud.

"How is there a 'but' in this situation? Did you fool

around with Nate? Get a little too close to be completely safe?" It was Hannah this time, probing, more critical than I'd ever heard her before, at least directed toward me.

"No, it's not that at all," I said, frustrated that I couldn't make them understand what I needed to say. But really, who *would* understand? Who could take any of this seriously? I mean, I probably wouldn't trust me if I were them.

I barely trusted me as it was.

A pregnant virgin? Unless I was an asexually mutated freak of a human, of course—some highly advanced form of the hydra we had learned about in biology—and a baby would just grow like a bud from my body and break away when it was fully mature, then quite frankly, the explanations for my pregnancy seemed a bit limited.

The fact that I was even considering the possibility only added to the inevitable diagnosis of psychosis and a future in a locked room covered in wall-to-wall white cushions. Maybe I had hallucinated that whole night with Iris; maybe she wasn't real and I had made up that whole conversation in my head, just me and myself. Too many hours on my feet that day, too much heat pouring out from the brick oven, too many vapors from the cleaning solution we used to bleach the rags.

"Then what is it, Mina?" Izzy yelled, cutting through my fantasy, her cheeks glowing red with hurt and anger. "Because you won't say you're not pregnant, but you won't admit to having sex, so what the fuck are you trying to say? We want to help you, but you're making that pretty impossible right now. Stop speaking in code and just tell us the goddamn truth, or I'm leaving, because I'm supposed to be one of your best friends and I don't deserve to be lied to."

"No, Isabelle, you're right," I said, meeting her gaze and forcing her to look, really look, at the sincerity in my big blue eyes that couldn't possibly be faked. She knew me too well, too long for any serious deceit to slip past her radar. That was my one hope, at least, and I clung to it.

"I'm scared to say what I'm thinking, because you probably won't be able to believe me. You'll think I'm crazy, or even worse, crazy *and* a liar, and I don't think I can handle that. Not right now, not with everything else going through my head." I paused, twisting a pillow with my sweaty hands to calm myself. "But I'm going to try. I'm going to tell both of you exactly what I'm thinking, what I know, because you deserve that."

And so, with much awkward fumbling and stopping and starting and backtracking, I told them about Iris. I told them every last detail I could remember, from what she wore to where we sat to every word and look she gave me. Strange, but even though I had rarely let myself think about her since it had happened, she was still there. Seared into my memory, as bright and vivid as the night we met, whether I wanted her there or not.

Neither of them said anything after I finished the story. Hannah and Isabelle sat in a daze, looking at the floor, the ceiling, anywhere that wasn't me. I didn't want to press, even though the desire to know what they were thinking about Iris, about me, was burning me alive, top to bottom.

Finally, right about when I couldn't possibly wait another second without combusting, Hannah spoke.

"I think we should go out and get you a pregnancy test. It might be nothing—it's probably nothing—but we need to know that for sure."

"You believe me?" I asked, so relieved and happy to have my best friend back at my side that the world almost felt right again.

Hannah bit her lip so hard that I could see a small bubble of bright red blood pool at the edge of her two front teeth. "I'm not saying that, Mina. I don't know what I'm saying, at least not yet. I want to believe you, but I have to think there's something to this story that you're not saying. Maybe there's something to this story that you don't even know." I could sense that a part of her wanted to stop there, go back, and rewind, but she took a breath and kept going. "I've heard that sometimes when something really bad and terrible happens, people block the whole thing out. Make themselves forget without even realizing. Maybe, I don't know . . . Maybe something like that happened to you?"

"Are you . . . are you saying I might have been raped?" I stammered, my air cut off, suffocated by the massive weight of my disappointment. She didn't understand, not at all. "You think I wouldn't know, wouldn't have felt something, some kind of pain that I would remember?" Of all the equally improbable theories, rape would never have occurred to me. Maybe it should have, I don't know, but somehow I knew—I knew without a doubt, with every part of my body, every toenail, every hair, every pore—that it wasn't the answer.

Hannah was crying now, almost as hysterical on the outside as I felt on the inside. But she couldn't reach out to me and I couldn't reach out to her, and so we both sat there—together but still so separate.

"Okay," Izzy said loudly from across the room, keeping her distance from the bed. "We're going to the pharmacy." She sounded matter-of-fact and in control, the Izzy I knew and loved so well. "Let's go. Now. I'll drive." And with that she grabbed her sneakers and her keys and walked out the bedroom door, not giving a single look back, not a hint of what was actually going through her mind.

Hannah sniffled a few times and stood up, sliding her sandals on and running a brush through her fluffy morning hair. She picked up her purse then, glancing over at me to make sure I was going to follow Izzy, too. I nodded and slowly pulled myself out from the tangled blanket, easing down onto the floor one leg at a time. The idea of doing something, anything, to finally acknowledge everything that was happening felt good. It felt right.

"Thanks," I said to Hannah so quietly that I wasn't quite sure I'd actually managed to say it out loud. But then she walked over to me and took my hand in hers.

"Listen. I don't know exactly what's going on with you, Mina. But I do know that no matter what shows up on that stick, whether it's a pink plus sign or a blue minus or even a big green damn squiggle, I'll be there right by your side and we'll sort it all out together. Okay?"

"Okay." I smiled for the first time that morning. "I should probably change out of this grotesque shirt first," I said, catching a glimpse of myself in her full-length mirror.

"Sounds like a good idea. Clean yourself up a bit, and I'll go down to the car and let Isabelle know that you're on your way. I give her ten seconds before she starts laying on the horn, and I don't want my parents asking too many questions about what we're up to." She squeezed my hand and let it drop, pulling the door closed behind her as she left the room.

I stepped closer to the mirror, so close that the tip of my still-red nose brushed against the cool glass, and my features became a hazy blur of blue and pink and milky white skin. I pulled back a bit, gripping the sides of the mirror so I could really see the girl standing in front of me. Frizzy nest of brown waves, swollen, red-rimmed eyes, cracked lips, stick-straight body without even the hint of any curves.

I couldn't be a mother. I was still a girl. A sloppy, filthy mess of a girl at the moment.

I stared blankly at my reflection for another minute or so, until I realized that, without thinking about it, I had moved my right hand off of the mirror and rested it against my stomach instead, my fingers spread wide in an embrace. I jerked it back down to my side and turned away, moving toward the dresser for a change of clothes.

I'd buy the test, pee on the stick—maybe two or three or four sticks just to be sure, just to quiet those ridiculous crazy voices in my head. I'd know without a doubt that I wasn't pregnant, and then I'd never have to think about Iris, not ever again.

chapter two

"I really wish we'd thought to bring ski masks or paper bags or something," I said, looking out across the parking lot at the all-too-familiar Reed's Pharmacy sign hanging above the faded brick storefront. This was where I'd gone with my mom when I was little to pick out bubble bath and candy bars, the store where Hannah and Izzy and I had bought our first glittery lip gloss and our first bottles of nail polish. The image of me buying a pregnancy test in those same aisles felt so wrong and so out of place, as ridiculous as the idea of my dad stopping for a quick post-work Budweiser at the dirty local strip club just outside of town. It shouldn't and couldn't happen, not ever, not in our predictable little Green Hill world.

Green Hill was like the flannel down comforter that had been on my bed for as long as I could remember—on some nights it was just what I wanted, a warm nest to burrow away in, so familiar and cozy and secure. But on others it was too heavy, suffocating me and trapping me in the middle of the night. I'd wake up sweaty and panicked with my legs captive under the weight of the feathers, my hands clawing at the folds to pull myself free. On those nights it was never easy to fall back asleep. I'd prop myself up with pillows on the ledge of my windowsill, staring out across the starlit fields that sprawled in every direction from my house.

Green Hill was my home, but even with all the wide, open spaces, I somehow still felt trapped sometimes.

And this—this was certainly one of those times.

"Izzy, *please*." I could hear myself whining, but I was desperate—close to unhinged, really, after everything that had already happened that morning. "There's no way we're not going to run into someone we know in there. I guarantee that the whole town will hear before noon that Mina Dietrich was spotted buying a pregnancy test from sweet old Mr. Reed. I can't. I can't do it, guys. Can't we drive to another pharmacy? Please? Somewhere outside of town?"

"Meen, no offense, but you're totally not in any position to be making demands of me right now," Izzy said, turning around to give me a pointed look from the driver's seat. Her brow crinkled, though, and she sighed. "But, as much as I hate to admit it, you do have a point. And it's not just your reputation at stake. People could think you're doing it for me or Hannah to cover for us." She put the key back in the ignition and started the car. "You win. We'll go to the Walmart in Kauffmanville." She turned the radio on, loud enough that any conversation was out of the question.

I rested my head against the cool leather interior of the door and tried to relax, closing my eyes against the blur of Main Street outside my window. I didn't want to see Frankie's and that front door that Iris had used to walk into my life. We'd be passing Nate's house in a few minutes, too, another sight I wanted to avoid. *Our anniversary,* I realized, my stomach instantly churning over the cruel irony of the date. I hadn't checked my phone yet that morning, and I couldn't bring myself to look now. How would he react if he knew what I was doing? If he knew that I was crazy enough to think that there was even the smallest fraction of a fraction of a chance that I could be pregnant because of what some random old lady had said to me at Frankie's a few months ago?

He would break up with me.

The words flashed in my mind, big and bright, before I'd even had the chance to realize I was thinking them. No. He wouldn't dump me. Not after two years. And regardless, the test would without a doubt—or at least only a very tiny, practically almost negligible, barely worth mentioning doubt—be negative, so I'd never have to tell him that any of this had ever happened. Hannah and Izzy would never tell anyone, even if they did have their doubts about my sanity. And if it came down to it, if I was pregnant—and I wasn't—but if I was . . .

I refused to finish that sentence.

Instead I forced myself to sing along with the radio for the rest of the car ride, forbidding my brain from saying anything but the lyrics. Someone else's words felt much safer than my own.

After what seemed like too much time and somehow still not nearly enough, we pulled up to the bright blue Walmart fortress that my dutifully ethical mom had raised me to always avoid. She'd search high and low in every last local, family-owned store in Green Hill or any of the nearby towns before taking a penny of her money anywhere else. She'd certainly never go to Walmart for something she could buy in Reed's, even if it cost half the price. But, given the circumstances, I'm pretty certain that even she would approve of this exception. At that moment Walmart was my only hope for any kind of salvation, at least in terms of my reputation. And reputation was everything in a place like Green Hill.

I grabbed at the door handle and leaped out onto the pavement before I could be paralyzed by any second-guessing. Izzy walked around to my side of the car, glancing at me for a second before she looked down at the ground and jammed her hands tight into the pockets of her green and gold school basketball sweatshirt. She had lived in that hoodie all of junior year, and had spontaneously cut off the arms a few months ago to make it short-sleeved and summer-proof, a crime of fashion that Hannah and I could never let go of, especially when we were out in public. I wanted to joke about the ridiculous frayed strings dangling around her arms, make her laugh like always, pretend that it was just another typical Saturday morning with the girls. But I couldn't make my lips push out the words, and I doubted she would have appreciated them much even if I had.

Hannah opened her door and stepped out between us, a few beats behind like always. The three of us stood there for a minute, still and silent, awkwardly unsure of one another. I closed my eyes to take in the moment—the moment of uncertainty that came before. Before whatever it was that would come after. Because in that moment, I could still have all my doubts. And in doubts, there was hope.

I heard Izzy start moving next to me, shuffling toward the entrance, and the moment faded away. The before was disappearing, the after fast approaching.

We walked in silence until we spotted the end of an aisle with a bright pink tampon display, which seemed like a reasonable place to start. I pushed past the basic monthly supplies into more unfamiliar territory—creams and suppositories for yeast infections, douches, deodorizing wipes, anti-itch powders and rinses. I cringed and moved farther along the aisle, deeper into the heart of the feminine mystique, and felt my cheeks turn pink as soon as I saw the rows upon rows of condoms in every shape, size, color, and texture imaginable. I felt nervous just standing there, that close to bottles of lube and warming gels, so entirely out of my element. I turned my head left and right to check both ends of the aisle, just in case someone had followed the three of us in. But no, it was just Izzy and Hannah. There was no one—well, no one but my two best friends—to judge me, and nothing to be nervous about.

But what about security cameras? Was this being filmed? My heart skipped, and I looked up to the ceiling and along the walls and tops of the shelves, but I couldn't see anything. *You're being ridiculous, Mina.* People buy condoms all the time. I'm *seventeen*, after all. It's not that crazy of a concept to think I might have sex someday.

Though I seriously doubted I'd even consider sex for years after all this.

I walked a few more steps and stopped when I saw a purple box with the words OVULATION PREDICTOR. I scanned the nearby shelf space. First Response, e.p.t., Clearblue. All words I'd heard in the background on TV commercials or seen in magazine ads, but nothing that had ever been remotely relevant to my life before.

I turned to Hannah and Izzy, both still staring, fascinated, at the rainbow of sex in front of them. I wasn't the only slightly behind-the-times seventeen-year-old in our little group—Hannah was still a virgin, of course, like me, and though Izzy had given it up last summer to her kind-of boyfriend at the time, a few rapid-fire hookups on the basement couch did not a seasoned expert make.

I coughed to get their attention, and they both snapped out of their dazes.

"So I'm assuming you're both as clueless about this as I am, but any suggestions?"

Hannah looked up at the boxes, squinting her eyes. "I know my sister was rambling about pink plus signs when she called to tell me the news. So I guess we could start with that? The test worked for her, at least."

"Yeah, that makes sense," I said, picking up the box that showed a magnified image of two sticks and a clear, irrefutable plus and a minus. It was a two-pack, which was good. The more evidence to prove that everything was normal, the better.

"But maybe you should get another brand, too, just in case?" Hannah suggested. "So you can be one-hundred-percent sure that they show the same result."

I nodded and grabbed another box that also showed two sticks on the front, but one had the word *pregnant*, the other *not pregnant*. Cut-and-dry, I liked that. No reading and rereading the explanation just to make sure I had the signs and meanings right. I glanced at the price stickers on each package. Almost forty dollars. Damn. That was a good chunk of tip money, but it was a small price to pay for my sanity.

Tip money. The thought reminded me of something awful—I was supposed to work the closing shift that night. But I'd have to worry about that later. After. One problem at a time.

"Okay then, I think I'm set," I said, trying to sound infinitely cooler and braver than I felt. "Let's get out of this place, please." I could do this. Pay for the tests, drive back to Hannah's, pee on the sticks.

Then this would all be behind me.

I wedged the boxes between my crossed arms and started toward the front registers, hoping that other shoppers passing by wouldn't notice what I was holding. *I'm a virgin*, I wanted to scream. *A virgin! Stop judging me!*

The whole confidence act crumbled as soon as I got in line to pay. The cashier looked sweet, plump and middle-aged—she was definitely someone's mom. What would she think of me? Would she say something? Ask me anything?

Izzy reached out and grabbed both boxes. "I'll do it," she said, avoiding my eyes. "Just give me the cash."

I was so stunned and relieved, I couldn't find the

words to thank her. I just nodded and fumbled through my purse for the wad of bills I had stuffed into an envelope after my last shift. Izzy took the money from my hands and stepped closer to the customer being rung up in front of her, casually putting both boxes down on the conveyor belt. She looked completely nonchalant and at ease, as if she were buying a box of Kleenex or a new toothbrush, not a test that would determine if another human being was growing inside of my body. *Yeah, lady*, her calm demeanor said, *I'm buying a pregnancy test. So what? Making babies is a natural part of life. Give me my change, and let's both move on with our days.*

God, I loved Izzy. I hoped that I would be half as composed and courageous as she was being if this was happening to her or Hannah.

The cashier didn't so much as blink when she scanned and bagged the tests. I guess pregnant high school girls weren't such a shock to her after all. Teens in small, backwoods places like Green Hill and Kauffmanville and most other towns within an hour or so radius of here didn't have many options when it came to entertainment. A few girls in my grade had actually already had babies, though I couldn't say that any of the pregnancies so far had been particularly surprising or newsworthy. They were the girls you'd expect it from, I guess, the ones who'd carried their *reputations* long before any babies came along—the girls who had worn eyeliner and pushup bras since fifth grade, bumming cigarettes from older boys and cutting as many classes as they wanted, because their parents either didn't notice or didn't care one way or the other what their kids did. They were the girls who no one expected to ever go to college, to ever leave our town at all. There were no shockwaves rippling around the halls when their bellies started to show. But Mina Dietrich—or better yet, *Menius*, as some of the kids still called me, short for Mina the Genius, a nickname from middle school that I could never seem to shake—with the highest grade point average in the class and who was the girlfriend of Nate Landis? It was safe to say that there would be a reaction.

"Where do you want to take the tests?" Hannah asked, her arm linked in mine as the three of us walked through the exit and into the brilliantly blue-skied and sunny late-August day.

The air was dense and sticky and infused with the smell of sweet, powdery doughnuts being boxed by the thousands at the factory on the next lot over. It felt too hot and summery to believe that senior year, our last year at Green Hill High, my last year with Izzy and Hannah by my side, could possibly start next week. I'd never been good with lasts, and the next year would be bursting at the seams with them. I shook the thought off, though—worries for another time. I had nine months of school to get through first.

Nine months. I cringed.

"I figured we would go to your house," I said, but then I noticed Hannah shooting Izzy an anxious glance. "Or... maybe that's a bad idea? I wouldn't want your parents picking up on anything weird."

"How about we go to your creek?" Izzy suggested. "The old tree house?"

"You're kidding, right?" I asked, almost laughing out loud. The warm, sparkling sunlight made everything feel slightly less frightening.

"Only half. I'd say our actual houses are out, since we don't want our families sniffing around. So that leaves some kind of public restroom, because I refuse to let you do this in the back of my brand-new car. And the idea of you pissing in some dirty McDonald's bathroom is way more depressing than even I can handle right now. The creek is looking pretty fantastic if you ask me."

Thinking about the tree house flooded my mind with a heavy, rushing stream of golden memories. Long, lazy summer days with Hannah and Izzy, digging for treasure along the soft banks of the creek, creating entire meals out of mud and twigs and stones, and having sleepovers up on those high branches. We'd lie awake all night telling ghost stories and listening to the eerie and beautiful chorus of toads and crickets and birds that swooped and hunted even in the blackness, the stars blotted out by the thick canopy of maple and sycamore leaves.

Izzy was right, as she usually was, and for once I didn't mind admitting it out loud.

"Of course that's where we should go," I said, looking over at Izzy. "That's a great idea." Her dark eyes were wary at first, softening only after she realized I was being sincere. "The creek is the perfect place. If there could be a perfect place for Mina Dietrich to be taking a pregnancy test, at least." Izzy choked on a laugh, which made me laugh, and suddenly the three of us were all giggling like the little girls who had played house day after day along that creek. We were practically skipping to the car, caught up in the thrill of an entirely insane and entirely ridiculous new adventure.

"Let's stop and pick up some coffee and sandwiches or something on our way back," Hannah said. "We can have a little picnic out there like the good old days. Plus it's almost noon and we haven't even had breakfast yet." She rubbed her hands against her stomach, which rumbled, precisely on cue.

I felt calmer than I had in weeks just picturing the way the sun danced along the ripples of the creek, the way the trees seemed to block out all evidence of the rest of the outside world.

In those woods it was only us: Mina, Hannah, and Isabelle. Nothing bad could happen, not there, not in

Immaculate

our special place. The knot that had been coiled up deep inside me for weeks released, and I grinned up at the sun in relief, because suddenly I knew.

Everything would be okay.

Everything was really going to be okay.

chapter three

"The good news, according to the instructions, is that the whole thing should only take about three minutes once Mina downs that liter of root beer," Izzy said, squinting at the little unfolded manuals fanned out in front of her on the picnic blanket. "So we won't have to wait long to get some results."

I nodded as I chewed on the same piece of bread that I'd put in my mouth a minute or two before, over and over into a tasteless mush, unable to make myself swallow.

We had stopped at my house first to pick up supplies and make small talk with my parents, who were both beyond thrilled that we wanted to eat lunch out by the old tree house—"the three princesses making an epic return to their kingdom," as my mom had put it. Thankfully, Gracie had just been picked up for a birthday party at a friend's house. She would have been begging to tag along otherwise, her impossibly gigantic blue eyes pleading with me, even though she'd never once showed the slightest interest in our precious fort before—she was more of a dollhouse girl than a tree house girl. I usually loved having Gracie follow me and the girls around, but I certainly didn't want my shadow trailing me to the tree house that afternoon.

My heart had already broken just watching my mom's grin as she'd put down her sacred Saturday morning newspaper and mug of coffee, her short brown hair still in a tangled frizz of bedhead curls like a cloud above her head. She had jumped up and started whirling about, pulling out our old wicker picnic basket and packing cloth napkins and fruit and little plastic baggies of chips to go with the sandwiches and sodas we'd picked up in town on our way back. She'd danced around the kitchen as she'd grabbed at drawers and cupboards, wearing her grungy floral sleeping gown that no one outside of the family but Izzy and Hannah would ever be allowed to see.

"Such a wonderful day to be out in the woods," she had said as she finally handed me the basket—so full that the folding wooden lid couldn't close over the top—and the quintessential red-and-white-checked blanket that had been dragged along on all our adventures. I could still make out splotches of spilled grape juice and Popsicle drippings that had resisted years' worth of bleaching and scrubbing. "My three girls . . . enjoy days like these while you can."

I had bit my lip as I'd looked down at our old farmhouse brick floor, unable to meet her gaze without bursting out into tears and wrapping myself in her soft pillowy arms.

"It's just so hard to believe that this time next summer, you girls will be getting ready to fly off on your own..." Her voice had cracked, and she'd waved us off toward the front door, clearly battling tears of her own. "The girls are off!" she'd called out to my dad, who had paused the baseball game he was replaying in the living room to come say good-bye. I was used to this kind of over-the-top attention and devotion, and generally it didn't bother me—it was pretty nice, actually—but in that moment I'd needed to be away.

I'd glanced back at the house for just a second as we left, and had seen her and my dad at the window, his arm tight around her shoulders, her head leaning against his chest, both of them watching us with such an overwhelming mix of pride and longing and sadness that my whole being had ached with love for them. I'd wanted to rewind a decade or so, be their little girl again, even for a day.

"What's the status of your bladder, Mina?" Izzy asked, her voice slicing through my thoughts.

"I... I don't know, Iz. I don't think I'm quite ready yet. Maybe another ten minutes or so?" I took a massive gulp from the soda bottle I was clasping in my clammy hands, and my stomach burned from the fizzle of carbonation. "I want to make sure that I have enough to cover all four test sticks."

"You don't have to be a perfectionist even about this, Mina," Izzy said. "Not right now. You're just putting it off."

"Let her wait ten minutes, Isabelle," Hannah said, shooting Izzy one of her most amazingly withering, mom-like looks before turning to me with a sympathetic frown. "I can never make myself go when they need a sample at the doctor's office. Remember, I had to sit in the waiting room for three hours at my physical last year? Three hours! Missed the whole afternoon of classes. Any other time, easy as can be, right? The mind is in total control over the body. Don't worry about it, Meen. Let's just think about something else for now."

"Not quite so easy," I said, forcing out a small laugh. "But thanks for the suggestion."

Hannah tilted her head for a minute, looking thoughtful, and then she smiled and stood up. She held out both hands to me, waiting for me to latch on and get up with her. "Let's climb up to the house, see how it's weathered all these years without us. How long has it been, anyway? Four years? Five?"

"Mina's thirteenth birthday," Izzy answered without hesitating, sounding surprised, almost annoyed, that Hannah wouldn't have remembered that obscure detail about our shared history. "We were sleeping out here like we did every year and decided halfway through the night that it was too cold outside and the floor was too hard, and then you said that no respectable teenager still slept in tree houses, anyway, so we packed up and that was that. Goodbye, lovely childhood."

"Oh, right," Hannah said, grinning as she kicked at Izzy's leg to urge her up off the blanket. "That does ring a bell. About time we go back up then, isn't it?"

Izzy sighed, but I could tell from the smirk on her lips that it was just for show. If Izzy had it her way, we'd all have stayed ragamuffin, hillbilly tomboys, digging in the creek and hanging around in the tree for the rest of our lives.

I thought back to the last time *I* had been in the tree house, and it wasn't my birthday four years ago. More like four months. Nate and I had climbed up one time at the beginning of spring, the first real warm night of the season, long after Gracie and my parents had gone to bed, and long after Nate had called his parents to say he was staying over at his friend Peter's house. I'm not sure why or how it happened, really, given that neither of us was particularly good at breaking rules, but I chalked it up to an overwhelming curiosity—what it would be like, what we would do if we were actually alone, no chance of my parents checking in to see if we wanted more soda or popcorn, no chance that they'd be able to overhear us through the gaps in the floors and the cracks in the walls of our early eighteenth-century farmhouse. Houses as old as mine typically felt like one big, open space—no walls, no closed doors. No matter what room I was in, I knew where everyone else was, what they were doing, what they were saying. Any sort of private life was impossible.

Anyway, nothing really happened that night, much to Nate's disappointment, probably, though he was too much of a gentleman to have ever said so. But it didn't seem like the right time to tell Izzy and Hannah any of that. I wasn't sure why I hadn't told them to begin with, actually—embarrassed by my own prudishness, maybe, or wanting some kind of secret that belonged just to me and Nate for once. Either way, I wasn't telling them today. It seemed too suspicious now.

Izzy was the first to start up the rickety old ladder, masterfully avoiding the rungs that had rotted and splintered over the years of neglect. "Let me test it out first, make sure it's all sturdy," she said, looking back over her shoulder at us as her arms and legs continued to climb, pushing and pulling, the familiar movements so etched into her memory. "I'll tell you when it's safe to come up." She pushed back the limp strings of colored beads still hanging in the doorway, the wooden strands bouncing against one another and tinkling like rain, and disappeared into the house. Hannah and I kept looking up, hands shielding our eyes from the sun peeking through the leaves, waiting for the all clear.

After a few long seconds, the house's faded blue shudders burst open in a flurry of paint flakes and leaf bits, and Izzy's grinning face popped out over the edge of the window. "Just like I remembered it, ladies, almost as if the last few years didn't happen." She sighed, her eyes glazed with contentment. "Anyway," she said, yanking her head back as she vanished into the house, "I think it's safe. The floors still seem solid enough."

Hannah motioned for me to go first, and we both started the climb up, more slowly and hesitantly than Izzy. I crawled inside and made room for Hannah to come in next to me, pausing then to soak in the makeshift all-in-one living room, kitchen, and bedroom that had been our home away from home for such a massive piece of our lives.

There wasn't much in the way of furniture, given the complexity of transporting it up twenty feet off the ground, and what we did have was a raggedy collection of well-worn, well-loved hand-me-downs that had been discovered stashed away in our parents' basements and attics. We had three assorted wooden chairs that my dad had somehow managed to carry up all by himself without toppling backward off the ladder—I can still remember that day, watching from the ground with my mom, petrified, hiding my face in her skirt while she assured me that he'd be okay. There was a "table" made out of planks of wood and balanced on two bright green plastic buckets, a few shelves that displayed the treasures we'd dug up along the creek, and a barrel of old cups and dishes that were probably still caked with strawberry Pop-Tart crumbs and hardened scraps of pizza bagels.

The walls, however, were our pride and joy, covered inch to inch in boy band posters and pages torn from glossy magazines that we'd slipped from our moms, our intricately hand-drawn maps of the woods, and other colorful drawings and photos that memorialized some of our greatest adventures together. I could have stayed up there for hours, poring over each page, each picture, remembering every detail of our past. But we weren't just in the woods for a pleasant stroll down memory lane.

I sighed. "I think it's time I head down and get this over with."

The girls nodded, and we each gave one final glance around the house before making our way back down to the ground. Who knew how long until we'd all be up there again together? Years?

Maybe never.

We walked back over to the blanket, and I skimmed through the instructions again to be absolutely sure I had the steps down. It all seemed simple enough: remove the cap and put the tip in my stream of pee for at least five seconds, lay the test down flat to develop, and wait three minutes for the results. The three minutes of waiting would no doubt be the trickiest part of the process.

"All right, then," I said, grabbing all four sticks from the boxes, two of each kind, and started toward the bank of the creek. "I guess you can just close your eyes or something? Or don't. I don't really care, to be honest. I'm just so glad you're both here, because there's no way I could be doing this by myself." I was shaking as I said it, the plastic sticks tapping against one another in my hands.

"I'll help you," Hannah said, jumping up from the blanket. "I'll grab the used sticks and hand you the new ones, make sure they're set up flat afterward."

"Count me out," Izzy said, her lips puckered in disgust. "I love you, Meen, don't get me wrong, but I do have my limits."

"Hannah, are you sure you're okay with that?" I asked, ignoring Izzy.

"I want to do it. Don't worry about it." Her voice was so calm and sympathetic, the way my mother would have sounded if this had been a moment I could have shared with her.

I hoped that the next time I'd be taking a pregnancy test—some day in the very ridiculously distant future—I'd be ecstatic and overcome with happy, excited tears. I hoped that the next time, I'd be able to call my mom afterward and scream the good news to her over the phone.

But I had Hannah and Izzy by my side, and in the moment they were more than enough. More than any girl in my predicament could have hoped for.

Hannah looked away and I squatted, willing it to happen despite the highly unusual circumstances. I held the first stick out as soon as I felt a trickle. Hannah grabbed it when I was done and handed me stick two, and between both of our efforts, there were four pink-tipped tests lying flat on top of their boxes before I even realized it had all happened.

"Thanks, Hannah." I grabbed her hand as we made our way back to the blanket. "You made that much easier."

"Of course, Meen. Now we just have to think about something else for a few minutes."

The three of us sat in silence, at a loss for what in the world we could possibly talk about for the next one hundred and eighty seconds besides those four sticks.

"So . . ." Hannah started, an unfamiliar grin spreading over her face. "I've decided I'm definitely going to apply to Ole Miss this fall. I'm sure I probably won't get in, and even if I do, I can't honestly imagine being that far away from you guys . . . wherever you guys will be, that is . . . But don't you think it would be fabulous to be surrounded by so many dashing Southern gentlemen? That'd be a nice change of scenery. And I'm pretty sure I could pass for a sweet little blonde Southern belle."

"Seriously?" Izzy choked out, her voice sputtering. "What happened to our pact to not be more than three hundred miles away from one another? What about our weekend road trips? I can't exactly hop in my Jeep and drive to Mississippi for a night if I end up at Penn State, can I?"

I looked up at Hannah, her cheeks blazing deep pink. I was just as surprised as Izzy. Hannah was supposed to be the predictable one, the stable one, the anchor of the trio. She wasn't supposed to drop bombshells, not ever, and *especially* not in the middle of my own massive personal crisis.

"I . . . I know we've always said that, guys, but I thought that was just us being scared. And naive. I would never discourage either of you from trying to go where you really wanted to go. You're my best friends, no matter where we live for those four years. Nothing's going to change that."

"Yeah. Okay. Thanks so much for the heads-up," Izzy said, refusing to look at her. "Has it been three minutes yet, Meen?"

I hadn't let myself peek at the sticks once since I'd handed them to Hannah. No easy feat, though Hannah's shocking news had, at the very least, distracted me better than I could have imagined possible. A cold, clammy sweat prickled down my neck as I nodded and pushed myself up off the ground, turning back toward the bank where we'd laid the sticks.

"So just a reminder: it's a blue minus sign if you're not pregnant, and a pink plus if you are. And the other test is pretty self-explanatory: pregnant, not pregnant," Hannah explained, her mothering instinct back in full force, as if the previous conversation hadn't ever happened.

I walked slowly, each footstep torn somewhere between running and freezing. I wanted the answer as much as I didn't want the answer. I could see the tests right below me, waiting to be read, but I didn't let my eyes focus at first, keeping the indicators a blurry haze. I closed my eyes and squatted down, taking a deep breath.

I opened my eyes.

Plus, plus, pregnant, pregnant.

chapter four

I was pregnant.

I, Mina Dietrich, an absolute and utter virgin, was pregnant.

Four tests couldn't be wrong, could they? Not with all the other symptoms I'd had during the past few months, and not with my fears about Iris's warning. But how could they *not* be wrong? How could any of this actually be happening to me?

"What should we do now?" Hannah whispered. She and Izzy were hovering over me, staring down at the evidence in front of us.

"I need to let Frankie know that I can't come in tonight," I said without even pausing to reconsider. For some reason that was the first and only immediate reaction that came to mind. The only answer, the only step forward that made any sense. Even in the face of the most fantastical crisis imaginable, I could still be relied on not to forget to call out of work.

Under normal circumstances, Izzy would have made endless fun of me for being so dedicated to Frankie's, but now she was ominously silent. I was afraid to look up at her face, to see whatever was lurking behind her eyes. Izzy couldn't hide anything, not from me and Hannah, no matter how hard she sometimes tried. Her eyes always insisted on telling us everything we needed to know.

"Let's get you back to the blanket," Hannah said, reaching for my hand. "Your cell phone is there in your purse, and then you can lie down while we . . . while we process everything."

I gave a weak nod and let them pull me up and steer me. My stomach pinched at the sight of the leftover food, the basket that my mom had packed less than two hours ago for our special tree house picnic. My mom. My adoring, gracious, astoundingly perfect mom. How could I ever possibly tell her about this? How could she believe me? How could she keep trusting me and loving me and being proud of me?

Too much. The idea of telling my mom was more than my mind could begin to comprehend, not when I'd only known the truth myself for a few entirely surreal minutes.

I pushed those thoughts to the furthest, blackest corner of my mind, and reached for my phone. I brushed past a few missed calls and messages from Nate, clearing my throat as I dialed Frankie's. The phone rang five, six, seven times, and I exhaled in relief. A voice mail would be much easier and faster: no questions, no elaborating. Just as I expected the beep of the automated message, I heard a sharp click and a breathless gasp on the other end.

"Frankie and Friends' Pizzeria. This is Jesse. How can I help you?"

"Oh, hey. Hi, Jesse," I said, flustered. I had barely talked to him since the night we first met. A few necessary words here and there about when to clean, what to clean, but nothing that didn't relate to dishes and mops and window spray. He was too intertwined with Iris in my mind. He was a witness—living, breathing, irrefutable proof that she had been at Frankie's, that I had talked with her. That she existed at all and wasn't a complete figment of my overactive imagination. Besides, I could only imagine what he thought of me afterward, running away from a harmless old lady, barely acknowledging his presence ever since. Though frankly, there seemed to be something a little off about him, too. He was friendly enough to the waitresses and to the other guys in the back, but he still seemed remote to me, distant, as if his body might be there, scraping pizza pans, but his mind was somewhere else entirely. I sometimes had to repeat his name a few times before he'd hear me, before he'd snap out of whatever cloudy daydreams kept him floating through his life.

"Mina?"

I almost dropped the phone, startled that he'd recognized my voice so easily. "Yeah. Yes. It's uh . . . me, Mina. I . . . I'm sick, Jesse. Really sick. Stomach bug or something. I was up all night puking, and I still am, actually, and really there's no end in sight, I don't think—" Hannah coughed, and I cut myself off. "So, yeah, please tell Frankie that I'm really, really sorry, but I just don't think I can make it in for my shift tonight."

"Sure, no problem, Mina. I'll help hold down the fort without you here. Feel better, okay?"

"Thanks, Jesse." I hung up and fiddled with the phone, pecking at random keys to avoid the awful, frightening silence that hung in the air between us.

"Say something, Mina," Hannah said. "Please, *please* say anything that makes all this more reasonable. You have to know how confusing this situation is for me and Izzy. I want to believe you. *We* want to believe you. Don't we, Iz?" She looked over at Izzy for encouragement, but it was obvious that Izzy was avoiding both of us, staring off toward the creek instead. Hannah gave up on her and refocused her attention back to me. "Help us to do that, Mina. *Please.* Help us." I barely recognized her voice, which was usually so warm and alive, like sunshine and bells. It was all hollow now, sad and desperate, begging for explanations I couldn't give.

"I don't know what else I can tell you," I said, lifting my head up to face them. I refused to cry again. I refused to look away. "Iris . . . What Iris said to me is the only answer I can think of, and trust me, I know how absolutely crazy that sounds, I do. I really do. But I didn't have sex, not with Nate, not with *anyone*. I didn't have anything even remotely close to sex. That's all that I know. That's all the explanation I have." I paused, grabbing, clawing at my mind for anything more I could give. "Maybe there's another reason besides pregnancy that I'd get those results? Some sort of sickness or condition that would cause a false positive?" I said it, but I didn't believe it. The words felt wrong, in my heart and on my tongue, but it was one small offering I could give them, however temporary.

Hannah looked almost satisfied, the corners of her tight, pursed lips relaxing as she considered this new and improved option. Izzy still said nothing. The silence had seemed best, preferable to confrontation at first, but it was starting to enrage me, scrape at my last bits of patience. Who was she to judge me? I had done nothing wrong, not to her, not to anyone. I didn't deserve her anger, especially not now, not on top of all the other emotions threatening to tear apart my entire world at the seams.

"Say it, Isabelle," I said out loud, surprising even myself with the sharpness of my voice. "Say whatever you're thinking. Let's just get it over with. In case you didn't fully realize, I have a lot to deal with at the moment, so let's get this conversation out of the way. Okay?"

She breathed in and out, balled her hands into fists, and turned her gaze toward me. For the first time in my life, I didn't recognize the look I saw in her eyes. I didn't see my Izzy. Her dark chestnut eyes were so cold and accusing, so hostile.

"Fine. You want to know what I'm thinking, Mina? You want to know what I'm *really* thinking?" She was yelling so loud that I worried my parents would hear all the way up at the house. "I think you're a liar. I think for the first time in your perfect existence, you made a mistake. Mina Dietrich made a massive, ugly, undeniable mistake. And instead of just accepting it and admitting it and handling it like any sane, normal person would do, you've decided to make up the most outrageous story I've ever heard in my life to cover yourself. I can understand you not wanting other people to know the truth. I get that. But I can't understand you looking your two best friends in the eye and telling them such a huge fucking lie. I can't understand, and I won't understand. You're so obsessed with being this perfect Mina who everyone expects you to be, but you don't have to act perfect for us. I don't care about any of that *Menius* bullshit. I just care about you being *real*."

She paused then, her eyes still drilling into mine, willing me to say something for myself. But there was nothing. She was wrong, but I had no way of making her believe that.

"Fine then," she said, pushing herself up off of the blanket. "If you don't want to make this our problem, you want to keep this to yourself, then great. You handle it. Best of luck, Mina. I'm out of this. Are you staying or leaving with me, Hannah?"

Izzy had wasted no time in establishing the line, making it clear that there were two very separate, very distinct sides. There was her and there was me. There were the nonbelievers and the believers. There was no middle ground, no space to be found in between.

"I'm staying," Hannah said. My heart banged against my rib cage, but I resisted the urge to fling my arms around her and hold on for dear life, at least while Izzy was still watching. I may have won the first battle, but I had the feeling that it would be a long, uphill fight.

Izzy stomped off toward my driveway without another word or a backward glance. I lay down on the blanket, knees tucked into my chest, and rested my head on Hannah's lap.

"Thank you." I closed my eyes and burrowed more closely against her, breathing in the familiar scent of lavender perfume and plain Dove soap. "Thank you for being here." She reached down and started stroking my head. We stayed like that for a long time: no talking, no analyzing out loud, just her hand weaving through my knotted hair, her occasional humming mixing with the soft ins and outs of our breathing.

I was just starting to nod off when Hannah's cell phone rang, breaking through our temporary peace.

"It's my mom," she said, glancing down at the screen, and I nodded, lifting myself from her lap. While she talked, I busied myself by packing up the food and the plates, accepting the inevitable reentrance into my real life waiting outside of our woods.

"I should go soon," Hannah said, squatting down next to me after hanging up with her mom. "I feel terrible leaving you, but my parents made these dinner reservations with my sister and our grandparents ages ago. It's probably the last time Lauren will be out with all of us before she has the baby." She flinched at *baby*, a look of guilt flashing across her face. "Is that okay? I'll stay if you need me to."

"No, you go." I patted her hand. "Really. You've already helped me so much today. You've been so amazing. Beyond amazing. I'll be fine by myself."

"Are you . . . are you going to tell your mom now?"

"No." I shook my head, adamant. "Not tonight at least. I need a little more time by myself to let it all sink in, consider all the possibilities."

"The possibilities," she said, nodding. "So do you think . . . Does that mean that you might get an abortion? It might be the easiest way, Meen, as hard as it might be at first."

"No," I said, without even pausing to consider. The

word sounded surprisingly sure and confident coming out of my mouth. But why? Why was that my answer? Hannah was right: it would be easiest. No one else besides her and Izzy would ever have to know about any of this. Not my parents. Not Nate.

But *I* would know. I would always know.

And I didn't think I could live with myself if I made the decision to make it all go away. I didn't feel as if it was even my choice to make.

"You don't have to decide right this second, Meen. But think about it, at least. Think about what it would mean for college, and for all your big plans, the books you want to write, the places you want to visit. Where would you get the money? And the kids at school . . . What will you tell them if you keep it? Or even if you give the baby up for adoption, everyone will be asking you for explanations once it's obvious you're pregnant."

It was too much, too many questions all at once, and I wanted to shove my fingers in my ears and scream as loud as I could to drown it all out. But I saw the tears on her cheeks, and I knew that it was only because she loved me. She cared about me too much to watch me throw everything away.

I took a deep breath and squeezed her hand. "I don't know. I don't think I can decide anything until I see a doctor and get some actual tests done. I guess I'll just go from there."

She nodded, satisfied for the time being. "Promise me you'll go soon, this week. I'll go, too, of course. I don't want you to be alone. And like you said, it really could be something completely different that caused those results. We don't know anything for sure, not yet."

"Of course," I said, though I hated leading her on.

"And promise that you'll call me absolutely whenever you need to talk. I don't care if I'm in the middle of dinner. I don't care if I'm sound asleep. Just call me."

"Yes, yes, I will. Promise. Now let's go back to the house. I don't want you to be late because of me."

While she folded the blanket, I walked to the creek bank and picked up the tests, stuffed them back into the boxes, and buried them at the bottom of my purse. I glanced up at the tree house one last time—we both did—and then we left, arm in arm, walking back through the trees.

Hannah was helpful in making excuses to my mom, building up the vicious stomach bug that had struck me down out of nowhere in the middle of our otherwise reportedly perfect picnic. I sat, pale and quiet, at the kitchen table. At least I didn't have to make any effort to act the part of the poor, sick girl.

"I'm so sorry that your picnic was ruined, girls," my mom said, resting the back of her hand on my forehead to check for a fever. "And only a few days before school starts, too. Such awful timing." She pulled back and frowned, her eyes looking misty, before leaning over to kiss the top of my head. She was so delicate, so careful, pecking me as if I was a fragile treasure that could crack under the weight of her lips at any second.

A horn honked from out front, and Hannah's face looked torn between relief and guilt.

"Have fun tonight, Hannah bear," I said, catching her eye. I winked at her and mouthed a silent thank-you, and she gave a small, tight smile back, probably more for my mom's benefit than my own. She didn't need to bother—my mom was too absorbed in her nursing duties, already taking inventory of whether we had enough saltines and ginger ale to get me through the night.

"Bye, Mina. Bye, Mrs. Dietrich," Hannah said, another round of honks firing from the driveway.

"Bye bye now, Hannah. Tell your parents I said hello, please, and thanks again for taking care of my Meen today."

"Of course, Mrs. D. Anything for your daughter," Hannah said, turning to push open the screen door that led to our side porch. "And, Mina, I'm sure I'll talk to you soon."

I nodded to myself as the door closed behind her, leaving me far too alone in the kitchen with my mom.

"Where's Dad?"

"Picking up Gracie from the birthday party and then bringing a pizza home from Frankie's for dinner," she said, distracted, her head buried in the depths of our cluttered, overflowing pantry. "They should be here any minute, actually."

I didn't want to see either of them, any of them, not then, not that night.

"I'm going to go lie down," I said, pushing myself up from the table. "I just want to sleep for a while, and hopefully I'll feel better when I wake up."

"Are you sure I can't make you something first?" She pulled her head out of the cabinet to face me, her brow wrinkled in concern. "Scramble some eggs, maybe? Chicken broth? I'd feel better if you had a little something in you."

"I'll take some crackers upstairs with me, okay? I'll be fine."

She nodded as she came over to give me a long hug, and I could feel her eyes following me as I disappeared up the narrow winding staircase.

I lay in bed until long after the sun went down and long after the hum of crickets and the flicker of fireflies started up in the darkness just beyond my window screen. I could have turned on the air conditioner, but I wanted to hear the sounds of the night, the familiar country chorus that made me feel less alone. I had listened, too, as Mom chatted to her sister Vera on the phone downstairs in the kitchen, and as Gracie and Dad laughed their way through *Toy Story*. I had listened to Gracie's inevitable grumbling as she was sent upstairs for bedtime against her will. She had tapped on my door a few times, cautiously called out my name. I could hear the worry laced in her soft, sweet voice, but I had still stayed silent, playing the sick girl who was too dead asleep to be disturbed, until she gave up and shuffled off to her room. Finally, sometime after nine, I had heard my parents both come up, brush their teeth, and talk quietly in their room for a few minutes before the bedside lamps clicked off.

After sending a few frantic apology texts to Nate for missing all his calls that day, and explaining how *terribly* sick I was, I shut off my phone for the night.

I couldn't think about him or about anyone else right now.

How? How could this be my life? How could this be real?

Miracles, divine intervention, supernatural phenomena, whatever you wanted to label it, didn't really happen—not in the real world, certainly not in the twenty-first century.

And even if somehow, some way, genuine miracles occurred that were totally inexplicable and defied everything we knew about science and the human body—and there couldn't be, my mind just couldn't comprehend that for a second—why would God, or whoever was in control of this decision, pick *me*? Who was Mina Dietrich in the grand scheme of things?

Sure, I was raised as a Lutheran, and my mom and dad were both fairly religious. I went to church a few times a month and volunteered at Vacation Bible School, more to appease my parents and to be a good role model for Gracie than because of any strict religious code of my own. Some of the stories were interesting and entertaining and all, but that was what they'd always felt like, ever since I was old enough to really think about them on my own—*stories*. Very old, very distant stories that had never seemed wildly relevant to my personal existence.

Had I ever *really* believed in God, though? In Jesus? Did I believe in them now—did I have to believe after this? The Virgin Mary had always seemed like a character to me, a sweet, muted woman draped in blue for the nativity play, a pretty porcelain face in old paintings and stained-glass windows—not a living, breathing woman who had once walked this very same earth. Who had once had her own life yanked out from under her and turned upside down by the truth of her destiny, a baby with no human father. Did I believe in *her*?

I realized now how odd it was that I'd gone through

the motions of Christianity for my entire life without ever really dissecting what I felt about any of it. There had always been more crucial things to think about—school and grades and cold, hard indisputable facts, geometry and physics, grammar and history. But there had to be something, didn't there? Some force that brought us here, some sort of higher power that knew what could become of all the atoms and molecules and compounds floating around in the universe?

It was unlike me to not have an answer. It was unlike me to have somehow let such a big question go.

My room was sweltering, but still I was wrapped up in my blankets, sweaty and buried, hiding beneath the nest of feathers. The person I wanted to hide from most was *me*, and I didn't know how to make that happen. Because even in my dreams—that is, if I would ever be able to fall asleep again—I knew I couldn't escape myself, my thoughts, my fears. My body.

By the time I counted twelve chimes from the old grandfather clock downstairs in our living room, I couldn't be alone in my room anymore. I couldn't be alone with myself. More than anything or anyone else in the world, I needed my mom. I needed her arms around me, and I needed her to know everything that I knew. Because as terrible as everything in my life felt in that moment, the most terrible, excruciating part was keeping it all a secret from my mom. I'd never hidden anything important from her before, and I couldn't hide this, either. Not even for a night.

I kicked off the blankets and rose from the bed like a sleepwalker, lifted up and tugged toward the hallway by invisible hands. A bright shaft of moonlight spilled through my thin, gauzy curtains, illuminating the full-length mirror that hung from my door. I reached out for the knob, but froze, caught by my reflection.

Was I showing? Could I see? Could other people see?

I was shocked that the idea hadn't occurred to me earlier, not once during the countless hours of solitude I'd spent in my room that night, reflecting and analyzing, poring over every last detail, every piece of evidence again and again and again.

Goose bumps prickled up my arms, the hairs standing on end, as I carefully, little by little, lifted up the edge of my T-shirt. I stared at myself, first from the front, then from the side. Front, side, front, side. My stomach looked so pale, so ghostly white against the shadows behind me. I cupped my hands over my belly and studied my profile. Was that a bump? A tiny, minuscule, almost entirely nonexistent bulge, but still, could it be the beginnings of a bump? I dug my palms harder, deeper against my skin, and closed my eyes to concentrate. I felt rounder, fuller somehow, I was sure of it. It was certainly nothing that anyone else would be able to see, not yet.

But it was only a matter of time.

I pulled my shirt back down and crept into the hallway, my bare feet knowing every creaking wooden floorboard, every slope and splinter, every inch of the way along the pitch-black path to my parents' bedroom. They always left the door slightly open while they slept, a habit from the days when Gracie and I were little and helpless—a nightly routine that they'd never been able to leave behind, no matter how old we'd gotten or how independent we'd become. I had hated this on the nights when Nate and I were downstairs together, cuddling on the sofa, wanting at least the veil of privacy, but seeing the crack now made my heart swell.

I pushed the door open farther, just far enough that I could poke my head through and peek into the room. My mom flinched and jerked herself up at the first squeak of the hinge. I could make out her panicked face in the moonlight, her eyes darting around the room until she found me standing in the doorway. I put one finger on my lips and pointed to Dad, and then motioned for her to follow me out. She fumbled for her glasses on the nightstand and swung her legs over the side of the bed, an instant transition from deep, sound sleep to active and alert motherhood. Within seconds we were both safely down the hall and inside of my room, and I closed the door behind us.

"What's going on, Mina?" she asked, her tired face tense with worry. I noticed wrinkles that I hadn't seen before, furrowed around her eyes and fanning out from her frown. "Are you feeling worse? Can I get you anything?"

"No, I'm fine. I don't need you to get me anything," I said, sitting down on the edge of my bed. "I just need to talk to you. I need to tell you something."

"Okay, then tell me something," she said, her voice sounding confused but still patient as always, and she walked over to lean in next to me. "What's this all about, Meeny? You're scaring me."

"I'm scaring myself, too," I said. My voice cracked. But I couldn't dissolve into tears, not until I'd pushed the whole story out into the void between us. I closed my eyes and forced myself to speak. For the second time that day, two times more than I would have ever liked, I described everything that had happened—meeting Iris, what she had said, what I had said. I told her about the last few months, all the strange symptoms, and I told her about that morning, that afternoon out in the woods.

She didn't say anything. No questions or observations. Not a single word the entire way through.

After I finished talking, ending right at the point when Hannah and I had walked back into the kitchen and lied about our day, I lifted my head up and turned to face her. She was staring at me, her golden brown eyes fixed on mine and burning with a kind of motherly love that even I had rarely seen, and only in fleeting glimpses. A look that was so raw and unfiltered, a look that captured so many instincts and so many emotions—passion, devotion, fear, distress, adoration, sympathy. I was stunned that someone could feel so much—feel so much *for me*.

"Mina . . ." she said, her voice quiet but firm.

I breathed in and held the air deep inside of my lungs.

"Mina, I believe you."

She *believed* me. And I hadn't even needed to ask.

She reached out before I could react, and rested her palm against my flushed cheek. "Mina, I may not understand one bit of why this is happening to you or how this is happening to you or what any of this craziness means for any of us at all . . . but I do know one thing in this world, without a doubt, without any uncertainty"—she shifted to face me straight on and wrapped her hands tight around both of my shoulders—"I trust in you. I believe in you. You're my Mina, my baby girl, and I can see right through those amazing blue eyes of yours. I can see exactly what's inside, and I know like only a mother could know for sure that you're not hiding a thing from me, not a thing. So if you're crazy, then I'm crazy, and we're just going to have to be crazy together, all right?"

"All right." I nodded hard, up and down, up and

down, still amazed by her reaction. "So . . . so what should we do next?"

We. The word felt so right on my lips.

"Well, I think I should call Dr. Keller on Monday, tell her we need an appointment as soon as possible. We have her run the standard tests, make sure we know exactly what we're dealing with. I think it's best we don't tell her too much at this point. Just the basics, the symptoms, the tests you took today. We'll fill in the gaps when we need to. I don't want to raise too many unnecessary questions—not yet, anyway."

I nodded again. She hadn't said anything that I wasn't already thinking on my own, but it all sounded much more solid and sensible coming out of her mouth instead. "And what about Dad?" I asked. And Gracie. I wasn't sure which of them would be the most agonizing to tell, both conversations feeling so equally impossible.

"I think . . . I think we should wait to tell Dad, at least until after we've seen the doctor," my mom said, her words slow, hesitant. I didn't think that she'd ever kept anything from my dad before, certainly not something this significant. I hated that I was the reason. "I think it's better to keep this between us and the girls until we know more."

The more I thought about my dad and Gracie and watching their faces as they heard my news, watching their eyes lose their glow, all their pride and trust, the more I started to shake—a shattering tremble from the tips of my toes to my knuckles to my eyelids. I could feel my heartbeat pounding, banging in my temples.

Why me?

I curled up into a ball on my bed, closing in on myself and hoping that I could somehow black out and escape my body, even for a few minutes.

But then I felt my mom curve herself around me, my smaller body completely folded into and against hers, my limbs, my head, my heart no longer just a part of *me*. With her touch we'd become one: my body, her body; my pain, her pain; and as she absorbed me into her, the shaking slowed.

Cradled like that, closer to my mom than I'd been in seventeen years, I drifted off to sleep.

chapter five

"I'm sure that Dr. Keller will be in to speak with you in just a few more minutes now," the assistant said, poking her head in to grin at us for what must have been the fifth or sixth time since we'd been escorted to the exam room an hour earlier.

"Oh yes, of course, not a problem at all," my mom said, smiling back, a few more teeth than usual showing between her tight lips. She had her eyes open wide, but I could see the hint of purple on her lower lids, peeking out from beneath the concealer she'd used to hide the past forty-eight hours without real sleep. "We're just so glad she scheduled us on such late notice."

I'd been glad, too, relieved when my mom had called the office Monday morning at nine o'clock on the dot, the minute they'd opened, and they told her I could be squeezed in at ten. But the gladness had faded as soon as I'd breathed in the office perfume of latex and rubbing alcohol and cheap citrus sanitizer, and felt the cold papery rustle of the exam table under the ultrathin cotton of my mint green gown. It had all become too real then, too official.

The assistant had handed me a plastic cup and pointed me to the bathroom straightaway—luckily, I'd prepared myself this time, and had drunk five solid glasses of water before leaving the house. I wanted to run back to my bedroom, lock the door behind me, and ignore everything for another few days or weeks or months. Ignore everything until it all disappeared and life went back to normal. I wanted to replay that last day of junior year all over again—ask off from my shift like I'd been tempted to do and celebrate the night properly, avoid Iris altogether. But no, here I was instead, sitting half naked with my mom in an OB/GYN office that was almost as cold as Frankie's walk-in freezer.

I had met Dr. Keller before, once or twice—she was the doctor who had delivered my Gracie—but I was only ten at the time, so I didn't remember much, really, other than a pile of flaming red curls and extraordinarily bright pink lips. I'd never had cause to see her for any other reason of my own since then, given that I was still under eighteen, and, despite the current circumstances, still not sexually active.

My dad was under the impression that my mom and

I were visiting the standard family doctor, seeing as my "stomach bug" had failed to improve at all over the last two nights. I'd done my best to avoid him the day before, hibernating in my room, tiptoeing to the bathroom, pretending to be sound asleep when he cracked my door to check in on me. But he had persisted, at one point knocking with a tray of scrambled eggs and cinnamon toast and chamomile tea, and I had no choice but to prop myself up against my pillows and smile weakly for at least a little while. Mom had taken Gracie with her to a charity luncheon she was hosting at the historical society, and afterward dropped Gracie off at Aunt Vera's house for a sleepover with our cousins, six-year-old Lucy and three-year-old Danny. I couldn't help but feel relieved—the longer I could put off being the big sister again, the better. I wasn't ready for Gracie.

But being alone together at the house had left Dad feeling even more determined to watch over me. He'd sat on the edge of my bed and done most of the talking while I'd taken tiny bites and forced myself to swallow. I'd tried my best to listen while he'd told me about his day, little anecdotes from church that morning—he'd put my name on the prayer list and Pastor Lewis had sent me his blessings for a speedy recovery—and his plans to clean the gutters and start repainting the garage walls that afternoon, before summer was over and he'd lost the motivation. His list of self-appointed chores never seemed to get any shorter. As an accountant, he spent hours every week hunched over a calculator, which was probably why he could never stop moving around on the weekends, fiddling with this, tampering with that.

But every time I'd looked at him, all I'd been able to see was the confusion and disappointment that would soon take over everything else that he felt for me. I'd kept thinking about how it could be the last simple, easy, lighthearted conversation we'd have for months, maybe even years. Because the truth was, even though I couldn't gauge exactly how he'd react, I did know that he'd never be as accepting as my mom. I wouldn't be that lucky twice.

The doorknob rattled again, and I looked up, expecting the assistant and more of her excuses. But this time it was Dr. Keller standing in the doorway, staring down with a furrowed brow at the clipboard in her hand. The nurse had weighed me and asked me to fill out a basic information sheet when we first got in—my age, the date of my first period, previous medical history, relationship status, the reason for scheduling an appointment. I had left the section about sexual history notably blank, even if it was just a temporary postponement of the inevitable. But I couldn't bring myself to add *zero sexual partners*, not on the same form that made it clear I was there for a pregnancy test. Writing the two entirely contradictory statements side by side in black and white was too ridiculous, too illogical, and I wasn't prepared for a stranger to look at me as if I was insane. Not yet.

Dr. Keller glanced up to smile at both of us, and my stomach lurched, dropping what felt like a solid six inches below where it rightfully belonged in my body. I couldn't do this. I couldn't have this conversation. Not with a certified scientific expert.

Breathe, Mina, breathe.

"Sallie! My goodness, it's been so long. And, Mina! I would never have recognized you. Gorgeous young lady! Sallie, how's the baby? Not a baby these days, I suppose, eh?" She grinned at my mom as she stepped into the room and closed the door behind her.

"Oh, Gracie's doing just fine, thanks. So hard to believe she's already seven this year . . ."

"This business certainly makes me feel my age, that's for darn sure," Dr. Keller said, settling herself down on the rolling stool and wheeling across the room until she was right in front of me. "Seeing all the babies who aren't actually babies anymore around town . . . Constant reminders of how many years have passed." She sighed, loud and long, a very dramatic sigh that I suspected was part of the doctor shtick she used with all her patients, an attempt to make us feel more comfortable and at ease. My mom chuckled, so maybe it worked. I was always bad at those sorts of predictable, rehearsed adult interactions—I just never knew how to play along. I wished that I had a script for that moment, a line-by-line manual to walk me through the entire appointment, help me to say all the right things, ask all the right questions. To save me from seeming like a totally delusional freak.

"So, now let's see . . . Mina, you're here for a pregnancy test, is that right?" She looked up at me, her head tilted and her eyes squinted in concern, all evidence of the grin from seconds before wiped from her face.

"Yes," I said, my voice cracking. I coughed and cleared my throat. "Yes, that's why I'm here."

"Well, then, my assistant, Jamie, will be joining us any minute now for the physical exam, and she should have the test results with her from your urine sample. But let's discuss some of the background first. What symptoms have you had? Why exactly do you think you might be pregnant?"

I mumbled through the list of mystery ailments from the summer—the fatigue, the sore breasts, the aches, the morning sickness—leaving the most obviously significant detail for last. "I also took a boxed pregnancy test over the weekend. Four actually. And they . . . they were all positive. But I figured those tests probably aren't always accurate?"

"Hm. I see." She looked away for a second, considering. "Actually, Mina, I have to say, the tests rarely give false positives. False negatives, on the other hand, are more common, but that's not what we're worried about today. I suppose there could be other reasons for a false positive... There are certain conditions, rare conditions, that can alter your hCG levels and affect a pregnancy reading. But let's not jump to that conclusion first. Like I said, very rare, and I doubt that's what we're looking at here." She paused to give me a quick polite smile.

"Now, Mina," she said, plowing ahead, "I notice you left the sexual history section blank, which I'd like to discuss. Do you know who the potential father would be?"

"Uh . . . no. No, I don't." My mom erupted into a coughing fit from her seat in the corner, and Dr. Keller glanced over at her, eyebrow raised.

"No!" I yelled, piercing the air, much more emphatic and desperate than I would have liked. "That's not really what I meant to say, Dr. Keller. I mean, of course I haven't had multiple partners or anything like that. I haven't . . . I haven't . . ." I sputtered, my cheeks flaming. "I haven't had any partners. Zero."

My mom and I had discussed this exact question in the car on the way over. We'd decided that it would be better to say I'd had one "sort of" partner, one "sort of" sexual encounter—make up a little lie, at least until we had adequate time for the massive amounts of reflecting necessary to come up with a better, more socially acceptable line.

But I couldn't. I couldn't lie. I couldn't do that to myself or to Nate or to whatever crazy, freakish slipup of nature had caused this all in the first place. It just didn't feel right.

"So you're saying that you haven't had sexual intercourse? That you're still . . . a virgin?" Dr. Keller asked, frowning in confusion.

"Yes? Yes. I am."

"All right, well, there are risk behaviors that wouldn't fully qualify as intercourse, but could possibly lead to pregnancy if the male discharge still penetrated the vagina. It's uncommon, Mina, but is that what you're suggesting may have happened?"

"No," I whispered, staring down at my lap. "I didn't do anything like that, nothing at all."

"I see. All right," Dr. Keller said, twirling her stool around to face my mom. "Sallie, I'm sorry, but would you mind waiting in the hall for a bit? I think it's best I discuss some of this with Mina one-on-one, if you don't mind."

My mom nodded, looking startled, and fumbled to pick up the strings of her purse. Just as she stood to leave, the door opened and the assistant stepped back inside. Her bright smile had disappeared, I noticed, and was replaced by an ominous look of total blankness. "I'm sorry to interrupt," she said, "but I wanted to give you the results." She held out a single sheet of paper in the air as evidence.

"Oh yes, thanks so much, Jamie," Dr. Keller said, taking it from her and scanning the details. She looked up at me, then over at my mom, hesitating.

"It's fine, you can say it in front of her," I said, steeling myself for the inevitable. My mom walked over to the exam table, clutching my hand as we waited.

Dr. Keller fixed her eyes on me, her lips a careful, practiced straight line. "The test clearly shows that you're pregnant, Mina." My mom's grip tightened around my fingers, and I squeezed back.

"Now, again, there is a small chance that it could be a false positive, so I'll need to check for a few things during the physical examination, and I'd also like to do an ultrasound today. I want to make sure we know exactly what we're dealing with."

"Whatever you think is best." I had nothing else to say. I wasn't surprised by the results—I was more surprised that I wasn't surprised, really. But I'd known the answer all along, hadn't I? Probably before Hannah and Izzy had even voiced their suspicions. Some small part of me had known. Some small part of me that I'd refused to acknowledge, not until I had to.

"Sallie," Dr. Keller said, looking over at my mom. "If you could just step out while I give Mina a routine physical and ask a few questions, I'll have Jamie come and get you for the ultrasound. It shouldn't be too long."

"I'll be okay," I said to my mom, tilting my head up to kiss her on the cheek. I hoped that was true.

"I love you, sweetie," she whispered. "I'll be right outside if you need me." She turned and walked out, leaving me alone with Dr. Keller and her doubting eyes.

I tried to detach myself from the room and the doctor and everything that happened next. I breathed in and out while she checked my heart and my lungs, and I leaned back as she kneaded my abdomen. I lifted my right hand, then my left hand after she pulled down the robe for my breast exam. I jolted a few times, her strong mechanical fingers jabbing too hard at my already sore and swollen chest.

"Relax now, Mina," she said, situating my feet into place in the stirrups, my gown tented over my bent knees. "I'm going to put the speculum in now, and you're going to feel some pressure. It may feel a little uncomfortable, but it won't be painful, I promise." I pinched my eyes shut as hard as they would close, but tears still leaked out, dripping down the sides of my cheeks. I tried to think of happier times, happier places—sitting on the counter in my grandmother's old kitchen, watching her cook her classic roast beef and mashed potatoes every Sunday afternoon, the sunlight from the window so warm and golden on my face; telling bedtime stories to Gracie, her soft little body propped against mine as she asked for *The Lorax* over and over and over; reading the first Harry Potter book out loud with Nate, an entire rainy Saturday on the couch passing the book back and forth, chapter by chapter, all the way through.

But the speculum was cold, so cold and so foreign, a piece of metal that didn't belong in my body. Dr. Keller was talking me through the exam, words like *spatula* and *wand, gonorrhea* and *chlamydia, standard procedure.* She used her gloved fingers next, less intrusive than the speculum, but still strange and unfamiliar, pushing against my cervix, my ovaries, my uterus. The sound of her voice fluttered around the edges of my subconscious, like a radio station coming in and out of service, clear to static, static to clear.

"Mina? Did you hear me? I said you can sit back now and put your legs down. I'm done with this part of the exam."

I opened my eyes and blinked a few times, readjusting to the present.

"Everything looks normal and healthy," Dr. Keller continued. "The uterus felt enlarged, which is to be expected. And I did detect that your cervix was softer than it would typically be in a woman who wasn't pregnant, and there was a bit of a bluish discoloration. This is called Chadwick's sign, and it's perfectly normal to find in the first trimester."

Dr. Keller pushed back her tray of tools that sat between us and wheeled herself closer to the table and to me. "Before your mom comes back in, I'd like to talk a little bit more about your sexual history. I know it's not an easy topic to talk about, especially as a teenager, and I didn't want your mother's presence affecting your ability to tell me everything. I'm your doctor, Mina, and you can rest assured that everything you tell me is entirely confidential. Because you're a minor, I legally should have a father's name to fill in our forms." Her clear gray eyes were locked on me, sympathetic and sensitive, but still determined.

"I wasn't lying to you earlier, Dr. Keller," I said, speaking slowly to keep my voice steady and strong. "I haven't had sex. I don't know why this is happening to me."

She opened her mouth to respond, paused in a silent O, and then closed her mouth and pursed her lips. "Mina," she started again, "when I was examining you, I did find that your hymen wasn't intact. Now, that in and of itself can't confirm whether someone is a virgin. Tampons and certain physical activities can cause the hymen to tear long before sexual intercourse. But you are pregnant, Mina. I can confirm that." She shifted on her stool, crossing and uncrossing her legs.

"I understand that you may be having some difficulty accepting the situation. It's not out of the question for people to deny what's happening to their bodies, especially if the circumstances leading to your pregnancy were . . . difficult or upsetting." I could see her hands fidgeting on her lap, and I watched as she spun her pen in circles like a miniature baton. I wanted to help her, wanted to somehow put her mind at ease, but I couldn't tell her any of the things that as a doctor she needed to hear. "Are you in a monogamous relationship currently, Mina?"

"Yes, I have been for two years."

"Heterosexual or homosexual?"

"Heterosexual."

"And have there been any instances of abuse, physical or verbal?"

"No! Absolutely not." My hands squeezed around the sides of the table. She was just doing her job. She was just trying to help. "Nothing like that at all. We're very happy and healthy. We're a normal teenage couple."

We were *happy and healthy*, I thought, correcting myself, my stomach turning over at the realization. We *were* a normal couple. *Were*. I didn't know what we would be anymore, if we'd be anything at all. I had avoided two more calls from Nate that morning, and I'd sent a single text back saying I was still too sick to really talk. It was a pathetic excuse, and if he wasn't so busy at the conference, he would have questioned me more. But I couldn't put him off for much longer, especially since he was getting back from DC that afternoon. We still had an anniversary to celebrate. I had a present for him, wrapped and waiting on my desk, a watch he'd been admiring at the mall over the summer. I'd spent so many shifts' worth of money on that watch; we couldn't break up *now*. The reasoning was so silly, so meaningless, that I almost laughed, but I made myself refocus on Dr. Keller and her sharp, curious eyes that seemed to be recording everything about me.

"Are there any problems at home?" she asked. "Any history of physical or verbal abuse that you want to talk about?"

Jamie shuffled her feet, and her shoes squeaked against the tile floor, breaking my attention. I'd forgotten that she was there, too, that it wasn't just Dr. Keller who was privy to every last intimate detail of my body and my life.

I looked back at Dr. Keller, my eyes pleading with her to believe me. "No. My family life is amazing. My parents would never in a million years hurt each other or me or my sister. I'm not lying to you, Dr. Keller. I'm not. But I can't expect you to accept that."

Dr. Keller sighed, a resigned exhale. "Mina . . . I won't ask you any more questions right now, because I think you need a little time and space to think this through. You've been hit with what I'd assume is a major shock, and we all need time to process these sorts of experiences. We all come to accept things at our own speed and in our own ways."

I nodded to appease her.

"But I am going to recommend that you talk to someone about this, Mina. Someone who's not a family member or a friend. Someone with experience who can help you to start sorting things out. I'm going to pass your name along to a counselor who works with a lot of other teens who have gone through the sorts of decisions and circumstances you're facing. I think it'd be incredibly helpful for you to talk some of this through with a professional."

I nodded again, though I doubted that I'd actually talk to anyone. I barely had the energy to convince *myself* that this was real, let alone a complete stranger who would be dead set on helping me to see otherwise—dead set on helping me to see a truth that wasn't actually true.

"Now, in terms of next steps, we first need to determine how far along you are. Can you remember when you had your last period?"

I thought back, squinting as I combed through my memories to the beginning of the summer. "End of May, early June, I think. Somewhere around then." Hannah's parents had just opened her pool, and I'd had to slip one of her mom's tampons from the bathroom cabinet.

"All right," Dr. Keller said, jotting down some notes on my patient sheet. "That means you could be as far as twelve or thirteen weeks in, near the beginning of your second trimester. The baby would be due in early March in that case, but the ultrasound will give us a better sense of more precise dates. You still have some time, Mina—you still have options in terms of how you handle this pregnancy. Do you want to discuss abortion now? I'm here to answer any questions you might have, any questions at all. I can give you information about adoption resources, too, of course."

"No," I said quietly, shaking my head. "I don't have any questions about that. Not right now."

"Mina, I really think you . . ." she started, but decided against whatever was next. Instead she just nodded, looking away from me for the first time since she'd sat down. "Unless you have anything else you'd like to talk about first, I'll have Jamie call your mom back in. But only if that's what you feel most comfortable with."

"Yes, definitely," I said. "I want her in here with me."

The sight of my mom reemerging a few seconds later was more of a relief than I would have expected. I hadn't realized just how much braver I felt when she was close to me.

While Dr. Keller and Jamie tinkered with a machine mounted on a cart in the corner, my mom and I hugged—a tight, desperate hug. I pulled back when Dr. Keller started wheeling over the ultrasound equipment, a computer screen and keypad with coils of cords and plugs and attachments hanging from the side.

My mom helped me settle into a prone position on the table, my feet propped back up in the stirrups. I closed my eyes as Dr. Keller ran a small device back and forth over my bare stomach, opening them only when she said that she wanted to try a transvaginal ultrasound, too. She showed me the probe she'd be using—a bizarrely penis-like stick covered in a condom and gel. I'd be losing my virginity to a machine. I almost laughed out loud at the thought, a deranged, crazy-lady laugh that I just barely stopped from reaching my lips. I squeezed my mom's wrist with one hand and grabbed the metal table rail with the other as the probe entered, pushing farther and farther in, making my body feel less and less like my own.

After a few tense seconds I heard a beep from the monitor and looked up as the screen came to life. I couldn't see much of anything at first, just darkness with a few hazy, wavy clumps.

"We should be able to detect the heartbeat in just a moment with the Doppler fetal monitor," Dr. Keller said, tapping at the keypad as she kept her eyes on the screen.

"See that?" she asked, running her finger slowly along the grainy image. "That's your baby, Mina. At first glance the size and formation is exactly what I'd expect for someone at the end of her first trimester."

I had stopped breathing, every last particle of my body suspended in disbelief, every last bit of energy focused on that strange tiny shape in the center of the screen. My baby.

My baby.

"And if you watch closely, you'll see a small flickering, a very rapid movement . . . See, right here? Like a little valve opening and closing, opening and closing. That's the heartbeat. That's your baby's heart, Mina, beating at just the rate I'd like to see at this stage." She turned a dial on the monitor, and it took me a few seconds to process what I was hearing. *Thump-thump, thump-thump, thump-thump,* much faster, louder than I would have expected, like a galloping horse or a train speeding down the tracks. That was the sound of my baby's heart.

I was listening to my baby's heart.

This was real. This was all real.

My mom choked next to me, a hiccupping sob that seemed to shake the entire room. But I couldn't tear my eyes away from the screen, couldn't stop listening to the thumping that seemed to ring louder and louder and louder in my ears. My whole body pulsed with the sound, every beat triggering a chain reaction, a tingling, prickling sensation that flowed, raced, and burst through my veins.

A heartbeat, a baby, a new life—inside of me. Part of me.

Though I'd already known deep down I couldn't possibly give this baby up, couldn't cut off its astonishing, miraculous little life before it began, couldn't hand it over to the arms of a stranger—if there had been any lingering doubt in my mind, it was gone. It was obliterated with that heartbeat.

Maybe my decision was selfish; maybe it was reckless and self-destructive and naive.

But there was no question, not a fraction of a second's consideration: I would have this baby.

I would be a mother.

chapter six

"You *believe* her, Sallie?"

The words made me flinch from my hiding spot at the top of our wooden spiral staircase. I pressed my head down between my knees and fought the urge to run back to my room, to blast music from my headphones and numb my eardrums with something other than the sound of my dad's angry, accusing voice.

"You're telling me that you honestly believe that this is, this is . . ." he stammered, sputtering, and I didn't need to see him to picture his frenzied gestures, his strong hands waving and clawing at the air for words. "You believe that this is some sort of *miracle*, Sallie? A sign from God? Who does she think she is, the leader of the Second Coming? Do you even hear what you're saying? This is goddamn ridiculous, and I can't believe you'd entertain any of it for a minute."

"She's not lying, Paul. She's not." Mom's voice was

quiet, a whisper in comparison to his roar. I edged farther out along the step, careful not to cause any creaking that would give away my position. I'd been in this same exact spot so many times over the years, waiting and listening for a hint of Santa or the Easter Bunny, eavesdropping on my parents' private conversations on nights when I wasn't ready or able to fall asleep. I'd overheard them bickering at times, petty domestic disputes, but I could probably count on one hand the number of times I'd actually heard my parents yell at each other.

My mom and I had seen this coming, which is why she had asked to talk to him alone first—to clear the way, to take on the worst of the initial shock and disbelief. I had argued that it wasn't fair to her, but after listening in on them, I knew that she'd been right. I wouldn't have stood a chance.

As soon as we'd stepped out of Dr. Keller's office that morning, I'd told my mom that I was keeping the baby. It didn't feel right, I'd said, to end something that should never have been able to happen in the first place. There had to be a reason for it that we couldn't understand yet, a reason that this was happening to me, to us. I couldn't give the baby away for the same reason—I couldn't live the rest of my life wondering who she or he was, why they were put here, how I had been chosen.

The wondering would make me insane. The wondering would ruin my life.

If Nate *had* been the father, if I'd gotten pregnant the *normal* way, would I have made this same decision? I still would have had to spend the rest of my life questioning who she or he would have, should have been. But I didn't know. And I couldn't know, not for sure. I only knew what I had to do now, in this very abnormal set of circumstances. I had no alternate reality.

Mom had nodded, and that was the end of the discussion. I would have to face the actual logistics at some point, some point very soon, of course: how to explain my situation to outsiders, how to support myself, where to live, whether to go to college next year or indefinitely postpone it. But those were questions for later, when reality—this brand-new form of reality—had time to settle in and slowly, little by little, mold itself into my daily life in a way that made any sort of sense. March. I would have a *baby* in March. I could already hear the frantic ticking in my ears, the countdown of the clock that was as real and as crucial as my own heartbeat.

My mom and I had spent the rest of the morning and afternoon curled up on the sofa together, waiting for my dad to come home early from work, all primed for some "news" that my mom had told him she needed to share. Talking and crying and replaying every part of the exam, the sonogram, the next steps. I had set up another appointment for the following week—my first trimester screening, a more specialized round of blood work and ultrasound evaluation to identify potential risks and abnormalities.

I had called Hannah afterward, too, since I felt guilty about ignoring most of her calls—practically on the hour, every hour—for the past two days. I could hear her relief rushing through the phone. Relief that I'd told my mom and taken the next step, and relief that she wasn't the only one looking out for me anymore.

Izzy, of course, hadn't called, and I hadn't called her, either.

"Stop it, Sallie, just stop it. Listen to yourself!"

My dad's yell brought me back to my precarious position on the stairs. I could hear his anxious footsteps battering against the tile floor, looping in circles around the kitchen table where my mom sat, soaking in his fury. "Our seventeen-year-old daughter fucked up, and she doesn't want to face the consequences. And you're accepting that. You're encouraging it! You're letting her live in a dream world where bad decisions and guilt don't exist." The pacing stopped, and suddenly everything was quiet. Too quiet. I couldn't hear anything but the late-afternoon breeze hitting the screen door at the bottom of the stairs, the rhythmic *tap-tap* as it flapped against the doorframe.

"I want to talk to Mina," my dad finally said. He was quieter, almost subdued, but his tone was colder, more demanding. I preferred shouting to the sound of this new voice, the voice of a stranger. "I don't want you doing her dirty work, Sallie. She can look me in the eyes and tell me the story herself. And then she's calling Nate and he's coming over here. We all need to have a serious family discussion."

"No!" I clamped my hand over my mouth as soon as I'd screamed it down the spiral tunnel of the stairwell, but it was too late.

"Mina?" both parents called out at the exact same moment.

I hopped to my feet and grabbed the banister for balance before turning and running back to my room. I slammed the door behind me and pushed my back up against it for support. The old farmhouse latches on our doors were worthless—a little well-placed banging made any lock reversible within seconds. I bent over, hands on my knees, gasping and heaving to refill my lungs with air. I could hear stomping on the stairs as my dad's feet got closer and closer, the softer steps of my mom just behind him.

"Mina! Let me in. *Now*. We need to talk." His fist pounding on the door sent a prickling wave of vibrations along my back. I stepped away and turned, holding my fingers down over the latch to keep the hook from coming undone.

"I'm not calling Nate, Dad. I don't care if you believe me or don't believe me. That's your decision and I can't change that, but I'm not bringing Nate into this. Not today, and not like this. I tell Nate on my own terms."

"I'm not having this conversation through a slab of wood, Mina. Open the damn door, or I'm getting the ladder and coming in through the window. Your decision."

I sighed, accepting my defeat. Hiding behind a closed door was pointless. I needed to change tactics and calm him down, start building back the trust somehow.

"Fine," I said, yanking the latch up and swinging the door open. His cool blue eyes opened wide, surprised that I'd surrendered without more of a fight. "Let's have a calm and rational conversation." I walked over to my bed and sat on the edge, hands folded on my lap, looking up at him. "Mom's told you everything that she knows and everything that I know. I didn't have sex with anyone, Dad. I didn't, I really didn't, as ridiculous as I know that sounds. I don't understand why this is happening either, or why me, why any of this, any better than you do."

He loomed over me, rigid and stone-faced, a statue with my dad's clothes and my dad's features, but still just an imitation, someone, something, very different from my actual father. My mom came over to the bed and sat down next to me, wrapping her arm around my shoulders. I could see my dad's eyes shift from me to her, his forehead crinkling in disappointment.

"I would like at least a little show of support in all this,

Sallie. I don't want to be the only sane parent in the house. The only person who sees that all this is completely ludicrous. Complete bullshit."

I winced, my ears unable to process my usually warm, devoted father talking about me like I was trash, a disgusting, despicable liar. I could feel my mom's body shaking next to me, but she stayed silent, letting him push all his ugly words out into the open.

He glanced back at me then, apparently finished with my mom, and cringed. "I can't even look at you right now, Mina," he said, turning to stare out the window instead, running a hand through his already rumpled thick brown hair. "I feel like I don't even know who you are." The words ripped through my chest, like an anchor being yanked straight out of my heart, leaving a big, gaping, bloody hole in its wake.

"I didn't sign up for a third kid, Mina. How are we going to handle this? Or, better question, how are *you* going to handle this? Are we supposed to play the daddy and mommy while you go off to college and have your own pretty little carefree life? Have you thought about any of this at all? Do you even grasp the fact that your life will never be the same? This changes everything, Mina. *Every* damn thing. All the dreams I had for you, all the dreams you had . . ." He choked up at the thought, putting his fist to his mouth to stifle the sob. "How could you do this, Mina? How *could* you?"

He started crying. My strong, invincible father. Weeping right in front of me. I had only seen him cry exactly four times before, twice for each of his parents—the moment that he'd heard each had passed away, and the point at the funerals when the caskets were lowered and the handfuls of dirt were thrown on top, forever separating my nanny and my pop pop from life on the surface, from green grass and sunlight and the first warm breeze of spring.

"I'm sorry, Dad," I whispered. "I really am."

His breath hitched and he looked up at me, expectant and hopeful. He thought that he'd cracked me, that I was finally going to confess all my horrendous sins.

"I'm sorry . . . but that doesn't mean that I did anything wrong. I'm sorry that I'm hurting you, but I can't apologize for being pregnant. I can't apologize that I'm having this baby. I didn't ask for any of this. Believe it or not, this wasn't my life plan either. This wasn't my big dream for myself. I may not have it all figured out, but I have six months to get my act together." I breathed in, balled my fists, and looked him directly in the eyes. "I can do this, Dad. I can. And I will."

As I heard those words come out from between my lips, felt the full shape and size and weight of them, I believed myself. I really believed myself. I had accomplished everything I'd ever put my mind to, mastered any class, any project, any hobby I'd tried, no matter how difficult it was at the start. I had always kept trying, kept pushing myself further and further. I'd never failed. And I wouldn't fail at this, either. I wouldn't fail when it mattered the most.

My dad lowered his eyes and shook his head slowly in a daze. "I thought I'd gotten through to you. But clearly I haven't even made a dent. I don't know what it's going to take." He sighed, lifting his hands to massage deep circles around his temples. "Call Nate and tell him to come over. Now. I want to hear what he has to say about all this."

"No." I crossed my arms tight to hide my trembling hands. I couldn't. I wouldn't. I needed more time.

"He needs to know, Mina. This is his problem, too."

"This is *not* his problem. It has nothing to do with him, Dad. It's not his child. It's mine. And yes, he does deserve to know, and yes, our relationship will change because of this, but I get to decide when and how he finds out."

"Give me your phone."

"Don't make her do this, Paul," my mom pleaded, speaking up for the first time since she'd come into the room. "You shouldn't force something like this on her, not so soon. Please, Paul. Give her more time."

"Now, Mina," my dad said, ignoring my mom.

"No!" My heart was skipping, banging in my chest, and I could feel the beads of sweat creeping down my neck.

He was quicker than I was, his eyes darting around

the room until they spotted my phone on the nightstand directly in front of him. He lunged for the phone and grabbed it, skimming through my contacts list. His fierce eyes locked on mine as his finger hovered over Nate's number, testing me, waiting for me to react.

"Are you asking him to come here, or am I? If you don't do it, I will, Mina. This is nonnegotiable."

My stomach was twisting and churning, but I couldn't stop him, I realized. This was happening, I couldn't fight it—I would be telling Nate that night. Though, if I was being honest with myself, it probably didn't matter when, where, or how I told Nate. I knew how this would go—how this would end—regardless of how we got from point A to point B.

"Fine," I said, my voice so thin and shaky, I barely recognized it as my own. "I obviously can't stop you. But I won't ever forget that you made me do this."

My dad nodded as he pressed the dial button and handed me the phone.

There was barely one full ring before Nate answered, like he'd just been staring at the phone, waiting all day to hear from me.

"*Mina!* Thank God. I just got home from DC a little bit ago and I was about to drive over there if I didn't hear from you soon."

"Nate . . ."

"I've been really worried about you, Meen. It's not like

you to get this sick. You scared the shit out of me when you were too sick to even pick up the phone to say 'happy anniversary.' But I guess that's why you were so tired last week. How are you feeling? Any better?"

"I'm okay. I'm . . . I'm so sorry I didn't call sooner." I paused, taking a deep breath, and forced myself to keep going. I could feel my dad watching me, waiting for me to say what had to be said. "Can you still come over now?"

"Yeah, of course. Do you need me to bring you anything?"

"No, thanks, though. I just . . . I just want to talk to you. About something."

"You need to talk about *something*? Is everything all right? What's going on?"

I started to say yes, everything was fine, I was all right, but I couldn't lie to him. Everything wouldn't be fine, and I wouldn't be all right, not after I told him.

"Just come over as soon as you can, okay? I love you." I hung up before he could say anything else.

"Are you happy now?" I asked my dad, tilting my head up to meet his eyes. *"Are you?"* I was shouting, practically spitting at my dad's face, but I didn't care. He deserved to feel at least a small piece of the pain and suffering that he was putting me through. "Are you happy that I'm about to lose someone I really, genuinely love and care about?"

He sighed. "This is his responsibility, too, Mina," he

said, as if he were explaining something entirely new and groundbreaking to me. "I expect that he's man enough to work through it with you. And I certainly hope for the child's sake that this isn't the end for you two."

I laughed, and it came out as a cold, hard shriek. "You don't get it. You don't get it, and maybe you never will." I pulled myself out of my mom's grip and slid farther down on the bed. She might believe me, she might be my most loyal ally, but she hadn't done anything to stop him. I knew deep down that she probably couldn't have fought him off any better than I had, but I couldn't be close to her, either, right now.

"Can you both please leave my room?" I asked, pointing at the door. "I need to be alone. You can call me down when Nate gets here, and then you can sit and watch the destruction for yourself. It'll be fabulous entertainment, A-plus epic drama, exactly what you asked for. Just you wait and see."

I wouldn't have needed to be in the room, sitting next to Nate on the faded gingham loveseat, my parents perched on the edge of the sofa across from us, to know exactly how the conversation would play out.

I felt my voice shift into automatic as I went through the details of the Iris encounter. On my third time telling it, the words all came out very neatly, streamlined, almost like a bedtime story worn in from being read out loud night after night. I saw Nate's perfect, beautiful face pinch up in confusion and disbelief, saw as it morphed into anger and repulsion and hurt, so much hurt, when he finally understood what I was trying to tell him, why I had called him over to my house.

"This isn't serious, Mina," he said at the end, his dark, bottomless eyes begging for me to tell him that this was all some elaborate, senseless joke, some strange fever-induced babbling that had nothing to do with our real lives. He wanted to prick a hole in the terrible bubble that was growing bigger and bigger, swallowing the entire room, and go straight back to normal—*pop! bang! swoosh!*—as if none of this had ever happened.

"It's serious, Nate. It's all serious." I wanted to reach out and put my hand on top of his hand, lock my fingers into his so that he couldn't get up and walk out the door. But I couldn't—I didn't think I could handle the rejection of him yanking his hand away.

Why didn't I have sex with him?

Why hadn't I just let it happen? Why not on that perfect night up in the tree house? I loved him, I definitely loved him, and he loved me. If we'd been having sex, he would have believed that the baby was his. We both would have, of course. There'd be no other option, Iris or no

Iris. Believing in anything Iris said was only possible in the absence of all other scientific explanations. It was a last resort, something to cling to when there was nothing else left.

But if I had lost my virginity to Nate, he would have stood by me and supported me. We would have raised the child together. Or we would have decided that I should have an abortion or give the baby up for adoption, but we would have made those decisions together, too.

But I hadn't had sex with him, and after this, I never would.

"Nathaniel," my dad said, clearing his throat to warm up.

I'd never heard him say Nathaniel before—it was always just Nate, to me, to everyone—and the sound of his full name felt so formal and unfamiliar, like someone I didn't know. My dad hadn't spoken once since we'd sat down in the living room, letting me tell the Iris story on my own, no interruptions, but I could tell from his constant squirming and foot tapping that his mind was leaping ahead to the questions he needed to ask and the answers he needed Nate to give.

"Now, Mina is fully intending on having this child. I respect her decision to not have an abortion, of course, but you can understand that I'm very worried about what's to come down the road. I think that the two of you need to very, very seriously consider adoption here. Recognize that it's the best option for both of your futures." He put his hand up, as if to stop any potential argument before it started. "You two kids have so much potential, so much life and opportunity ahead of you, that you owe it to yourselves to at least think about giving this child to some other responsible, grateful couple, instead of raising it on your own. There are so many families who would be much better equipped to give this child the life he or she deserves."

I thought again of my baby growing up as part of someone else's life, completely removed from my own, and my stomach twisted. *No!* I wanted to scream. This was *my* life. *My* baby. There was a reason. There had to be a reason.

"Mr. Dietrich . . ." Nate started, and my muscles tensed, knowing what would undoubtedly be coming next.

"I know this is a lot to be hit with all at once, so I don't expect you to have any immediate answers," my dad said, plowing on, too absorbed in his own monologue to notice anyone's reactions. "But six or so months will be over before you know it, and you need to start planning now. Mina may be the one carrying this child, but these decisions clearly involve you, and I'd like to see the two of you make it through this together. You know, I've always liked you, Nathaniel, and this doesn't have to change everything. We all make mistakes, and life is about how you react to those mistakes." He folded his arms and tilted his head toward Nate, signaling that now, finally, he could take the floor.

"I appreciate everything you're saying, Mr. Dietrich," Nate said quietly, "but this is not my child. Without getting graphic, there is absolutely no conceivable, scientifically possible way that this is my child. So you're wrong. These decisions have nothing to do with me. None of this has anything to do with me, not anymore." He stood up, looking back down at me with tears spilling from his eyes. I'd never seen Nate cry before.

"Nate, please," I said, whimpering, as I stood up to face him. "Please believe me. Please give me a chance to prove myself."

"You're pregnant, Mina, and I'm not the father," he said, his voice shaking as he tried to fight back a sob. "How do you think that makes me feel, Mina? I loved you so much, *so much*, and you . . . How could you do this to me?" The last words came out louder, angrier, and he looked over at my parents, weighing the fact that they were listening to all this. He kept going, though, clearly unable to leave without telling me exactly what he thought about everything. What he thought about me.

"You cheated on me, Mina, and now you don't even have the decency to admit you did anything wrong? I can't believe you—you of all people—would ever be capable of doing something like this. You weren't having sex with me, but you'd sleep with someone else?" He put a fist to his mouth and looked down at his feet, cheeks flaming red. "You're disgusting. I don't want to talk to you ever again. And after we graduate, I never want to have to see your face for the rest of my life."

Something inside, something deep down and dangerously fragile, collapsed, and I started sobbing. I didn't care how desperate I looked. I didn't care that my parents were watching from just a few feet away, jaws dropped, totally unsure of how to respond to a scene that no parent should ever have to witness. I grabbed at Nate's arms, his T-shirt, his jeans, clawing at some small piece of him to hold on to, some small piece to keep for myself—until I looked up, straight into his eyes, and saw them burning with a hatred I'd never have been able to imagine him feeling about anything or anyone in the world. I had to step back, my whole body scorched from his glare. My fingertips were numb where they'd last grazed his skin, and the feeling was spreading up through my arms and across my chest, into my heart.

"Good-bye, Mr. Dietrich, Mrs. Dietrich. I'm sorry I can't help you. And I'm sorry it had to end like this." He started for the front door and I stumbled after him, my mind still racing to think of something I could do, something I could say to make this any less final.

"Nate," I said, grabbing on to his shoulder. He flinched

and shook me off, but I realized that I still needed to ask him one favor—one incredibly important favor—before he left me.

"Nate, wait," I said, gasping. "I just have one thing to ask. And then I'll let you go, I promise. I won't bother you. I'll leave you alone." He stopped moving, but he didn't turn around to face me.

"What, Mina? What could you possibly have to ask me?"

"Please don't tell anyone about this. Please let me figure out how I'm going to explain this to everyone at school."

"You didn't have to ask. I'm not going to run around telling everyone that you're pregnant with some other guy's baby. It doesn't exactly make me look good either, does it?"

I nodded in gratitude, relieved, before remembering that he still had his back to me. "Thank you, Nate. I really appreciate that."

"Whatever, Mina. It's your business. But you won't be able to hide this for long. It's going to be obvious to everyone soon enough that you're pregnant, so good luck figuring that story out. Good luck with your baby and good luck with life." He pushed open the screen door and stomped across the porch, head down, eyes fixed on the ground.

I stood there for a moment, stuck in the doorway, unable to pull my eyes away from him until he disappeared entirely.

"Mina?" a small, hushed voice called out from somewhere outside, just beyond the door. The sound was so familiar, but I couldn't label it, not instantly, because it had no place in that moment. My hand rose to my lips in panic, and I bit down on my fingertips.

"Gracie?" *No, please, no. Don't be there. I imagined that voice. Please let me have imagined that voice.*

"Mina . . ." she said again, stepping out into the soft twilight glow of the porch. "Why did Nate just say that you're having a baby? Is it true? Are you really pregnant?" Her big crystal blue eyes were wide and watery, staring up at me, waiting for my answer.

My aunt Vera shifted from the shadows just beyond my vision and stood next to Gracie, putting her hands on Gracie's shoulders to keep her steadied.

"Mina, oh God, I'm so sorry . . . I didn't mean to interrupt. I should have called before I dropped her off. I didn't know—I thought you had a stomach bug, and I figured you knew I'd be bringing her home sometime this evening . . ."

"Mina?" Gracie asked again, her little voice faltering. I could see her petal pink lips trembling, but she was fighting her tears, holding out for whatever I was about to say.

"Gracie?"

I jumped at the sudden sound of my mom's voice. I turned around to see her and my dad standing just a few feet behind me, their faces looking as horrified as I felt.

"Somebody tell me what's happening," Gracie demanded, sounding older and more grown-up than I'd ever heard her before.

I didn't want her to have to be older and more grown-up. Not because of me.

"Gracie . . ." my dad started, pushing me aside to be closer to her. "We're not talking about this right now, sweetie. I'm sorry, but I don't think you're ready for this conversation."

"Stop, Dad. Just stop," I said, stooping down so that I was at Gracie's height. "There's no point in keeping it a secret. Gracie, it's true. I am pregnant. And it's not Nate's baby, it's not anyone's baby but mine."

"Mina, don't tell her this nonsense!" my dad yelled. "You're going to confuse her!"

I put my hands on Gracie's shoulders and pulled her toward me. "This sounds crazy, but I think that this baby might be some kind of miracle, Gracie."

It was the first time I'd said the word out loud, the first time I tried it against my lips. "A miracle," I said again, letting the word sink in. "I don't know why it happened to me, but it has, and I just want you to trust me and have faith in me. Even if that takes a little time for you to come to, I'll be here. Okay?"

She stared at me, completely silent and unreadable.

Everyone else on the porch was frozen in place, waiting for her to react.

"Okay," she said at last, her strawberry-blonde pigtails bobbing as she nodded at me, a very solemn look spreading over her rosy freckled face.

"Okay?" I asked, still waiting to take my next breath.

She stepped in closer to me, so close that the tips of our noses were practically touching. So close that I could see one small tear slowly rolling down her cheek.

"You're my big sister, Mina, and for you, I'll believe in miracles."

the second trimester

chapter seven

"I think they all know, Han, I really do," I said under my breath after a few furtive glances behind me—just to be positive that no one was lurking around, eavesdropping. "I swear, I can just feel people staring at me. It's like little lasers pricking the back of my neck. They won't make eye contact when I pass them in the hall, and then they whisper as soon as I've walked by—as soon as they think that I can't hear them anymore." I opened my mouth to take a bite of my peanut-butter-and-banana sandwich, but I couldn't do it. I couldn't force myself to put food in my stomach. I had no appetite, not when I was sitting in the middle of a crowded cafeteria overflowing with all the people whom I was most afraid of at the moment.

Hannah noticed my resistance and gave me a pointed look, a look that she'd been perfecting over the last few weeks: *This isn't just about you. You have to think about the baby.*

"You're so controlling," I muttered, shoving the sandwich in my mouth and flashing a sarcastic grin as I chewed.

"Good girl. Anyway, I think it's all in your head, Meen." She lowered her voice and leaned in closer to me. "Besides, how would anyone else know? Even I can't see the bump you're talking about, though it would be hard to see much of anything under all the baggy mom shirts you've been wearing. So that leaves me, your family, Dr. Keller, Nate, and Izzy. Your family is automatically ruled out because they're your family, obviously. Dr. Keller would be breaking all sorts of doctor confidentiality rules if she told anyone, Nate would look too pathetic and bitter, and Izzy . . . Izzy would never do that. I don't care how upset she may be right now. She wouldn't ever be that disloyal to you."

I hoped that she was right, of course, even if I wasn't nearly as confident about the last two suspects as she was. But I still couldn't shake it, the feeling of being watched that had followed me everywhere since the first day of school.

"And let's be real, Meen," she said, popping a few red grapes into her mouth. "There are plenty of other reasons for people to be talking. You and Nate broke up out of absolutely nowhere, and neither of you will say why or how that happened, and Izzy hasn't so much as waved at you in the hallway since we got back. And, to top it off, you and I are sitting alone at lunch like some rejected, pathetic castaways. Everyone is obviously wondering what you did to annihilate two of the three closest relationships you had. And they're probably wondering about me, too, by association." She paused, looking away from me to stare down at her plate. "Honestly, you know you'd be whispering about someone else, too, if their life took such a dramatic downhill turn."

"Wow. Thank you, Hannah," I said quietly, shoving the rest of my sandwich back into the brown paper bag and crumpling it up into a tight ball in my hands. "Thanks for putting my life so perfectly into perspective for me. I needed that."

She winced and I looked away, frustrated with both of us. In a moment of weakness, I couldn't stop myself from peeking over at the exact spot that I so painstakingly avoided each lunch period, the big oval table closest to the counter where Hannah and I had sat every day for the last three years of high school. It was the traditional home table for the popular kids—not necessarily the trendiest or the most attractive or the most intimidating, but the kids who were the full package deal. The best athletes, the best students, the best of the best all around in everything there was to be best at, really. Smarts, talent, ambition, good looks—all wrapped up together, a killer combo. They were the people who most of the other tables aspired to be and aspired to be friends with. The people whom they wanted to be partnered up with for projects, wanted to hang out with on the weekends, wanted to be seen with in the hallways. I had always secretly questioned if I would ever have made it there on my own—my perfect grades alone weren't enough, not without other, cooler attributes to round me out, make me more of a Renaissance girl. Izzy had her dazzling athletic talents and Hannah was blonde and blue-eyed, but they were both so much more than that. They were intelligent and outgoing and confident. They lit up rooms. Between them and then Nate, I was carried along by association. And I had convinced myself that I belonged in that crowd, no matter how I'd landed there in the first place.

But now, after seeing how quickly and neatly I could be removed from the equation, I couldn't help but think I'd never belonged as much as I had let myself believe. They looked unchanged to me now, sitting there at our old table, as if nothing at all had shaken up the established equilibrium. Sasha, Molly, Quinn, Erin—we'd sat together in classes, cheered at Nate's soccer and basketball games, celebrated birthdays, primped for dances. But maybe I'd still been *Menius* to them all along, the nerdy good girl who probably thought that she was above everyone else. Only I had never thought that—I was just proud of my grades and proud of how hard I worked. Maybe I could have gone to more Friday night football games, said yes to more shopping trips to the mall, cared more about hair and makeup and girl talk with anyone besides Hannah and Izzy. But I'd stupidly felt secure about my place there. And even if I *had* tried harder to fit in, I'd still be sitting at a different table right now, wouldn't I? I'd still be the girl who used to date Nate, the girl who used to be friends with Izzy. I couldn't have altered the natural order of things, not permanently.

I watched Nate and Izzy, their chairs on opposite ends, as far apart as two people could be without sitting at two different tables. I could tell, even from my position halfway across the room, that they were carefully avoiding each other. They'd nod and laugh along with the group when the other talked, but they didn't go out of their way to say anything one-on-one—probably because the one thing and the one person they'd most like to talk about wouldn't make for appropriate lunchroom conversation. Otherwise, they looked entirely normal, happy, and at ease. No one would ever have guessed that either of them was secretly torn up on the inside, devastated with missing me. Maybe that was because they weren't. Maybe they'd both already moved on.

A sudden thought banged against me like a fist to the gut. Had they been talking outside of school? Were they comparing notes about me? Going over all the reasons why I was a horrible best friend and a horrible girlfriend?

The idea of the two of them bonding over some newly discovered mutual hate made me feel sick. And it also made me furious. I had done *nothing* wrong. Not a single thing. They just couldn't believe that—they couldn't believe *me*.

But I wouldn't cry. I wouldn't cry. I wouldn't cry.

"I'm sorry, Mina. I didn't mean for it to sound like that," Hannah said.

I tore my eyes away from Nate, who was in the middle of telling a story that had the entire table in hysterics. But just as I was about to turn back to Hannah, I noticed that *I* was being watched, too, the target of a too-pretty girl with glossy black hair and red lips twisted up in a smirk. Arielle Fowler—I'd known who she was since the first day of kindergarten, but we'd never been friends, or anything close to friends. She hadn't sat at our lunch table before, though she moved in the same circles as most of the people who did. But there she was now, taking up a spot that would have belonged to me or Hannah before.

Arielle was the head cheer captain and the shoo-in lead for school plays, a blending of after-school worlds that usually didn't collide. But she was unnervingly beautiful—a real-life Snow White with her wavy raven hair and flawless porcelain skin—and so normal rules didn't apply to her. Though unlike Snow White, she had never been friendly, at least not to me. I had always gotten the feeling that she could see right through me with her dark-lashed doe eyes—that she knew I didn't really fit in. That she, too, wondered why Nate would choose someone like me, when she'd openly had a crush on him for as long as I had.

"Meen?" Hannah asked, forcing me to break away from Arielle's unsettling stare. "Are you listening to me? They have no clue what's really going on, so you need to just do your best to ignore them. You can't let them bother you and stress you out too much . . . It's not healthy." There was the look. Again.

I took a deep breath to stop myself from exploding, to remind myself that her intentions were good, even if they weren't always spectacularly executed. She was trying her best; she genuinely was. She could have sat at our old table with all her other friends who didn't hate her, but she hadn't. I doubted that the idea had even crossed her mind. I exhaled and looked into her brilliant blue eyes.

"But it's not just how it looks from the outside, is it, Hannah? Nate really did break up with me, and one of my best friends really does hate me. My dad can't bring himself to look at me, let alone speak to me, and everywhere I turn, I find my mom hiding out somewhere and crying to herself. Last night I found her sitting on the washing machine in the basement and sobbing when she thought I was up in my room doing homework."

"You have Gracie, though."

She said that as if it made up for everything else—as if this one vote of support in my favor could make all the difference. And maybe it did, to be honest, because I don't know how I could have woken up every morning if Gracie had turned against me, too.

"Seriously, Meen, little kids are like a litmus test for right and wrong. She believes you because she knows that you're a good person and that you wouldn't lie to her. She's not old enough or jaded enough to question it."

"And you're not old enough or jaded enough, either, I take it?"

"I have a uniquely optimistic sensibility. I like to hope for the best in people." She smiled and squeezed my hand under the table.

I smiled back at her, a real smile, even though I still sensed her uncertainty. "I can live with that answer."

And I meant that—for now, at least. I didn't know what she did or didn't believe, but as far as I could tell, she didn't know either. She may have still thought that I was repressing the real explanation, locking the traumatizing truth away so deep and dark in my mind somewhere even I wouldn't know where to find it again. But in that case, she wouldn't think I was straight out lying to her, or at least not any more than I was lying to myself. I wanted her to know as absolutely as I did that that was *not* what had happened, but I had no proof. I could accept whatever doubts she had, though, because she was still sitting there next to me. That mattered most.

"So your dad . . . He isn't budging at all, then?"

My smile evaporated as quickly as it had appeared. "Nope. Still a total stalemate. I don't think he's looked at me, not once. He won't even sit at the dinner table with us, just gets his food and goes straight to his office and shuts the door. My mom and Gracie both keep a straight face and chatter away while we eat as if everything's all normal, but I know they miss him, even if they're angry at him, too, for my sake."

"I'm sorry, Meen . . ."

"Don't be. It'll be fine. He has to come around at some point." I hoped that if I thought and said that out loud enough, it would inevitably become true. I could make it true; I just had to want it and will it with everything I had in me. But I couldn't know anything for sure, obviously. I couldn't predict how my dad or Nate or Izzy would ever come to terms with my pregnancy, or if they would ever come to terms with it at all. There wasn't exactly a precedent to guide me for this type of real-life drama. Except for the Bible, I suppose, but the people in my life didn't seem to swallow the magic miracle pill quite as easily as they did back in the day.

Go figure. Mary had it so easy.

Not that I thought that I was *actually* the next Mary. I didn't know what I was or what I was doing, but to even think for a second that I was carrying some world-altering gift from God—not just a gift, but the next *Jesus*, the next Messiah, the almighty savior of the whole damn universe—seemed like total blasphemy, a surefire way to send myself straight to the Devil's flaming lair of tortured souls. If I even believed there was a Hell to be sent to, anyway, let alone a God, or at least a God in the way that the Bible described.

I didn't know what I really thought or what I really believed about anything anymore. I couldn't separate absolutes from myths, facts from fiction. I couldn't say what was real and what wasn't real.

How could anything in the world ever be predictable after this?

How could there ever be any certainty? Any guarantees?

Maybe I'd wake up tomorrow and the sky would be tangerine orange and dotted with fluffy green clouds. Grass would be hot pink, puppies would be singing, kittens would be dancing with top hats and canes, and we'd all be soaring like eagles through the sky, flying with our arms fanned out behind us to catch the gusts of wind.

If a virgin like me could suddenly wake up pregnant, wasn't *anything* possible?

A nearby chair slammed against the tile floor—along with the unlucky but deserving football hero who had been leaning too far on its back legs—and the cafeteria broke out in its typical round of applause and catcalls. I shook off my questions like an odd, hazy dream and looked back over at Hannah. She still seemed caught up in our conversation, hesitant to say anything too hopeful or too positive for fear of misleading me. I saw the struggle going on behind her eyes, the internal battle as she tried her hardest to think of an optimistic follow-up.

"Hannah . . ." I started, then stopped, debating what I actually wanted to know and what would be better left unknown. Curiosity won out—I was never one for tucking questions away for later. "Can you tell me what people are really saying about me and Nate, and me and Izzy? They must be coming up with some sort of creative explanations, right?"

She sighed and stared out the big bay window next to our table. I already wished I hadn't asked—I didn't want to push between her and everyone else at school any more than I already had. Her reputation and social ranking were in free fall, plummeting just as fast and steadily as mine were, like a tiny, fragile hummingbird chained to a massive barbell. Not quite the golden senior year we'd been anticipating.

"I'm sure they are, Meen, but no one's saying anything

in front of me, either," she said, turning back to look at me. She didn't seem angry that I'd asked, thankfully, but I could still see unfamiliar shadows on her face—it was like a sparkly, glowing piece of the Hannah I'd known forever had somehow gotten lost, had faded away. Because of me and because of everything she was putting herself through to make my life easier. "I think I've made it pretty obvious whose side I'm on. And to be honest, I don't even want to know, since it'd be all lies, anyway. Hearing it would just make me hate people for gossiping about something they know nothing about. It's easier to pretend that they're not talking, to smile along like everything's fine, everyone's okay, and just get on with this last year together."

She was right: it was probably better not to know. But I still couldn't help the urge to find out more. I could ask someone else, but I had barely talked to anyone but Hannah and my teachers since classes had started. I didn't want to do or say anything that would put the spotlight on me, at least not more than it already was.

"Yeah, we'll see. But you're probably right. Best not to know." I looked over at the clock and leaped up, scrambling out of my chair. "We should head out now, ahead of everyone. The more I can avoid all their beady eyes in the hallway, the better."

We grabbed our trays and started toward the exit,

my head ducked to avoid any accidental interactions.

"Hey, Meen, isn't that the busboy from Frankie's? What did you say his name was? Jesse Spero?"

I jerked my head up, almost smacking straight into the bright yellow trash can in front of me. It *was* Jesse, wearing the same green cap and another blazer, though this one was a faded camel brown with a matching bow tie at his neck.

"*Shhh!*" I hissed at her, turning my back to him. "I don't want him to see me." I threw the rest of my sandwich in the garbage and ducked behind a nearby pillar. "I didn't realize he went here. I thought he was homeschooled or something like that." Not that we'd had much actual conversation—but I could have sworn I'd overheard him mention homeschooling to one of the guys in the kitchen. Obviously, things had changed, because here he was at Green Hill High.

He was sitting alone at the table closest to the trash and the dirty tray counter, which was, hands down, the least desirable property in the cafeteria. It was the zone where all the loners sat, scattered a few seats away from one another at the long rectangular tables, a random mix of goth hermits and special needs kids and the occasional new student, like Jesse, who either hadn't found any potential friends to rescue them, or didn't care to be rescued in the first place. I had always felt a small burst of shame when I rushed passed their tables, wondering if there was anything I could or should do to make their lunches even just a little bit less lonely and miserable. But I was realizing now that that was probably presumptuous of me—that maybe they didn't mind being alone. That maybe not everyone cared about everyone else's opinions as much as I did. Jesse certainly didn't seem to notice or worry that his social status was at any sort of risk. He had a thick book in his hand with an unmistakably sci-fi cover, and he looked far more interested in that than the fact that he was potentially hurling himself into isolation for the rest of his high school career.

I envied him. I wished that he could teach me to stop caring. To let go.

The end of lunch alarm blared, and students started swarming from all directions, buzzing in circles around me. Just as Jesse put his book down and glanced up, I ducked my head and ran. I pushed through the double doors and into the hallway, leaving him and every other face I couldn't stand to see safely behind me.

A few hours later, back in the sanctuary of my room, I stared down at my backpack, deliberating: to open or not to open. To face reality, or to keep pretending that grades and GPAs had ceased to exist. The zipper was stretched dangerously close to splitting from the jumble of textbooks and notebooks and folders that I had somehow managed to magically squeeze inside. I'd been in school for almost a month, but I couldn't recall learning much, if anything at all, and I'd barely so much as touched a textbook outside of class. I had, of course, signed up for almost all advanced-track classes. And while this meant less day-to-day busywork, hugely significant essays and tests and projects were looming on the horizon. The exceptionally close horizon.

Before I could change my mind, I yanked the zipper down and dumped every last spiral pad and piece of paper out onto my bed. I couldn't put off what I could see with my own eyes, the physical evidence of just how momentously screwed I'd be if I didn't start being the student everyone expected me to be again, and soon.

It wasn't that I was doing nothing with my nightly study time in my room. I was reading and researching into all hours of the night, every night, but I wasn't enlightening myself about the finer points of European history or calculus or classic American literature.

I had two tall stacks on my desk, towers of books I'd ordered online and books I'd scavenged from my parents' bookshelves. A–Z pregnancy guides with week-to-week growth charts and how-to's and suggestions: what to eat, what not to eat, caffeine or no caffeine, how much exercise is too much exercise and how much weight is really acceptable to gain? I had already read through five different books, highlighting and penciling notes in the margins, notes that I'd typed up afterward so that I could reread the most important ideas again and again and probably even again until I was convinced that they had been permanently seared into my memory.

I didn't know why I was having this baby, but that only made the whole process infinitely more terrifying. What if I did something wrong, one tiny little thing, an innocent accident, and that ended up hurting or . . . ? Just thinking of anything worse made me break out in cold sweats. The fear hit me harder every day, every morning when I woke up worrying that I would somehow let this baby down. Let Iris down, disappoint whoever or whatever was holding the strings behind all this.

How could the War of the Roses or the limits and infinitesimals of calculus possibly rank on the priority list? No matter the exact cause or the exact reasons behind it all, I knew that this baby was more important than getting straight As—becoming a mom was more important than becoming the valedictorian. Because who was I in all this? Who was I in comparison to the life I was carrying?

I was a vessel, a mode of transportation, a way for this child to get from one place to the next, one world to another. I was a human incubator, a machine that just happened to have lungs and a brain and a beating heart.

Did all soon-to-be mothers feel this? All of them who had conceived in the normal way? Whether it was intentional or a slip, whether it was a one-night stand or a loving husband, a defective condom or a perfectly laid-out plan—did every pregnant woman feel as if she had suddenly stopped existing as an individual? That she had handed over the keys to her independence the moment she decided to keep the baby? I couldn't imagine *not* feeling this way because, really, when it came down to it—wasn't *every* baby its own kind of miracle? Just because science could explain the hows and whys of reproduction didn't make it any less amazing that a sperm met an egg and nine months later a living, breathing baby was born. My hows and whys were unusual, yes, but maybe the end result was the same.

I liked this, the idea that I wasn't the first or last new mom to feel this way—so selfless and humbled in the face of something much bigger than I was.

My baby was, according to my reading, roughly five ounces, five inches long that week, or about the size of an onion or a small potato—for whatever reason, every pregnancy source liked to compare the fetus size to fruits and vegetables, though there was nothing particularly cute to me about measuring my baby against a lumpy brown root vegetable. She or he was just beginning to start forming body fat, rubbery cartilage was turning into bone, and tiny ear bones were developing, which meant that maybe, just maybe, my voice was being heard. Was becoming familiar, even. Little eyes had moved to the front of the face, complete with eyebrows and eyelashes—eyes that could now sense light and make small side-to-side movements. Eyes that would maybe look just like mine, wide and blue and relentlessly curious. She or he could wiggle fingers and toes, and sometimes, if I closed my eyes and really focused on the inside of my body, I swore I could feel the movements.

Those were the facts that really mattered. *Those* were the details I needed to be learning and absorbing every spare minute I could find.

But pregnancy books weren't the only books I was fixated on. I'd slipped into the church library two Sundays before—my first and only time there since it had all began—and taken out as many books as I could find about miracles in general and about Mary and the Immaculate Conception—which, contrary to what I'd spent my whole life assuming, was a doctrine concerning Mary's mother's conception of *her*, not Mary's conception of *Jesus*. It was *Mary* who was born free of any original sin, free of all stains and blemishes—blessed with the purifying grace normally conferred in baptism. From the moment she was born, from the very beginning of her life, Mary had already been chosen.

And what about me? When had this become *my* fate? *My* path to stumble down?

I was desperate, ravenous for clues. I'd pored over the books, searching for whatever slivers of insight I could find. I'd read and reread different translations of each passage in the Bible that centered around Mary—the conception, her fateful meeting with Gabriel, the reactions of the people who loved her. But I kept coming back to Luke, the passage that was most familiar to me:

> *In the sixth month the angel Gabriel was sent by God to a town in Galilee called Nazareth, to a virgin engaged to a man whose name was Joseph, of the House of David. The virgin's name was Mary. And he came to her and said, "Greetings, favored one! The Lord is with you." But she was much perplexed by his words and pondered what sort of greeting this might be.*
>
> *The angel said to her, "Do not be afraid, Mary, for you have found favor with God. And now you will conceive in your womb and bear a son, and you will name him Jesus. He will be great and will be called the Son of the Most High, and the Lord God will give to him the throne of his ancestor David. He will reign over the house of Jacob forever, and of his kingdom there will be no end."*
>
> *Mary said to the angel, "How can this be, since I am a virgin?" The angel said to her, "The Holy Spirit*

will come upon you, and the power of the Most High will overshadow you; therefore the child to be born will be holy; he will be called Son of God. And now your relative Elizabeth in her old age has also conceived a son; and this is the sixth month for her who was said to be barren. For nothing will be impossible with God." Then Mary said, *"Here am I, the servant of the Lord; let it be with me according to your word."*

Then the angel departed from her.

But what did Mary *really* think after the angel just up and departed, vanished back into thin, heavenly air? I wanted to read about her struggles, her shock, her disbelief—that she was "much perplexed" didn't quite cut it for me. I wanted thoughts and feelings that would make her real and three-dimensional, a human being rather than a character meant to impart some kind of lesson in faith and obedience.

After I exhausted the relevant Bible passages, I started reading about miracles across the centuries, across religions, and across the globe, the history of the beliefs and the history of the word *miracle* itself. *Miracle*—mir-a-cle—a mid-twelfth-century Middle English word derived from the Old French *miracle*; from Latin *miraculum*, "object of wonder"; from *mirari*, "to wonder at"; and from *mirus*, "wonderful." Mary, it turns out, wasn't even the first symbol of miraculous birth to be found in historical and religious literature—the idea of divine conception had been around long before her, in Assyrian, Babylonian, Egyptian, Japanese, Greco-Roman and Hellenistic mythologies, Hinduism, and Buddhism. There were commonalities laced throughout all of these ancient belief systems—deities emerging through physically impossible conceptions, and the inexplicable nature of divinity itself.

But why is this a narrative that human beings keep latching onto, keep grasping at as truth, as proof of some supreme being? Why did the divine need a womb at all, really? Why not just spring out of the ground, or fall from the sky? Materialize out of nothing and nowhere?

I kept hoping that something would jump out at me from a page, a word or an image, some cryptic message that would somehow illuminate everything I was going through. But so far—nothing. I wasn't closer to any sort of explanation than I'd been in August, staring at those damn pee sticks in the woods.

I grabbed my English notebook from the rubble pile and flipped open the front cover. An essay with a big red *C* stared up at me, and I quickly jammed it in the back pages where I could at least temporarily pretend it didn't exist. It was my first C in the history of my education, and in English of all classes, my strongest subject. My favorite subject. Reading and writing had always just come so naturally to me, so effortlessly, like breathing and walking and eating. English was the only college major I had ever seriously considered, the only future I could picture for myself. Teaching, editing, writing—anything that involved words on paper, thoughts pinned down in black and white.

But now I had proof that I couldn't even count on a guaranteed A in English, not if I planned on doing nothing to really earn it. This particular essay had been the first of the school year, written about *The Scarlet Letter*, appropriately enough—an analysis of knowledge, sin, and the human condition. One would think I'd have excelled at the topic, but the C seemed to say otherwise. I had already read the book on my own two years earlier, so I'd figured it was reasonable to rely on online summaries and critiques the second time around. I'd been so proud the week before when I'd managed to cobble together the entire paper in less than three hours. Safe to say, all pride had vanished.

I felt as if I should care more than I did. I should care enough to beg the teacher for a redo. I should care enough to start reading the copy of *Heart of Darkness*, the next book on our list, that was sitting on my nightstand. I should care—but I didn't. I was scared of what my parents would say if they knew, and of what other students would think about my stunning fall from the top. But when it came down to me and what I really felt, the part of me that had held so much stress and ambition and fear about school . . . that place now just felt hollow. Perfect grades had lost their power over me. Grades couldn't define me anymore. It was petrifying, all of a sudden existing without the clear spectrum of success that I'd held myself up to for the last twelve years. Grades made it easy to label yourself: As meant you were a success, you were smart and capable and in control. Cs meant you were mediocre. You needed to study longer, try harder.

I was on my own now, with no clearly set marks to validate my progress. Real life didn't quite work like that, I was learning. Real life seemed much more pass or fail to me.

I sighed and tossed my English notes back in the heap. Tomorrow would be Friday, and then I'd have the whole weekend to catch up. I would make to-do lists for each of my classes and systematically cross off each assignment, one by one, powering through all of Saturday night if I had to. I'd worked too hard for too many years to ruin it all so close to the end. I didn't need all As, but I still needed to pass. I still needed to get into college. As soon as the most urgent schoolwork was done, I'd go back to the applications. Reassess, reevaluate. Come up with a new, more functional plan of attack. A plan that somehow figured in caring for and supporting a tiny, helpless, fatherless baby on my own.

I sat down at my desk in front of the computer, scanning mindlessly through a few e-mails before my fingers typed in *modern-day miracle* on autopilot. I'd searched slightly different combinations and variations of the same words almost every day, hoping each time that I'd find a story I'd somehow missed before, some hint that even one other person in the entire world had experienced something remotely similar—that genuine miracles were happening if people were open and willing enough to believe.

There were the standard stories about miraculous healing, and who was to say what really happened in those cases? Amazing genius doctors and brain-numbingly innovative medications and procedures? Pure and simple good luck? The human body could perform some pretty spectacular, awe-inspiring feats sometimes—that much seemed inarguable. But the spontaneous growth of a baby sans sexual reproduction? That would be a first—or a second, depending on who you asked.

A knock at the door made me jump.

"Mina?" my mom called out from the hallway, her voice low and tentative. Before this had all happened, she would have opened the door without giving me the chance to respond, the knock more on principle, an alert rather than an actual question. But privacy lines had changed. My life inside my room was suddenly much more my own, my one free space to think and cry and breathe.

"You can come in, Mom," I said, closing the window on my computer screen and turning in my seat to face her. She stepped in and shut the door, glancing at me briefly before looking away, her eyes twitchy and unfocused.

"What's up?" I asked, nervous because she was nervous. Her anxiety was contagious. "Is there something you want to talk about?"

She nodded as she perched herself on the edge of my bed. "I've been wanting to talk about this ever since . . . well, ever since we found out the news. But I also wanted to give you time to think on it by yourself, to come to your own decisions. I didn't want to push you." She paused, and we both stared down at her hands, her fingers spinning her thick band of bracelets in jangling circles around her wrist. "The thing is, sweetheart, you're going to be showing any day now. To be honest, this morning at breakfast I thought I noticed a bump for the first time. A very small bump, but this is just the beginning. It's only a matter of weeks, maybe even days, before people start to talk. Before they start to ask questions. And I just want to know that you're prepared to give them some sort of answer. Now, I will fully support you on whatever answer you want to give—that's your decision—but I don't want you to be caught off guard when it does happen. And it *will* happen." She exhaled for what seemed like the first time since she'd walked into the room, her face flushed from the exertion of pushing it all out.

"It's not as if I haven't been thinking about this, Mom. Trust me," I said, my voice shaking. "I've gone over it so many times in my head, played through every sort of answer I could give. No one will believe that I'm a virgin if my own dad and boyfriend and best friend can't even have that sort of faith in me. But I don't want people to think that I cheated on Nate. I don't want people to think there's a random daddy running around out there, some kind of meaningless one-night stand. How do I win, Mom? How do I make people hate me the least? Because that's the best I can hope for."

My mom kneeled next to my chair, wrapping her arms around me. She burrowed against my chest, not bothered by my tears streaming down through her hair.

"We'll give it a few more days, Mina. We'll both think about this over the weekend. We'll come up with something. I know we will, Mina. We will."

I wanted to believe her. She was my mom—she had always been able to solve every problem, to make everything wrong become right again. But this time I wasn't so sure. Because this time, a solution might not exist.

Not without another miracle.

I couldn't fall asleep after that, not as I kept replaying what my mom had said, brainstorming one impossibly lame explanation after another. At midnight I gave up and kicked off my blankets, quietly making my way down to the kitchen to heat up a glass of milk on the stove. I hadn't resorted to that since I was little, afraid of monsters and ghosts and every little sound that came out of an old house at night, and it was always Mom or Dad heating the milk up then. It had worked, though, every time, whether it was the milk itself or just the idea of it that made it so effective. The warm mug cupped in my hands, the warm milk against my throat—I barely had time to swallow the last sip before I'd be passed out on top of the pillows.

As soon as I stepped into the kitchen, before I even flicked on the light, I realized that I wasn't alone. My dad was sitting in a chair by the window, his silhouette dark and hazy against the backdrop of pale moonlight. I jumped in surprise, my hand smacking against the doorframe behind me as I started to spin back around. My dad started, his chair scraping against the tile floor as he stood.

"Mina?" he asked, his face turning toward me, though I couldn't see his eyes in the darkness.

"Sorry, I didn't mean to disturb you," I said, backing away toward the hallway. "I just wanted some warm milk.

I couldn't sleep, and I remembered how well that used to work when I was a kid."

"No, it's fine. Don't leave," he said, his voice sounding too tired and worn to hold any of his anger right now. "I was actually down here doing the same thing. The pot's still on the stove. Sit down. I'll heat it up for you." He pushed his chair forward, motioning me toward it.

"No, it's fine. I can make it," I said, starting toward the stove.

"Sit down, Mina. I got it." The gruffness I was used to hearing lately was back, and I was too exhausted to fight it. I sat down as he grabbed the milk carton and flipped on the small light over the stove, leaving the room still mostly in darkness. It was better that way, I thought, easier not to be able to see each other in too much light. I waited for him to say something, anything, but he didn't. I listened instead to the tap of the wooden spoon as he stirred in slow, careful circles so that the milk wouldn't scald at the bottom of the pot. I watched as he stuck the tip of his finger into the milk, cocked his head, and stirred for another minute or so before testing the temperature again and then, deciding it was just right, poured it into the same mug he'd used. He clicked off the burner, walked over to me, and handed me the mug.

"I hope this helps," he said, his eyes looking out the

window just behind me. "Good night, Mina."

I wanted us to say so much more, but I just nodded as I took the milk, our hands brushing for one precious second.

"Thank you, Dad. Good night."

I really miss you, I almost said, but the words caught in my throat as he disappeared down the dark hallway. *Do you miss me, too?*

chapter eight

I woke up the next morning with the sort of grotesquely ballooning eyelids and blotchy cheeks that made it obvious to anyone with eyes that I'd spent most of the previous night wide awake and drowning in tears. That, of course, only added to my fears that everyone was analyzing my every movement, speculating about what devastating secret could possibly be putting me through so much anguish. And so my Friday at school passed, as usual, in a blur of dodging glances in the hallway, head tucked like a defensive linebacker as I sprinted from class to class. I was desperate to avoid Izzy and Nate, and now Arielle Fowler was on that list, too—I could swear she had been staring at me during lunch again. But why? She'd certainly never shown any interest in me before. She'd barely ever acknowledged that I existed at all. What would she be saying now to all her sycophantic cheerleading and drama groupies about me? Just thinking about those cool, calculating blue eyes from across the cafeteria gave me the chills for the rest of the afternoon. The three-o'clock bell that marked the official start to the weekend did little to comfort me, not with a long closing shift at Frankie's to get through first.

I had considered quitting countless times, probably twenty times a day, give or take a few—throwing in the apron and finding a new job that didn't involve working in a crowded, claustrophobic room with everyone I'd ever known in the entire community of Green Hill. People staring at me, waiting for me, shouting out my name across the busy restaurant for more ice in their Coke or an extra side of ranch. Leaving would be the easy choice. But I needed to be saving money now, before I was too far along to be on my feet. The tips weren't a fortune in the grand scheme of things, but they were still much better than nothing, and they were more than I'd make in any new job I could find in Green Hill.

And there was something more that kept me there, another reason to keep pushing through. There was a powerful, almost masochistic need to be connected to Iris. I was scared by the memory of her, terrified, really, but I still clung to it, wrapped my arms and legs around it like a little kid hanging onto her parent's leg. I needed that memory as validation—the clear, definite moment that marked the beginning of my new, alternate existence. It's not that I expected her to walk back through the front door—I had a sickening feeling that that was a one-time-only appearance—but I was desperate for more answers. There were so many questions and explanations that I needed to hear, and being at Frankie's gave me a small seed of hope—as if by going back to the beginning, I could gradually start to unravel the middle and the end.

I drove straight to the restaurant from school and changed into my bright green Frankie's T-shirt and my alarmingly tighter-than-usual jeans in the staff bathroom. I couldn't stop playing over what my mom had said the night before, and no amount of sucking in made me feel safer or more invisible. Tucking in our shirts was mandatory, but I tugged the extra material out from my waistband, carefully bunching and scrunching, making a loose, billowy cloud of cotton to block what may or may not have been a conspicuous bump. As a secondary precaution, I tied my apron on above my hips a good few inches higher than usual so that it flapped down over my stomach. Slightly awkward-looking, sure, but better than the alternative.

Satisfied that I'd done the best I could do with my limited wardrobe options, I stepped out into the kitchen, already warm and sticky from the heat of the brick ovens, and went to help Frankie prep the counter.

The first few hours melted away before I'd had the chance to even think about looking up at the clock. At eight or so, when there was a small lull between the main dinner crowd and the second string of stragglers, mostly kids my age and younger couples, I pushed through the back kitchen door and stepped out for some cool, clean, pizza-free air. The worst of the nausea had passed by then, thank God, though the omnipresent, stinking haze of oozing mozzarella and garlicky tomato sauce still didn't smell nearly as good to me as it had a few months ago. But I could fight through it. I could smile while I sliced up steaming hot pies for customers, swallow the gag reflex that threatened to come out with an especially strong whiff from the ovens.

I closed my eyes as I leaned back against the outside brick wall, breathing in the scent of the late-September evening, the smell of grilling steaks from a nearby backyard barbecue, fresh grass clippings from the soccer fields across the back alley. It would have been so easy to walk just a few more feet to my car, to drive away and lose myself on some winding back country roads with old-school John Mayer blaring from the speakers. But I couldn't let myself give in to that impulse, just like I couldn't quit altogether, not yet. There was more money to make first, before I was too far along, before the jig was up and all eyes really would be on me. And I knew I would need that money, when I had a newborn to support. Besides, I was getting so used to fighting myself—I seemed to be doing it all day every day lately. It was getting harder to separate what I actually felt from what I thought I should feel, or what I actually wanted from what I thought I should want. The line was so faded and fragile, I could blink and miss it, almost like it hadn't existed in the first place. And maybe it hadn't. Maybe I'd never really listened to myself before now.

The door next to me swung open with a bang, colliding with the wall only a few inches away from where I was leaning. My eyes split open and I jumped forward, startled.

"Oh, hey, Mina, didn't mean to scare you there, kiddo," Carl said in his jolly round voice that so perfectly suited his jolly round body. Sweat was pouring from under his white cook's cap as he heaved a massive carton of what looked like plates and glasses from the top of his shoulder down to the pavement in front of us. "Just getting ready to clean out the back of my van and load up some supplies. Frankie's catering a party in the morning, before the lunch rush." He paused, huffing as his bright red cheeks mellowed back to their more normal shade of light, rosy pink. "Jesse should be right behind me with another big box. He has a list with him. Would you mind seeing if he needs any help? I know he's been here a few months now, and he's a smart enough kid, don't get me wrong, but his head's not always on the ground if you know what I mean. Too much of a thinker and a dreamer for his own good, that one. He looks like a space cadet most of the time, floating around the kitchen here with stars in his eyes. I don't know where he actually is, but it sure isn't Frankie's," he said, chuckling as he winked at me conspiratorially. "Must be from his mom's side of the family. Didn't come from my brother or me, that's for sure."

I grinned at him. Carl generally had that effect. Everyone loved Carl. He was like a younger version of Santa, a big, happy man who made everyone else around him happy, too, just by the sheer proximity of his presence. It was a shame he was hidden away in the back, slaving in the kitchen, but he seemed perfectly content dicing onions and frying cheesesteaks on the griddle, as if there was no better job to be had anywhere in the whole entire world.

"Sure, no problem," I said, slapping him on the back as I reached behind him and pulled the door open. "Whatever Carl asks, I do. You know that. I'll keep tabs on that nephew of yours."

I sounded more confident than I felt, but that was the power Carl had over people. As soon as I'd set foot back in the kitchen, my stomach fluttered with doubt.

I was being ridiculous, I reminded myself. I could talk to Jesse. We were both outcasts, so why not at least be friendly to each other? So what if he thought I was a little weird, especially since it seemed as if he was a little weird, too, based on what Carl had said and my own observations.

And besides, it wasn't as if I could really have avoided him altogether forever, given the fact that we worked at the same restaurant and went to the same school. I wasn't even sure why it mattered that I tried to anymore.

I walked across the deserted kitchen and poked my head into the storage closet. He was sitting on top of another enormous box, his forehead wrinkled in concentration as he stared down at a grease-stained, crumpled piece of paper. His fingers were knotted up in his dark brown mop of hair, a Medusa-like mass of wild curls that looked outraged by the steamy heat pouring out from the kitchen.

I bit back the small smile that was creeping up my lips. "Hey there."

He jumped up in surprise, his customary distracted haze slipping off as his eyes focused on me.

"Your uncle . . . asked me to check in. Give you a hand if I can."

He grinned at me, the same grin I suddenly remembered with a flash from that first night, so shockingly bright and genuine. Infectious smiles seemed to run in the family.

"Old Carl doesn't trust me, does he?" He shrugged, waving the paper in the air. "I'm just going over the list for the last time, but I think everything's crammed into this box now, so I should be all set. But thanks for the offer. Really. I appreciate it."

He put a slight emphasis on those last words, like he wanted me to know that he really meant it. That he was touched that I'd gone out of my way to help him, probably because it was so entirely out of character based on the Mina he'd witnessed for the past few months. I blushed and looked down at the ground, scraping my foot against the light dusting of flour.

I watched from the corner of my eye as he folded the paper into his apron pocket and bent over, hunching his shoulders as he started to pick up the box.

"Let me help with that at least," I said, rushing forward to grab the other side. My fingers had just barely grazed the cardboard when Jesse put his hand on my wrist to stop me.

"Wait," he said, sounding panicked. "You shouldn't be lifting that."

I looked up, confused. My eyes met his, dark honey brown and rimmed with worry.

"What's wrong?" I asked. "I know I'm not exactly Superwoman, but I think I can help you move this box to the back door."

"No, it's just that . . ." he started, and stopped, his cheeks flushing a deep red.

"It's just that *what?*" A slow burning ache gnawed at the pit of my stomach.

"It's nothing. I mean, I shouldn't have said that. It's

not any of my business . . ." His face was tilted down, his eyes hidden from me behind thick black lashes.

"What were you going to say?" I needed him to answer. Now.

"It's just something I overheard," he said, still refusing to make eye contact. "Two girls sitting in one of the back booths yesterday, at the very end of the night. They were the only two people in the restaurant at that point. I was wiping down a table near them, but I don't think they even realized I was there. I tend to be kind of invisible, I've noticed . . ." He was still staring down at the floor, where his ragged blue and white Converse sneakers were rocking back and forth to a nonexistent beat.

"What did you hear?" I asked, more hesitant this time.

"I . . ." He broke off as he raised his eyes to face me. There was so much regret and sympathy looking out at me that I gasped and stepped back to move away from him. I felt entirely too vulnerable, as if he was gazing straight through my clear blue eyes while I laid out every last intimate detail of my life for him to see all at once. I couldn't look away, though, either unwilling or unable to break the connection, I wasn't sure.

"I heard you were pregnant, and I just assumed it was true. It seemed as if the girl knew what she was talking about, but that was still really out of line for me to say to you. It's your business, not mine. I just got nervous when I saw you trying to lift such a heavy box, and I didn't think before I spoke, that's all."

The words fell on me like a collapsing ceiling, as if the whole restaurant were crashing down, beam by beam and brick by brick, burying me in the wreckage. But I had to keep going before I was cut off completely. I had to know everything.

"Is that all she said? If she said more, I really want you to tell me. I can handle it."

His cheeks turned an even more intense shade of red. "The girl, she said that you were claiming to be . . . Jesus, this is hard to say out loud. I mean . . . *shit*, no, not *Jesus*. No. Bad word to use there."

He winced, cursing under his breath before he composed himself and started again. "The girl said that you're claiming to be a virgin. That you didn't have sex, and there's no actual dad. That's why you had some big breakup recently, because the boyfriend didn't believe you." His body slumped as he exhaled, emptied of all the details. I watched as he reached out to touch my arm and then stopped his hand midair, shoving it back into the pocket of his jeans.

"What did they look like? The girls who were talking about me?" I forced myself to ask, even though I already knew the answer. There was really only one possibility.

He shook his head at me, his eyes glazing over. "I

didn't pay that much attention at first, and after I overheard them, I kind of rushed off before they could realize I'd been there. But they were our age, I guess. The girl who was talking had dark hair pulled back in a ponytail, and I don't really remember the other girl. She didn't say much, just a lot of gasping and squealing while she listened. I wish I could give you more. I'm sorry. I really am. I don't know anyone around here yet."

Dark hair was enough evidence to clinch it. Though he could have said red or blonde or white or even hot pink for that matter, and I still would have found a way to link it all back to Izzy.

Tears started pricking at the corners of my eyes, and I turned toward the door.

"Thanks for telling me. Really. It was only a matter of time before it got out anyway, and you just confirmed my suspicions. It's almost a relief to know that there's nothing I can do to stop it now. Do you know how impossible it is to keep secrets in this town? Everyone in Green Hill will probably know about this by the time the first bell rings on Monday."

"So . . . it's true then?" His question was so faint, I almost missed it under the hiss of the old air vent on the ceiling above us.

I opened my mouth to respond, but something inside of me snapped before I could speak. I couldn't be standing here in this dingy back room for a second longer, crying loud enough for everyone in the restaurant to hear me. I ran through the kitchen and out the back door, but I only made it as far as the stoop before I couldn't go any farther, not without completely falling apart along the way. I sat down on the cold cement step and cradled my head in my knees, rocking myself back and forth as the tears ran in sloppy streams down my arms and legs. I heard Jesse step out and close the door behind me, but I didn't move or look up to acknowledge him, even when he sat down next to me and put his arm around my shoulders. I heard Carl come and go, too, and heard Jesse mumble something about him needing to cover the front for the rest of the night.

After what could have been ten minutes or an hour, the tears finally seemed to reach their peak—all of the water had been drained from my body into a puddle on the pavement beneath me. The orange light of the streetlamps sparkled against the slick asphalt, lighting up my tears with a fiery glow.

"You didn't have to be out here with me," I said at last, when I was able to speak again. "But I'm glad you were. Thanks for that."

"No problem. I didn't want you to be alone. You can talk to me if you want. Or we can just sit here. Your call."

I sniffed, wiping my dripping face and nose against

the sleeve of my T-shirt. "You don't have to believe me, of course. I don't expect you to. But everything you heard that girl say was true, even the part about me claiming to be a virgin."

He didn't say anything to that, just sat there staring out at the fields across the street, a faraway look in his eyes, as if he was on some other stoop, in some other place entirely.

I realized suddenly how much I wanted him to believe me. Needed it, even. It didn't matter that I barely knew him, that I'd ignored his existence for the last few months. There was something about him, the sense that he was so much older and wiser than his years, maybe, or the feeling that there was something so genuine and real and good about him, despite or even *because* of his quirks. He didn't seem to care about what other people thought, at least not superficial high school kids. I wanted him on my side. I wanted him to trust me. Before I could stop myself or rethink what I was actually asking, I opened my mouth.

"Do you remember your first night here at Frankie's? The old woman I made you more or less kick out while I ran away through the back door?"

He nodded, and I could see the surprise on his face, that of all the questions or things to say about what was happening, I was babbling about that strange old lady.

"I was running because she scared me. What she said

to me scared me." I paused, picking at a hangnail on my thumb while I collected my thoughts. "She told me that I would be pregnant, and that it was her job to keep me safe. To protect me. She said that it was time, and that they were ready—whoever *they* are—that the whole world was ready for it to happen. For me to have this baby. Then she asked for my approval, and I said yes. I said *yes* to her. You were there already when that happened. I ran out saying *yes*, just to make the getaway easier. I didn't have time to think about any of it. Not that any amount of time thinking about that question could have helped me to answer better."

I watched his profile while I talked, trying to gauge at least some tiny piece of what he was thinking. There was no gaping jaw, no crinkled forehead, no squinting eyes. That alone gave me hope.

"Something happened that night. I don't know why or how or any of the questions that really matter to everyone, but it did. I had a strange dream afterward, too, strange but beautiful, with all sorts of bright, amazing colors I can still see every night when I close my eyes." I sighed, wishing that those colors would suddenly light up the whole sky above us—that life and God or whatever and whoever was in control of all this would give me some kind of sign. Give me some kind of proof that I wasn't just creating some insane fairy tale in my mind. Didn't I deserve that? Didn't

I deserve some reward for *trying* to believe? For fighting through the doubt? But the sky stayed dark, the same old stars and the same old moon shining down on me. I guess that was maybe how faith worked, though. Faith was trusting in the absence of all the facts; it was an active, constant attempt at believing in someone or something I couldn't understand.

Faith, I was learning, wasn't easy. But then again, wasn't I carrying around the proof of a miracle, every minute of every day for these nine months? Wasn't that why I had a bump that I couldn't hide anymore? Maybe it was selfish of me to think that I needed more evidence than what I already had. Maybe this baby had always been more than enough.

After all, people had believed—had had faith—without this kind of tangible proof for thousands of years. People had believed enough to start wars over it, to lose their lives for it. Faith in something more had been part of the human race from the very beginning of existence. If anything should seem strange to me now, shouldn't it be that I'd never believed in anything more than my everyday life before this baby?

"She talked to me," he said, turning to face me, instantly pulling my mind back to that stoop. His cheeks were strangely white, drained of any color in the hazy light. "She talked to me after you left. I would have told you sooner . . . I wanted to, actually, but you haven't exactly seemed interested in talking to me, so I guess I sort of forgot about it somehow. Until now."

"What did she say?" I could feel my heartbeat soar, could hear the rapid thudding in my ears. He knew something. He held another piece of the puzzle.

"She said that when the time came, I shouldn't be afraid to believe in you. That I should support you and trust in whatever you'd have to tell me." He stared at me as if he was seeing me for the first time, his eyes scanning over every curve and every shadow of my face. I wanted to hide, cover myself with my hands, but I stayed still. I let him look.

He laughed then, but it wasn't the sort of hostile laugh that I'd come to expect. He sounded amazed, like a little kid almost, excited to have made some awesome new discovery.

"Well, now," he said, one of his trademark grins slowly spreading across his face, lighting up the dark stoop. "I guess I have to believe you, right? No choice in the matter, it would seem. That solves that for us."

I heard myself giggle in response. The sound was completely foreign to me after the last few weeks.

"It's that easy to convince you?" I asked, savoring the unexpectedly easy, happy moment. "For all you know, that was my grandma and I begged her to go along with this whole incredible, elaborate story, just to keep myself entertained. You never know."

"I may hardly know you, Mina, but something tells me that you're not the kind of girl to take the risk of ruining your image quite so lightly, not for the sake of some ridiculously premeditated practical joke." He paused to beam at me again, dimples on full display, and had we been anywhere else, talking about anything else, I would have thought we were flirting. But we weren't. We couldn't be, not here and now. "It all sounds pretty outrageous, I know it does. But it feels good to believe in something this crazy, you know? To believe that there's something in the world that we can't explain. I like it. I want a little crazy in my life."

"Ha. Be careful what you wish for," I said, though *crazy* didn't sound so bad to me, not when he put it like that. Maybe I needed more crazy, too. Maybe I always had, and this was life's over-the-top way of giving it to me.

"I warn you, once the entire school knows—and they will know very soon, I'm sure, because Green Hill plays a pretty vicious game of whisper down the lane—all bets are off. You'll be putting your whole reputation on the line to be seen anywhere near me. I don't want to suck you into my mess."

"Reputation? Please. I don't have a good reputation now. I don't have *any* reputation at all, in fact. So you definitely don't have to worry about that, trust me. But this will all add some nice color to my first and last year in public high school, that's for sure. I've been homeschooled my whole life, up until my parents very recently decided that sending me off into the real world for senior year would be a good way to prepare me for college life. Just in time to be your bodyguard and knight in shining armor, it seems. Everybody wins."

"How are you winning?" I asked.

"Well, now you *have* to be my friend, of course." His lips were still curled up in a smile, but his eyes looked dimmer, as if part of him had crawled off into that other world he so often seemed to live in. "You probably haven't noticed, Mina, but I've yet to make any of those at our school. And if I'm being totally honest with you, despite my pretty tremendously charming personality, I've never had many friends to begin with. I blame the homeschooling, but I think it's probably my wicked intelligence and dashing good looks, too. Deadly combo. Scares people away." He laughed then, softening the blow of such a sad, intimate detail about his life. It surprised me to think that the boy with the beautiful smile could be so lonely.

But I could see, I suppose, why people would be put off by his spacy, zoned-out way, his offbeat sense of style that made it clear he didn't follow anyone else's rules. As soon as someone reached out to him, he snapped out of his shell, and he was warm and friendly and interesting—but that was just it. Someone else had to make the effort first. And in a new high school filled with strangers, that could be a lot to ask for. After all, even I had taken this long to come around.

"I'm glad we have it all sorted out then," I said, nudging him with my elbow as I looked down at my wrist to check the time. I'd gotten into the habit of wearing the gold watch I'd bought Nate for our anniversary—silly, I knew, but somehow having it there, on me, tracking my days, made me feel as if Nate wasn't lost for good. At the very least, it had been too expensive to just waste away in a drawer, and I couldn't bring myself to return it to the store. Just in case. Just in case Nate ever found a way to forgive me. But now, sitting so close to Jesse, the watch made me feel almost guilty. As if I was betraying Nate somehow, feeling this connected to a boy who wasn't him.

I spun the watch, hiding the face along the inside of my wrist. "We should probably go back in now. Save your uncle from the mountain of things I'm sure he still has to do. I believe there's a big box that needs carrying, too. But I promise to only watch from the sidelines while I direct you." My hands automatically flew to my stomach as I said that, cupping the tiny bump that was hiding under my apron.

His eyes followed my movement, and we both sat there

staring at my hands, thinking about what was actually under them, just inches beneath the surface of my skin. No matter how many times every minute of every day I'd thought about that baby, that little miniature person growing inside of me, it never felt any less mystifying or any less spectacular.

"I'm not far enough along for the baby to kick," I said, filling the space with the first thought that came to my head. "But soon, I hope."

"Can I . . . Can I touch it?" He looked away as he asked. "I'm sorry, that was probably a weird thing to say. I don't want to make you uncomfortable."

"No. No, it's fine," I said, though the idea of his hand on my stomach actually terrified me. "You can touch it." My mom and Gracie and Hannah were the only people I'd let get that close. But I couldn't say no to Jesse. And I didn't want to, I realized.

He reached out and I moved my hands off to my lap to give him room. His fingers were light and cautious, landing on my stomach one tip at a time. Neither of us said anything for a minute or so, letting the full weight of everything settle on the stoop around us.

"Why do you think . . ." He paused, his hand still resting over the baby. "Why do you think Iris needed the child to be born from a virgin? Or from a person at all? Why not just have him or her delivered down to earth by, I don't know, an angel or something? Some kind of divine messenger?"

I sighed, so heavily that I felt his hand carried by the rise and fall of my belly. I closed my eyes, trying to be less aware of his touch, his warmth spreading through the thin layer of my cotton T-shirt. "Trust me. I've asked myself that question. It doesn't really make sense, does it? Why does there have to be a carrier at all? What am I? Why me? Why any of this? But I'll never understand. I don't think I'll ever get an answer."

"I wonder then, if you *hadn't* been a virgin . . ." My eyes snapped open as he trailed off again, blushing profusely. "Sorry." He shook his head, looking down as his teeth clenched in an awkward grimace. "Too personal maybe."

"It's fine. Really. None of this feels personal anymore anyway. But if I wasn't a virgin, would they not have picked me? I don't know that, either. I didn't not have sex because I thought it was dirty or sinful or anything like that. I just wanted to be perfectly sure, I guess. I wanted to be completely in love."

"Yeah," he said. "That's how I've always felt, too." He turned back to face me then, his eyes wide and curious. "But do you ever wish that you'd said no that night? To Iris? That maybe if you had, none of this would have happened?"

It was the first time the question had been said out

loud, the first time I'd even really let myself analyze the possibility. There was no point in asking, not if I couldn't change that first response. But I had the answer, I realized. I didn't need to think about it.

"No," I said, and I knew right away that I meant it. "Maybe if you'd asked me when I'd first found out about it. But now . . . No. I think it was the right answer. Or the only one, maybe."

He nodded, as if it was just as simple as it sounded. "Well, it's been a pleasure meeting you, little one," he said, grinning over at me as he moved his hand back. He stood up, reaching both arms down to help pull me to my feet. "Go home and get some sleep. I'll cover for you inside."

I nodded, at a loss for expressing everything I was feeling in that one moment. "I don't know how to thank you."

"Perfect, because you don't have to thank me. So don't waste any more time trying to come up with anything good, okay?" He put one arm around me and squeezed, an awkward half hug that left me feeling prickly and overheated. "I'll see you Monday?"

"Monday."

I had an awful feeling about Monday, a horrible, creeping suspicion that everything was just a weekend away from erupting all around me. But the idea that Jesse would be there helped, made the day feel at least a tiny bit less ominous. And there was Hannah, too. There was always Hannah.

I gave one last wave before walking off to my car, my head whirling with everything that had happened in the past two hours, good and bad. My secret was officially out in the open, and the rest was just a matter of time. On the flip side, I'd made a new friend who believed me, or at least seemed to believe me, and who could verify that Iris had definitely existed.

But I'd also found out that Izzy had done the unthinkable, that not only had she abandoned me, she'd snuck around behind me and stabbed me in the back.

The sting hit me all over again. I had to see her. I needed her to admit to my face that she'd betrayed me. I needed her to feel ashamed when I walked into school on Monday or whenever that day would finally come, mobs of people pointing and judging me. Because of her. Because she didn't even have enough loyalty to keep my secret.

But most important, I needed her to know that I was fine without her.

Because if she thought that, maybe I could believe it, too.

chapter nine

I woke up at four the next morning with my arms wrapped tight around my belly and a smile on my lips, the wisps of a happy dream I couldn't quite remember floating above me, just barely out of reach. I thought again about what I'd said to Jesse the night before, about how I wouldn't trade in my answer to Iris, not anymore. I was relieved to realize that it was still true this morning. I still believed. I believed in the miracle that was this tiny baby inside of me right now, right here in my bed with me. I curled to my side, hugging myself into a ball.

But just as I let my eyelids close again, willing myself back into my cozy, sunny dream world, I remembered what Izzy had done. I had no chance of falling back to sleep after that, tossing and turning in my sweat-soaked sheets as I went through the list of everything I wanted to say to her. I was tempted to drive to her house at that very moment, before the sun rose up above Green Hill, ring her cell phone over and over or toss pebbles at her window—do whatever it would take to make her come outside and face me. But I promised myself that I'd wait it out until at least nine, when I could knock on her door in broad daylight like a normal, civilized human being. I didn't want to raise any unnecessary suspicions with her parents, assuming Izzy hadn't already told them everything on her own.

I doubted that she had, though. On the outside, she and her mom and her stepfather were the perfect upper-middle-class family unit, about as shiny and pristine-white-picket-fence and four-car-garage as it could get in our town—the mini-mansion, Hannah and I liked to say, since it was easily the biggest house in the area, and reminding Izzy of the fact always got her hilariously worked up. One if not both parents came cheering with bells and whistles to all her many sporting events, no matter what time of day or how far the drive. They hosted over-the-top birthday parties each year without a blink at the price tag. Ponies, clowns, Moon Bounces, a mini petting zoo . . . what Izzy asked for, Izzy got—and what she didn't ask for, she still got. Her parents took her on a glamorous vacation every single summer that made my family's annual trip to the Jersey Shore feel like a few nights at an Econo Lodge in the middle of a toxic wasteland.

But everything wasn't quite that glossy when you stripped away the top layer, even if Izzy very rarely went into details. It had taken until a few years into middle school of collecting bits of evidence for Hannah and me to really piece together how the family operated: a mom who needed a water bottle filled with white wine to kick-start the day, every day, and a stepdad who seemed to forget that he had a family at all when they weren't busy performing at public appearances.

Izzy had always had us as her second family, ready and waiting to fill in for her real one on the bad days. Me and Hannah, and my parents, who had treated both of them like special bonus daughters for as long as they'd known them. But apparently none of that had meant anything to Izzy. Or at least hadn't meant enough to stop her from abandoning all of it the second I didn't live up to her unfair expectations.

By eight thirty I put down my old tattered copy of *Anne of Green Gables*, the most reread and well-loved book of my childhood. I'd hoped that it would distract me, that the cozy, familiar words would calm my nerves, but I'd been staring at the same page for the last hour. I propped it back on the nightstand where I usually kept it, and pulled on a sweatshirt over my pajamas. I had kept the window next to my bed open all night, and I could feel that a cold front had moved in while I'd slept. The air was crisp and cool, the sort of perfect early fall morning that usually made me giddy with cravings for steaming pumpkin spice tea and cozy frayed flannel shirts. But it also reminded me of Izzy, of haunted hayrides and horror movie marathons, of weeks planning and coordinating and agonizing over our Halloween costumes. That Izzy was gone, though. The Izzy who was still walking and breathing and living was someone else entirely.

I stopped by the kitchen on my way out to tell my parents I was going to see Izzy, even though I'd considered slipping out the front door and bypassing the conversation altogether. My mom raised an eyebrow in a silent question mark as she stood up to hug me good-bye. My dad, however, continued reading his newspaper as if I'd never walked into the room at all. The blatant indifference made the knot in my stomach pull even tighter—I had thought I'd gotten used to him ignoring me, but after the other night, my hopes had shot up too dangerously high. Had I imagined it all? Was that image of my dad at the stove just a dream I had desperately wanted to make real?

No. It *had* happened. Maybe to him it had been a small, meaningless gesture, but to me it had been a gigantic one. I brushed it off, though, waved to them both anyway, and pulled myself together for the bigger challenge ahead.

I'd traveled the seven-minute ride to Izzy's house hundreds of times, the curves and dips in the roads connecting us as natural to me as the freckles dotting the backs of my hands and the blue veins running along my pale wrists. That morning was no different, and I found myself pulling into her driveway before I'd consciously recognized that I'd even turned onto her street. My sweaty palms slid along the gear stick as I shifted into park and stared out over the towering three-story stone house, the thick white pillars lining the porch like a row of royal guards.

I will not cry, I will not cry, I repeated silently, looping in sync with each step along the brick sidewalk that carved through the deep green of her perfectly manicured lawn. The strong scent of boxwood and chrysanthemum, usually so fresh and welcoming, gagged me as I stepped up on the porch and banged the brass knocker against the front door.

"Coming!" I heard Izzy's voice call out, followed by the stamping of hurried feet down the front stairs that led into their foyer.

The door swung open, and Izzy nearly barreled into me before looking up, an expression of total shock flooding across her face as she registered whom she was seeing.

"I didn't think it was you," she said in explanation, her hard eyes staring directly into my own. "I was expecting someone else."

"We need to talk. Can I come in?"

"Now isn't a good time. I have a hockey tournament today, and my ride will be here any minute. That's why I answered the door. That's the *only* reason I opened the door."

"Fine," I said, wedging my foot against the door's lower hinge. "Then we'll talk on the porch."

She looked surprised, maybe even a little impressed, by my defiance. "Fine then. You have a few minutes. Talk."

"I know that you're telling people, Isabelle. I know that you're telling them everything, that I'm pregnant, that I'm claiming to be a virgin, that it's the reason that Nate and I broke up. I knew that you were angry with me and that you might never trust me or want to be my friend again. I'd come to terms with that, or at least done the best I could to ignore it most of the time, because, really, what else could I do? Beg for forgiveness? But I never, not in a thousand years, would have expected you to betray me like this. It's so low, Izzy. So despicably, disgustingly low." I could have stopped there—should have stopped there—but the more I let go of everything that had been bottled up inside me, the more invincible and the more justified I felt.

"You've always been jealous of me—admit it. My family, my grades, my boyfriend, my life—all of it. And the first time something happens that makes you feel better than me, what do you do? You throw me in the trash and make sure that everyone else in Green Hill knows it, too. You make me sick, Izzy. Sick. I can't believe it took me this many years of friendship to see you for who you really are—a sad, desperate, pathetic little girl who's so lost in herself that she can't honestly give a damn about anyone else in her life. I don't need that. I don't need you."

I'd been looking straight at her the whole time I'd talked, but I was so high on my words that I'd barely noticed her reaction until I'd finished, my monologue neatly wrapped and tied up with a bow.

Izzy's usually golden, rosy complexion was so milky white that it was nearly translucent, drained of all expression. Her eyes were open, but they might as well have been closed for all they were holding back from me, like a filmy veil had been pulled down to protect her from the world outside. To protect her from me.

"Izzy?" I stepped back, pulling my foot away from the door. I wanted to undo it all, every last word. I wanted to start the whole conversation over—tell her what I'd heard, ask her for an explanation. My hands tingled to reach out and wrap themselves around her, but I held back.

"I never told anyone, Mina. Not a single person, not even my parents." Her lips were moving, but her face was still stiff and bare. "I would never have done that to you. Never. I would never have disrespected our history together, and I would never have just stopped caring about you."

A light flush was slowly starting to circle her cheeks, and her pupils seemed to focus and sharpen in the dim light of the porch. I was relieved—an angry Izzy I could understand, I could face. "Do you think this has been easy on me? Going through my senior year without my two best friends? I mean, seriously, how insensitive and clueless are you?" She laughed, a cruel, unfamiliar sound. "And you think I'm the one who's lost in herself . . . Priceless, Mina. Priceless. This conversation is over. Please be off my porch by the time my ride gets here."

She slammed the door, and I stumbled back, almost tripping down the first step before I turned and ran to my car. The drive back to my house was even more of a blur than my trip there—I was lucky that some subconscious part of my brain managed to navigate stop signs and turns and passing cars, flashes of shiny metallic reds and blues that streaked past my windows.

As I parked in our driveway, I saw my dad puttering in the flowerbeds in front of the house. I fixed my eyes on the stone path as I walked up to the porch, refusing to give him any kind of acknowledgment. I was vulnerable enough as it was without adding his rejection on top.

"Mina," he called out.

I nearly tripped over a loose stone as I froze midstep, completely knocked off balance by his greeting. I kept my head down, waiting for his next move.

"Mina," he said again, more quietly, as he wiped his hands against his mud-and-paint-splattered work jeans. "I hope everything went okay with Izzy. Your mom . . . She told me after you left that you girls haven't been talking. I didn't realize."

I jammed my hands into my pockets, biting back any of the bitter words that had raced to the tip of my tongue in response. He was trying, and I could, too. "Yeah, she's, uh . . . She's had a tough time wrapping her head around this. I can't say I completely blame her. And I guess I can't say I completely blame you, either." I let it all out in one breath before I could convince myself to keep it in.

He was silent for a moment, probably because our dialogue had gotten so rusty and out of shape from disuse. "I see," he said, nodding, as if each word was a weight lifted, a gasp for air. "I see. Well, I hope things are better after your talk. She'll come around. Give her time."

Does that mean you'll come around, too? I wanted to ask. But I didn't, because maybe this conversation was already enough of an answer.

"Thanks," I said. "I hope so, too."

We gave awkward nods to each other then, and I started toward the house, still in a confused daze. This morning I was invisible to him, and now he was consoling me. Step backward, step forward. But I was glad to be stepping, period, after standing still for so long.

My mom was sitting in the kitchen exactly as I'd left her, a half-full mug of what I was certain was lukewarm coffee still clutched in her hand, staring down at the newspaper.

"Mom?" I said, stepping so close, I was just inches from where she sat.

She jumped in her chair as she finally looked up, startled, and a small splash of coffee ran down the side of her mug and dripped onto the table.

"Goodness, sweetie, way to give me a scare. I didn't even hear you come in," she said, dabbing at the spill with a napkin. She shook herself, and the fear seemed to leak away, replaced with a concern that lined the crinkles of her eyes. "Do you want to tell me about what's going on with Izzy?"

I nodded and slid into the chair across from her, resting my forehead on the smooth, cool wood of the tabletop. "People know, Mom." The words felt sour as they slipped through my lips. I wanted to spit them out, fling them as far away from me as possible. "People know."

"Oh, Mina." She sighed. "I'm so sorry. I'm so sorry that it's out." Her words sounded more resigned than surprised. "What happened?"

"Jesse . . . the kid I work with, the one who was there that night I met Iris. He overheard two girls talking about it at Frankie's. He said that the girl who did most of the talking had dark hair up in a ponytail. And she knew everything, Mom. She knew I was claiming to be a virgin. So I assumed it had to be Izzy, right? Who else?" I lifted my head up, meeting my mom's wide, somber eyes. "So I went over there this morning and freaked out on her, accused her of betraying me and a whole lot of other nasty things that I probably shouldn't have said. She told me that it wasn't her, that she hadn't told anyone. And as unlikely as that seems, I still think I might believe her . . ."

My voice faded away as I turned toward the window, staring out at the sunny fields next to our house as my mind scrambled for new answers. "But if it wasn't Izzy, who else could it have been? No one else makes sense. But it doesn't even matter, I guess, because either way it's out there now. If Jesse knows about it and he doesn't have a single real friend at Green Hill, then everyone in the entire town will know soon enough, and there's nothing I can do to change that."

"Oh, Mina, I'm so, so . . ." my mom started, but she was cut off by a loud thudding noise from across the room. We both looked over to see Gracie on the floor, slumped into a tight ball in the hallway just beyond the kitchen entrance.

"Gracie?" we both said at the same time, kicking the chairs back as we ran over to her.

"Gracie, sweetie, what's wrong?" I asked, kneeling down low to get closer. I reached out to smooth her tangled blonde curls. "Are you hurt?"

She said nothing back, and though I couldn't actually hear her crying, I could feel her little body trembling under my hand.

My mom crouched down next to me. "Baby, you need to tell us what's wrong. Please. Sit up and talk to us." She latched on to each of Gracie's balled fists and slowly started tugging, urging her up.

After a few seconds Gracie gave in and let my mom lift her like a puppet, but she yanked her hands free as soon as she was upright. She pulled her knees in tight and stared down at the floor, refusing to look up at either of us. This wasn't her typical fighting style. Gracie got angry and upset, of course, like any seven-year-old girl, but usually the more upset she got, the more she talked. Gracie never had any trouble telling us exactly what was on her mind.

"Gracie. Look at me." I put my palm under her chin and gently tilted her face so that I could see her eyes. As soon as she looked up at me, she broke, a sudden stream of tears pouring down her cheeks. "I . . . I . . ." she stuttered, her porcelain face flushed with the effort.

"I did it!" The confession exploded from her mouth in a scream. "It was me! It was me, Mina. *Me, me, me, me,*" she yelled, slapping frantically at her legs each time she repeated herself, the hits getting harder and louder as she went along.

I grabbed her wrists to make her stop. "I don't understand, Gracie, what did you . . ." The question froze on my lips. A hot tingling knot gnawed at my stomach, and I dropped her hands. "No," I said, and gasped, putting both palms on the floor in front of me to steady myself.

"No, Gracie," Mom said. "You didn't. It wasn't you. It couldn't have been . . ."

I watched my mom's face as everything clicked into place, the open-mouthed shock replacing any lingering confusion.

"How could you?" I yelled.

Gracie bit down on her lips and pressed her hands against her ears to block me out.

"Damn it, Gracie, answer me!"

She lurched away from me, her beautiful blue eyes wide with fear. Guilt instantly washed over every last bit of me. I hadn't meant to sound so cold and demanding, not to my little sister. Not to my Gracie.

"Mina," my mom said, a note of warning in her voice.

"I'm sorry." I reached out to touch Gracie's cheek. "I am. I didn't mean to yell at you. You just really surprised me. I need you to explain this to me."

"I told Ava," she said, her voice tiny and fragile. Ava was her best friend, had been since the first day of kindergarten. "I know you told me not to tell anybody, and I wasn't going to, I promise. I was just so excited! And I hate secrets. I don't keep secrets from Ava, not ever. I wanted her to know how special you were, too. It was like something burning up in me like a fire, and I had to let it out."

She was looking right at me while she talked, and even

then I could still see the pride glowing though her red-rimmed eyes. I wanted to sweep her into a hug and tell her that it was all okay, that she had done the right thing. But I couldn't. I was still too numb to move or speak.

"I made her swear on her grammy's grave that she wouldn't tell anyone. That's what she always swears on when she really means it, and she's never gone against a swear before. But I guess she couldn't keep this secret either. I want to be mad at her, but I did the same thing she did. We both told a secret we weren't supposed to tell. We're both bad people." Her eyes welled up again, and she looked away.

"But, Gracie," my mom said, "I still don't understand. How did telling Ava spread the story to girls in Mina's school?"

"Arielle," I said, the name dropping from my lips the second the pieces all lined up in my mind. Ava—Ava *Fowler*. "Ava told her cousin Arielle. Arielle has dark hair, too." I always forgot that Ava and Arielle were related, because the two were so different, so separate in my mind. But that was why Arielle had been watching me. She knew. And she would do anything to make my life harder—anything that would make her look better than me in Nate's eyes.

Shame squeezed my lungs, cutting off my breath.

Izzy hadn't told my secret after all. Izzy had been loyal. And I'd screamed in her face, said the worst things I could have imagined saying to her, things that I'd known weren't true but had said anyway. Just to hurt her. And it had worked.

I stood up. I needed to be somewhere by myself, away from Gracie.

Gracie rushed to her feet, too, and wrapped her arms around my waist. "Do you hate me, Mina?" she asked, the question muffled against my sweatshirt.

"I don't hate you. Of course I don't hate you," I said, hanging my arms loosely around her shoulders. "I just need to be alone right now. I need time for everything to settle in my mind, okay?"

She nodded and released me. I turned away and picked up my purse from the table, still unsure of where I was going but knowing I couldn't face Gracie's eyes.

"I'll be back in a little," I said to my mom, who was still sitting cross-legged on the floor. She looked bleary-eyed and exhausted, blinking at her two daughters as if she'd been woken up in the middle of a bad dream and still couldn't sort out fiction from reality.

I flinched and turned my back to her. *I* was the one putting my mom through this—it was my decision that was making her life so difficult.

I could only hope now that I was right, that what I'd told Jesse last night had been true: I'd made the best choice.

That there had been no other answer.

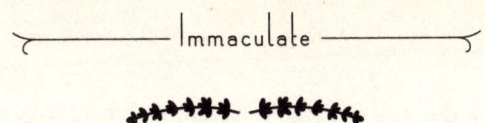

I hadn't expected to be back in the tree house again so soon.

But after sitting in my parked car in the driveway for twenty minutes with absolutely no idea where to go and less than a quarter tank of gas to get me there, the woods just outside my window seemed to be the easiest solution.

I was sprawled on my back on the dusty, splintered floor, torturing myself by reading through old notes from Nate that I had kept stuffed in the glove compartment of my car, a scattered collection of ripped notebook pages and ratty old napkins that I had expected to treasure for the rest of my life. Some were tedious, practical check-ins he'd snuck to me in the middle of class and probably didn't merit the storage space—*Meet me at my locker after third period* and *Need a ride home?*—but others were much sweeter, more personal messages that seemed to reach out from the page and punch me in the gut every time I read back over them. We had written to each other as if we had all the time in the world. There was so much love on the pages, and so much trust in our future. Gone now. All of it. At least for Nate. *I* still had love, and I probably always would. He was every first for me, except for the one that would have changed all this. The one that Nate and Izzy and the rest of the world thought mattered most.

Before I could stop myself, I started ripping every last

note to shreds. If he could cut me out of his life without any hesitation, then I could cut him out, too. I wanted to be completely clean of him, scrub every last touch from my skin.

After the final letter was destroyed, I grabbed my phone from my pocket and grinned at the pile of tiny paper scraps scattered all around me. I had just barely finished deleting his number—one final tie to him—when the phone started ringing and vibrating in my hands. I jumped, startled by the sudden noise, and the phone slipped through my fingers and landed on my stomach with a jolt.

A cold, panicky sweat swept over me as I sat up and wrapped my hands around my belly. That wasn't enough to hurt my baby, was it? It was just a little phone, and it hadn't fallen from more than a foot in the air. Surely that wasn't enough to cause any actual damage. *Right?* I breathed in and out ten times, slowly, trying to convince myself that everything was absolutely fine.

And I knew it was, of course—but still all I could think about was what and where exactly the phone had hit. Was it his or her tiny, delicate head? Fragile little fingers or fragile little toes?

"I'll be more careful," I whispered, rubbing my stomach in soft, soothing circles. "I promise I'll be more careful."

His or *her* head, fingers, toes . . . ? Did I want to know which pronoun it would be? Did it matter, really? I could know soon, very soon, if I wanted to. I closed my eyes and tried to picture myself holding a baby in my lap. Did I see a little boy in a sailor shirt? A little girl with a bright pink sparkly bow on her head? *Probably a gift from her aunt Gracie,* I thought, smiling to myself. Gracie would much rather have a tiny niece to fawn over, that I knew for sure.

Gracie, I thought, my stomach suddenly clenching with guilt. I hadn't been spending enough time with her lately. I'd been too busy thinking about myself and the baby, and worrying about Dad, Izzy, Nate—the people who weren't behind me. I had it all wrong, I realized. The people I should focus on were the ones who were still there. And Gracie, despite her slipup with Ava, was most certainly still there. She deserved a big sister who appreciated her.

My phone buzzed again, and the screen lit up with a missed call from an unknown number. From the area code and the first three digits, I could tell it was someone from town. I read back over the numbers and froze. The last four numbers looked familiar. Very familiar. Was it Nate? I'd gotten so used to calling him on my cell, his digits always safely stored and accessible with a single tap, that I couldn't remember the full number. I knew that there was a seven and a nine, I could remember that much. But the rest was fuzzy in my mind, a clump of random numbers that I'd never bothered to memorize.

Of course he would call then, right after I'd finally found the strength to erase him. It was as if he'd known somehow—he'd known that I was ready to let him go, and he wasn't ready to let that happen. A small flame of hope flickered in my chest. *Nate wanted to talk to me.* He still cared.

I held my breath and stared at the phone, willing the voice mail alert to pop up. Instead the phone started ringing and shaking again, the same mysterious number glowing up at me from the screen.

"Hello," I said, gasping, answering before I could convince myself to resist. If Nate wanted to talk to me, then I would talk to him. I owed him that much. We owed each other that much.

"Mina?" The voice sounded husky, familiar, but it wasn't Nate's.

My hope was extinguished just as quickly as it had been lit, a burst of icy cold disappointment filling the dark empty space left behind.

I recognized the voice, though. It was, it was . . . My mind scrambled to match face with tone, trying to pull itself together in the midst of all my crumbling excitement.

"Mina? Are you there?"

The connection snapped together in my head. Jesse. It was Jesse.

"How did you get my number?"

"I'm doing great, actually, thanks so much for asking." He laughed, and I could feel him grinning through the phone.

"Sorry, Jesse, I didn't mean for it to sound that way. I was just . . . I was expecting someone else, that's all. You surprised me."

"Yeah, no problem," he said, his voice sounding slightly deflated. "I got your number from the call list at work. I just wanted to check in after last night and make sure you were okay." He paused. "Are you? Okay, I mean?"

I smiled, leaning back to prop myself against the wall. "I'm okay. Better at least. Thanks for asking."

"Yeah, no problem. We're in this together, remember? I mean, I'm not letting Iris down, *no way*. I listen to a lady who can implant innocent people with babies at will."

The laugh that burst from my mouth was so loud and so unexpected that I had to glance around the tree house, just to be certain that the sound had actually come from me.

"Thanks for that. Really. I think you're the first person to successfully make me laugh about Iris, and I wouldn't have thought it possible. But can you watch that whole 'we're in this together' business, at least in public? I wouldn't want people getting the wrong idea, if you know what I mean." I blushed at the thought, glad that he couldn't see my cheeks through the phone.

"Don't worry about that. Firstly, I have no one to tell. No friends, remember? Total loner?"

He was joking, trying to make light of his situation, but there was nothing funny to me about him being so lonely. I barely knew him, though I already knew without a doubt that he didn't deserve that kind of solitary existence.

"And secondly," he started again, "this isn't my story to tell. It's yours, Mina. Your story. And that's all there is to it."

"Thanks," I said, whispering into the phone. I wanted to say more, but he'd managed to catch me entirely off guard. Again.

"Anyway, I'm in the middle of a shift at Frankie's right now, so I should get back to work. But I wanted to ask if I could give you a ride to school on Monday, so we can at least go in together. I'm sure no one really knows anything and it's all going to be fine, but . . . I don't know, you seemed pretty nervous last night. I just thought you might not want to be alone Monday morning, that's all."

"Sure," I said, nodding to the empty tree house. "That would be nice."

Nice wasn't the first word that had popped into my mind. The idea of driving to school *with* him made me much more nervous than the idea of driving to school *without* him.

The mildly offbeat boy who grinned all the time and spent his lunches with sci-fi books rather than human beings made me so nervous, I realized, that the phone was suddenly hot against my ear, the hand gripping it prickling with sweat.

We hung up after I gave him my address, and I sat for a minute staring at my phone, replaying the conversation in my head.

Jesse? Was I . . . Did I *like* Jesse? I stared at my still-clammy palm as if it had betrayed me somehow. I couldn't like Jesse, not now, not when I was still just getting over Nate. And certainly not while I was pregnant and trying to sort out my already too complicated life.

Jesse was my new friend. That was all.

That had to be all.

My stomach growled, thankfully, because I was happy to think about something else, anything else. I realized I'd never thought to eat breakfast, not between the fight with Izzy and Gracie's confession. I stood up and stretched, my back aching from lying against the rough wooden floor. After doing my best to shove most of the note scraps into one of the buckets from the makeshift table, I gave the room one final glance and made my way toward the beaded doorway.

A flash of neon pink on the mossy ground below caught my eye and I froze, one foot perched on the top rung of the ladder.

"Gracie? What are you doing here?"

She looked up with a small, hesitant smile. "I was waiting for you. I wanted to see if you were okay, but I didn't want to bug you and make you even madder."

"You've been sitting here this whole time?"

"Almost. Mom got on the phone with Aunt Vera a few minutes after you left, and then I snuck out. I followed you when you finally left your car. Are you angry still?"

"I'm not angry," I said, slowly edging down the ladder on the heels of my feet, keeping my eyes on Gracie the whole time. And I wasn't. Looking at her rosy cheeked, freckled little face peering up at me from below, all I felt was relief that she was still there, even after I'd yelled at her.

"Everyone would have found out sooner or later, Gracie. Because of you, it's just a little sooner, that's all." I grinned at her as I stepped off the last rung, and she ran over to me, a mesmerizing smile lighting up every last inch of her face.

"If anyone deserves an apology right now, it's you," I said, pulling her in for a hug. "I've been so busy with worrying about the baby and about school, I haven't been spending enough time with you. And I'm sorry about that. I miss you. You need your big sister."

"It's okay," she said, wrapping her skinny little arms tightly around me. "I forgive you. I know you have to spend time on the baby now, too." She pulled back and grinned up at me. "No, wait. I forgive you *if* . . . you let me pick the baby's name!" She giggled, tugging at my sweatshirt sleeves as she twirled herself around in happy circles.

I laughed. "We have a few months to go, still, sweetie. And we don't even know if we're naming a boy or a girl yet. But you can start a list, and I promise to give your suggestions *very* serious consideration when the time comes."

"Yes!" Her scream rang out through the quiet woods, and we both laughed again, listening as the echoes seemed to bounce along the trees surrounding us.

"Well, now that we've decided that," I said, reaching out to grab her hand, "I think it's time we go make some peanut butter chocolate chip pancakes, and then we build a pillow fort and watch movies all day long. Sound good to you?"

"Sounds very good," she said, dragging me as she skipped toward the grassy field waiting just ahead of us. I moved my legs faster to keep up, but then she stopped so abruptly that I bumped against her, almost knocking her to the ground.

She turned to face me, her little forehead suddenly scrunched in worry.

"Mina," she said, her voice hushed. "I just thought of something bad. What if when people find out your secret, they get mad and want to hurt you or the baby? Like they did to Jesus in the Bible, when they . . . when they put him on the cross to die?"

Her question felt like stepping under an ice-cold shower, every muscle and nerve and thought seizing up in shock. My breath stopped, and my heart stopped, too, I swear—either that or the second itself became some strange, mutilated section of time that didn't have to follow any of the normal rules, didn't have to pass to the next second in any kind of predictable pattern.

"That's not going to happen, Gracie." The words somehow found their way to my lips even if my brain hadn't consciously delivered them there. "I'm going to be fine. *We're going to be fine.*"

She nodded, but I could tell that neither of us really believed what I'd said.

Because Gracie was right. When the news got out, some people would be angry.

Very angry.

But she was wrong about one thing—no one would hurt this baby. Not unless they killed me first. I would leave if I had to, run away somewhere no one would ever find me. I'd be a new person.

I'd live a new life, if that was what it would take to keep my baby safe.

Immaculate

After three back-to-back Disney movies, two towering stacks of syrup-drenched pancakes, a plate of brownies, and one very buttery bowl of popcorn, Gracie and I were curled up in her bed, my eyelids heavy from too much fatty food and too many corny love ballads.

"How did you know, Mina?" she asked, my eyes blinking back open. "How did you first know about the baby?"

I held my breath, trying to decide how much Gracie actually needed to be told. I was surprised it had taken her this long to ask, though I suppose seven-year-old brains processed the *why*s and *how*s of miracles differently than the rest of ours did.

"Well..." I started, flipping onto my side so I could see Gracie's face. "One night while I was working at Frankie's, I met an old lady named Iris. She was very strange, and very old, with bright white hair and a funny-looking ragged old jacket." Gracie curled up closer against me, and I relaxed. I pretended that I was just telling her a made-up story, as if Iris was just another magical character from a fairy tale, and the words rolled easily off my tongue. "She didn't quite seem real to me from the second she walked in that door. There was something different about her. Something special. She ordered a water with sugar and lemon," I said, smiling to myself. "She asked me to sit with her for a little, and then she told me that I had been chosen. That the world needed me and this baby. I don't know why, Gracie, but that's what she said to me, and when she asked if I would do it, I said yes."

Her golden eyebrows crinkled as she very solemnly considered everything I'd said. "But why did you say yes, Mina? If she was strange and you didn't really know what she was saying?"

Nothing slipped past her—I sometimes didn't give my little sister enough credit. "Honestly, Gracie, I don't know exactly. *Yes* just felt like the only answer. Maybe because I was a little scared of telling her *no*. But I think also because I just needed to get away from there, and saying yes seemed like the easiest, fastest way out."

She looked up at me, her blue eyes squinting as big, heavy thoughts shifted around inside of her head. And then she nodded. "I think I would have said yes, too."

"You would have?" I asked, feeling relieved at her approval. "Why?"

"She said the world needed you," she said simply. "You can't say no to that."

"No," I said, leaning back against the pillows. "No, when you put it that way . . . I guess you can't."

chapter ten

I woke up to my alarm Monday morning feeling stiff with dread and exhaustion, though I was relieved that I'd managed to get any sleep at all. I'd spent most of Saturday night and Sunday working dutifully on schoolwork, burying my nose in textbooks and trying to ignore Gracie's scary question, that terrifying vision of Jesus dying in agony on the cross. I had hoped that I could somehow shove it back out of my mind if I just distracted myself enough, pretended that it had never been there at all.

But I couldn't. Now that the seed had been planted, the fear was there to stay.

I refused the plate of sunny-side up eggs and bacon that my mom held out to me when I walked into the kitchen, my stomach churning at even the idea of eating. But I did allow myself a small cup of milky vanilla coffee, a habit I'd otherwise cut after all the prenatal research I'd done. I squeezed my eyes shut and savored each sip, trying to visualize the caffeine slowly flowing through my body, working its glorious magic. Gracie was perched on the chair across from me, elaborating on her schedule for school that day in great detail, and I was trying my best to focus on what she was saying. Trying and failing, apparently.

"So which of those ideas do you think I should use for the diorama, Meen? I can't pick." Gracie stared at me over the table, her face and lips scrunched up in a look of agonized indecision.

"I . . . um . . ." I squeezed my mug and frantically tried to pull up what Gracie had just been saying. Science, I think. Ocean? Space?

A cheery loud knock came from the front door. My mom dropped the spoon she was rinsing and Gracie jumped from her chair, the question over the diorama already forgotten. I exhaled, relieved to be off the hook. But then I remembered.

Jesse. My heart thudded. And my palms—those damn palms—were already sweating again. I had never mentioned Jesse's offer to my mom. And now he was here, on my porch, ready to take me to school.

"Oh, right. Mom, I forgot to tell you that a friend was picking me up today." I pushed my chair back and stood up so fast, I almost spilled the rest of my coffee on Gracie's curious upturned face. "A friend from work. Jesse. The boy who, you know . . ."

Recognition flashed in my mom's eyes before I had to finish, along with a suspicious glint that made my cheeks burn.

Jesse knocked again, and I grabbed my backpack from the floor as I rushed to get the door. I looked over my shoulder to say bye, and jumped when I saw that my mom and Gracie were both right behind me, following me down the hall.

My stomach flipped and I almost tumbled over the step leading up to the front door. I forced myself to smile as I swung the door open.

"Hey, Jesse."

"Hey, Mina." Jesse smiled back at me, of course, and I couldn't help noticing that he looked especially adorable, standing there in a faded vintage bomber jacket and dark green pinstripe pants, his curly hair still wet and tangled from the shower. His warm brown eyes shifted from me back to my mom and Gracie, who opened the door wider as they huddled behind me.

"Hi, I'm Jesse," he said, reaching out his hand to my mom. Gracie latched on first, pushing her way past me as she pumped his arm vigorously up and down.

"I'm Gracie. Mina's little sister. Well, not that little anymore. But still her sister."

I could tell Jesse was holding back a laugh, but he caught himself, mirroring Gracie's own very serious expression. "It's a pleasure to meet you, Mina's not-so-little sister."

My mom gently pulled Gracie away from Jesse. "Thanks for picking Mina up, Jesse. I hope it wasn't too far out of your way."

"Not at all, Mrs. Dietrich. I actually just live a few roads over, so I'm happy to give Mina a ride whenever."

My mom chuckled and draped her arm around my shoulders. "That's lovely, really, because between you and me, Mina's father and I breathe much easier when she's in the passenger seat. A little too skittish to be behind the wheel, if you ask me."

"I am standing right here, Mom, so I can actually hear you," I said, shooting her what I hoped was a subtly threatening look. "On that note, time to go." I kissed my mom and Gracie on the cheeks and darted across the porch, motioning for Jesse to follow me.

He still beat me to the passenger side of his fire-engine-red pickup truck, which, based on the rust around the headlights and the dents clustered along the rear, was quite the antique.

"I wouldn't have pegged you as the pickup truck type," I said, ignoring the hand he held out to help me climb up to the seat. "Seems too—I don't know—rural and uncivilized for you." I cringed, wondering if that had sounded more judgmental than I'd intended. "I just mean that you seem like more of an old rusty Beetle or Saab type of guy. You know, smart, edgy, a touch of Euro cool."

He laughed as he started toward the driver's side. "It's the newsy cap, isn't it? Or maybe it's the whole mysterious loner thing, am I right? I'm just one big walking stereotype."

"No, not at all, I . . ." He was right, it was *exactly* that. I was kicking myself for saying anything about the truck at all—kicking myself because once again I'd assumed I'd known more about Jesse than I really did. I'd assumed he was just that easy to read.

He saved me, though, continuing on as he climbed into the seat next to mine. "Well, my dad's certainly not a Beetle type of guy, and this was his for the past fifteen years or so before he bequeathed it to me. He's in construction, so it's always a pickup truck. And it's not so bad, really; it's actually pretty useful. I have an uncle on my mom's side of the family who does a lot of camerawork in the Philly area for low-budget indies—documentaries, things like that—and I help him out a lot on nights and weekends when I'm not at Frankie's. The truck comes in handy for carting around cameras and props and whatnot. There's no money in it for me and I'm basically everyone's slave, but I want to major in film at college next year. I figure I should soak up whatever experience I can."

"That's really cool," I said quietly. My lips suddenly felt

too dry to speak actual words. What was wrong with me? *Pull yourself together, Mina.* I glanced around the front seat as he pulled out of my driveway, searching for anything that could possibly be the next subject of conversation. It was surprisingly nondescript and neat for a guy's car, especially compared to the scattered hoodies and empty coffee cups that rolled around my backseat every day.

He reached out for the radio, twisting the knob until the static dimmed and the sound of "Sweet Home Alabama" covered any awkward silence. I grinned and rolled down my window, letting the cool morning air mix with the smell of soil and metal that hovered in the truck. There was something about the scent that I liked—it smelled real and earthy and made me feel protected from the world outside.

We didn't talk the rest of the way to school, though we both tried our best to sing along with the random oldies station he'd landed on—me humming through the vague parts, Jesse creatively improvising the lyrics he didn't know. For those ten minutes I could almost forget that it was a Monday morning, that we were on our way to school, and that I'd soon inevitably be seeing Izzy and a whole crowd of other undesirable faces. Almost.

I resisted the urge to slouch down and duck as we pulled into the school parking lot.

I had no one to hide from. I hadn't done anything wrong.

Jesse turned the music down to a barely audible buzz. "Are you okay, Mina?"

"I'm fine," I said quickly, more for myself than for Jesse. "I'm totally fine. Really."

I pushed open my door before Jesse could ask any other questions. I scanned the lot and saw Hannah standing alone at her car in the next row, lost in her usual morning daze as she mentally ticked through the list of everything she might have forgotten already that day. All her books and assignments? School ID, lip gloss, lunch money? I smiled to myself, relieved that Hannah was still so completely familiar to me—relieved that some people and some things in my life hadn't changed.

"Hannah!" I called out, my hands cupped around my lips. She looked up, turning her head left and right as she searched for my usual silver Jetta. When she zeroed in on me standing in front of the red truck, her head tilted in confusion.

I'd talked to Hannah on the phone the day before, but I'd been too distracted by other things to mention Jesse—I told her about Gracie and Izzy, of course, but most of the conversation revolved around the fact that Hannah had finally become an aunt that weekend. She'd spent most of the time at the hospital with her sister, Lauren, and her precious new baby niece, Ella, and was busy cooing to me about everything I had to look forward to—and how much love I would instantly feel for such a tiny little human being.

"Babies are such miracles, Meen!" she'd screamed into the phone, cracking up when she realized the irony of her words. "Though maybe yours qualifies just a *bit* more than Ella."

So, comparatively—Jesse's offer to drive me to school ranked low on the list of pressing news. I mean, really, it was just a ride to school. Her sister had had a *baby*! That had clearly been a terrible oversight on my part, though, given the evil squint she was giving me as she marched across the parking lot in my direction.

"Mina," she said, her voice probably sounding calm and even to a casual observer, though my well-trained ears could detect the angry questions swarming just beneath the surface. Before I could make any quiet pleas for forgiveness, Jesse came up behind me, my backpack dangling from his arm.

"Oh, hey there," he said, giving Hannah a small wave with his free hand. "I'm Jesse."

"Of course." She beamed at him before glancing at me, lips pursed and hands perched on her hips. "I've heard *so* much about you already." She turned away and focused her bubbly golden energy back on Jesse. "It's great to finally meet you. I'm Hannah, Mina's best friend."

Jesse looked back and forth from me to Hannah, eyebrows lifted in amusement.

"So . . . are you ready to go in, Mina?" His question was discreet—he wasn't sure what Hannah knew or didn't know about Arielle and the whole story coming out. But he locked his dark eyes on mine, and I could feel the full force of his concern pour over me, making me more nervous than I already was.

"It's okay, Jesse," I said, looking toward Hannah. "She knows everything, too, so you can say whatever you want in front of her."

Hannah nodded at both of us, her eyes softening. "I'm here for you, Meen. We're both here for you."

Her anger at being left out of the Jesse loop had passed, at least for the moment.

They both stayed close as we pushed through the crowded front doors and walked along the main hallway to our lockers. We didn't talk much as we went, too preoccupied watching and listening to everyone around us, waiting for that moment—that first accusation, that first sharp bite of reality. They both stood with me while I emptied my backpack and piled up everything I needed for the first half of the day. When I was finished, we made the rounds to both of their lockers, too, Jesse only just clicking in his combination when the first bell rang.

"You guys go," Jesse said, yanking his locker open. "Don't worry about me. I'll catch up with you later this morning sometime."

The idea of leaving Jesse behind felt wrong somehow,

made me feel oddly unbalanced, but Hannah nodded and started dragging me behind her to European History.

Nothing happened anyway, not during history, not during lit or my drawing class either. Hannah was in total mother bird mode all morning, fussing and hovering so much that I almost wanted something to happen, anything that would distract her long enough to give me a second's breath of alone time. We were in all the same classes, a feat we'd pulled off for sophomore year and junior year, too. Izzy was only in our lunch, a detail that had horribly disturbed me when we first set up our schedules last May, but now was an incredible relief.

By the time I was at the sandwich bar in the cafeteria, layering thick globs of peanut butter and jelly onto slices of whole wheat bread, the day was starting to feel like every other Monday. Hannah was complaining next to me about the mysterious clear flecks of gel on the turkey lunch meat, even though she still ate a turkey sandwich, gel and all, almost every day.

We steered our trays toward our table in the back of the cafeteria, where I saw that Jesse was already waiting for us. He had a massive forkful of the cafeteria's crusty orange macaroni and cheese in one hand, and a small handheld camera in the other. The lens was pointed toward the tables near the trash cans, the area where he usually sat. He gave a shy smile as we settled into the seats across from him, clicking off the camera as he shoved it back into his messenger bag.

"Sorry, I just like to film random things sometimes. I need the editing practice. Anyway, I hope it's okay that I sat here," he said, not quite meeting my eyes. "I usually just sit by myself and read, but I don't know, I thought—"

"Of course it's okay, Jesse," Hannah cut in, rescuing him. "You're totally welcome here. Though I'm not so sure about that despicable excuse for mac and cheese. I guess you're still learning the ropes here, so I'll let it slide for today."

We all laughed at that, which is why I didn't notice at first when Kyle Bennett came up behind me, two of his absurdly square-shaped friends flanking him on either side. Kyle was our senior football quarterback and he was also, in a nauseatingly predictable high-school-movie kind of way, Arielle Fowler's sometimes boyfriend—they were more off-again than on-again, and judging by the way she had started sitting at my old table, at *Nate's* table, I was guessing they were off for the time being.

Kyle, it should be said, was also the mastermind behind the nickname *Menius*, which I was positive he had never once intended as a compliment. I had made the fateful mistake of telling our seventh-grade math teacher halfway through the year that Kyle had been copying my test answers all along—he was already a giant for his age and quite an expert at leaning over my desk. I'd had a crying meltdown to my mom about it after we both got the only As on a particularly brutal quiz, and she had insisted that telling Mr. Thompson was the right thing to do. Right in her adult mind, maybe, but after Kyle got a week's detention and a seat alone next to Mr. Thompson's desk for the rest of the year, he certainly didn't think it was *right*, and neither did any of his many cool influential buddies. And so *Menius* had started—and spread—and Kyle had gone out of his way to torment me ever since. Until I started dating Nate, that is, and he'd finally backed off.

But now he had free reign again, and he looked alarmingly smug about it. Darren Reed stood on Kyle's right in a skintight black T-shirt, ruffling his signature messy blond fauxhawk, and to the left was Eric Andrews, a stocky guy with a buzz cut and a grass-stained football jersey who was probably oblivious to the fact that he'd lived on my street for our entire lives. We had even played by the creek together a few times when we were little kids, though I doubted he remembered any of that now. To him, I was just the girl who told on his friend once years ago, and the girl who spent too much time studying and caring about school.

Kyle cleared his throat as soon as he caught my eye, and clapped his hands for attention. Darren yelled, "Quiet!" and the cafeteria buzz instantly dropped off.

What felt like hundreds of eager eyes turned to our table.

"We have a brief but exciting presentation for everyone today," Kyle called out, his shiny white grin blinding me as he stepped even closer. He swept his arms around the cafeteria like he was greeting old friends—like these were people he'd actually talk to or acknowledge on a daily basis, not just slam against lockers as his jock parade powered through the hallways.

Eric pulled his hands from behind his back and pulled out what looked like an old mini boom box. He put it down on the table next to ours and shot Kyle a thumbs-up.

A song started playing quietly through the speakers, and Eric turned a knob until the volume was so high that static vibrated under the music. The opening instrumental part sounded strangely familiar, and my mind raced to put a label on what I was hearing.

Classical music?

Why were they playing classical music in front of the whole cafeteria?

And then the lyrics started, and every part of my body, every last molecule, froze solid, like I had been transformed into a stone statue after looking into the eyes of some horrible mythological creature.

We three kings of Orient are
Bearing gifts we traverse afar.

Field and fountain, moor and mountain,
Following yonder star.

My hand flew to my mouth to trap the scream I could feel rattling up my throat. All three of the boys got down on their knees and leaned forward into bows, their arms fanned out on the floor below me.

O, star of wonder, star of night,
Star with royal beauty bright,
Westward leading, still proceeding,
Guide us to thy perfect Light.

Darren pushed himself up off the speckled linoleum and stood. He fiddled with a knob on the speakers, lowering the volume, then reached into his front pocket slowly. "I present you, my fair Virgin Mina, with gift number one." He pulled out a handful of condoms and held them above his head for everyone to see. "Very valuable to have around. Too late this time, of course, but I'm sure there will be plenty of other opportunities." He laughed hysterically at his joke, tossing the shiny gold foil packets onto my lap before lowering back down to his knees.

Eric stood up next, opening his hand to reveal a small

pink plastic bottle. "Perfume for your purse, Virgin Mina. I hope you like the scent I picked. It's called Seductress. Sounded just perfect for you."

I balled my fists against my eyes to block out everything that was happening, as if it would all cease to exist if I couldn't actually see it anymore. This wasn't real. It couldn't be. *Please let this be a nightmare.* I was dreaming, and I'd wake up soon.

> *Myrrh is mine: its bitter perfume*
> *Breathes a life of gathering gloom.*
> *Sorrowing, sighing, bleeding, dying,*
> *Sealed in the stone-cold tomb.*

The music clicked off, and I dropped my hands from my face.

"That's enough!" Jesse's voice, strong and angry, filled the sudden silence.

"Yo, asshole," Kyle said, standing up and getting so close to Jesse that their chests nearly touched. "We haven't finished yet, so sit the fuck down and mind your own business." He gave Jesse a small push backward, throwing him off balance as he stumbled over an empty chair.

"And for Virgin Mina's last gift," Kyle continued, holding up a small clear bottle, "I present her with Johnson &

Johnson's finest baby oil. Very important for the baby on the way, obviously, and I'm sure she'll find lots of other creative uses, too."

Jesse lunged at Kyle, and they tumbled against the wall behind our table. Jesse was a few inches taller, but he still had nothing on Kyle and his overmuscled football player's body, especially with Eric and Darren just waiting for the right moment to jump in. Kyle punched once, hard, his fist landing on the edge of Jesse's cheek.

I felt Hannah push her chair back and get up beside me, and I followed her motions without thinking, hurrying to catch up with her as she ran over to Jesse.

"Stop it, Kyle! Stop hitting him!" she was screaming, hands thrashing at both sides as she flung herself into the middle of the action. I was just steps from joining her when my hands rushed to cradle my stomach. I couldn't help break up the fight. I couldn't risk the chance of Kyle's fist anywhere near my body. I backed away, frantic to be as far from danger as possible.

"Help," I said, gasping, looking around me. No one seemed to notice, even though their eyes had been glued to me just seconds before. I was nothing now, invisible compared to the drama of the fight.

A shrill whistle blew from across the cafeteria, and I looked over to see two aides rushing toward us. Kyle stepped back as they approached, fists clenched at his sides in surrender. Relief swelled through me and I moved closer to Jesse and Hannah, needing to make sure that they were both okay now that the baby was safe.

A heavyset aide with cropped black hair stepped up beside me and spit out her whistle, while the second aide, white-haired and petite, hung back, keeping her distance. As my eyes landed on her and her face came into focus, I froze.

Iris.

She was here.

In my cafeteria. Almost swallowed up in the background as my classmates seethed and roiled like a wild, stormy sea around her.

She was looking at me, too, those same piercing green eyes, as her lips twisted up in a smile. A friendly smile. A reassuring smile.

I looked down for a second to steady myself against the table, and when I looked up again, there was no Iris. There was still a second aide, small and white-haired, but her face looked nothing like Iris's. And she was too far away for me to even see her eye color—how had they looked so green before?

I shook my head, dizzy from the image.

"All right, show's over, men. You're both coming with me."

"Jesse," I said, my heart still racing as I tried to bring myself back to what was happening around me. "I'm so sorry. Let me come with you and explain."

"Mina, it's fine." His jaw was already bruising from the hit, and a few spots of blood had been smeared above his top lip. "I'll go with her. You don't have to worry about me."

I wanted to protest, but I couldn't think about anything except Iris, that overwhelming belief that she had been there, watching over me somehow. I nodded my silent agreement, stepping toward Jesse and wrapping my arms around his neck in thanks. He stiffened at the touch, and I pulled back, realizing that everyone was staring.

"I'm sorry," I whispered. My cheeks were flaming, and I couldn't meet his eyes. "Everyone's watching . . . and I didn't mean for anyone to get the wrong idea about you. About us."

"Don't worry about it," he said, giving my shoulder a soft tap before turning and following both aides through the maze of tables toward the side door, Kyle close behind him. I stood looking out over the eerily still cafeteria, blinking as reality slowly started to settle, a few whispers giving way to the normal sounds of chatting and laughing and yelling across the tables. When my daze lifted, I realized I was directly facing my old table. I looked for Arielle's face, the reason this had all just happened to me, but she wasn't there—she was probably too busy slapping hands with Kyle's friends on the other side of the cafeteria.

But Izzy and Nate were there. They were staring into each other's eyes from across the table, their faces hard and pale under the fluorescent lights. People talked around them, to them, but they both seemed too lost in their mutual thoughts to notice. They were sharing something, some deep, unsettling vision, and I ached to grab both of them, shake them out of their stupors—make them look at me and listen to me and understand just how hard this was for all of us. But they looked so far from me now, so removed from all my pain. I couldn't worry about them, not anymore.

And though part of me wanted to find Arielle and scream at her, yank her perfect, shiny hair, I knew it wouldn't do any good at this point.

I had to let everyone go, everyone but Hannah and Jesse and my family. Everyone who didn't and couldn't believe in me and my story. Seeing Iris, whether I had imagined her there or not, had made it all so much clearer. I couldn't worry about changing anyone else's mind. I only had the power to change myself.

I wasn't ready to talk about Iris, though—about that second of absolute certainty, not even with Hannah. She reached out from behind me as if she'd heard my thoughts, pulling me down onto the seat next to her.

"I wanted to help," I said, "but I didn't want Kyle to accidentally hurt the baby."

"I know. Trust me, I would have gone totally psycho on him if he'd laid a hand on you, so we're all better off that you stayed away."

I squeezed her hand, weaving my fingers through hers. "Everyone knows now, Hannah. Even if some people were confused when it was happening, I'm sure Kyle and his friends will be screaming the whole story through the halls until every last person in this building knows everything. I mean, they blared 'We Three Kings' and threw condoms and baby oil at me, Han. Who the hell does something like that to someone they barely even know? I mean, obviously I know that Kyle and Arielle and their friends never really liked me, but still? This? This much?" Saying it all out loud made me want to crawl into an infinitely deep, dark hole in the cafeteria floor and stay there until no one even remembered that Mina Dietrich had ever existed in these hallways.

"They're such immature shitheads that they'll do anything to put someone down." She sighed. "But you're right. There's nothing we can do to stop the news from spreading." No frills to pretty up the truth, no silver lining.

"What am I going to do now?"

"I know what you're not going to do. You're not going to run away. You're not going to hide. You're not going to let any of these damn idiots think you have anything to be ashamed about or sorry for. Okay, Meen? You keep doing what you're doing. You go to class, you make plans for the future. You take care of yourself and that baby growing inside of you. You keep living. And you hold your head up high because you are so much more special than even I could have ever imagined. And I picked you as a friend the first second I met you, so that's saying something."

I nodded and tried to smile, but my lips refused. "You're right. I don't hide. I live my life. Fuck them, Han. Fuck them all." The words sounded harsh and more powerful than I felt, but they filled me with a burst of hope—hope that I really could rise above the judgment and criticism to come. I could be strong. I could be courageous.

A bright white paper plane flashed out of nowhere and soared toward me, the nose making a small jab against my forehead before the plane tumbled down my face and chest and landed on top of my untouched food. Heat prickled along my neck as I felt eyes turning back to me. I picked the plane up and unfolded the paper, careful to hold my trembling hands steady.

ALL, BEWARE:
THE SECOND COMING IS NOW UPON US.

I smiled as I tore the paper in half, and then in half again and again, until the plane was just a pile of shreds on the floor below me. And then I blew a kiss to no one in particular, nothing but the air, and picked up my sandwich to start eating.

chapter eleven

"It's hard to believe that you're already twenty-two weeks in," Dr. Keller said, flipping her folder open as she rolled her stool over to the exam table to face me. Her assistant Jamie hovered just behind, a quiet, obedient shadow. "How have you been feeling? Anything concerning you?"

"No, nothing I didn't expect at this point. A little aching in my back, some soreness and swelling in my feet, but otherwise I've been feeling good. Much better than the last few months, actually." I was surprised to hear myself saying that out loud, and even more surprised to realize that I actually meant it. It had already been more than a month since the Three Wise Men debacle, and so far, *miraculously*, nothing else too cataclysmic had come out of the big reveal. Jesse, fortunately, had got away with only a warning, given that he'd had an unblemished record and Kyle had already been an established troublemaker.

People stared at me more maybe, whispered more, but I was becoming a master at tuning them out. I hadn't seen visions of Iris again, either, and no matter how illogical I knew it was, a part of me hoped that she'd actually been there, even for a second. I wanted to believe that she was watching me, that she hadn't abandoned me to deal with all this on my own.

"Good. And have you felt the baby move at all yet?"

"No," I said, my hands automatically settling around my belly, a position they were in more and more often lately. I usually woke up that way, holding my stomach in my sleep. My arms felt too heavy and inconvenient, unnatural even, if I just left them dangling at my sides. "But that's not abnormal, right?"

"No, not for a first-time pregnancy. It's true that most women feel movement closer to twenty weeks, but it's nothing to worry about right now, Mina. I expect it'll happen soon. Can you lie back for me?"

She was quiet as she and Jamie went through the motions, taking my blood pressure, feeling my abdomen, checking my hands and feet for any swelling. When it was time to use the Doppler to listen to my baby's heartbeat, I closed my eyes and let the sound flow through me. The perfectly rhythmic *thump-thump, thump-thump, thump-thump* was just as mind-blowing to me as it had been the first time I'd heard it, maybe even more so now. The more I processed and accepted what was happening to me, the more amazing it became. I wanted to carry the sound with me all day, a constant reminder that there was a real miniature person with a beating heart growing inside of me. Before now I had never thought about the fact that pregnant women held two working hearts—and I was pretty sure that even after the second heart was no longer physically inside my body, emotionally I would have double the hearts, double the love within me for the rest of my life.

"Well, Mina, everything is looking good, perfectly normal for this stage. I've gone over what the hospital sent me from your midpregnancy ultrasound, and your baby seems to be developing perfectly on cue. Speaking of the ultrasound, I take it you're still planning on waiting until delivery to learn the baby's sex?"

"Yes. Definitely waiting." Everything else about this pregnancy was a mystery, so it only seemed fitting to keep this a secret, too. "You know, I never peeked at my Christmas presents early either. And I still refuse to help Gracie now when she begs me for hints. Surprises make life so much more interesting." I smiled—that was certainly an understatement.

"Of course," Dr. Keller said, her bright pink lips attempting a smile in return, though it didn't quite reach her eyes.

She looked back down at her papers, jotting down a

few notes, and I pulled myself up onto the edge of the exam table. I looked down and started to pull my gown closed in the front, but I stopped when I realized just how obvious my bump had become. How had my body changed so quickly? I'd already gained more than twelve pounds according to Dr. Keller's scale. What would I look like next week? Next month?

"Jamie," Dr. Keller said, nodding toward her assistant, "you're free to go prep the next patient. I'll take it from here." She waited for the door to click behind Jamie before she turned to face me.

"I've been wanting to check in with you about the recommendation I gave to talk to a professional counselor about some of what you're going through. I received the message that a coordinator has tried to reach you several times now, but they've yet to hear anything from you. Did you get the voice mails, or is it possible they were using the wrong number?"

"I did get the messages, yes," I said, pulling my gown tighter around my chest and belly. "And while I really do appreciate the suggestion, I think I'm going to pass for now. I have the support I need and, to be perfectly honest, I'm really not in the mood to have one more person think I'm crazy. If you have any other questions you'd like me to answer for you, I'm happy to, but I'm not telling my story to some counselor who's going to send me off to the psych ward."

"That's not what a counselor would do. They would just help you get to the bottom of some of what you're feeling right now. No one thinks you're crazy."

"You mean by get to the bottom of it, they'd help me uncover what awful truth I'm actually hiding from myself, right? Like this is all some delusion I've created to cover up who really made me pregnant?" I could feel my cheeks burning, and I regretted the decision not to bring my mom into the room with me. She was out in the waiting room—she'd insisted on driving me—but I'd told her I wanted to do this part on my own. That I had to start feeling more independent and comfortable handling these sorts of things by myself. But I wanted her in here now, holding my hand while she made all of Dr. Keller's questions disappear.

"Oh, Mina," she said, her voice low and subdued. "I don't know what I'm saying. I'm sorry, I really am. The truth is, I don't know what the best thing to say right now is. I don't know the best way to help you because, quite honestly, I still can't really wrap my head around what you're telling me, and what all this means. I want to take you at your word as my patient, but . . . we both know that you're an unusual case. One of a kind. I don't exactly have a lot of experience with handling this kind of . . . *situation*." She paused, her hands flying to her face, covering her cheeks, which were now as red as mine felt. "I shouldn't even be saying any of this out loud. But you know what? Doctors are humans, too. And I want to be understanding and supportive for you. I want to know what you're really going through every step of the way."

"I get that, really I do," I said. "I'm sure they don't teach divine intervention as part of the reproductive unit in med school. You're not trained to deal with someone like me. And honestly, I can't expect you to believe me. I mean, my own dad thinks I'm a liar, and he's my *dad*. All I want is to not have to defend myself every time I come here to see you. Because now that everyone in Green Hill knows what's going on, I spend way too much of my time defending myself. I don't need that here, too. I look forward to this, you know, hearing the heartbeat, knowing everything is normal and healthy and happening like it should. It's when everything feels most real. Most special. So please, can we agree to that?"

She looked at me, her eyes red-rimmed and watery beneath her pink plastic eyeglass frames. I could practically see straight through them to the struggle happening beneath. Was it more important to get to the bottom of what could have happened, to some dark, repressed sexual memory? Or to stand by me? Focus on me and the baby, the future—not the past?

Dr. Keller nodded, coming to her decision. "Absolutely, Mina. I want you to feel safe here. I want you to be able to say what you're really thinking and feeling. You know that everything is completely confidential."

I nodded, and I could feel my own tears pricking at the corner of my eyes. "Thank you. That means a lot to me."

"Of course." She reached out to me, her hand grasping mine as our fingers briefly interlaced. "So I'll see you in another four weeks, Mina, but please know that you can call whenever you have any questions. I'm here. I'm always here."

I could see the mystery green car sitting in our driveway from a quarter mile down the road.

"Mom? Who is that at our house?" I asked, turning to get a clear view of her expression. She bit her lip and looked out the driver's side window, avoiding my eyes.

"I think it's . . ." She trailed off, ticked her fingers against the wheel. "Well . . . Mina, your father mentioned something this morning about *maybe* having Pastor Lewis stop by. You've had such a long few weeks at school, and you had your appointment today, and I just . . . I don't know, I didn't want to add to everything else. I figured he'd probably even change his mind, or that the pastor would already have plans."

"And why would he have Pastor Lewis come to our house?" I asked, a burst of anger pouring through me so red-hot that my hands were already shaking as I balled them into fists. Pastor Lewis had tried calling me a few times, had left a few polite messages to check in, but I had never followed up with him. I was too scared to hear what he might have to say. "Does Dad think the pastor will talk sense into me? Make me confess or something?" And, silly me, here I'd thought my dad and I had been slowly working our way to an understanding. Clearly, I'd been mistaken. He was just trying to soften me, maybe. Knock down my defenses until I was ready to finally tell the truth.

But I'd already told him the truth. I'd told *all* of them the truth. He just didn't want to hear it.

"No!" I yelled, my voice so unexpectedly loud and high-pitched that my mom jumped, banging her shoulder against the window. "No," I said, steadier this time. "I have nothing to say to Pastor Lewis, Mom. I'm not defending myself."

"You don't have to defend yourself, Mina. He's not going to interrogate you. You know Pastor L. He might be able to help you make more sense of all this. Maybe he'll give you more perspective."

I snorted. "Perspective, huh? So you agree with Dad on this one?"

"Mina, I know this may be hard for you to believe, given how strained things have been around the house. But your dad still wants what's best for you. He cares about you, and he's worried. He's incredibly worried, Mina, about how stressful all this has been for you."

"Well, if he's been so *worried* this whole time, why hasn't he just talked to me about it? Asked me how I'm doing? I can count on one hand the number of times he's said a word to me in the past few months."

She sighed, finally turning to look at me as she parked the car and turned off the ignition. "I don't know, Mina. He has a different way of dealing with things. I know it's not the best way, but we can't force him into this, sweetie. He needs to find his own path back to you. He loves you. You have to remember that."

"Loving someone means having faith in them. Trusting them. Supporting them. Last I'd checked, he's failed to do much of that over the last few months."

"Please just give this a chance, Mina. Talk to him and Pastor Lewis. Just for a few minutes at least. For me."

I could hear the tremor in her voice, the needy, pleading undertone, and I wanted to give her some kind of relief, some kind of hope that things would get better. I knew that this wasn't easy for her, either, her husband and her daughter barely speaking.

"Fine. A few minutes." I clenched my sweaty hands as I got out of the car, kicking the door shut behind me. As soon as I stepped into the cool damp of our foyer, I could hear voices from the kitchen, Gracie and Dad with Pastor Lewis. They were all laughing, joking about something I couldn't quite make out. The sound of it hit me like a kick to the stomach. How could my dad sound so happy? Why wasn't he as torn up as I was?

Their laughter stopped as soon as they heard my footsteps in the hall. Gracie ran to me, wrapping her little spindly arms around my waist and burrowing her head into my side.

"Hi, Pastor Lewis. Hi, Dad," I said, nodding toward both of them. "You wanted to talk to me?"

"Yes, Mina, I think that a family talk with Pastor Lewis would be a good thing for all of us," my dad said, his gaze fixed somewhere on the yellow-checked wall behind me.

"Well, you know, Dad, I have been here since August, living in the same house as you. You haven't seemed all that interested in talking to me." I bit down on my lip to stop myself. I would be mature about this, at least in front of Pastor L.

"Let's go sit in the living room," I continued, starting for the hallway before either of them could respond. I was suddenly feeling exhausted and every bit of twenty-two weeks pregnant. I pressed my hands against my back as I walked, rubbing out the dull, persistent ache. My baby was now roughly the size of a papaya, or (finally!) a much more appealing description—a small doll, coming in at a whopping one pound, eight or so inches long. A doll that was developing senses, a doll that was beginning to touch, see, hear, taste.

I settled onto the sofa with a pillow behind me,

propping my feet up on the coffee table. Pastor Lewis and my dad sat on the love seat directly across from me, while Gracie and my mom hovered for a minute before deciding to join me on the couch.

I had known Pastor L for my entire life, and I'd never seen him look nearly as uncomfortable as he did right then. He was always so calm and composed, as if he had all the secrets of the world just waiting for you behind his bright twinkling eyes. But he looked very uncertain and very out of place in our living room, picking at the white clerical collar around his neck like it had suddenly become a few sizes too small. I had always loved Pastor L—he was a warm, big-hearted teddy bear of a man who had a hug and a kind word for every person who walked through the church doors. But as I sat there watching him fidget and perspire, thinking about the role he'd played in my life, I realized that a big part of why I had loved him so easily was because he made religion feel simple. He didn't push envelopes, he didn't ask hard questions. He had never made me face my doubts, had never made me even consider that I had any doubts at all.

Hopefully he wouldn't finally start with the hard questions now.

Pastor Lewis coughed, clearing his throat. "It's good to see you, Mina. I've been keeping you in my prayers these last few months. You and the baby, too, of course. I was glad that your family invited me here today, though, so I could ask for myself how you're doing." He paused, waiting for me to respond.

"I'm doing okay, Pastor L," I said, forcing my lips into a smile. "Considering the circumstances, anyway."

"Very good, very good," he said, knotting his fingers so rapidly that his knuckles made a fierce cracking sound. "Your father tells me, Mina, that . . . How do I say this? The child was conceived in a rather miraculous way. That there's no father. And that this all started with the appearance of a mysterious woman at the pizzeria one night."

"That's all correct," I said. "I don't mean any offense to you, Pastor Lewis, but I have nothing to add to that."

"And I'm not here to disagree with you, Mina," he said, his voice deeper, more mellow and assuring, like he'd started acclimating to the bizarre surroundings. "I'm here just in case you have any questions, or anything at all you want to talk about. You should know after, what—nearly eighteen years now?—that I'm not a fire-and-brimstone kind of preacher." He leaned back into the chair, propping one leather loafer against his knee. "I have to admit, even as a Pastor, I'm not the most literal of biblical scholars. Do I believe that God created the entire world in seven days and seven nights? Do I believe that Noah actually loaded up an ark full of animals? That Moses parted the Red Sea?" He cocked one eyebrow dramatically and wriggled his shoulders. "Literally? No, probably not. To be perfectly honest, Mina," he said, putting a finger to his lips as he leaned in and whispered, "I'm not even sure that I believe in *Hell*."

I heard my dad gasp next to him, and I pressed my lips together, stifling a laugh.

"But that is a discussion for another day. My point is that faith isn't a rigid book of rules to me. I believe in a compassionate, loving God. And I believe in a compassionate, loving Jesus. I might have a fancy certificate saying that I graduated from seminary school, and I might have this fancy collar around my neck, but I don't have any answers for you today, Mina. I'm as dumbstruck as you are. Faith is one heck of an interesting journey sometimes," he said, chuckling to himself as he reached out to pat my knee.

"Thank you," I started, grinning at him in relief. "I was a little—"

"Pastor," my dad interrupted, his face flushed as he leaned forward to intrude upon our cozy powwow. "I don't want to speak for you here, but I was hoping you might have a little more insight into what is really going on."

"And what do you mean by 'really going on'?" I asked, turning to look at my dad.

"I'm worried," he said, his blue eyes drilling into mine. "I am scared every second of every day, Mina, worrying about what God is thinking about all this. About how these—these *lies* you're telling—could . . . could change your path forever. Pastor," he pleaded, tilting his head toward Pastor Lewis, "can you really sit there and not be terrified for my daughter's future?"

"If by 'future' you mean whether she'll make it to Heaven, then no. I'm not scared," Pastor Lewis said simply, his voice like a smooth touch, gently nudging my father back toward his seat.

"I'm not sure that I believe in Hell either," I said, feeling encouraged and emboldened by everything Pastor L had said. It felt good to say the words aloud, as if I was freed from something I had never realized was holding me back before now. "I'm not scared, Dad, and I don't want you to be scared for me either. I just want you to be in my life again."

"Do you think I don't want that, too, Mina?" he asked, his voice breaking as he buried his face behind his hands. "It's tearing every last piece of me to shreds to ignore you like this. This isn't what fathers do. It's at least certainly not what I do. I've watched you and your mother deal with this for the last few months, and I'm so damn proud of you for fighting through it all, holding your head up high, but I don't understand why you keep hiding behind lies, Mina."

I couldn't begin to respond, not right away. I closed my eyes first, trying to relax my abdominal muscles and breathe in deeply from my diaphragm, a meditation practice I'd been turning to whenever I felt the stress closing in on me. It seemed so simple, but it was more helpful than I would have ever imagined, giving me the strength and calm I needed to make it through my days at school. *Ten.* I inhaled, exhaled. *Nine.* In, out. *Eight.*

"Mina?" My mom laid her hand on my elbow. "Are you okay, sweetie? Does something hurt?" Gracie leaned in against me, curling up alongside my belly.

"I'm fine, Mom. Just trying to stay calm for the baby's sake." I took another deep breath in and opened my eyes, locking them on my father's face.

"I can't explain why this is happening, Dad, but it doesn't feel wrong to me. It doesn't feel bad or dirty or freakish. It feels . . . it feels amazing, actually. It feels like it was meant to be for some reason, like this was meant to be my life. And maybe someday I'll understand all of it, or maybe I won't. I don't know. But either way, this is my life now. This is what I've chosen."

I turned to Pastor Lewis to thank him again, but before I could say anything, I felt a strange tickling in my stomach—like a tiny, fragile butterfly was fluttering its wings for the first time, flapping its way slowly into life. I looked down and grinned, a golden, sunny happiness flooding through my body.

"Did you feel that, Gracie? The baby just kicked!"

"I didn't feel anything!" Gracie squealed, pressing her

head more heavily against my stomach. "Do it again! I'll listen harder this time!"

"I don't think it quite works like that, sweet pea. I can't tell the baby what to do. He or she has a mind of their own. But it'll happen a lot more, don't worry."

I smiled over at my mom and saw that her eyes were wet and shining—she was crying, too, excited, happy tears as she pressed a warm hand next to Gracie's head on my belly. I could see my own grin mirrored on her, no sign of the pursed lips and tight lines that had become such a permanent fixture on her face.

"Congratulations, Mina. I'm glad to see you're doing so well," Pastor Lewis said, rising from his chair to leave us to our family moment. "You're truly glowing."

"I know it's hard to believe, given that I've destroyed my social life and I have a whole school filled with people who think I'm crazy . . . but I *am* doing well. I'm happier than I would have thought possible right now."

From the corner of my eye I saw my dad stand, too, and for a second, for one glorious, shimmering, perfect second, I thought that he was coming over to join all of us. I thought that he was going to accept me and the baby, even if he couldn't accept my story. But he wasn't coming over to me. He wasn't accepting anything.

Instead he simply left the room without another word, his footsteps echoing through the hallway and out through the foyer. The front door banged shut behind him. Pastor Lewis watched him go with a small frown on his face.

He glanced back at me, his eyes creased with a new-found sympathy. "Please call me, Mina, if you ever want to talk more. I'm here for you."

I nodded, waving as he turned to follow my father out the door.

I wouldn't let him destroy the moment. The memory of that first kick, the feel of their hands on my belly, Gracie's sweet, sticky breath against my face as my mom pulled us all together even closer. This was more family than some people would ever have in their lifetime.

Like my mom had said earlier, my dad had to find his own way back.

All I could do was hope that he somehow found a compass.

I sat alone on the front porch later that night, curled up on a rocking chair with an old quilt and a mug of hot chocolate. The early November breeze was cool and crisp, laced with the rich, oaky scent of nearby wood smoke and the dizzying sense of imminent change. The leaves were becoming brown and brittle, and those that had already dropped were swirling in circles across the dark lawn. I realized, watching the leaves dance, that I had barely noticed the reds and golds of October, hadn't had even one cup of cider or eaten a single caramel apple. I had dreaded everything about Halloween, convinced that someone, Kyle or one of his clones, wouldn't be able to pass up the opportunity to dress like Mary or Joseph or baby Jesus. I'd stayed home on Halloween as a precaution, and kept the door locked and the lights off while my parents took Gracie out trick-or-treating. Nothing happened, no jocks cross-dressing in a long blue Mary tunic caroling at my doorstep, thank God, but I wouldn't have had the heart to celebrate, anyway. And besides, soon enough my Halloweens would be very different—next year I could be dressing my seven-month-old baby in a fluffy orange jack-o'-lantern costume. It was time to change, along with the season. Time to let go, time to make new traditions.

An owl hooted from high up in a nearby tree, and I shivered, pulling my mug closer to my chest and inhaling the warm sugary vapor. It would be my birthday in a few weeks, and Thanksgiving, then Christmas right around the corner. I couldn't imagine celebrating any holiday without my dad. He would be there, yes, sitting in a chair at the table eating turkey, driving the car to church on Christmas Eve, but he still wouldn't really be *there*. Not in a way that mattered. I set the mug down on the porch rail and squeezed my eyes shut as I rocked back in the chair, willing away the tears that I refused to cry. Not anymore.

A soft knock drummed against the front door behind me, so quiet that I didn't hear it at first over the tapping of my chair.

"Um, yes?" I said, confused. People knocked to come *in* to the house. "Come . . . out?"

The door opened and my dad stepped out onto the front stoop. I tensed, not willing to start another round of the evening's conversation. He'd disappeared for the rest of the night, hadn't even come out of hiding for dinner. "I'm too tired right now, Dad. I don't want to fight with you anymore tonight."

"I just came out to check on you. It's late, Mina, and cold out. That blanket's not enough. I think you should head back inside."

"Oh," I said, too surprised to say more.

"I also came out . . ." He paused, scuffing his slipper back and forth against our worn WELCOME TO THE DIETRICHS' mat. "I came out here to say I'm sorry. About some of the things I said earlier. Pastor Lewis just threw me off, I suppose. I was expecting him to have very different advice from what he gave. But he chased me down after I stomped out of the room like a child, and he said a lot of things that I needed to hear." He glanced at the empty rocking chair next to me, hesitating for a few seconds before sitting down on the edge of the seat.

"I want to try to be more a part of all this, Mina. Even

if I can't agree to believe everything that you're saying, I still want to support you. I'm your dad. I want to start acting like one again."

"Okay," I said, nodding in the dark. "I'd like that. A lot. And . . . and I want to apologize, too. I told you that I'd never forgive you when you made me call Nate that day. I wish it hadn't happened quite that way, yeah, but we were both angry. Neither of us could be completely rational. Nate had to find out one way or the other, and it was probably better it happened sooner rather than later. I needed to let him go so that I could start moving on."

There were a few beats of silence before he spoke. "I appreciate that. But I'm still sorry that it hurt you." He settled a little farther back into the chair, kicking the runners up as he rocked in a rhythm that seemed to directly oppose my own. I watched his silhouette in the dim porch light, slowing my chair until the pace better matched his beat.

"How are the college applications going?" he asked, his voice still just a little more polite, a little more formal than I was used to.

I grinned to myself in the dark, wondering how long this question had been gnawing away at him. Usually this kind of conversation annoyed me, but now—I felt practically giddy. My dad was harassing me about college applications again. It felt beautifully, fabulously normal. "Just

Penn State. Following in your footsteps, of course. The application barely took any time at all, and I figured I would go to the branch campus near us, at least in the beginning, take some English classes and knock out other general requirements. As lovely as it would be to move away, get a fresh start somewhere else, I obviously can't do that. Firstly, I don't need to explain to you that I'm broke and need state tuition, and, secondly, I need to be near Mom and Gracie. And you. I can't do this alone, even if that means I don't get the Ivy League degree I always imagined I would. Dreams change, Dad. They get rewritten so that we can create new dreams instead. I think that's the secret to growing up, right?"

"You can be very wise sometimes, daughter," my dad said, and I didn't have to turn my head to see the tiny smile on his face. "One more thing. I want you to know that your mom and I have talked about some of the . . . arrangements. And I want you know that you're welcome to stay here after. After the baby is born." He paused, probably as surprised as I was to hear those words out loud—those words out of *his* mouth. He was acknowledging my decision. He was acknowledging my *baby*. "We of course want you to continue with your studies and to continue with a job on the side that will help you to contribute. But we don't want you to worry about living on your own and funding everything by yourself. Not right now. This can still be your home. Okay?"

"Okay," I said, reaching over to squeeze his hand in mine. We were both quiet then, and I closed my eyes, lulled by our synchronized rocking, the creaking of the old porch planks with each sway and tap of our chairs.

"Well, you may be wise, but you're not wise enough to make all your own rules yet. You're not even eighteen," he said, pushing off the chair to stand. "So it's time to get inside and get to bed. Father's orders. You need to stay healthy, got it?"

I nodded, swiping at a tear on my cheek with my sweatshirt sleeve as I stood to follow him in. "Got it, Dad."

In all of my almost eighteen years, being sent to bed had never felt so amazing.

chapter twelve

In my dream I was perfectly skinny again, straight up and down from shoulders to toes, no round belly or swollen chest. I was flat and hard and entirely naked, standing with Nate in the middle of the tree house. A cool, early spring breeze ruffled the curtains, and goose bumps raced along my arms and legs. Nate saw me shiver and stepped closer to me, pulling me against his bare chest, warming me with his body heat. This was the night we had planned, the night all those months ago when I'd had my real chance. *This could be so different,* I thought, looking up into his eyes. There was no hate there, no disgust or bitterness. Just pure, raw love and desire. *We could be so different.*

I wound my fingers through the hair at the base of his neck and tilted his face down, pressing my lips hard against his. They were so sweet, so familiar. He moaned into me, and I started pulling him with me lower, to the

— Immaculate —

ground, our bodies becoming tangled on the bed of old sleeping bags.

I can do this. I will do this.

But suddenly, just as I started to crawl on top of Nate, everything felt wrong. His skin became rough and coarse, like sandpaper scraping bits of me off with even the slightest brush of our bodies. His breathing and groaning was loud, too loud, so piercing and terrible that I wanted to put my hands against my ears and scream at the top of my lungs to hide the noise. When I opened my eyes, his face was entirely blurred and unrecognizable in the moonlight that spilled through the tree house window. Shapes, lines, colors that had just been Nate's features, all shifting and transforming right in front of me.

I tried to push away, but Nate—or the boy who had been Nate at least, had looked like him on the surface—whispered that he loved me, wrapped his rough arms around me even tighter.

But did I really love him? Did I even know him at all?

My phone rattled against the nightstand and I jerked up from my pillow, my heart still thudding fast and heavy against my rib cage. A wave of chills swept up my spine, tingling along the back of my neck. The dream had been too real and three-dimensional, the senses all so magnified and heightened, swirling around me still as I lay shaking under my covers. The sounds, the smells, the heat.

Suddenly the idea of touching Nate, of being with him like that, felt abhorrent. I was never more glad that whatever had happened—whatever was happening now, this little human kicking inside of me—hadn't been confused with other potential explanations. If Nate had been the father, if he even just *believed* he was the father, I would have been tied to him forever, our lives sewn up for good. It scared me now, that I'd come so close. It scared me to think that just one night together could have changed everything. Nate could have been my first, and my last.

I pushed back the strands of sweaty hair that clung to my forehead and reached for the phone. Hannah was calling. It was just barely past six, way too early for any normal morning check-ins.

"Han?" My throat croaked, and I realized how dry my entire mouth felt. The dream flashed in my memory, the horrible sounds, the screaming.

"Meen. Listen to me. Start getting ready, and I'm going to be at your house in ten minutes, okay? And I need you to promise me something really important."

"What's going on? What am I promising?"

"Seriously, please just trust me on this."

"Okay. I'm playing along. I promise."

"Thank you. Don't touch your computer until I get there. Nothing, okay? I'll be there soon."

She hung up and I glanced over at the computer resting just a few feet away, the screen black in sleep mode. Why couldn't I touch my computer? What couldn't I see without Hannah being there first? Every last part of me wanted to frantically start scouring any recent e-mail, news, classmates' blogs—but I made myself look away. I had promised.

I threw on a loose sweater and a pair of stretchy jeans, and ran a brush through my tangled hair. Without even a glance at the computer, I grabbed a pen and crossed out another day on the pregnancy countdown hanging above my desk—Friday, November 16. Sixteen weeks until my March 7 due date. It was a morning tradition I'd started when I'd realized just how quickly the days were flying away from me. I had my midpregnancy sonogram hanging above the calendar, a constant reminder that this was real. This was happening.

I still had time before Hannah would get there, and I couldn't wait around in my room, staring at the computer I wasn't allowed to touch. I went to the bathroom and splashed cold water on my face, still trying to wash away every last trace of that dream. I didn't want to think about how good it had felt at first to have Nate's skin against my skin—or how horrible it had felt by the end. I had been getting better at keeping that part of my brain locked up, and I wanted it to stay that way. A few swipes of mascara and a little blush made me look slightly more awake, but nowhere in the mirror did I detect the glow that Pastor Lewis had claimed to see. It was funny to me that my face could still look the same as it had months ago—just a bit paler maybe, more tired-looking—when the rest of me was so entirely different.

There was a knock at the front door, and within seconds my mom was in the foyer, greeting Hannah. They started talking in hushed, hurried whispers. Cold beads of sweat prickled along the back of my neck. What could have happened since last night?

Their footsteps started up the stairs, and I walked toward them, meeting my mom and Hannah at the top. One look at both of their anxious faces, and I knew that something was most definitely wrong.

"What is it? What's happening?" I gripped the banister next to me.

"Let's go into your bedroom, sweetie," my mom said, her eyes blinking down at the carpet. "We'll talk there, okay?"

I followed her numbly into my room and leaned against the edge of the bed. Hannah shut the door behind us and turned to face me.

"So I was up pretty late last night, working on that essay for Sweeney's class, and I was chatting with Elise, you know, the girl who sits behind me and always has a thousand questions." She paused, twisting a spiral of hair

Immaculate

so tightly around her finger, I could see the tip losing color. "Anyway, she asked if I'd heard about the website that everyone was talking about. The website . . . It's about you, Mina. It was two a.m. when I saw it, so I decided I'd wait until this morning to tell you about it."

"A website about me? What kind of website?" The words sounded tinny, distant in my ears, as if I was anywhere else but in my own body.

She sat down at my desk, typing on the keyboard as the computer flicked back to life.

"Here it is. I think you should come see for yourself."

The first thing I could clearly make out was a picture of me at the top of the page, a photo from last year's Halloween party at Peter's house. Izzy had dressed as the devil and Hannah and I were angels, and the three of us spent the entire night mock-fighting one another with cheap light-up plastic swords. The picture showed just me, though, dressed in a puffy short white dress that I'd coated in clear iridescent sparkles, big yellow wings strapped to my back, and a pipe cleaner halo hovering on the side of my head. Someone from the party—a *friend*—must have taken that picture. And now they'd posted it here, for anyone in the world to see, with the caption THE VIRGIN MINA in massive capital letters that screamed at me from the screen.

There was more just below it, a long paragraph. The

letters were swimming in circles in my vision, and I closed my eyes.

"I'll read it out loud to you," Hannah said, her voice shaking.

> All Hail the BLESSED VIRGIN MINA, the miraculous Mother Mary of the twenty-first century! At long last, after two thousand years of waiting . . . the promised second coming of the Messiah is upon us! (Repent, repent!) With his all-knowing wisdom, God has chosen Mina Dietrich of quaint but lovely Green Hill, Pennsylvania, to be the blessed mother of this sacred child. Mina is a senior at Green Hill High, a straight-A student in line to be the class valedictorian, admired throughout the community for her many achievements and aspirations. Beauty and brains, kindness and virtue, a solid gold reputation—it's no surprise that the Father would choose Mina out of every other female on the WHOLE ENTIRE PLANET to help him in his holy plan. Though Mina was in a long-term relationship at the time of the Second Messiah's conception, she claims that she has never engaged in any form of intercourse, and thusly, there is NO OTHER EXPLANATION other than DIVINE INTERVENTION for the creation of the child that she is now carrying. (Side note: this relationship has

since been terminated, as for some inconceivable reason way beyond our grasp, the partner refused to BELIEVE that such a miraculous event could ever happen in these modern times. Shocking! Outrageous! Ex-boyfriend, be damned!)

Mina has been reportedly carrying the Lord's child since the beginning of the summer, which means, oh dear world, that we can expect the baby's grand arrival in early March. We see it as our divine duty to spread the TRUTH as far and wide as possible, and ask that you please do the same. We have created this Virgin Mina website to explore Mina's nine-month journey, and we ask you to leave your observations, questions, concerns, etc. in the comments section, as we want this to be a forum for group discussion. We also ask you to send any pictures and suggestions for the site to the e-mail address provided on the contacts page.

Please note: ONLY BELIEVERS MAY ENTER. (And for all you nonbelievers—SERIOUSLY, ARE YOU F*#@ING CRAZY?! Who doesn't believe that babies can magically appear out of thin air without sperm or penises or any kind of sexual interaction?! Didn't you read the BIBLE?!)

Our most sincere blessings to all,
TEAM VIRGIN MINA

Hannah's voice stopped reading, but I could still hear all the words, looping and weaving like bright red ribbons through my mind.

Who could have started this? Who would hate me this much?

I mean, even if everyone thought I was lying, why couldn't they just ignore me? Leave me alone? I hadn't asked for any of them to believe me. I hadn't asked for them to worship me.

I hadn't asked them for anything.

"How many . . . ?" The question froze on my lips, but I didn't have to finish. I'd seen the answer for myself as Hannah silently clicked on to the comments page. Nine hundred people had already left responses. Did I even know that many people, even if I counted every single person in my high school?

"It was at around eight hundred last night when I first found the page. It seems to be . . . spreading pretty quickly, I guess. From the posts I saw, I think it's been around for a little while now, a month maybe, but it seems like it's just starting to pick up speed. I'm so sorry," Hannah whispered, her head in her hands. "Do you want to read any of it? What people are posting? Or is it too much right now?"

"Now. I might as well see it all now." My mom reached out and squeezed my hand, steadying me.

Comments varied on a spectrum from incredibly shocked and entertained to incredibly cruel and hateful: *OMG, this bitch needs a TV show!* to *I can't believe she hasn't been struck by lightning yet, but I guess Hell will be burn enough.* There were plenty of pictures, too, on the dedicated photos page. Me in a tight hot pink minidress and matching heels, a Barbie costume I wore for a party last year, the caption saying THIS IS OUR VIRGIN?!!? A classic painting of the Virgin Mary with my face Photoshopped in over hers, *Menius* scrawled along the bottom; another photo of me and Nate at last year's prom, a bright red line drawn in between us and the words I'M NOT THE DADDY written in a bubble above Nate's head. The most recent was a picture that must have been taken just yesterday, judging from the outfit—I was standing at my locker, Jesse holding my books as I was reaching out for something on the top shelf. Jesse's eyes were on me, and we were both grinning. I hadn't noticed at the time, but my shirt had ridden up, leaving the bottom of my stomach exposed for somebody's waiting camera. That was my bump, right there on the screen, for the whole online world to see as proof of my pregnancy. The caption made the post infinitely worse: COULD THIS POSSIBLY BE THE REAL DADDY, *VIRGIN* MINA?

The idea that someone had been watching so closely, holding a camera for just the right angle, just the right pose, made my stomach erupt in hot swirling waves. I put my hands on my bump, holding my baby to ground myself. To remind myself what really mattered. But I could still taste bile in the back of my throat. There were no boundaries anymore. I was public property.

As Hannah scrolled through more of the posts, I realized that I barely recognized most of the names—it seemed as if the majority of comments came from people who were from other schools and towns, other states, even. This wasn't Green Hill's secret. Not anymore. The names that I did recognize were mostly strangers or very casual acquaintances—no sign of any of my old *friends* yet. They were probably just too scared to get publicly involved, too worried that I'd try to get them in trouble once I discovered the page's existence. No doubt they were all sitting around that very morning checking for updates, prepping for in-depth conversations about the most recent posts.

"What's going on?"

I jumped at the sound of Jesse's voice from the doorway. I'd forgotten that school would actually be starting soon, that time had been moving while we'd sat there staring at the screen. He'd had his camera out, filming his walk up the stairs, probably—I'd gotten used to its constant presence, his constant need to document—but he shut it off now and dropped it onto my dresser.

"Look," I said, waving my hand at the screen. "Just look."

Jesse came over to the desk and hovered behind Hannah as she clicked and scrolled, silent as he took in everything there was to see on the screen.

"You should call the police, Mina," he said, turning to face me, his cheeks splotchy and red. "This is slander. This is harassment, and you can't let them get away with it. Whoever started this deserves to be punished. I'm sure the cops can easily trace this."

I looked away, his steely, penetrating gaze more than I could handle at the moment. "But they're doing this for a reaction, aren't they, Jesse? They want me to freak out. They want me to scream and cry and run away with my hands up in the air. I don't want to give them that. They don't deserve that much from me." Could Kyle be smart enough to make an entire website? Maybe if some of his friends helped, too—he had always been good at getting people to do his bidding.

"So what, you're just going to walk into school today with all these terrible people and act like everything's fine? Act like it's okay that they're doing this to you?" Jesse's hands were knotted up in his unruly dark curls, and I could tell that he was struggling hard to keep his voice level. "Mrs. Dietrich, you agree with me, right? It'd be crazy to not report this. It's practically a hate crime."

"I don't know," my mom said, shaking her head as she reached across the desk and closed the web page. "I don't know the right answer yet. I think we need more time to think about it before we make any rash decisions."

"I agree. What if the police getting involved just makes everyone even angrier?" Hannah asked, wrapping an arm around my shoulders. "I don't think that we can stop people from having a reaction to Mina's story, and the bigger deal we make out of all this, the louder and more cruel their responses might be. I think Mina might be right, at least for now. She keeps holding her head up, she keeps pushing through. We keep pushing through with her." She gave me what I knew she meant to be a reassuring smile, but I could see the strain of her lips, the worry clouding her eyes.

"This is absurd," Jesse said, "completely and ridiculously absurd." He latched his hands on to my window ledge, his knuckles white from the pressure, and stared out at the fields, shaking his head. "But it's not my decision to make, is it? So do what you think is best, Mina. It's your life, and I'll stand behind you. I promised you at least that much, and I promised Iris, too."

I blinked at the sound of her name, the ring of those two syllables that had become so significant, so earth-shattering when strung together side by side. *I-ris*. I wanted to tell them all that I'd seen her, that she was still around, somewhere, hovering in the air around us like dust particles, but I couldn't. Not until I saw her again. Not unless I was sure.

"I just hope that everyone at school gets bored with it when you don't react, so they can turn their attention to other things and other people." Jesse paused, pulling his gaze away from the window to meet my eyes. "I hope that *this* is as bad as it gets."

There was no denying the tension as we walked through the school hallways that morning. The blatant stares, the judgments, and the jokes that no one even bothered to whisper anymore. How had I been naive enough to think that Kyle's performance was just a blip in everyone's memory? It was obvious that I was now a public entity, like some C-list tabloid celebrity who had ceased to be a real person and had instead become something less than human. Something that didn't deserve respect or compassion, something without feelings or emotions or a living, beating heart.

The three of us stared straight ahead as we made our way to my locker, Jesse and Hannah flanking me on either side like bodyguards. I tried to still the shaking in my hands as I fumbled over the combination, cursing under my breath when the lock refused to snap open.

"Mina . . ." Hannah said, "I think—"

"Hold on for just a minute," I said, frustrated. "I can't get my damn locker to open." I spun the dial back through the familiar pattern, and after a few tries, the lock clicked open against my palm.

"What were you saying?" I started to reach for my books on the top shelf. "Han?"

I froze, my calculus book suspended in midair. The hallway around me suddenly felt too quiet, expectant, as if everyone but me was holding their breath.

I lowered the book and slowly turned around.

Nate. Nate and Jesse, face-to-face, standing barely a foot apart in the middle of the hallway. Everything else had ceased to matter—all eyes and attention focused on them, waiting for whatever movement or word would come next.

"It was you," Nate said, his voice low and threatening and almost entirely unrecognizable. Though I hadn't actually heard him speak since August, I realized. Maybe I'd already forgotten what he sounded like. Maybe a few months was all it took to make someone a complete stranger. "You're the father, aren't you?"

Jesse laughed in surprise. I flinched, tilting my head down. The laugh sounded nervous to me, a twitchy giggle stemming from his social awkwardness, but that was because I knew him. To a stranger, to Nate, I was sure it sounded mocking. "Of course not. Don't be ridiculous. Mina and I weren't even friends until a few weeks ago."

"It's just a little funny to me that out of nowhere you've

suddenly become her biggest defender. You're a little too protective for someone who barely knows her, don't you think? A little too possessive, maybe?"

"Seriously," Jesse said, stepping back, hands fanned out in front of him, "you're way off. I have nothing to do with what's happening with Mina."

"And why should I believe you?" Nate asked, taking a few steps forward to close the distance. "Who else could it have been? I don't exactly see any other guys trailing around behind her like a desperate little puppy. You're making it a little too obvious, don't you think? I know that you work with her. Were you there at the beginning of the summer, when she . . . ?" As he asked that question, I could see in his eyes that something had clicked. The details were spinning into new, terrible possibilities for him. He looked so sad suddenly, so broken, that I fought the urge to run to his side. "That night you came to my house crying," he said, slowly turning to face me. "Was that when it happened, Mina? Was that *guilt*? Were you going to tell me something then?"

"Nate, no!" I yelled, pushing my way through the throngs of gawkers to wedge myself in between the two of them. I couldn't stand that he thought that—I hadn't, I never would have. "Jesse and I are just friends. Nothing happened between us. You have this all wrong. I promise."

"You *promise?*" Nate asked, his voice breaking so loudly and so obviously that his entire face flamed red with embarrassment. "Sorry, Mina, but your word stands for very little these days."

Someone in the hallway laughed, a hollow sound that set off a round of murmuring all around us.

"Can we talk about this somewhere else?" I pleaded, blinking to keep the tears back. "Somewhere where we're not on public display?"

"That seems unnecessary. It's not like any of this is a secret. Not anymore. And the way I see it, you deserve for everyone to see you for who you really are."

"Nate, stop," Hannah said, stepping up beside me and squeezing my hand. "You're making a complete ass of yourself. Just let it go. You're hurt. I get that. But this isn't going to make things any better."

"Just *let it go?* Like it's that simple? She lied to me and to everyone else, and she's still lying. We can't all be as naive and forgiving as you are, sadly, though I guess life must be much easier that way. I envy you a little."

Hannah's fingers gripped my hand tighter, the bones of my knuckles grinding into one another. "This isn't your business anymore."

"Not my business? Not my business that my girlfriend is parading around right in front of me with the guy she cheated on me with?"

"Ex-girlfriend," I said. "And that was entirely your decision."

"Like I had a choice."

"You did." I choked on the words, swallowing hard as the tears finally rolled down my cheeks. "You definitely did. But that's in the past. *We* are in the past. Please, please just leave me alone. Please, Nate."

Nate looked away, and I thought that he was finished. I thought that he had scraped together enough decency to back off. Nate wasn't an aggressive person—it wasn't in his nature. Or so I had incorrectly thought, because before I could even take a full deep breath, Nate lunged forward, shoving Jesse stumbling back through the crowds until his back slammed against the lockers.

"Just admit it!" Nate yelled, angry tears streaming down his twisted face as he pinned Jesse by the shoulders. "Just admit that you slept with my girlfriend, you fucking coward!"

"Nate! Stop!" Izzy appeared at Nate's side, her strong, capable arms tugging him away from Jesse. "You have too much to lose to get caught in a fight. Think about sports, about college. He's not worth the punishment. You're better than this. You're better than *all* this."

Her words must have worked some sort of spell on him, because he seemed to instantly transform back into calm, sensible, predictable Nate—it was as if Jekyll and

Hyde had stepped right out of the pages of our English lit reading. He shook his head a few times and stepped back, letting Izzy pull him in more closely against her. I stared at their hands, their fingers interlocked, so close and familiar, their cheeks nearly touching as Izzy whispered something into his ear.

My stomach tumbled and turned as I stood there watching them. I could handle not having either of them in my life. I'd accepted that that was the way things were, the way things would probably always be. But the two of them together? Kissing, cuddling, and, *oh God*, going further than Nate and I ever had? I couldn't. I couldn't handle that. I shut my eyes and turned away, trying to block the flood of images that were spilling across my mind.

"Mina? Mina, are you okay?"

I opened my eyes to see Jesse staring down at me, frowning, Hannah close behind him.

"I should be asking you that, Jesse, seeing as you just got in your second fight because of me. Did Nate hurt you?"

"No, I'm fine. Really. Don't worry about me. But the way you looked just now, with your eyes closed, and your skin that pale, I don't know . . . I just thought something was really wrong. You scared me."

"Sorry about that. I just got really anxious, that's all. I try to close my eyes and deep breathe whenever I get stressed out. Keep calm for . . ." My gaze turned down toward my stomach, and I could feel Jesse's eyes following the movement. "Keep calm for the *baby*." I didn't care if anyone heard me, because Nate was at least right about one thing. None of this was a secret anymore. There was no point in walking on eggshells, pretending that the obvious wasn't happening in front of all our eyes.

The first warning bell rang, and the crowd splintered off in all directions. Someone knocked me from behind in the frantic rush, and I turned to see Sara Fritz timidly peering up at me through her long, floppy bangs. Sara was a quiet, solitary sort of girl who had transferred in from a private Catholic school only at the beginning of our junior year. She kept to herself mostly, spent her lunches and free periods hunched over a keyboard in the computer lab. I barely knew her, though I was pretty certain she was right behind me in class rank. Had been, anyway, before our current grades were factored in. I was doing decently enough, given the circumstances, now that I was more settled into the semester—a B average in most of my classes, thanks to some extra credit and to what I suspected were a few sympathy points from teachers who pitied the not-so-private derailing of my personal life. That wouldn't be enough to keep topping Sara, but I was surprisingly proud of those Bs, as proud as I used to be of my standard 100s. I was keeping my head above water, despite everything.

"So s-sorry," she stuttered, dashing off down the hall before I could respond. I stared after her, confused by how jittery she'd seemed. Or maybe that was just her way—after all, I'd never really talked to the girl, and I had been her competition.

"Maybe you should go to the nurse, just in case?" Jesse asked. "Go home and take it easy for the rest of the day?"

"I think I should stay." I turned back to my locker and reached for the last notebook.

"You don't have to prove anything to anyone, Mina. Like you said, that was a lot of stress for one day."

"Jesse's right," Hannah said, picking my backpack off the floor. "It's one day. No one's going to think you're weak. I think you've already more than proven that you're not running away. But between everything you saw online this morning and everything that just happened with Nate, and, well, Izzy, too . . . it's just a lot. A lot to take in, even for a superhuman like you. Go home, Mina. Do it for the baby if you won't do it for yourself."

Do it for the baby. I forfeited my armful of books over to Jesse, who started loading them back into my bag. That was all it took. Hannah knew that I couldn't say no, not when it came to the baby. Not when it came to protecting and nurturing the little life growing inside of me.

"Fine." I sighed. "You guys win." Though now that I'd decided—or had been decided for, more accurately—I was relieved to have a whole day by myself to catch up on homework. "But just for today. And I expect a full report this evening, Han, about anything that you happen to hear about me. I want to know what people are saying. I want to know what I'm up against. No secrets, okay?"

"No secrets," Hannah said, slipping the backpack around my shoulders.

"No secrets," Jesse echoed. "Now let me walk you to the nurse."

"Absolutely not. You two are already going to be late."

"I have Mrs. Royer for Physics II first period, and we're totally compadres. We share a very deep, obsessive love of old-school science-fiction novels. Anyway, she won't be upset. She'll understand when I explain that you needed an escort."

I nodded—because he was right, I really didn't want to be alone—and gave Hannah a quick hug before she ran off to first period. Jesse and I started for the nurse's office, walking the first few minutes in silence.

"So do you think Mrs. Royer knows all the rumors?" I asked. "About me, that is. Do you think all the teachers know about the baby, Virgin Mina, everything?"

"No secrets, right?" he asked, glancing over at me. "Yes, Mina. I think teachers know about all of it. I think they know a lot more about all of us than we'd like to think, and this doesn't seem like a story that could slip past their radar. But it's like that old saying—'those who mind don't matter and those who matter don't mind.' My mom's favorite catchphrase for my entire childhood and, even if I wouldn't admit it to her, pretty mind-blowingly true, don't you think?"

But Izzy and Nate had definitely mattered, I wanted to say. Hadn't they? I nodded anyway. We were already outside the nurse's office.

"Thanks for walking me, Jesse. And thanks for . . . for putting up with all this. I still say it's not a fair trade-off, not anywhere close, but I hope you at least know how grateful I am to have a friend like you. I hope I can pay it all back someday."

"Mina, stop, you don't—"

"Things won't always be this hard. Life will settle into place, and then it will all be different for us. You won't always have to be guarding me like this, I promise." But as soon as the words were out of my mouth, I realized how hollow they were. When would things stop being hard? When would life be any shade of normal? When would people stop talking, stop staring, stop pointing their bored, ignorant little fingers?

"You're not forcing me into anything against my will, Mina. I like you—I really like you—complicated or uncomplicated. And you're right, things will settle down someday. And maybe when they do . . . I don't know, maybe when they do things really can be different for us."

I wanted to ask exactly what he meant by *like*, wanted to pore over every last bit of it with a magnifying glass, determine the exact tone and emphasis and meaning behind each individual word, but I couldn't. I couldn't even meet his eyes, not without giving away every thought spinning through my mind.

So instead I muttered a quiet *thanks* as I gave him a weak, one-armed hug and ducked into the nurse's office, my head so dizzy with a weird blend of confusion and curiosity and hope that, suddenly, I felt quite in need of a sick day after all.

chapter thirteen

After Hannah showed me the Virgin Mina website, I couldn't stop myself from compulsively checking for updates every opportunity I had. Refresh, refresh, refresh—attached to my computer for hours on end with the fear that if I got up, walked away, I'd miss the latest, most horrendous accusations yet. I had to know what they were saying about me, and I had to know as soon as it was said. It became an addiction, and I knew it couldn't possibly be healthy, not for me, certainly not for the baby, but I couldn't stop. I couldn't stop waiting for whatever was going to happen next, because it was becoming clearer every day—every hour, really—that this was growing to be much bigger than any high school kid's amateur web page. This was becoming a national story. *I* was becoming a national story.

I watched the number of comments grow—nine hundred to twelve hundred, two thousand, five thousand—as more and more sites spread the link across the Internet. My parents had both started to press the idea of involving the police, now that it was clear that we had, in fact, not reached "as bad as it gets" after all. Or anywhere close, for that matter. Jesse had been keeping constant tabs on the Virgin Mina page, too, and he cited the numbers in my ear so often that it was almost pointless for me to check on my own. I knew, of course, that something had to be done—but what could I do, *really*? Maybe we could have the website taken down—the police could do that much—but it wouldn't stop people from talking. It wouldn't erase the whole story from their minds. Where did the line of free speech cross over? What was slander and what was just plain old permissible cruelty? I couldn't very well slap handcuffs on practically the entire school population.

Regardless, it was Thanksgiving Eve, and I would have the next four days of refuge at home, four days to breathe the delicious fresh air outside of the suffocating school hallways. Four days to pretend that things were okay, that life was normal.

And it was also my birthday today, the big one-eight. Eighteen years old. I was officially an adult—a full-blown, baby-carrying adult—though other than my mom's traditional pancakes that morning, served on a faux silver platter with globs of homemade vanilla icing and rainbow sprinkles, the day hadn't really felt like much of a birthday, let alone a landmark, monumental birthday. No one at school other than Hannah or Jesse showed any sign of caring or remembering. Not that I'd expected anything from Izzy, but there had been nothing, not even a birthday wave, from any of my former friends—people who had seemingly erased all memories of the last decade's worth of celebrations together.

Hannah and Jesse came over after school, and the three of us hung around the living room for a few hours, chugging hot apple cider and eating our way through a box of ginger snaps while we helped Gracie make a chain of construction paper handprint turkeys to string along the fireplace. Jesse had brought a flashy new camera along that he was testing out for his uncle, and insisted on filming clips throughout the birthday night—a recording made much richer with Gracie performing a rousing song and dance routine to "Over the River and Through the Wood," the only Thanksgiving song she could think of. Even if, she said with a big frown, we wouldn't be riding through woods, over rivers, or to a grandmother's house.

My dad picked up a few pizzas from Frankie's, my ritual birthday dinner for as long as I could remember, and he sat next to me at the dining room table while we ate. That was the only gift I really needed this year. He had been warming up in tiny but still noticeable increments each day since his talk with Pastor Lewis, but my birthday was the most normal day in a while by far. He sang "Happy Birthday" as loudly as ever, cut me the first piece of banana chocolate chip cake, and topped it all off with a quick kiss on my forehead. I could still feel exactly where his lips had touched, the sweet mark they'd left like a drop of perfume on my skin.

I had explicitly told my mom not to get me any presents, given all the inconceivable baby expenses to come. But after disappearing with my dad to clear away the pizza boxes and the remains of my cake, she reemerged with a beautiful white wooden cradle, and I burst out in tears.

"What's wrong, sweetie?" my mom asked. "Do you not like it? I know we said no presents, but your father and I would have wanted to buy this for your shower anyway, so why wait?"

"No, I love it," I said, jumping up to wrap her in my arms. "Thank you. It's wonderful. Perfect. All of you here, my birthday, Thanksgiving. I'm just happy. I'm really happy." I realized that my dad was still in the kitchen, though, and I wanted to thank him, too. "Where's Da—?"

"This is from me!" Gracie squealed, interrupting me. She pulled out a small yellow present from behind the sofa and shoved it into my hands. "Open it! Open it!"

I opened the box slowly and pulled out a thin, delicate silver bracelet from the puffs of tissue paper. I held it up to look at it more closely—a charm bracelet with tiny silver letters strung along the chain, spelling out *Dietrich*.

At either end was a charm, one of a heart, the other of a little house.

"I wanted you to have something that could always remind you of us, even when we're not right next to you," Gracie said, curling herself up on my lap like a cat. "So now you can never really feel alone."

"I'll wear it every day, sweetie. And you are absolutely right. It will always remind me just how lucky I am to have you." A tear rolled down my cheek, and I buried my head in Gracie's hair to hide my face.

"Well, my present feels a bit anticlimactic after both of those gifts," Hannah said, tapping my shoulder with a sparkly gold gift bag.

I reached inside and pulled out a bright pink T-shirt, the words SEXY MAMA printed across the front in white cursive letters. I tugged it on over my sweater, and by the end of my runway stroll around the living room, we were all laughing so hard that my crying had become contagious.

"I figured it's time to be living out loud and proud, you know?" Hannah said, grinning through her tears.

"I would love to see how everyone at school would react to me prancing down the hallways in this. Maybe one of these days, hm?"

Loud, stomping footsteps from the kitchen made us all turn toward the hallway. My father appeared from the shadows at the edge of the room, his face drained of color.

"What is it?" my mom asked first. "What's wrong?"

"I . . ." he started, taking a few clumsy steps forward as he cleared his throat. "I had the news on in the kitchen while I was doing the dishes, and . . . and there's something that you need to see. Your story, Mina. Your story is on the news tonight."

My breath hitched, and I forced myself to swallow. I couldn't possibly be surprised, could I? How could the local news, the national news even, not pick up on a story like this? This was the headline that golden news stories were made of, a scandalous human interest piece that seasoned reporters and rookies alike would battle over—who would get the first public interview, the most intimate details, the most stunning accusations.

Jesse jumped up to turn the TV on and quickly started scrolling through the channels, stopping when he landed on KBC and the feature we were waiting for: *Pregnant Teen in Pennsylvania Claims to Be Virgin.* My picture—the photo from the top of the Virgin Mina website, that atrocious Halloween angel costume—was radiating from the TV screen, and the reporter's voice was reading through some of the more repeatable posts. *Almost six months in, and she still hasn't cracked. Will she ever give it up?*

"They can't . . . They can't do this without my approval, can they?" I felt as if my heart had stopped beating, my blood had stopped flowing, but somehow I was still alive, still sitting on the sofa and watching what was on the TV in front of me. Gracie stiffened on my lap, clamping her arms protectively around my shoulders. I couldn't look down, though, couldn't bring myself to see the terror I was certain would be flashing across her eyes.

"You're eighteen now, Mina," my mother said, her words quiet but steady. She said it so immediately, so absolutely, that I knew she must have been thinking about this for a while, worrying about what my birthday could bring.

Eighteen didn't just mean becoming an adult—it meant no longer being untouchable. No longer being protected or coddled by the law. I was fair game.

My picture vanished from the screen, replaced by an overly polished-looking middle-aged reporter standing in front of Green Hill High. "According to the heavily trafficked website, eighteen-year-old Mina Dietrich, lifelong resident of rural Green Hill, Pennsylvania, has remained strong to her claims of virginity since the news of her pregnancy first broke to the public in October. We've heard from several sources today in the small, tightly knit community of Green Hill, and by all accounts, Dietrich has always been a role model and source of pride for the town— at the top of her class, well liked by her peers, and actively involved in various volunteer organizations in the school and throughout the community. However, most Green Hill residents we've spoken with seem hesitant to believe any part of the story, and are instead outraged by the sacrilegious nature of the claims. In just a few minutes we'll be speaking with a few of them directly—Tana Fritz, mother of one of Dietrich's peers, and Kyle Baker, a longtime acquaintance and classmate of Dietrich's. For now Dietrich continues to attend classes at the high school, seemingly determined to go about 'life as usual,' as one classmate reports. But many, such as Fritz, wonder if that will change, especially now that the story is quickly gaining ground throughout the country. Fritz even suggests a petition to the school requesting Dietrich's removal, citing the potential for safety issues as the story continues to strike up controversy. More from Green Hill after the commercial." The reporter gave a tiny wink and a flash of her glowing white teeth, and then the screen clicked off into blackness.

"That's enough of this," my dad growled. "That's *enough*. We've let these people talk about you right in front of our faces for too damn long, and I've had enough of it."

"Tana Fritz?" I asked, shocked by the utter randomness of it. Kyle—yes, no bombshell there. But Tana? "Why does she get to have a say about me? Why should anyone listen to her opinions?"

I knew of Tana, but had never once spoken to her personally. She was the mother of Sara Fritz, the odd, loner type who'd bumped into me in the hallway after Jesse and Nate's fight. But unlike her timid, reclusive daughter, Tana had a reputation for throwing herself into the limelight—she was the type of parent who volunteered for every school event or activity across the board, and her name was a regular on the list of editorial letters printed in the local paper. She had an opinion about everyone and everything, so I guess I shouldn't have been entirely surprised that she'd have a hand in this.

Was that why Sara had looked at me that way? She'd felt guilty, of course, guilty that her own mother had tried to sabotage me with a stupid petition. She'd already known the plan. Did our class rank have anything to do with this? Knocking out the competition? Or maybe that was just a side bonus for a much larger religious grievance.

"They called today," my mom said, her voice so low that we all leaned in to hear better. "KBC left a message today asking to talk to Mina, to us, but I didn't call back and I didn't say anything. I didn't want to ruin your birthday. I had no idea it would be happening this fast, especially without them getting through to you first, Mina. I'm so sorry I didn't warn you earlier."

I was silent for a few seconds, my thoughts too mixed and messy to pin down. "It's okay, Mom. I don't know what I would have done differently if you had told me earlier. I couldn't have just jumped in front of the camera today. I'm not ready for that. I'm not sure if I'll ever be ready for that. What would I say?"

"Well, you need to say something, Mina, because

they're sure as hell not going anywhere until you do," my dad said, pacing behind the sofa in small, anxious circles.

I stood up, too angry and jittery to sit. "I can't lie and make up a daddy just to make them go away, Dad. I can't do it. I've gone this long, and I'm not changing my story now. That's not an option."

"I think it's a little late for that anyway, Mina," my dad responded, pausing to look me straight on. There was a rage in his eyes, an anger that didn't sit right on his usually soft and open face. "I say we wait to see what other requests come in from KBC or from other news outlets, because there *will* be other requests—that's one thing we can be sure about. And then you go on, you put yourself out there, and be the confused, honest girl who can't exactly explain what's happening."

"But you're my father and *you* don't believe my story, so what chance do I have of convincing strangers who know nothing about me that I'm sincere? That I'm not just some stupid, scared little girl who made a mistake and lied and now doesn't know how to backtrack? Doesn't know how to undo all of the damage she's created? And why do you even want me on TV spreading a story that you still think is a lie? Not just a lie, but a sacrilegious claim that will have me burning in Hell."

"I don't know, Mina." He sighed, rubbing his eyes with his palms. "I don't know. You're my daughter, and I can't watch strangers tear you apart like this. I don't think we can sit back and do nothing, I really don't, and this is the best that I have right now."

"I think it's worth a try, Mina," Jesse said. "I think you're going to have to put yourself out there and say something at some point if this keeps up, or your silence is going to raise even more questions and suspicions. You'll have to issue some sort of statement at the very least. But maybe you should talk to a lawyer first. This feels way out of our depth."

I looked to my mom, waiting for her to weigh in with some of her softer, more cautious maternal insights, but she looked too exhausted to disagree.

"Hannah? What do you think?"

Hannah hesitated for a moment, a lock of hair wound tightly around her fingers. "Your dad and Jesse make sense. But I don't want to interfere with the family decision-making."

"You are family, Han." I almost said, *And so is Izzy*, because that was how I'd always thought of it—Hannah *and* Izzy were family, a pair, a full set—but I stopped myself just in time.

"Whatever you do," Jesse cut in, "however you handle it, you all need to be behind it, a unified front."

"Exactly," my dad said, nodding in approval.

The room was silent then, all of us lost in our own

murky thoughts. Jesse and Hannah got up to say their good-byes soon after, and I walked them both out to the porch. I blew a few misty white *O*s with my breath, the frosty night air feeling amazingly clean and refreshing in my lungs. Hannah gave me a last birthday hug—her eighteenth hug that day, she'd been counting—and looked toward Jesse to start off together for their cars.

Jesse shrugged and shook his head, shoving his hands farther into the wooly pockets of his brown leather jacket. "I'll leave in a few minutes, but you don't have to wait. I wanted to just talk to Mina about something first."

Hannah's shivering lips turned up in a tiny, fleeting smirk. She blew me a kiss as she turned away, leaving Jesse and me alone in the darkness.

Jesse was standing just a few feet away, but I'd left the porch lights off and it was too shadowy to make out his expression. There was only a soft, muted glow from the front windows, the light from the kitchen filtering out through lacy curtains.

"The present giving got a little disrupted earlier. And I wanted to wait, anyway, to give you my gift when we were alone."

My breath caught. "You didn't have to give me anything."

He didn't respond, just reached into his frayed canvas camera bag and pulled out a flat, rectangular package wrapped in old newspaper comics.

"It's nothing much," he said, clearing his throat as he handed it to me. "But I hope you like it."

I peeled the paper back carefully, not wanting to tear through any of the cartoon faces or word bubbles because I already knew that I would fold this up and keep it tucked away somewhere safe in my room. When the paper fell away, I could see that it was a canvas underneath, a painting of some sort, but I had to walk over to the window to make out the details. It was a young woman—no, it was *me*, it was definitely me, *I* was the young woman—and I was standing by the window in my room, gazing out over the fields, a peaceful, satisfied little smile playing on my lips. My hands were wrapped around my stomach, cradling my precious bump, and in this portrait it looked like everything made sense. I was a glowing, confident pregnant woman who was looking out over the life and the future that she wanted for herself.

"This is incredible, Jesse," I whispered. "I knew you were a film guru and everything, but you never told me that you were a painter, too. This looks exactly like me. Or exactly like I wish I could be."

"You're becoming her, Mina," he said, the words sounding so simple on his lips. "And I wouldn't call myself a painter. I'm in a painting class right now at school and, I don't know . . . I guess you just inspired me."

I looked back down at the painting, too lightheaded

and giddy to string any adequate words together. As my eyes pored over the finer points, I realized that there was a phrase written in delicate cursive letters along the bottom of the canvas.

"*Dum spiro spero*?" I asked, squinting in the faint light. "What does that mean?"

"Oh, that . . . It's a little corny, I guess," he said, pausing as he fiddled with a zipper on his bag. "Kind of a Spero family saying. *Spero* means 'I hope' in Italian and Latin, and it's a Latin proverb: 'While I breathe, I hope.' I thought it fit with the painting's theme. It fits with you."

While I breathe . . . I hope.

I set the canvas down on the windowsill and slowly moved closer to him. "Jesse. This is the most special gift anyone has ever given me."

I smiled up at him in the dark and watched as his head dipped down toward my upturned face. Before I even realized it was happening, his lips brushed against mine, warm and pillow soft, still so sweet with frosting and cider. His hands brushed lightly against my cheeks, and I instinctively wrapped my arms around his neck, pulling him closer as I kissed him back. I reached up to twist a strand of his hair, his striking black hair, the color of fresh ink and midnight sky. And for a few seconds I was completely happy, spiraling and soaring in sparkly golden clouds, angels singing, every cliché I'd ever heard suddenly becoming strangely, brilliantly true. It was as if something had burst open inside of me, some radiant sparkle of joy that had never had a chance to show itself before that moment—a prize, a reward, for finding my way to this place, this person.

But then, in a sharp flash of reality, I could feel my belly pressed oddly and uncomfortably against him, the unnatural fit of his flat stomach clashing with my round one. The entire moment dipped and swayed and slipped out of my grasp.

I was pregnant, and the baby was not his. I was pregnant, and my life was a mess.

I was pregnant—and I had no right to be kissing anyone at all.

No matter how much I wanted to be.

"Jesse, *no*." I forced myself to pull back. "We can't be doing this. It just doesn't feel right. I have too many things to figure out, and I won't drag you into it. You're too good of a friend, and I don't want to jeopardize that."

"What if I want to be dragged into it?"

"It's not fair to you. And people are already talking enough as it is. We don't need to add fuel to their ideas."

"I don't care what people are saying. You should know that about me by now. We know the truth, so screw their lies."

"I *do* care. This is my life."

"Are you worried about what Nate would say?"

I laughed without meaning to, and the sound of it made me wince. "Nate? No, of course not. Nate can say whatever he wants. Nate and I have nothing anymore."

He paused a few beats too long.

"Okay. I understand." He turned around and looked out over the pitch black of the driveway. "It's too much right now. I'm sorry if I made you uncomfortable. I shouldn't have just kissed you like that."

"You didn't make me uncomfortable. I just . . . It can't be like that. Right now my life has to be about the baby. Only about the baby."

"I get it. Don't worry, really. I get it. Let's just pretend that never happened, okay? It's cold out and you don't have a jacket, so you should get back inside, anyway." He gave a small wave and tugged his hood up as he jogged toward the truck.

A nauseating swell of regret made me want to call out after him, but I pushed it back down. I would have to erase that kiss from my mind. An eighteen-year-old single mom didn't have time for romance and all the complications that came along with a relationship. Especially not when she had an angry mob of strangers to deal with first and foremost.

Jesse would understand. Jesse would move on.

And hopefully, someday, I would, too.

the third trimester

chapter fourteen

Ten days.

Ten flaps left to open on the Advent calendar hanging on the kitchen wall.

Ten more pieces of star-shaped chocolates to pop out of the ten remaining small windows that opened into the cozy winter village scene—round puffs of smoke rising from the chimneys, bundled-up carolers open-mouthed on front stoops and grinning children peeking from behind curtains, a glowing tree in the center town square.

Ten days before Christmas and then maybe, just maybe, life could get a little bit easier. Not surprisingly, the whole "pregnant virgin" story seemed especially popular during the holiday season. But soon it would be a new year, with its own new stories. People disappeared come January. Crawled back into their own little houses and their own little lives and didn't poke their heads out into the fresh air again until the first early spring breeze come late

March. And by late March, I wouldn't be a pregnant virgin anymore. I would be a mother, and maybe at some point the media and all the thousands of people who couldn't get enough of Virgin Mina would become bored. They wouldn't forget—the story, the idea, the image of my face would still linger in their minds, a memorable curiosity to turn over through the years, to pull out occasionally when dinner conversations became entirely exhausted—but I would no longer be a subject for prime-time TV. Reporters would run out of angles, the story would be flat and stale. The well would run dry.

And then I would get my life back.

The house phone started ringing, and two chimes in I remembered that I was home alone and that no one else would be answering. My parents and Gracie were Christmas shopping at the mall, but after the news broke, I'd stopped going most public places other than school, really. Shopping online might lack Santa's village and twinkling greenery, but it also lacked gawking moms and wide-eyed kids without filters—kids like the boy last week who stopped me at the grocery store and asked how I knew that my baby wouldn't be a flesh-eating alien who could eat its way straight out of my belly. Oh yes, online shopping would most definitely do just fine.

I'd left my job at Frankie's behind, too, in the aftermath. It was hard to put an end to the income flow, but it had all become too much—the stares, both real and imagined, and the religious imagery plastered all along the walls. It wasn't only the eyes of the customers I could feel tracing my movements around the room. The life-size Madonna portrait was like the Mona Lisa, her gaze pinning me down no matter where I stood. And besides that, the need I'd had to stay connected to Iris, to catch her again on that off chance—it felt less confined to Frankie's now, after that moment in the cafeteria. Maybe she was just as likely to show up anywhere at all. Maybe she'd know where to find me no matter where I went.

I sighed as I pushed myself up from the kitchen table, where I'd been flipping mindlessly through a special new mothers magazine Hannah had picked up for me at the pharmacy. My mom was still collecting last-minute RVSPs for a holiday party that she was holding at the historical society the next week, and I felt guilty ignoring a call from any of the sweet old ladies who generally attended my mom's events.

I grabbed for the phone right before the answering machine could click on.

"Hello?"

"I'd like to speak to Mina Dietrich, please." The voice was high-pitched and booming, and I detected at least a slight Southern accent in those first few words.

"Mina speaking. And this is . . . ?"

"Gladys from Richmond. Richmond, Virginia."

"Hi, Gladys from Richmond. Can I . . . can I help you with something?"

"I'm just calling to tell you that I think it's downright disturbing, this blasphemous black Devil lie you keep on spreading around our God-fearing country. During the very season of Our Lord, nonetheless! You ought to be so powerfully ashamed of yourself. And your parents! I don't know how your parents sleep a wink at night."

My blood chilled, froze solid like tiny piercing crystals of ice lodged in my veins. She might have been hundreds of miles away, but her voice, coming from the phone in my kitchen—my family's very own kitchen, our safe haven—made me feel completely violated.

"How did you get my number?"

"Well, I'm sure I could have found it in the phone listings on my own if I'd tried, but as it is, it was just posted on the Internet this morning. It was the latest post on that Virgin Mina website that everyone's been talking about. They're encouraging people to speak out directly—you know, have a real dialogue with you about our thoughts."

"Your thoughts?" I hissed into the phone. "I don't know you. You don't know me. You're not entitled to call me in my own home with your thoughts about my life."

She snorted, a sort of *harrumph* sound, and then continued. "I saw that piddly fluff ball of an interview you did for KBC last week, and let me tell you, it was obvious from where I was sitting that you really have nothing to say for yourself. 'I can't explain how this happened,'" she quoted, her voice taking on a nasally, offensive edge as she attempted to imitate me, "'but no, I'm not claiming to be God's chosen either. I'm just trying to do the right thing.' Because that's just plain old nonsense. If you knew—if you really knew with every fiber of your being, your soul—that you were innocent, then how could this be anything *but* a miracle? How could you be anything *but* chosen? But you won't say either of those things because you know that you're lying, and I suppose it's good to see that you at least have enough decency to close your mouth when it comes to the most sacred claims. Mind you, I still think you'll be going straight to the Devil if you keep up with the path you're on now, and . . ."

I hung up and threw the phone down onto the counter, watched as it skittered and spun in precarious circles edging closer and closer to the sink. Good. Let it get ruined. Let me be inaccessible to the whole world of strangers who now had our number, just in case they wanted to "dialogue" with me this morning, tonight, tomorrow, whenever they so desired. I edged my back along the cabinets as I sank to the floor and buried my head in my hands. Her patronizing tone still rattled in my ears, making my whole body shake.

Immaculate

She was right. The KBC interview I'd agreed to last week *had* been a joke. A totally insubstantial, useless filler story that did little if nothing to help my case. I blushed, stuttered, rambled about my good grades and my regular church attendance while my hyperdilated eyes darted everywhere but at the camera or the reporter sitting across from me on our living room sofa. Based on the feedback I saw on the website after the report first aired—and again after the reposting of the video online—the majority of viewers concluded that the nervous tics more than proved my guilty conscience. Only a few outsiders suggested I was endearingly confused, crazy and delusional rather than an outright pathological liar.

"You'll just have to do better next time," my dad had said under his breath, all of us gathered in front of the TV, stone-faced and hushed, for the first prime-time viewing. So far, I hadn't let there be a next time, despite the daily flood of new requests. One failed attempt was enough to convince me that there was nothing I could say to change the public opinion. My story was weak. There were no facts. There were no theories. I had no supporting evidence, no photographic proof, no witnesses other than Jesse, and I refused to let him burn under the spotlight next to me.

But as I played over Gladys from Richmond's call, I was most upset, I realized, by her claim that if I was so certain, if I was *so absolutely positive* that this baby had come about by nothing short of divine intervention, than I would be claiming my "chosen" status with pride and courage. That there could be no room for uncertainty.

But how could I know—how could anyone in the world know—that miracles were, by necessity and without a doubt, the plan, the doing, the sign of God? Of a god, of any god? And if so, which god? Whose god? Last I checked, there was more than just one perception of God, so why should I assume that this was the work of the same god as in *my* Bible? The god I learned about in Sunday School and the god who almost everyone in Green Hill considered to be the "true God"—the "one and only God."

Perhaps there were miracles *outside* of the church. Miracles outside of any realm that we knew, and outside of any logic system that we as mere humans could even begin to wrap our heads around. I was starting to think that ancient cultures—the Maya, Celtics, Egyptians, Buddhists, Native Americans—had a much more sensible view of the way things worked, the divinity to be found in nature, the world all around us, the sun, the moon, the trees, the changing of seasons and the forces of weather.

"Miracles are not contrary to nature, but only contrary to what we know about nature."

It was a line I'd stumbled across over and over during my online scouring for miracles, a quote from Saint Augustine of Hippo, born in the fourth century, a Latin philosopher and theologian from the African Province of the Roman Empire often considered to be one of the greatest Christian thinkers of all time. I had researched him afterward, excited that he had so eloquently summed up my own thoughts—my hopes that there was more to nature and its phenomenal possibilities than met the eye—but I didn't see much else in his writings that I agreed with or could absorb as my own belief system. But I still had this one quote, this sentiment of faith, a new perspective for the kind of miracle I was experiencing in my here and now.

And I needed that, desperately. Needed something to cling to, nails dug deeply in, no matter how insubstantial or removed the idea might be. It's not as if Iris had outlined the greater scheme to me. There was no name-dropping, no finger pointing to who exactly was calling the shots or if "they" had any concrete plans for the baby once he or she was walking, breathing, living on planet Earth alongside me. After nearly seven months of pregnancy, I still hadn't come to many conclusions. What I knew, or thought I knew, to be true on some inner, metaphysical level, came to a very short list: This, this baby, this *asexual* form of reproduction, was an inexplicable, unprecedented scientific phenomenon. It was the work of some power—some much, much higher power—beyond our limited understanding as the insignificant peons temporarily wandering around this planet. For reasons that were entirely undecipherable to me, I was the person who would bring this mysterious creation into life.

And I would care for this creation, protect and love this baby, for the rest of my life, regardless of whether or not I ever came any closer to understanding the heart of it all: *why?*

Why, why, why?

One syllable, three letters, yet it still had more power over me than any other word I'd ever known. I'd always been the type of person who needed answers, which is probably why I'd been such a naturally good student. Teachers asked questions, and I'd study until I could answer them. But then came this question, the biggest question of my life, and I would probably never have an explanation, any real sort of resolution. My own *sort of, kind of,* innate and intuitive answers would have to be good enough. Somebody or something was clearly trying to teach me a lesson.

There was no perfect answer. Just like there was no perfect way to *live*.

I had tried, after all, for almost eighteen years. And now, with more ups and downs and unexpected loops than in the rest of my life combined, I somehow, oddly, felt more alive than ever.

The phone rang again from the counter and I held my breath, counting the rings as I waited for the answering machine to pop to life. Eight, nine, ten. Gracie's sunny, giggly voice chirped from the speakers and made me feel even more alone. I needed the real Gracie. *Hiyah! You've reached the Dietrich house! We're not around to talk right now, so pretty please leave us a message. Bye!*

"This is Elliot Ste—err—Elliot S from Ohio." He spoke in a hurried, breathy whisper, his words smeared through the speakers from holding the phone too close to his anxious lips. "I'm calling for Mina. I wanted to say that it's not too late to be forgiven. Not *quite* yet, not without one last warning. Come clean with the Lord and let Him back into your life. Open your heart to God, and let Him wash away this blackness from your soul. Acknowledge your sins to your family, to yourself, and to your country. You're on a very dark and dangerous path, Mina Dietrich. And if you don't repent soon, if you don't admit to your Devil's lies, then you deserve to be punished. I know where you live. We all do. And we'll find you, Mina. If you don't stop on your own, then we'll find a way to stop you." He finished with a flourish, breathing into the phone raggedly for a moment before the machine finally beeped and fell back into silence.

Within seconds the phone wailed at me again, and I pushed myself up to stand, arms reaching toward the shiny silver base mounted on the wall. I grasped at it with both hands, tearing it from the wall with a loud snapping of plastic brackets, and slammed it down against the floor. It slid against the tiles and I chased it, my feet, my legs, my entire body burning with the need to see it smashed into as many pieces as possible. I jumped on top of it, stomped again, right foot, left foot, kicked it against the bricks that lined our pantry and watched a spray of plastic chips fly into the air with an ecstatic sense of satisfaction. I lunged again, sending the machine rocketing toward the kitchen table. I was so focused that I didn't hear myself screaming, didn't hear the front door click open or the sound of my family's footsteps pounding down the front hallway.

"What the hell, Mina?" my dad shouted, running at me and wrapping his arms around my shoulders and my chest, lifting me up so that my feet dangled above the ground. "What are you doing? What the hell do you think you're doing?"

He spun me around and I saw my mom and Gracie, slack-jawed and cowering by the door, Gracie's face half hidden as she pressed against my mom's puffy winter jacket.

"I'm sorry," I said, my eyes meeting Gracie's in apology. I swallowed my terror, willed Elliot S's cold, brittle words from my head. I didn't want to add even more fuel to her fears. I didn't want her to know how right she probably was to be afraid. "I didn't mean to get so . . . so violent. But people are calling me, and I just couldn't hear one more ring right now. I just couldn't." Dad's stiff hold softened.

My feet hit the ground, but he kept his arms around me. I breathed in the smell of him, the scent that I realized just now how much I'd missed—cool evergreen pine and spicy clove that somehow clung to his sweaters and T-shirts for days after he'd worn them. I inhaled again, savoring the closeness. I felt protected. Shielded from everything that lay beyond our front door.

"Who?" he demanded. "Who's been calling you?"

"Strangers." The word felt frigid, grim when I heard it on my lips. "Our number was listed on the website, apparently."

At that, I heard a distant, muffled ringing—the phones in my dad's office, my parents' bedroom. I hadn't even thought about the other extentions, I'd been so caught up in my fury. But I wasn't inaccessable, not even close. It would take much more than annihilating a single phone to actually cut myself off from the rest of the world.

"Damn it," my dad snapped, his arms dropping to his sides. I shivered, suddenly cold without the comforting warmth of his hold. "I knew this would happen. I knew it."

"What do we do now?" my mom asked, her face as pale as the stark white fur lining her hood.

"I'm calling the phone company and finding a way to block or change our number. And then I'm calling the police, because this is harassment and I refuse to let these ignorant sons of bitches invade our family home." My dad ducked his head and started for the hallway, boots stomping across the tiles. But then he turned back to face me, an afterthought, his eyes burning into mine so fiercely, I had to fight not to look away.

"Let me say this. I may still not know what to believe here, Mina, and I'm well aware that I haven't been one of your biggest supporters. But I would never—*never*—do to anyone what these people are doing to you right now. I would never force my religious opinions on a complete stranger. I would never disrespect another family's right to privacy. Because from where I'm standing, these people are committing much graver sins of their own, casting judgment on you like they have the authority. Acting like they have the right to make God's own decisions. I won't stand for it, Mina. I won't." With that he started back down the hall, his footsteps dying out with the slam of his office door.

"Can I go on the news for you, Meen?" Gracie asked, pulling me over to sit with her at the kitchen table. "Maybe they'll believe you if I tell them all what a good sister you are. I'll tell them that your eyebrows always get all funny and squiggly when you lie to me about something, and that's how I know you're not lying about this."

I laughed, though I stopped myself after I saw the look of hurt on Gracie's stoic face. "That's very sweet of you, Gracie, but they'll probably just think I brainwashed or blackmailed you. Honestly, I'm not sure there's anything that any of us could say to change their minds."

"You could tell them about Iris," my mom said, her voice wavering and paper thin, like I could poke right through it if I so much as lifted my finger. "You didn't say anything about her at all in the KBC interview. The way you told it to the reporter, you more or less woke up one day with all the standard pregnancy signs. *Poof.* Not pregnant one day, pregnant the next. Maybe people need to hear that there was *something*—some event, no matter how vague and inexplicable—that was the catalyst for all this. Iris was your Gabriel, Mina. That conversation was your own kind of Annunciation, as insane and sacrilegious as that sounds. And I think that's what people want to hear. That's what people need to hear."

"Let me get this straight," I said, trying my best to keep the words flat and even. "You think people are *more likely* to believe me if I say that an odd old lady came into the local pizza shop and told me I'd be having a baby?"

"I'm not saying that everyone will believe you, Mina." She sighed. "I'm not even saying that most people will believe you. But I think that there are people out there, people who want to *find something* to believe in. Anything, some sign that there's more to life than we have right here in our mundane and predictable day-to-day existence. Maybe if you say it, tell them all about Iris, maybe, just maybe, a few people will stop and think. Some small piece of them, buried somewhere beneath all the cynicism we're trained to carry around from the time we're supposed to *know better*, will hear what you're saying. Will open up to you, to the idea that there may not be a black-and-white explanation."

"And if they think I'm just crazy?"

"Then they think you're crazy. They're already hell-bent against you, Mina. The way I see it, a few desperately hopeful people switching over to your court is better than nothing. We can use whoever we can get on our side." Her voice was getting stronger, the argument in her mind fully clicking into place as she put it into words out loud. "And there are decent people out there, too, people who still may not believe a word you're saying but will believe in your personal right to say it without getting attacked by the media and the country's conservative zealots. You need to face the camera and pour it all out, Mina, let America see that you're not holding anything back anymore. Let them know what this is really doing to your everyday life."

"So you think I should have cameras follow me around all day? Some sort of warped teen pregnancy documentary?"

"I wasn't thinking of it quite like that, no. I meant that you could verbally and metaphorically walk them through your day." She paused, her thumb drawing tiny circles along her palm as she considered. "But maybe what you're suggesting is a much better idea. Maybe if people see the real you, your life, you'll be more humanized. Less of a publicity object and more of a normal teenage girl going through a very abnormal experience."

"Nice idea in theory, Mom. But seriously, think about how the media tears people apart, scatters their shreds across the tabloids. I can't trust a reporter to do me any favors. I was just a prop to KBC. They all have their own motives and their own angles, and the bigger the scandal, the better for them because that's what their viewers want, right? They'd turn my life into a total joke. Any dignity I have left—and that's assuming I have any left at all—goes straight out the window."

"Maybe we don't have the typical reporter film you then."

"Meaning . . . ?"

"Jesse."

"*Jesse?*"

"Yes, Jesse. You told me that he helps out with a film crew, right? And he had that camera glued to his hand on your birthday. Why not have him record some of the day to day? You at school, you at home, pull some other interviews together, and then we could talk about submitting it somewhere. If it feels right, that is, after we've all looked it over. At the very least it'll give you practice talking on camera. You can trust him to show the real Mina. That's what matters. That's *all* that matters."

"I don't know." Sweat was already prickling along the

back of my neck just at the thought of it. I wasn't sure what made me most nervous: the idea of Jesse observing my life so closely, observing *me* so closely, or the idea of sending the final project out to the public. Things had been different since my birthday—cooler and more polite. We were still friends, of course. He drove me to school and sat with me and Hannah at lunch. Jesse had promised me—had promised Iris—his support, and he wasn't the type to break his word. But after that kiss . . .

"I have to think about it," I said, not meeting her eyes.

"Of course. But I think having Jesse film you couldn't hurt, even if we don't end up sending it out or posting it anywhere. It might be good to have this period of your life recorded. It's a special time, Mina. Strange and terrible at times, yes . . . but definitely still *special*."

chapter fifteen

Jesse didn't waste any time leaping full speed ahead into my mother's grand plan.

I spent the next week and a half living on the opposite side of Jesse's camera, trying my best to pretend that he wasn't there and that there wasn't a tiny machine recording every movement, every expression, every word. I was used to seeing the camera in his hand—it was more unusual to see him *without* his second set of eyes—but I wasn't used to the lens being focused so exclusively on *me*.

Our classmates weren't fazed by Jesse filming me, probably because he was either A, invisible to them, or B, already the weird kid who always had a camera in front of his face. Whichever reason, the camera definitely didn't curtail any of their typical behaviors. If anything, the pre-Christmas hype had made some of them even more determined to harass me. Kyle and his crew fell to their knees and hailed me whenever we crossed paths in the hallway, and I was getting more notes jammed in my locker, more balls of paper wadded up and thrown at me during class or in the cafeteria. I'd stopped reading the messages altogether after catching Jesse recording over my shoulder, making a point of throwing them away unopened. I had always suspected that some of my classmates thought I was a bit of an outsider, maybe, a grade snob who didn't dare to step outside of her little social circle. But I'd never realized how outside I'd really been. How detached I was from all but a measly little handful of companions. It's funny, really, the kind of pseudo-safety a few qualified close connections can give you. Nate, Izzy, Hannah. They'd been my guardians, and I'd never once stopped to think about who I'd be without them. But now I knew. Now I had no delusions.

There were, thankfully, some people who cruised right past me in the hallway, too—as if I was anyone, or maybe even as if I was no one at all. Kids who'd either gotten sick of the hype or had never really cared in the first place. They cared about Christmas, exams, college applications, their own best friend and relationship dramas. Their *own* lives.

Sadly, though, those indifferent classmates were still in the minority.

Jesse met me at my house each weekday morning, but instead of just waiting outside for me to hop into his truck, he'd come in first, take random footage of me getting ready for the day, reading over the latest Virgin Mina web posts, talking with my mom and Gracie at the breakfast table about nothing and everything—what kind of pizza we'd have for dinner that night, or how my mom had woken up one day to find BURN IN HELL written in bright red spray-painted capital letters on our porch.

We'd had it painted over that same day—the same day that we also, not so incidentally, ordered the installation of a new state-of-the-art home security and surveillance system—but I still saw the words every time I stepped up to our front door. They couldn't be painted over in my memory. I couldn't stop thinking about the stranger who had prowled across our lawn the night before, wondering who and why—and what he or she might do next. Maybe this had just been a warning, like Elliot S's cryptic call. A preview for something much bigger than a few nasty words. I hadn't watched the footage, but I already knew how petrified my face would look on playback. I was completely vulnerable—my entire family was vulnerable. We were never safe, not even in our own home. But other than a few slips on mornings like that one, I kept a straight face. I pretended to be brave.

Jesse shadowed me over the weekend, too, when he wasn't working at Frankie's or schlepping around for his uncle. Me wrapping presents on my mom's bed, pretending not to cry as *It's a Wonderful Life* played in the background. Me watching birthing videos in our living room, my substitute for actual group instruction because I refused to go to any public classes, no matter how enthusiastic my mom and Hannah had both been about filling in for the "daddy" role. Jesse never offered, but I think we both more than understood that his role in all this was already suspicious enough. And after that birthday kiss, I had a feeling that playing mommy and daddy together, even for a ninety-minute class, would topple our fragile balance.

I had a hard time, though, believing that this was the kind of real-life drama strangers would want to watch—that there was something compelling to be gleaned from my morning bowl of cinnamon and brown sugar oatmeal. But I didn't want to challenge Jesse's vision for the project. And as much as I refused to admit it, out loud and just barely to myself, I didn't want to say anything that would make Jesse stop. I didn't want to say anything that would mean us spending less time together. Because despite what I'd said—and how I knew things had to be—it was hard to imagine starting and ending my day without him.

"Are you coming to church with us, Jesse?" Gracie asked, looking around behind her to make sure my mom was nowhere around. Satisfied that there was no imminent risk, she reached into the tin of freshly baked cutout sugar cookies we'd be giving to our pastor's family later that night, swallowing a sparkly blue snowman in two massive bites.

"Oh, I wouldn't want to intrude on your Christmas Eve family time," he said, glancing up from his camera, where he'd been replaying some of the day's footage for Gracie to see.

"Does your family go to church, too?" Gracie asked, licking a few stray sugar crystals from her thumb.

"Yeah, but not until much later. Midnight mass. It's a tradition in my family."

"Weren't you ever worried that Santa would come while you were still at church?"

Jesse put the camera down on the kitchen table and looked over at me, fielding the question in my direction. Gracie was just on the outer cusp of no longer believing— or maybe she *had* stopped believing but wasn't ready to admit to it, not yet, just in case that would mean fewer presents under the tree.

"Santa knows to come late enough," I said, ducking my head below the table as I pretended to tighten my bootlace. I didn't want Gracie, the human lie detector, to spot my giveaway "squiggly" eyebrows, as she'd put it. "He knows when everyone is tucked in their beds and fast asleep. All part of the Christmas magic."

Gracie nodded, content with that answer. "So will you come with us then, Jesse? Please? If you don't have to go anywhere until midnight?"

"Gracie." I sighed, squinting at her. My nerves were wound too tightly to be patient. "Don't pressure Jesse. He probably wants to be with his family for Christmas Eve."

"Well, I'd be happy to go," he said, his eyes still on me. "As long as that's okay with you and your parents."

"Oh," I said, hoping my cheeks weren't as red as they felt. The room was suddenly ten degrees too warm for the scarf that I'd wrapped around the top of my chunky black sweater dress. "Of course you're welcome to come with us. I didn't know you'd want to come along, or I would have asked sooner."

"Awesome. Then I accept the invite." Jesse smiled and turned back to the camera.

I'd always loved the Christmas Eve service, but I was anxious about tonight. I hadn't been to my church in months now, and I didn't know how everyone would react to my being there. My parents had assured me it was fine, and regardless, I couldn't imagine not being there, with them, for the first time in eighteen years. But I felt better knowing that Jesse would be there, too. I felt even more secure.

Fifteen minutes later we were all bundled in our thickest, puffiest jackets and piled into the minivan: Gracie, my mom, and Jesse in the back, me in the hallowed passenger seat next to my dad because it required the least amount of squeezing and squishing for my awkwardly round belly—which, according to my most recent visit with Dr. Keller, now carried my massive three-pounder of a baby. How the baby could still more than double in size in the next two months before delivery left me equal parts mystified and horrified.

My dad dropped us off at the front steps of the church, insisting that I not have to walk too far in the bitter cold. I opened my mouth to argue, but the look of genuine concern in his eyes made me stop myself. I nodded instead, stepping out onto the sidewalk as my mom took my arm and ushered me through the twinkling entrance lined with boughs of evergreen. I started to duck my head, screening my eyes from any open hostility—but then the homey piney smell washed over me, reminding me of everything that I loved about Christmas Eve. Even this Christmas Eve, which was so different from every one that had come before it—but still so similar to them, too. My family, my church, the same carols and the same familiar faces of people I'd known my entire life. But there was *more* this time. There was my baby, of course. There was Jesse. I liked to look at it that way—I had more than instead of less than. I had gained rather than lost.

So I kept my head up. I didn't want to miss anything about this night.

As people passed, I smiled and waved along with my family, and while eyes maybe lingered on me for a few beats too long, no one seemed offended by my presence. We sat right in front of the altar in our family's regular pew—or at least what *had* been my regular pew, too, before I'd stopped going every Sunday with the rest of them. Church was still, miraculously, a safe place for my parents. Church was about listening, singing, letting all the day-to-day worries and hopes go. It was about drifting to a better, more purposeful place. I envied them that kind of devotion, and that kind of certainty in an actual *doctrine*, a rulebook to play by. I had my beliefs centered on my baby—my own individual, tailor-made kind of faith—but that didn't translate to a neat and orderly way to worship.

I couldn't call myself a Christian, not anymore; that much I was certain of. And even though I would have previously considered myself a Christian, in my life before this baby, I'm not sure that it would have been accurate, looking back now. It had been a stamp without real meaning, a word I'd carried with me because of my parents and my upbringing—because it was *expected* of me—rather than a realization I'd come to on my own. If I'd never really thought about my beliefs, how could I have known? How could I have been classified as anything, really?

I certainly couldn't give myself any kind of traditional label now. I just *believed* in the power of something beyond myself, something beyond the physical world of science and math and predictability. What did that make me? Was I the sole member of a radical new religion?

Aunt Vera and Uncle Teddy and the kids swept in, interrupting my thoughts with big, jolly Christmas hugs as they settled into the pew behind us. I'd last seem them at Thanksgiving, when both Vera and Teddy had locked me in a fierce hug the second they'd walked through the front door. I was their niece, they'd said, and they would always love me no matter what. Nothing was said after that. But nothing else *needed* to be said. Vera rested a hand on my shoulder now, and I squeezed it, silently thanking her for being there. They didn't usually come to church, not even on Christmas Eve—but they were here tonight, and I had a feeling that I was the reason. The opening music started up, and I felt my mind and my body soften, the usually nonstop anxiety easing away. Tonight was about family and tradition and cozy carols by candlelight—everything else could wait.

I smiled up at Pastor Lewis during his readings from the Bible, the oh-so-familiar Gospel of Luke, and the sermon that sounded more or less identical to me every year. He ended the message with a few moments of silence, and then, as part of the Christmas Eve tradition, we all reached down for the miniature white candles placed at each of our seats. The lights overhead dimmed as ushers carried a lit candle to each pew, their flame passing down the line until every face in the room was lit from below, golden balls floating eerily in the shadows.

This was always my favorite part of the service by far, a moment that I looked forward to all year. *This* was Christmas. This was happiness—pure, simple, unconditional happiness. Standing shoulder to shoulder with my family, singing at the top of my lungs, knowing that Christmas morning was just around the corner.

The choir stood from their mounted pews behind the altar as the first few notes rose up from the piano. "Silent Night." Just like always.

A small figure emerged from the dim corner of the pews, her head down as she edged slowly forward to stand ahead of the rest of the singers. As she stepped into the glow of the candlelight, I could see her face clearly.

Iris.

She was luminous against the darkness around her, her white hair glistening and her pale face like a moon hovering above the altar. Her green eyes landed on mine as she opened her lips and the first words poured out, fuller and richer than I could have ever imagined coming from her petite, fragile body.

Silent night, Holy night,
All is calm, all is bright

The song somehow sounded new coming from Iris, so much more profound, entirely raw and visceral, as if she were singing the words as they came to mind—as if the lyrics and the melody were being created right then and there. As if she were weaving them all together. For me.

Round yon Virgin Mother and Child,
Holy Infant so tender and mild.

I was terrified to look away, to risk losing her again, but I needed to know that Jesse was seeing her, too. That I wasn't imagining her, not this time, not last time either. I looked up at him, squeezing his elbow to get his attention. "Do you see, Jesse? Do you see?"

He looked down at me, head cocked in confusion. "See what?"

"Iris," I said, fighting to keep my voice low as I pointed at the altar. "It's Iris. Singing."

He glanced at the altar and back at me, his face looking even more bewildered.

I turned back to the choir, frustrated. How could he not have noticed as soon as I did?

But as my eyes fell on the woman singing, I realized why Jesse didn't understand. She wasn't Iris, or anyone who looked remotely similar to Iris. She was a tall blonde woman, curvy even in the folds of her oversized choir gown, who had been my fifth-grade Sunday School teacher. The same woman who had sung the "Silent Night" solo the year before, and the year before that, and every other year for as long as I could recall.

What was *wrong* with me? Was I going crazy?

Throughout all this—through Iris, the pregnancy, the idea of an actual *miracle*, all the absurd and all the irrational—I had always trusted in myself. I had always believed in my own mind.

Because if I couldn't do that, how could I believe in anything?

My throat clenched around warm bile, and I shut my eyes, the pinpricks of flame all around me suddenly too much to take in. Tiny lights everywhere, flashing, flickering behind my eyelids. I needed to leave, needed to be anywhere that wasn't this room, this song. I blew my candle out and pressed Jesse back so that I could slip out from the aisle.

"Mina," he said, breathing against my ear, his fingertips brushing my wrist.

"Never mind what I said. I just need some fresh air," I whispered, pushing past him. "Stay here. I'll be right back."

I ducked my head and pushed through the side entry, careful to close the door softly behind me. I started toward the bathroom, but as I rushed through the hallway, my eyes were drawn to the dimly lit cement stairwell that led down to the lower level of Sunday School classrooms. I veered off down the steps, to guaranteed solitude. The hallway was pitch-black when I reached the bottom of the stairs, and I groped along the wall, fingers fumbling until I found the switch. A lazy bluish light spilled over the walls, every inch lined with bulletin boards and crafts, watercolor Bethlehem scenes and sparkly pipe-cleaner angels. The air was damp and cool, permanently infused with the scent of glue sticks and markers.

The doors I passed were all a blur, until I reached the room clearly marked as the second-grade classroom with a six-foot number two in bright red glitter—Gracie's class. I pushed the door open and flicked on the lights. As I stepped inside, my eyes instantly froze on the elaborate display in front of me, a life-size nativity scene that spanned the entire length of the back wall. Gracie had come home from Sunday School for the last few weeks gushing with enthusiasm. She was so proud of their work, and now I could see why. My feet drifted forward, one step, two, until I could reach out and rub my hand along the crinkly blue construction paper of Mary's tunic, the prickly bits of real hay glued inside of the manger that held a smiling baby Jesus. I'd seen so many versions of this scene in the books stacked in my room, my online scouring for answers—so many different interpretations from every artistic period of the last two thousand years. But none of them had held this kind of power over me. None of them had ripped through my chest, squeezed and pounded at my heart like this second-grade art project. Maybe it was the sheer size of the display, or maybe it was because it was Christmas Eve, and I was still shaking from seeing Iris. Maybe it was because it had been pieced together by seven-year-old hands, Gracie's hands, so sweet and innocent, with its asymmetrical faces scrawled with crayons, the jagged scissor cuts.

"I'm not crazy!" I yelled to the mural, to no one at all. "I'm not! I'm *not* . . ."

My knees caved and I sank to the ground, my outstretched hands sliding down along the bottom of Mary's thin paper robe. The tears came fast and heavy, and I pressed my lips against the top of my shoulder to muffle the sound. Not that anyone could hear me from the basement, not as they sang their hymns and recited their prayers above me. I cried, even though I didn't know exactly who or what I was crying for. For me? The baby? Our future? For all of it, maybe—for every struggle I'd been through already and for every struggle I knew we'd still face.

I needed Iris to *really* come back. I needed her to explain things, to make it all easier. I needed to know why my baby and I were meant to fight through this. What were we fighting *for*?

"Mina?"

A sob caught in my throat, and I wheezed as I lifted up my head.

"Mina, are you okay?"

Jesse was hovering over me, his lips and eyes and forehead all sharp and pinched toward the center of his beautiful face.

I looked away. "I told you not to follow me."

"Yeah, well, I'm glad I didn't listen. You shouldn't be alone down here. Not like this. Not on Christmas Eve. Come back upstairs with me."

"Like it's that easy to just put on a happy face, right?" I could feel the anger rising through me, the anxiety and resentment I had hidden so well and for so long. "How do you think *Christmas* makes me feel, Jesse? You can't understand. No one can."

He opened his mouth to respond, but I cut him off. "I mean, seriously, for two seconds pretend that you're me. Pretend that you're some potentially crazy modern-day Mary impostor who believes—who *actually fucking believes*—that she could be the human carrier for some kind of twenty-first-century miracle baby. Another Jesus type maybe, but who the hell knows? Maybe it's the Devil, maybe it's a demon spawn, some sort of evil black angel who will take over the whole—"

"Stop it, Mina!" he yelled, wrapping his hands around

my shoulders and snapping me upright to face him. "Stop it. You know you don't mean any of that. You're not crazy and this isn't some demon baby. I don't know what this is, Mina, but it's not bad. It's not, and you know that. You can feel it, just like I do." He paused, loosening his grip on me. "I know that whatever is happening to you is somehow good. It's meant to be. You just have to believe that. It's the only way, Mina."

I closed my eyes for a few seconds and breathed. I wanted to believe him. And I did, in my strongest and best moments, the times I was convinced that miracles could exist and that I—I was lucky. I was part of a life that would be everything but ordinary. But seeing Iris up at the altar had made me question myself—and questioning any piece of this led to a slippery slope.

"I'm sorry, Jesse," I said, reaching out for his hand as I pulled myself to my feet. "I shouldn't have talked like that, not to you. You didn't deserve any of that."

"Don't worry about it. All forgiven. Really. 'Tis the season and all that." He smiled at me, his eyes crinkling at the edges, and I realized that his hand was still wrapped in mine. I wanted to pull him closer, lean my cheek against his thick red sweater. I could feel myself moving in, the air between us tightening.

"We should probably head back upstairs," he said, taking a step back as he dropped my hand and pretended to study the nativity scene. "The service might be over by now."

I nodded dumbly and started toward the door, unable to meet his eyes.

My family had been looking for us, their jackets already on as they stood waiting by the front doors. The lobby was mostly emptied at this point, which was a relief. I was in no state to mingle with the merry crowds.

"Where were you guys?" Gracie asked, pulling away from them to hand me my coat. "You left during your favorite part."

"I'm sorry, sweetie. I just needed someplace quiet for a few minutes to be alone."

"But you weren't alone. Jesse left, too."

I felt my cheeks flush with embarrassment. The tears, the awful things I'd said. I needed to apologize. I needed to tell him about that glimpse of Iris, about how unsteady I was afterward. He would understand.

As we made our way down the steps to the sidewalk, I leaned in, careful not to brush against him as I whispered. "I'm sorry again, about all that. I need to tell you something later. About . . . Iris."

Before he could answer, a blinding flash came from somewhere in the dark lot in front of us. I jumped, grabbing on to Jesse's arm to steady myself.

The light flashed again, and this time I saw the person

directly behind the flash, the man holding the camera in front of his face. A photographer was there to take a picture of me on Christmas Eve. The new virgin worshipping the old. Too sickeningly appropriate for him to pass up.

Jesse moved to block me from the camera, but the flashes kept coming, faster, closer.

"Leave my daughter alone," my dad growled. I peeked from behind Jesse's shoulder to see him approaching the photographer, who was much shorter and smaller than my dad's solid six-two frame. The man cowered and brought the camera down behind his back, protecting his goods.

"I'm done, I'm done," he said, taking big steps backward. "I'm leaving now."

"I want those pictures deleted first." My dad was matching him step for step, the distance between them shrinking. "Give me your camera."

"You're crazy, man. No. I didn't do anything wrong."

"You're stalking my daughter and taking pictures without her permission. Outside of church on Christmas Eve, damn it. Don't you have any decency? Any respect?" He was spitting, he was yelling so hard, angry white flecks glistening under the streetlamps.

"I'm just doing my job. I have kids, too, you know. We all have our work to do. You do yours, I do mine." The man's voice was louder now, less shaky and intimidated, and he'd stopped moving away.

"I feel sorry for your kids then. I feel sorry that their dad puts food on the table with money he made taking advantage of innocent people's lives."

"And I feel sorry for you that you actually believe your daughter is innocent."

In a hazy blur, my dad hurled his head toward the man like a bull, knocking him flat on his back against the pavement.

"Dad, no!" I screamed as Jesse lurched forward.

"Paul! Paul!" My mom's pleading shrieks cut through the darkness, and Gracie's softer, weaker cries followed like an echo.

I stood frozen where I was, too numb to react. They were fighting because of me. I was ruining Christmas. My hands rushed to cover my stomach. My belly looked so big under the padding of the jacket, a ball that seemed too impossibly round to be a part of my actual body.

"Jesus! You're fucking crazy!" The man screamed as he picked himself up, camera nestled protectively under his arm. Jesse was fighting to keep my dad controlled, tugging his arms back to lock him in place. "You're just lucky my camera didn't bash open on the ground, or we'd be going straight to the police station right now, you asshole."

My dad was seething, but he'd stopped fighting against Jesse's grip. "You tell the cops. They haven't done a damn useful thing for my family. They haven't lifted a finger to stop people like you from intruding in our lives."

"If you want us to go away, tell your pretty little daughter there to give up the bullshit. If she admits that she had sex, she's suddenly just like every other stupid knocked-up kid out there. But as long as she gives us a story, we're not going anywhere." He spit on the ground, just barely missing my dad's shiny brown oxfords, before spinning away from us and jogging across the dark lot.

"Merry Christmas, everybody!" he called out over his shoulder, leaving the five of us standing there, silent in his wake.

Christmas morning was anticlimactic after that—no calls from the cops, thankfully, though we all flinched every time the phone rang. Police, angry zealots, reporters who would stop at nothing to get a holiday feature. There were too many potential land mines lurking behind each ring to risk picking up the phone. Family or friends calling to wish us a merry Christmas could be filtered through the answering machine.

The present opening was somber, except for Gracie, who still squealed over every shiny pink package she tore open. Her big gift—a baby doll that ate, drank, peed, and pooped—seemed a bit young for her, considering that she'd cried last spring when my aunt gave her a doll for her seventh birthday, saying that she was a big girl, too old for dolls anymore. But she'd insisted on this particular doll, plastering wish lists to Santa on the refrigerator, the kitchen table, my parents' nightstand, the bathroom mirror—anywhere and everywhere to make sure the request couldn't possibly be overlooked.

"I need practice to be the most perfect aunt ever," she had said to me when the commercial for the doll played on TV. "I can feed her, hold her, put on diapers—just like I will with your baby, Meen. *Our* baby." I hadn't known if I'd wanted to laugh or cry when she'd said it.

Everything Santa brought me was baby related, too—a few red and yellow unisex footy jumpers, a night sky–themed mobile with a smiling man in the moon and twinkling stars to hang over the crib, and the crowning present, a beautiful bright green stroller with every kind of attachment and compartment that a new, helpless mom could ever possibly need. Gracie proceeded to push around her doll—"Baby Mira for miracle," she proclaimed—in the stroller for the rest of the afternoon, making tireless laps around the living room and kitchen.

Aunt Vera and Uncle Teddy came over for Christmas dinner with Lucy and Danny—both of whom immediately pounced on Gracie, begging for turns at pushing Baby Mira around. I did my best to look merry and bright with the rest of the adults, hovering around my mom and aunt in the kitchen. But when I saw my phone light up with Jesse's name, I was thankful for a good reason to excuse myself.

"Merry Christmas," I said, closing my bedroom door behind me.

"Merry Christmas, Mina."

"It's strange, you know, a full day without having you and the camera shadowing me. I'm not used to going unrecorded."

He laughed on the other end, but I knew him well enough to know that his eyes and his lips didn't match the sound.

"Is everything okay?" I asked. "About last night—"

"Mina, it's fine, really. Don't worry about it. I called because I wanted to ask if you've . . . if you've checked out the website at all today."

I hadn't. A day without Virgin Mina updates was my Christmas present to myself. I hadn't even felt the urge, not really. Christmas was always that way for me, a day to feel entirely disconnected and removed from the outside world, to soak up every minute with my family, lying around in pajamas eating cinnamon buns and candy canes until we all passed out on the couch, deep in our sugar comas.

"No. I'm afraid to ask."

"Damn," he said, sighing. "I knew I probably shouldn't

have said anything until tomorrow. But I was worried that you did see it and were too upset to call, and I didn't want that to happen either."

"What does it say, Jesse? Just tell me." I sat down on the edge of my bed.

"It's us. From last night. A few of them, actually. You're leaning in pretty close to me in one of the photos. I know you were just whispering something to me, but in the picture . . . in the picture it looks like we're about to kiss. And the others . . . Well, your arms are wrapped around me. It was after the guy with the camera popped out and scared you. But we look pretty close in the pictures, Mina. We look a little more than friendly."

The phone was suddenly blazing hot in my hands. I wanted to look, but I didn't want to look. I could already imagine the scene in my head more clearly than any photo could have captured. This was why I had said no when Jesse had kissed me. This was why I had pushed him away. It wasn't right, dragging him into the spotlight next to me. I hadn't been careful enough, but I would try harder. I had to.

"I'm so sorry this is happening," I said, the guilt swirling in my gut. "Where did you see the pictures? Where are they posted?"

"They're on the Virgin Mina site, which is where I first saw them. But they're on a few news sites that I've found, too. No respectable ones, but they're definitely up there pretty widely for people to see. There's a lot of speculation about me now. About us. And the fact that I'm with your family for Christmas Eve makes it look like we're pretty serious, I guess."

"Did they say anything about my dad? About the fight?"

"No, actually. At least not from what I've read. The cameraman probably didn't want to admit that he was wrecked by your dad, and on top of that, it is in exceptionally poor taste that he was lurking outside of a church to catch you. He probably didn't want to bring any extra attention to that."

"So people think you're definitely the dad now?"

"More or less."

"I'm sorry that you're becoming such a big part of this," I said, my face hot with shame. Even now I couldn't stop thinking about our kiss, remembering the way his lips had felt so perfectly shaped to match my own. How sugary sweet they had tasted, how silky his hair had felt between my fingers. I pinched my eyes shut, willing it all away. "I never should have let you get close to me, Jesse. This is my fault. This is exactly what I didn't want to happen to you. Your reputation—"

"I already told you, reputation means nothing to me," he said, cutting me off. I could practically see his head shaking through the phone line. "It was my decision to get close to you, Mina. We know the truth, and once we put our video out there for people to see, maybe at least a few of the intelligent people will, too. Besides, there are worse things in the world than people thinking I'm your boyfriend."

"Maybe that would be true if I wasn't some insane pregnant virgin."

"Pregnant and a virgin, maybe, but not insane."

"But aren't you upset that people think you could be the dad? That you're just as much a part of this lie as I am?"

He paused, a long breath crackling through the phone. "I mean, sure, I wish that total strangers wouldn't make accusations about me. But I can't stop them from making up their own stories. I *can* refuse to let them change the way I live my life, though. I'm not going to stop spending time with you. I'm not going to hide."

I smiled, even as a tear dripped down my cheek. "I don't deserve you."

"I think we've had this argument before. Get back to your family, okay? We can talk about this tomorrow. Let's do something fun this week—go on a day trip or something. We need to get you out and about before you're too pregnant to move."

He hung up before I could pretend to yell at him, and after a few minutes of staring blankly out my window, I drifted back downstairs. I decided to not tell anyone else about the photos, not until after Christmas was officially over.

And even though a large part of me knew I should be upset by the pictures, upset that people would jump to the wrong conclusions about Jesse's role in all this, I couldn't completely ignore the bubble of happiness floating above my head.

Jesse was right.

There were far worse things in the world than having people think that he could be my boyfriend—a girl could only be so lucky. But I still couldn't let it happen. I couldn't let myself be that girl. He deserved a normal high school relationship. He deserved to be happy without all the complexities and all the conditions.

And most of all, he deserved to love someone who wasn't too scared to love him back.

chapter sixteen

"So, Mina," Dr. Keller asked, wheeling her stool around to face me. "Have you given your birth plan much consideration since we last met?"

We'd already finished the rundown of checkups—weight and blood pressure, size and position of the baby, and the heartbeat, always my favorite part. Jamie had left to help with another patient down the hall, leaving the two of us alone in the exam room.

"I wrote some things down," I said, pulling the paper out of my purse and handing it to her. "I've given a lot of thought to pain medication, and I've decided not to take it. I want this to be as natural as possible, unless of course something goes wrong and it's absolutely necessary. It just doesn't feel right to go about this in an unnatural way, if that makes any sense. I want the full experience, for better or for worse."

Dr. Keller nodded, making some notes in my file.

"And I know I've been a little back and forth about this, but I need this to be a home birth. I'm positive about that." I paused, bracing myself for any resistance. Dr. Keller looked up at me, calmly pushing a few stray red curls away from her eyes as she waited for me to continue. "I know there are risks involved, but I've had a normal, healthy pregnancy so far, and the hospital is only fifteen minutes away if there is an emergency. I can't have reporters waiting outside of the hospital, outside of the room, Dr. Keller. The attention is only going to get worse the closer I get to labor, and I'm not putting my baby in the public's hands like that. I want to be at home, in my own bed, with you and my family there. If you can't be there, I understand. But I need to have this baby in private, one way or another."

"I'm not going to lie to you, Mina. It's not exactly . . . standard protocol for me to do that, to come into your home for the birth. But I've put a lot of thought into this, too, you know, because you're not exactly my standard case." She smiled, looking just as nervous as I felt, and I couldn't help but smile back at her. "I want to do this for you. We'll make it work, okay?"

I unclenched my hands from the sides of the exam table, relief spreading through me. I'd been certain that she was going to try to scare me out of the home birth, convince me that a traditional hospital birth was the better, safer choice. But I'd started having a recurring bad dream—our driveway so mobbed with reporters that I couldn't get to the hospital fast enough, and I went into labor right there, right in front of hundreds of flashing cameras. I shuddered even then, fully awake in the brightly lit exam room, blinking my eyes to flush out the image.

"How are things, Mina?" she asked, closing her folder, a sign that the question was more personal than professional. She'd been different, less hesitant, since our talk, and she hadn't brought up the idea of counseling since. She was still my doctor, serious and efficient and as crisp as her white jacket. But she was more than that, too. She was another guardian standing next to me and my baby, another defense I hadn't expected to have.

"I can't stop thinking about you, I have to say. Worrying about all the stress you're going through, wondering how you're able to hold your head up high with everything that's been happening. You're amazingly strong."

Her expression was so sincere that I had to fight the urge to hop up and kiss her on the cheek. It wasn't that Dr. Keller was ever a cold woman, because she was always very friendly. But to see her that concerned, to know that she cared about me, that I wasn't just a random patient to check off the to-do list—it made me appreciate her in an entirely new way.

"It's not easy," I said. "But there are good days, too."

"I wish there was more I could do for you, Mina, I really do. I mean it when I say that you can call me whenever, even if it's after hours. I'm always available."

I nodded, afraid to speak, because if I did, I wasn't sure that I'd be able to stop.

"Your mom must be very proud of how well you're handling all this. I see a lot of twentysomethings and thirtysomethings even who aren't halfway as put-together as you are at eighteen."

The dam burst, and there was no more holding back. I gave in to it, let all my deepest, darkest thoughts and fears escape out into that exam room. "I'm just scared sometimes, Dr. Keller. All the time, really. I'm scared that I'll do something wrong, that I won't be a good enough mother. I'm scared that somebody will try to hurt my baby, and that people will never leave us alone. We'll never have a normal life. We'll never be safe."

The worries dropped out, hot and heavy, one after another, words that I'd never said out loud before. I sagged against the back of the exam table, feeling drained from my confession.

"Oh, Mina. Oh, Mina, Mina," Dr. Keller said, her voice a soothing purr as she stood and leaned over me, her hands smoothing my hair behind my ears, just like my mother would have done. Dr. Keller, my mom—they were so effortlessly maternal. Strong, nurturing, sensitive by nature. I knew from my mom that Dr. Keller and her husband had two adopted children, and I'd always wondered if she couldn't conceive—a sad irony for someone who spent her days bringing other women's babies into the world.

But what if I wouldn't be like them? I didn't feel ready to be a mother, but I hoped that it would click, that it would all fall into place once the baby was in my arms. But maybe I wouldn't be enough. Maybe I'd already made too many mistakes.

"Every new mother is scared, Mina. Every single one. She wouldn't be a good mother if she wasn't. Being a mom means a whole lot of being scared for the rest of your life. But one thing you need to realize now to save yourself a lot of time and stressing for the rest of your life—there's no perfect mom. Not possible." She smiled down at me, her eyes twinkling behind that day's thick green frames. "Every mom makes mistakes, a hundred little ones every day, probably. Trust me. My kids could tell you. But that's okay. A mom learns, she moves on, she makes another mistake. That's life, Mina. You can't put so much energy into worrying about all the little details. A baby isn't like a final exam. There's no perfect answer for every decision. You make the best out of what you're working with. You cut yourself some slack, and you forgive yourself. Got it?"

I nodded, letting her words soak into me, willing them

to stay trapped deep inside where I couldn't let them go. I needed them—needed their truth to keep me sane.

It was terrifying, but it was freeing, too, not to have one clear "perfect" to aspire to, no set 100 percent to always be reaching for. Not anymore.

"And everything else that you're experiencing, Mina, on top of all the normal mom fears . . . that's why I'm just so amazed by you. It's good that you're letting it out. You can't keep all this bottled up."

"I know," I said, knotting my hands around my stomach. "I know it's not good for the baby that I have all this stress. But I can't pretend it's not all happening. I can't not be scared when I have so many people all around the world who hate me. Do you see the things they say about me online, Dr. Keller? Do you read the messages that complete strangers post about me?"

"I do," she said, her voice a whisper. "I hate reading them, but I hate not reading them, too. I want to know what people are saying, just to know what you're up against."

"I check them every day, too. Have you seen the latest?" I laughed, in spite of the fact that nothing was funny. "The Christmas Eve photos of me and Jesse in what everyone thinks was a compromising position, but what was really just me whispering a stupid apology to him. Scandalous, huh?"

"There are very cruel and very ignorant people in this

world, Mina. Your pregnancy is making that horrifyingly apparent."

"I just don't understand, Dr. Keller. I don't understand the kind of anger—the kind of *passion*—that drives complete strangers to feel this involved in my life. Who are these people, really? Do they seem normal in their everyday life? Are they schoolteachers, nurses, lawyers—people who seem completely rational and stable? And then they come home at night, or they take their lunch break, and they go online and they write that I'll burn in hell? That my baby will burn in hell with me? I just don't understand where it comes from. The fervor. The idea that it's their duty, almost, to condemn me. Or maybe it's just sick entertainment for them. They're bored or they're angry at their own lives somehow, and I've become some kind of outlet. It's unreal, Dr. Keller. It's just so unreal to me that these people . . . they actually exist. And they think *I'm* the one who's doing something wrong?" I laughed again at the irony of it all, swiping at the tears dotting the corners of my eyes.

"Technology," Dr. Keller started, voice trembling and her cheeks splotchy red as she fought to compose herself. "Technology makes people feel too powerful, Mina. They can say things online that they'd be too cowardly to ever say to someone's face. It's a cheap, artificial kind of strength. These people who hate so much, hate without even really knowing . . . their hate is more about them than you, Mina. They're weak. And they're scared. People like that, they always need a target. They need to point a finger at someone besides themselves. You're so much better than they are, Mina. Deep down maybe they know that. Maybe that's why they're so angry."

I hopped off the table and crossed the floor to face her. I reached my arms out and hugged her, wrapped myself tightly around her as I closed my eyes and leaned into the fresh lemony scent of her coat.

"Thank you, Dr. Keller."

"Like I said before, Mina—anytime. I mean that."

I gave one more squeeze and pulled back, my head still too busy spinning with her words to speak.

"I'll see you in two weeks, Mina. Be safe, and keep on doing what you're doing." She smiled and reached out for the handle on the door. "You're getting so close to the end now."

"I have to say, Jesse, when you first suggested a trip to Long Beach Island, I thought you were crazy," Hannah said, stomping through the hard, wet sand in her furry black winter boots. "But now that we're here? It feels perfect. Insanely perfect."

"Good to hear, Hannah. So glad you approve." Jesse

grinned at her, kicking a soft spray of sand in her direction. She shrieked and kicked back, running to the water's edge as he chased after her.

I smiled, pulling my hood tighter around my face. I'd thought the idea was crazy, too. A deserted vacation town at the end of December, temperatures hovering in the low twenties. Jesse and I had discovered on one of our morning car rides that we had both spent our childhood summer vacations along the sacred beaches of LBI, a skinny stretch of island off the New Jersey coast. It was always bursting with people during the summer, mostly families with lots of sticky, screaming kids in tow, but it was a ghost town in the winter. Restaurants and stores boarded up until Memorial Day weekend, houses dark and stripped of the usual kitschy island decor, driveways emptied of boats and cars. I would have expected to be depressed to see my golden summer world so gray and desolate, but now that we were there, I loved it, loved the peace and solitude. I could breathe here in the winter—I could let my hair blow in the cold, salty wind, stare out over the water, and scream at the top of my lungs if I wanted to. No unsupervised kids ramming against me with their boogie boards or sobbing about the fierce green bottle flies.

This was the island at its most pure and most raw, and the effect was amazingly cleansing. Revitalizing. I felt more spiritual standing by the brutal, beautiful force of the ocean than I had at church on Christmas Eve. Maybe this was how I would worship from now on. Not in a pew, contained by walls and a roof, but out in nature instead, surrounded by water and trees and birds, all reminders of just how many pieces came together to make up our world. All the little miracles that came together *just so*, by chance or by will, at random, or according to plan—I wasn't sure that it mattered. Whichever way, the world's creation was nothing short of miraculous.

I spread our old red-and-white-checkered blanket along a patch of dry sand and plunked down on it, stretching out as I lay on my back and knotted my hands on top of my belly. The sky was bright blue and cloudless, a perfect beach day even if the winter sun couldn't warm my upturned face. Hannah and Jesse gradually made their way over, settling down next to me. Not the tree house but the beach, and a new threesome of friends, but it was the same ratty, well-loved blanket that had seen us through so many adventures. Jesse, it seemed, had effortlessly filled in that third spot of the trio. But no matter how much I appreciated him, he could never be Izzy. No one would ever be Izzy.

We lay there in silence for a while, all of us lost in our own thoughts as we stared out at the ocean. The sound of the waves crashing felt more important than any words I could think of to say over them.

But then Hannah cleared her throat, and I looked over to see her winding a finger through a loose curl of hair. I tensed, waiting for whatever announcement was coming next.

"So I know I haven't really talked about the whole college application thing much in a long time. It just hasn't seemed as . . . I don't know, as important as everything else, Mina. Plus I know it's all probably kind of weird for you, since you're still not sure what you're doing next fall . . ."

"Hannah." My cheeks burned, the sudden warmth at odds with the cool of the sea winds. "Seriously, please don't think that you can't talk about college in front of me. It's fine. I'm fine. I'm still planning to commute to the Penn State branch next year and try to take as many online classes as I can. I've already been accepted, so there's really not much else to decide about for right now. One step at a time, that's all I can do. So what about you, Han? What's the latest?"

Maybe I had avoided—we had avoided—the topic of college. I hadn't intended to, not consciously at least. I cared about my friends' futures, where they were going, what they'd be doing in the next eight months. I just couldn't stand to think about Green Hill without them. Of course they'd want to move on, just as I had wanted to six months ago. The difference was they still could.

"Well, I don't know anything yet, but I just finished my

application to NYU for their journalism program. It's my top choice by far."

"What happened to Ole Miss?" I asked, afraid to feel too relieved. "Becoming a belle? I thought that was your new dream?"

"Oh, that. That was just a silly summer notion. I don't want to go that far, Mina. New York is only two hours away, so I can come back all the time. And you can come visit, too. You and the baby, of course," she added. "It's a great school for journalism, hopefully not too great for me to get into. But more important, I can still see you when I want, not just on the major holidays and summer break."

"Firstly, with your SAT scores and GPA, I'd be floored if NYU would be stupid enough to reject you. But secondly, I only want you going there if it's what you want, Hannah. This can't be about me. I can't let you do that."

"It's about both of us. You're not *letting* me do anything." She was using her mom voice on me, the tone that meant there was zero room for debate. "So, Jesse, how about you? Have you heard back from anywhere? You've been pretty silent about the whole college thing so far."

"Yeah, well, I don't like to get my hopes too high. And I don't like to tell other people and then risk disappointing anyone else when it doesn't happen. I'll be disappointed enough on my own." He took a deep breath and exhaled into the wind. "But, since we're all being pretty open and honest here . . . I guess I can make an exception. I want to be in New York, too. It's the only place other than LA to be for film, and I have family in Brooklyn, so I figure I could maybe live with them and save some cash. I have my submissions in at NYU, too, like you, and then Columbia, Pratt . . . But it just depends on what kinds of loans I can lock down. My parents aren't able to help, so . . . So yeah, we'll see. No promises."

"So I might have a friend in New York!" Hannah squealed, her face lighting up. "That's so awesome! Now Mina has double the reason to visit, and we can come back together on the weekends."

"Hannah, seriously, dial it down a few notches," Jesse said, tossing a handful of sand at her. "You're jinxing both of us. It's just a possibility. A maybe. We'll see." Jesse turned to me then, eyebrows cocked, and I knew he was waiting for my reaction.

I pressed my lips together and made myself smile. "That's so exciting, guys, seriously. I would love to have both of you just a few hours away. And in New York City, too! You'll be my tour guides."

The words felt false on my lips, and I was furious at myself for not feeling happier about their news. Why didn't I? Why couldn't I be thrilled for them—following their dreams, moving to a big, bright new city, and studying at fantastic schools? I wanted to believe that I was only jealous because they'd be going off to all the excitement of New York while I'd still be in Green Hill.

But it was more than that; I knew it was. I couldn't stop the shiny montage spinning through my mind: Jesse and Hannah laughing together in class with their brilliant, interesting new friends, exploring Central Park on the weekends, lingering in a downtown bookstore on a lazy Sunday afternoon as they drank overpriced French press coffee and talked about which indie movie to see in the Village that night.

They would not only both experience so many amazing new things—they'd experience those amazing new things *together*.

Without me.

Sure, they'd think about me, talk about me, call and visit and write e-mails with clever observations about their day, but it wouldn't be the same. *We* wouldn't be the same.

The beach day suddenly felt much less perfect and exhilarating. The air felt downright cold rather than refreshing and invigorating, the sand felt too dense and difficult to walk through, and the little grits I could feel gathering inside the edges of my sleeves made me want to be curled up in my clean, smooth sheets with a warm mug of chamomile tea in my hands. I wanted to be anywhere but there, with anyone but the two of them. And I felt even more terrible for wanting that—for wanting to be away from two of the best friends I would probably ever have. But it made me feel nauseated watching them, noticing now just how close the two of them had gotten. It wasn't me and Jesse and me and Hannah. It was me and Jesse *and* Hannah. A full set of three, not two separate pairs. That realization should have made me happy, an old friend and a new friend getting along so well.

But I wasn't happy, not at all, and I was ashamed of myself for it.

After we all started getting too cold to pretend we wanted to stay much longer, we piled back into Jesse's truck. Hannah squeezed in the middle seat between us—which bothered me, though it hadn't caused a second thought on the drive there that morning. We drove up the strip in silence until we found the first open restaurant, a tavern that would have looked entirely forlorn and vacant if not for the bright yellow OPEN flag flying by the front entrance. The restaurant looked just as abandoned inside. There was only one other customer being served—an old, grizzly looking man dwarfed beside his massive plate of battered fish, absorbed in the newspaper he had spread across the table. The sole waitress in sight was a frowning middle-age woman with purplish auburn hair to match the dark circles under her eyes.

The atmosphere couldn't have been more perfectly aligned with my mood. But after brooding over the menu,

I was determined to at least pretend that everything was normal.

"So . . ." I started, staring down at the heaping plates of fried, unrecognizable bits of seafood that the waitress had dropped onto our table. "You're both still coming over for New Year's Eve, right? Wild night at the Dietrichs'?"

"Wouldn't miss it for the world," Jesse said, squinting at the misshapen lump of batter he'd just speared on his fork.

"Actually . . ." Hannah's voice faded out as she bit down on her straw. "I wasn't going to mention anything until I was absolutely certain, but I just found out before we met up today that Lauren and the baby are definitely going to be staying over that night, so my parents want me to be at home. I'm sorry, Meen. I feel bad, and trust me, it's not really my dream New Year's either. Quite a difference from Nate's awesome party last year." She cringed as soon as she mentioned Nate, her cheeks reddening as she looked back down at her soda. "Anyway, I've just been so busy lately with everything, I haven't spent much time with little Ella. Or Lauren, for that matter. Don't be mad at me?"

"Of course I'm not mad," I said, and I was relieved to realize that I meant it. And I was also relieved to realize that the sound of Nate's name no longer pummeled me in the gut just to hear it. Progress. "Now if you were jumping ship for a kegger at Kyle Baker's house . . . then

I might hold a grudge. But it's family. It's Ella. You have my blessing."

"So it's just you and me then, Meen?" Jesse asked.

I bit into a big piece of what I assumed was fried scallop to hide my nervous grin. "Looks that way. Oh, and there's Gracie, who I'm sure will at least pretend she's going to stay up until midnight. My parents will be out of the house for some party with a few of my dad's coworkers. They're clearly cooler than we are." So I would be alone with Jesse, or practically alone at least, on New Year's Eve. But it was just like any other night, only with a ball dropping on the TV screen and some fake champagne. No big deal, right? I swallowed and smiled at him from across the table.

"That's you, isn't it?" a rough voice croaked from the aisle just behind me. I jerked my head back, startled, to see that the tiny, birdlike old man had gotten up and was now standing just inches away from me, his newspaper clenched in his fist and dangling in front of my face. "That's you, that's both of you, isn't it? Together like that in front of church on Christmas Eve. A church! A church of all places to be going about your shameful business . . ."

The tips of my ears and my cheeks were scorching hot, and it took every ounce of focus I had left to keep the last bite of fish batter down my throat.

"Yes," Jesse said from across the table, not missing a beat. He stared the old man straight in the eyes. "Yes, that *is* us. Thank you for saying hello. Now, if you wouldn't mind leaving us alone, we were having a private conversation."

"It's not right," the man spit out, his thin, withered lips twisting, adding to the many folds and wrinkles already etched across his leathery brown face. He had spent too many hours under the sun, out on his boat, deep-sea fishing and sailing away the weekends.

"I tell you, you're both playing with the Devil, and I have no doubts that you'll both come out burnt for it." He turned to Hannah then, ticking a knobby finger in her face. "And I don't know who you are, but get away. Get away from these two before it's too late for you, too."

"We're leaving," Jesse said, shoving back against the booth as he rushed to his feet. "Now." He reached into his pocket and tossed a few bills onto the table.

I had gotten used to the kids at school talking about me, had gotten used to the website posts and even the unanswered calls that still somehow came through, even with our new number. But a stranger yelling accusations in my face?

No. I would never get used to that.

I was shaking by the time I had my jacket and purse in my hands, and Jesse looped his arm around my back as the three of us walked to the door. The old man was still calling out behind us, and I couldn't stop myself from glancing back one last time. The waitress was trying to block him from me, it seemed, her hands waving in front of his face to make him shut up. But the waitress looked smaller, her hair looked whiter . . . *Iris.*

I sucked in my breath and closed my eyes to stop the dizzy feeling that washed over me. And sure enough, as soon as I opened them again, Iris was gone, the tired-looking waitress in her place. But the waitress was still doing her best to silence the man, shooing him away to get his jacket and leave her restaurant.

"He doesn't know you, Mina," Jesse said, pulling me out into the frigid night air. "He's a crazy, lonely old man."

I nodded, still trying to shake Iris out of my mind. *No.* She hadn't been a hallucination. I had to trust myself. But even so, she seemed to be appearing more and more often, which terrified me. What if Iris was trying to tell me something? What if I was missing something important that connected all these moments? I was torn between wanting to tell Jesse and Hannah and not wanting to worry them. I worried them enough already without these Iris sightings tacked on to the list.

"He's right," Hannah said, wrapping an arm around me. "You can't let that awful old man bother you."

Of course the old man had bothered me. Of course I was bothered that a total stranger hated me, a stranger who probably had grandkids who called him Pappy and visited him every summer for boat rides and sand castles and double scoop ice cream cones.

His judgment made me want to prove myself somehow, to march back in there and convince him that I wasn't the blackhearted heathen he thought I was.

"Your video," I said, gasping as I took a deep breath of the frosty air. "People need to see me. They need to *really* see me. We have to finish it and get it out there. Soon. But do you . . . do you think it'll even work? Will it make any kind of difference?"

"I hope so," he answered, tilting his head against mine so that his thick curls brushed along the top of my forehead. "I really do."

He talked about the project for much of the ride home—the footage he was using, the editing finished and still to be done, the music I might want to add, where and how to post it, any people or ideas or moments we could have forgotten to include. Hannah gave good answers, and I chimed in when I had to. But for the most part I was more caught up in the reflection of my face in the passenger-side window, the faint outlines of my lips, my nose, my windblown hair, competing for visibility against the dark blur of shapes in the passing scenery outside.

I couldn't look away from that girl in the window. How could the rest of the world see someone so different from who I saw? How could a face, a body, a person—an entire *life*—become so distorted and grotesque in other peoples' eyes?

We passed a brightly lit rest stop, and my face blinked out of sight, the reflection lost in the yellow glow of restaurant signs and street lamps. I disappeared, just like that. Just that easily.

Maybe, I thought, the realization crashing with a sickening thud to my stomach—maybe that really *was* the only solution. The best way to move on for everyone involved.

I would disappear, slip off the radar. I would stop weighing down my friends and my family, all the people who were the most loyal to me—all the people who least deserved this kind of punishment. I would run away, find a new place, make a new name. And I would be just like any other single mom trying to make it work.

I couldn't keep doing this to all of them, and I wouldn't. If the video did nothing, if the pressure and the scrutiny kept getting worse and worse . . .

I would leave. I would let them live their lives.

And the baby and I, we would live ours, somewhere far away from Green Hill.

chapter seventeen

I observed the scene in Frankie's from the passenger seat of Jesse's truck, glad that it was dark, that no one would see me staring in, slouched in my seat like some Peeping Tom. I hadn't been in once since I'd quit. Frankie had seemed sad to let me go, but I could see the relief in his face, too. He was devoutly Catholic, and I'm sure that having a mockery of his much-beloved Mary running around the restaurant wasn't sitting well with his conscience. My decision to leave was a favor for both of us.

But Jesse and Gracie had both wanted Frankie's pizza to ring in New Year's. I went along for the ride, and that was as far as I'd go. I could see Jesse in the long line for the register, waving and making small talk with Frankie and the guys in the back. Two heavily bundled-up customers turned away from the crowd to leave, tall stacks of pizza boxes in their arms.

As they walked through the lot and got closer to the

truck, I realized with a stomach-turning lurch whom I was watching.

Izzy.

And Nate.

Izzy and Nate, together, carrying enough pizza for Nate's annual New Year's house party. I shimmied down lower in the seat until only my eyes and forehead were above window level, my face pushed up against the glass for a better view.

They had stayed close after all, even if their cafeteria interactions had seemed limited. That was for the public, maybe, and the private was a different story. Their moment together in the hallway, after Nate's argument with Jesse—I had been right to read into Izzy's power to instantly calm him. There *was* something there, more than they wanted to let on to anyone else.

Nate balanced his boxes on the hood of his car, which was parked only a space away from where I was sitting. I wanted to pinch myself for not noticing it there sooner, after all the hours I'd spent riding around in it.

Nate opened the car door and waited as Izzy loaded her boxes into the backseat, adding his to the pile after she stepped back. He snapped the door shut and turned to her, his now empty hands grabbing at Izzy's waist, pulling her closer in a gesture that looked nauseatingly familiar. She didn't flinch or step back. The touch was normal, expected. Wanted. She let herself lean against him and tilted her face up, meeting his as he curved his head down to reach her. Their lips brushed, softly at first, and then more demanding, her hands reaching to circle his neck and pull him in deeper. A car door slammed from somewhere across the lot, and they pulled apart, each moving away so quickly that I almost could believe that the last thirty seconds hadn't happened. The kiss had been some trick of the eye, my imagination taking advantage of the dim lighting.

It *had* happened, though. It definitely had, and I'd probably suspected it on some level all along. Nate and Izzy had always gotten on so well. Maybe too well, since they had more in common with each other than either ever did with me. They liked the same sports and the same movies and TV shows, even had the same favorite kind of pizza—way too extra-extra pepperoni for any normal person. They were both so outgoing, always making friends so effortlessly, and they both plowed through life like nothing ever scared them. I'd just been some unnecessary middleman, and the big falling out had finally made them realize what and *who* had always been there.

I wanted fresh air to stop the sweaty chills that were wracking my body, the ache that seemed to come from everywhere and nowhere at the same time. But Nate and Izzy were still parked just feet away, and I refused to be caught.

I tried my deep breathing trick, inhaling and forcing myself to count the seconds, but it didn't work. My mind was too thick and muddy to focus.

The driver's-side door clicked open with a burst of cold air and I jumped, my heart pounding at the sudden movement.

"Oh my God, Jesse!" I yelled, gasping for breath. "You scared the absolute shit out of me."

His smiling face seemed to fold in on itself. "Um . . . I'm sorry? I should have knocked?"

"No, I'm sorry, it's okay," I said quickly, already embarrassed by my rudeness. I was the one who had been too busy staring at Izzy and Nate to pay attention.

Izzy and Nate. I whipped my head back around toward their car, just then realizing that I'd come out of hiding, sitting upright in a fully lit interior.

Nate was looking toward the street, but Izzy's eyes were locked straight on mine. She wasn't smiling, but she wasn't frowning, either. Her mouth was a straight, unreadable line. There was nothing there for me to read, not a trace of the easy communication we'd always had in the past. Nate looked front, then back, as he started pulling the car out of the lot, still oblivious to the blazing cord linking me to Izzy. I wouldn't look away, not before she did. She refused, too, and we stared until the car was too far gone and our necks couldn't twist any farther.

"So you saw them?" Jesse asked, hesitant.

I nodded, my face still turned toward the window. My eyes couldn't seem to unstick themselves from the space where Nate's car had just been, where Izzy had just been.

"I'm not upset that I saw Nate kissing someone else," I said, feeling that I had to justify myself to Jesse. I sucked my lips in and bit down, refusing to give in to the tears threatening to spill out. "I'm upset that they can still be so close, when they both chose to be cut off from me. It makes me feel like they never cared about me that much after all, like I'm just so completely easy to let go of. I'm so easy to lose."

"I'm sure that's not true, Mina. I'm sure they miss you, they just never wanted to let you see that. They didn't want to seem weak."

I didn't say anything else during the drive home, and I barely said two words while we ate dinner with Gracie around the coffee table in the living room. But I kept catching Jesse glancing over at me with a worried expression on his face, and I tried my best to shake it off for the rest of the night. I was fine then, or at least seemed to be fine, once I set my mind to ignoring that kiss, which I had already replayed at least a hundred times since it'd happened. I pulled out Candy Land and was the loudest, most enthusiastic of the three of us, insisting that we play round after round. It wasn't until after the Funfetti cupcakes and sparkling cider, and after Gracie had passed out sprawled across the sofa, that I could feel the gnawing ache starting up again—the hollow feeling in the pit of my stomach that made me feel as if I had lost Izzy all over again.

Jesse kept trying to pull me out of it, making running witty commentary on the New Year's Eve live performances and Times Square coverage we had on the TV, poking at my belly and whispering little jokes to the baby. The baby must have been in a strange mood, too, based on the flurry of kicking and squirming around I could feel all night. I usually loved the feeling, the reminder that this little person was actually there inside of me, but it felt like too much at the moment—I wanted to just be selfish, to be alone and sulky if that was how I felt, and Jesse and the baby were both making that impossible.

I couldn't stop thinking about Nate's party. It was hard to believe that only a year ago I was in the center of all of it, glued to Nate's side for the entire night as the hostess of the evening. He had yanked me away just before midnight, pushed me into the small, pitch-black laundry closet so that we could have our midnight kiss alone, away from the rest of the party. "I want this moment to be just about you and me," he had whispered, just before giving me the slowest, warmest, most tingly and amazing kiss we'd ever shared.

Thinking about that kiss, about him and Izzy and how

they'd be kissing that night—maybe in the very same laundry room, maybe with the very same quiet words—made me feel suddenly so desperate to do something, anything, that could help ease the sharp, burning pain even just a little. I looked over at Gracie, a small smile on her lips as she dreamed on the sofa, and then back at Jesse.

"Hey," I said, struggling to push gracefully off the couch. I silently cursed at my belly for making me so completely unbalanced and unsexy. "My phone's in my room and I want to call Hannah to wish her a Happy New Year. Can you come with me?"

Jesse looked up at me. "Do you just want me to run up and get it for you? I don't mind."

I shook my head. "Nah, I want to move around anyway. The baby's antsy, too." He followed me up the stairs, both of us stepping carefully so that the creaking wouldn't wake Gracie.

After we were both inside my bedroom, I closed and latched the door behind us. Jesse stared at me, confused, but I pretended not to notice as I pulled back my curtain to let in the moonlight. I felt so bold and so reckless and so helpless all at the same time, as if my nerves were screaming at me, and I was powerless to do anything but obey. They wanted me to let it all go, every last rule and boundary I'd built up for myself—for once to be just in that moment, that minuscule fraction of time that existed right here and now, never before, never again after. There was no tomorrow and no yesterday, no Izzy and Nate, no college plans, no impending baby bills, no threatening calls from strangers or cruel Virgin Mina posts online for anyone in the world to see. There was no planning, no right or wrong, no perfect.

I wasn't perfect, not anymore. And I didn't want to be.

I took a few shaky steps toward Jesse, who was still standing by the door, his puzzled face pale in the moonlight.

"Mina, what are you . . . ?"

I tapped my finger to his mouth, and the question dropped off. His lips felt so soft and so warm, I suddenly wanted them to touch every last part of my body. I felt him as he swallowed, his throat tensing at my touch. We stayed like that, hovering in front of something bigger and scarier. My finger, his lips—nothing more than that one simple gesture. I couldn't tell which one of us moved first, who tilted their head and crossed over that space between us. Because all of a sudden we were kissing, our lips moving together in a way I'd never imagined possible, so effortlessly in sync, shaping and reshaping. We were on my bed then, and Jesse delicately lowered me, so careful and aware of my stomach. I was surprised that I didn't feel more self-conscious about my belly, the awkward bump that was always there between us, reminding us both that there was a third person to be considered.

I ran my fingers along the top of his jeans and his waist, and then reached up under his shirt, his back so hot and solid beneath my hands. I was pulling his shirt up without even realizing I was going to do it, tugging it up inch by inch to bring our skin even closer.

"Mina," he whispered, his breath warm in my ear. "Mina, I don't think we should . . ."

I pressed my lips harder against his, pushing the words back into his mouth. I felt so in control for once, so free, and I didn't want to let that go so soon.

"Mina, seriously," he pushed himself up on his forearms, suspended above me. "This probably isn't a good idea. Gracie could wake up at any minute and come looking for us, and . . . and you've made it pretty clear that you don't want this. At least not right now. Not with everything else that's going on."

"Maybe I've changed my mind," I said, circling my arms around his neck and trying to tug him back down.

"Really?" He looked hopeful, and nervous, too, and I wanted to close my eyes and go back to just feeling, no more thinking. "Why tonight, Mina?"

When I couldn't respond, I saw something click in his expression, the confusion replaced by disappointment as he pulled away from me.

"Because of Izzy and Nate. Of course." There was disgust in his voice, and I wanted to undo that last moment, I wanted to say the right answer, the one that he needed to hear. The one that I was so afraid to say out loud.

"No, it's not like that," I said, my voice shaking. "It's not like that at all." *I love you, Jesse, not Nate. Don't you see?* But the words caught in my throat. I couldn't give in.

"It's not? Then what is it like? Because you've rejected any possibility of us since I first put it out there, Mina, and suddenly, the night you see your ex-boyfriend kissing your ex–best friend, you're bringing me up to your bedroom and practically throwing me on your bed. So please, explain to me what's really happening then if I'm so completely wrong."

His words stung, more so because I knew part of what he was saying was right. I had feelings for him, of course, though my motives for tonight, in that moment, had been questionable. But I couldn't stand feeling so wrong, so worthless and rejected. It was easier just to feel angry instead—enraged.

"Everyone thinks that I'm a whore anyway, that we've already slept together, so why not just do it, Jesse? If everyone's going to think it's true, we might as well just give in to it, right? I might as well enjoy being slutty."

He leaped off my bed—he couldn't have looked more stunned if I'd slapped him straight across the face. Already I wanted to beg him to forget what I'd said, to plead for his forgiveness, but instead I just yanked at the blanket under me, wrapping it around my body like armor. I needed to hide. I needed to disappear.

"I c-can't . . ." he stuttered. "I can't believe you just said that to me. I can't believe that's what this meant to you."

"It's not," I said, pleading. "I didn't mean that. I care about you, Jesse, I really do, I just—"

"I can't talk about this right now, Mina. I can't even look at you right now." His feet fumbled as he backed away from me toward the door. "I just need to go."

"Don't . . ." The word cracked on my lips. He stepped out of the room, leaving me, his footsteps quiet and cautious down the stairs.

I was mad at myself for yelling at him, but at the same time—didn't I deserve to be angry? Didn't I have that right?

I'd never asked for any of this, and now I was rebuilding my entire life. For a decision that had never really been mine to make. I hadn't gotten drunk or been knocked up by some stupid one-night stand. I hadn't even had sex—let alone unprotected sex—with a serious boyfriend.

I'd be fast-forwarding through the college years, the years where it was okay to be a little bit irresponsible, reckless. Selfish. There'd be no becoming best friends with my freshman roommate, no flirting with the cute boy sitting behind me in English Theory 101, no getting too drunk and making careless, awful decisions, and spending the next morning laughing over all of them with my new friends, glad—proud even—to have made them.

I'd spent my whole life walking a narrow line, trying not to make mistakes—not to make a *single fucking mistake*. Was that why I was chosen? Because somebody up there thought I was so goddamn perfect?

"I'm not perfect, Iris!" I screamed, shaking off the blanket and grabbing at the first thing my eyes landed on to throw—Nate's anniversary watch, still on my nightstand, though I'd stopped wearing it weeks ago. I hurled it across the room, gloating at the satisfying thump as it hit the wall. "I'm not fucking perfect, and I want my fucking life back!"

Silence. Nothing but the dark, empty house to answer to me.

"Did you hear me?" I yelled, louder this time. My throat burned. "Take it back, Iris! Take it all fucking back! I know you're there. I've seen you. I've seen you, Iris! Stop hiding!"

"She won't come back, Mina, not when you talk to her like that."

I shrieked, my heart pounding in my chest, before I realized that it was Gracie. She was standing in the doorway, soft light from the hallway framing her tiny body.

"What are you talking about, Gracie?"

"Iris. She won't come if you're screaming at her like that."

"What do you know about Iris? You've never seen her. I do. I see her, Gracie. I haven't told anyone, but I still see her sometimes."

"I see her, too, Mina. She's everywhere."

A chill prickled along my spine as I stared at her, my mouth gaping open.

"How . . . ?"

"She's there when you need her most, I think. When you're really sad, or maybe when you're really happy, too." She pushed herself onto the bed and crawled to squeeze in next to me. "When I get mad at school about something somebody says about you, or when I can't sleep at night because I'm scared about what's going to happen to you and the baby . . . that's when I see her. She never says anything, but she smiles at me. She smiles with those happy green eyes. And that's enough. I always feel okay again when I see her."

"But I don't get it. How did you know it was Iris? How did you know about her green eyes? I never told you that."

"I just knew." She shrugged. "Who else would it be?"

"Why haven't you told me?" I asked, my lips still shaking.

She scrunched her face. "I don't know. I guess I was worried you'd think I was making it up, maybe. Because even though I think she's real when I see her, she always disappears right away. Like a ghost or something. I was scared no one would believe me."

"I believe you, Gracie," I said, and sighed. "I'll always, always believe you."

I knew that I hadn't just imagined Iris at school or at church, or in that depressing old restaurant. She was real, just like my baby was real.

I don't really want Iris to take you back, I said in my head, desperately hoping that the baby could somehow hear me. I felt hot and sick with shame, as if flames were burning holes through my stomach. *I didn't mean that, not at all. I wouldn't trade you in for anything or anyone.*

Both of us were silent after that, and when Gracie's breathing fell into a slow rhythm next to me, I closed my eyes and prayed.

Not to God, because I still wasn't sure who or what that was.

But to Iris. I prayed to Iris.

I woke up on New Year's Day puffy-eyed but determined—determined to make the best of a fresh start. I wrote up a list of resolutions, which I'd never done before, and every single one revolved around the baby. Because that was what this New Year would be: all about the baby. Not about me. Not what I wanted. Not *who* I wanted. There would be time for that—for me—later, after the baby was born, and after life settled again. But I couldn't sit around sulking and brooding. It was a relief, really, to have no choice but to pick myself up and move past it all. Just one more reason I was glad to have this baby growing inside of me. I was learning what it really meant to be *selfless*.

I needed to apologize to Jesse, but I didn't know where to begin. I didn't know of any words that could possibly undo the ones I'd already used. So I decided not to call, not right away. I needed time to get the apology right, and besides that, he deserved some time away from me. I didn't have to wait long, though, because he called me the day after New Year's, the day before we'd be going back to school for the new semester.

"I finished the video," he said, all businesslike and matter-of-fact. "Do you want me to come over tonight to show you guys?"

"Sure. That sounds great," I said, cringing at the false, cheery ring of my voice. I opened my mouth to say more, but the words stuck in my throat. Jesse was silent for a few awkward beats, too, before he said a clipped good-bye and the line went dead.

I sighed, frustrated with myself. I needed to say something—he deserved that much at the very least. I was scared to lose him, but I was just as scared to get any closer.

There seemed to be no winning here, no easy way to crawl out of the big hole I kept on digging.

I called Hannah and invited her over, too, hoping that she'd buffer at least some of the awkwardness. I still hadn't told her about any of it, not even that first kiss on my birthday. She suspected something, I could tell, but she hadn't asked, and I hadn't offered. I was too conflicted—and now too ashamed—to explain myself, even to her.

Jesse and I barely glanced at each other when he walked into the living room a few hours later. Hannah filled the void, just as I'd predicted, telling us all in great detail about her resolution to read a book every week for the next year, fifty-two books in fifty-two weeks. As she rambled, my whole family huddled around Jesse and the TV.

"I'm pretty excited about how it turned out," Jesse said, sounding anxious as he inserted a disc and fidgeted with the settings on the screen. "But don't be afraid to offer up any constructive criticism. You all need to be happy with it, too, of course."

We all fell silent as the video started playing—a shot of my house with the rising sun glowing just behind it, squares of light shining from my bedroom window and the kitchen, where my mom was probably standing, pouring her first mug of coffee.

And then, in a blink, it was my face, my voice. "I wake up every morning and the first thing I think, every single time, is *I'm pregnant. I'm having a baby.*" I was sitting at my desk, my hair still wet from my shower, just about to read through the newest website posts. "At first, in the beginning, that was a bad thing. Like I was waking up from a nightmare, and then I'd remember that it was my reality and I'd want to pull the covers over my face and hide from everything for the rest of my life." I smiled as the camera zoomed in, a small, sad smile that didn't reach my eyes. "But it started getting easier every day, a little bit more and more. Now when I wake up, I think *I'm having a baby!* and I remember that I'm not alone in my bed, that there's this little human being right there inside me. I hope that every mom feels that. That every mom feels like her baby is her own special miracle, just like I do."

I talked about Iris next, though I didn't use her name, and I didn't reveal everything she had said either, or all the little, more peripheral details—the way she dressed, the way she talked, the way the blue of her old veins had almost shone through her translucent skin. Somehow it didn't feel right to tell the camera everything. I wanted to keep most of Iris for myself. But I did explain, of course, that she'd left me with a cryptic message about the world's troubles, and about the mysterious baby to come. I told them about the dream I'd had that night, the symptoms that popped up one by one soon after. Watching myself on the screen now, studying each tiny twitch, I could see fear etched on my face, but there was more than that—reverence, maybe. Awe.

From there, viewers would quickly get a heavy dose of the many low points to come—me reading some of the more disturbing online posts, including a note that suggested I actually be crucified in public, both as my punishment and as a lesson to others. "If we let her go, we're just begging God for an apocalypse." There were many less sinister, just plain cruel posts, too, about my baby weight, about how ugly and pathetic I was, about how desperate I must be for any kind of attention. I wasn't crying while I read any of them out loud, which I was proud of—I looked surprisingly calm, actually, just exhausted.

The camera moved on as Jesse guided us through a standard day, Gracie chattering about baby names over frozen waffles, blatant stares and whispers as we navigated the hallway to my locker. I pulled out a note that had been wedged in the locker vent, tossing it on the ground without bothering to read it. I hadn't realized at the time, but Jesse had panned the camera down and focused on the sloppily scrawled message: *You're not special. You're just a slut.* Not one of the more eloquent letters, but at least not as damning as some. There was a rapid montage of me in classes—a lot of yawning and staring off into space, slouched at my desk and avoiding any kind of student or teacher interaction. Doing my best to be invisible. I hadn't realized how obvious I'd made it that I was so completely detached from all of it—except for one brief slip in European History, the frown on my lips as I looked down at the graded exam that had just landed on my desk, a bright red *C* at the top.

As difficult as it was to see myself on film—my expressions, the way the world responded around me—the interviews that followed were even harder to watch. Jesse had done most of the shooting without me in the room, so the footage was new to me.

"It's hard to be in school sometimes because of what some of the other kids say." Gracie was curled up in a ball on the sofa in our living room, her little fingers twisting the frayed blanket on her lap as she avoided looking up at the camera. "Like today . . ." She paused, and I could tell from the pink in her cheeks that she was trying her best not to cry for the recording. "Today someone asked me how I can still love my sister when she's such a liar. They said I was just as bad as her for going along with everything, and that our whole family should just leave Green Hill. Even my best friend won't talk to me, but you know what? That's okay, because I don't want to talk to her, either. I can't be friends with anyone who is mean to Mina."

"Are you excited, then? About the baby?" Jesse's voice came quietly from behind the camera, prompting her.

Gracie's eyes lit up. "Of course I'm excited! I'm going

to be an aunt! I know that Mina is really young to have a baby . . . and that there's been a lot of bad things happening because of it. But I think that this baby happened for a reason, and that it's meant to be this way. And I also think that Mina is special. This baby will be special. I just want to be the best sister and the best aunt I can be, because Mina needs me. My family needs me."

My mom came next, talking about how she had believed me from the very first second—trusted with her all-knowing motherly intuition—and how proud she'd been to watch me, my transformation from daughter into mother. My dad was more vague regarding what he believed or didn't believe about my story, but he trembled as he admitted that he'd turned his back on me for too long. He'd let his own expectations get in the way of protecting and supporting me.

"I will never, ever abandon my own family again," he said, staring unblinking into the camera, even as his voice broke and a stream of tears ran down his cheek. "Not for anything. Not even for a moment. I've learned a very valuable lesson from my role in all this."

I looked over at him as the video played, at his face hidden behind his palms, hands kneading into his tired eyes, and I felt myself step toward him. I had already forgiven him that night on the porch. Or at least I'd said the words out loud then, because I'd wanted to wash it all off.

I'd wanted to take us back to normal as quickly as possible. But I felt it again now—I *really* felt it. We—every one of us in that room—had learned lessons. We were all changed, and we were probably better people because of it. My dad wasn't perfect, but he was trying his best. That was all any of us could do.

"I forgive you," I whispered, wrapping an arm around his waist as I leaned into his chest. "It's time for you to forgive yourself, too."

He didn't say anything back, but he didn't have to. He hugged me, and we stayed like that, tangled up together, as the footage played on.

Hannah was up then, telling the camera about the day I took the pregnancy test, the first moments of realization for her and for me. It hadn't been easy, she said, none of it, but staying by my side was the right thing to do. I had been so strong and courageous that it had inspired her to be strong and courageous, too, even if that meant losing every other friend she had. Or more accurately, "redefining friendship and what loving someone unconditionally actually means, when you strip it out of the hypothetical and give it real-life context."

Jesse flipped the camera around to himself after that, and I tensed, surprised to suddenly see him staring out of the screen. I didn't recognize the backdrop behind him, but based on the numerous overlapping movie posters tacked along the wall, I suspected it was his bedroom. I hadn't realized, not until that moment, that I'd never actually been to his house and that our friendship was so conspicuously one-sided. The thought made the guilty knot in my stomach twist even tighter, and I watched his warm, adorably sincere face while he described Iris and that night we first met. He swore that even though we'd worked together through the summer, we'd never had a real conversation until a few months ago. We had been complete strangers at the time I would have conceived.

"I came to this school not knowing anyone, and Mina . . . she took me in. I may have only known her since this fall, so I can't comment on her past here and her reputation through the years, but I know who I've seen—I know this Mina, today and now, and she's one of the strongest, sweetest, most genuine and good people I've ever met." He smiled, distracted, as he swiped a hand through his knotty curls. "I hate that our friendship has started even more rumors about her and the baby, and honestly, if I were the father, I'd be proud to admit it. Any guy should be with a girl like Mina. But I'm not, at least not biologically speaking. Emotionally, though . . . emotionally I already know that I would do anything to keep both of them safe. So maybe I'm protective like a father, and care like a father, but I'm not—I am *not* the father. And I don't think we'll ever fully understand who is."

The film kept playing from there, artfully jumping through various scenes from the past few weeks: me taking notes on my faux birthing class DVDs, a trip to Dr. Keller's office, my birthday night and our shocked reactions to the first news report, which I hadn't even noticed him recording. But I could barely absorb any of it, not after listening to Jesse talk about me—not after knowing that he'd said those things before our fight, and probably wished he could take them back now, rerecord his statements about an idolized girl who didn't actually exist.

A clip with Pastor Lewis brought me back, though, and I leaned forward for a better view of the screen. He looked stiff and uncomfortable behind his glossy wooden desk, as out of place in his own office as he had been that day in our living room. He was fidgeting in his seat, the leather squeaking slightly as he spun the chair in tiny half circles, left and right. But his light hazel eyes, solemn and wide, were fixed on the camera as he opened his mouth to speak. He talked about how he'd known me since the day I was born, baptized me in that same church eighteen years ago, and watched me grow up through Sunday School and choir, youth group and catechism classes.

"I won't say that I believe unequivocally that Mina is carrying a baby conceived through some sort of divine intervention, because I can't be sure of that. No one can be sure of that. But I will say that in our times, I think we've reached a sorry, sad state of cynicism. That we've stopped believing that miracles—any miracle, no matter how small or large—are inherently possible. We've become so obstinately certain that we can explain every last detail about the world around us, and I think that in doing so, we've lost some of the magic and the beauty that God intended for us to have in our lives. We've lost that humble, grounding belief that there are things and acts outside of our power to comprehend—that as men and women we still have limits in what we can perceive of God's plan.

"So is it possible, could Mina actually be the virgin mother of a child who comes to us through some higher being? From God Himself?" He paused, knitting his hands together on top of the desk to steady himself, but his eyes never left the camera. "I think it is. Or at the very least, I think it's outside of our right and our authority to question and criticize what is or isn't God's doing. This is not for us to judge. We cannot condemn. We can only hope and pray and open ourselves to the possibilities that God can still reach down—can touch our everyday lives in ways that we've maybe never dreamed possible. We believe in the ideas that we read in the Bible. We believe in Jesus, in his mother, Mary. Why is it so hard to believe that miracles can still happen today, in our modern world? Ask yourself that, if nothing else. Why? Or, more appropriately, *why not?*"

Pastor Lewis's lips stilled, but Jesse kept the camera on him for a few more silent seconds, allowing the full effect of his words to linger, dense and electric in their implications.

Just as I was thinking we'd reached the end, the scene changed again. It was me, on Christmas Eve, hands dragging down the mural of the nativity as my sobbing body sagged to the floor. I gasped, pressing against my dad's arm to steady myself. I hadn't thought Jesse had been there that long before he'd called out to me—would never have guessed that his camera had been on me that whole time, the bright recording light blinking red as he captured my fall.

My first instinct was to scream, to accuse him of completely violating my privacy. But then I saw the reactions that Hannah and my entire family were having, and I held myself back. Every cheek was shiny wet with tears, all eyes riveted by the scene—the round-bellied girl, the mother-to-be, so symbolically close to another mother. Another mother who mirrored so much of what she was experiencing in her own extraordinary life, two thousand years later.

And I realized that maybe—just maybe—that scene could actually change peoples' minds. Soften them at the very least. Because how could that girl, that poor aching, breaking girl, be a fake, an impostor? And why would she? Why would she, or anyone, willingly put themselves through this experience? This kind of judgment?

That girl, that girl up on the screen, she was real. She was real, and she was hurting, but she was also determined and resilient and proud. She was the Mina I wanted to be. She was the Mina I wanted the world to know.

chapter eighteen

I don't know how the girl knew where to find me, but she did. She was sitting on the steps outside of Dr. Keller's office, her small chin propped in her small hands, waiting as my mom and I made our way to the door. I didn't pay any attention at first, not until she jumped up and latched on to my waist.

"Mina, Mina, Mina!" she screamed, her whole face lighting up in a big smile, adorably crooked from her two missing front teeth.

I stepped back a little, startled. I looked to my mom, and she shook her head at me, just as confused.

"Excuse me. I don't think I know you?" I put one hand on her shoulder as I gently pushed her back to get a better look. Red braids, freckles, a sparkly pink jacket. She could have been Gracie's age.

"No, but I know all about you. My whole family does. And I need to ask you a really important favor." Her grin disappeared, and she looked suddenly much older, more serious.

"My mom is the one who needs you, but she was too sick to come. She's really sick. And they won't tell me much because they think I'm too little, but she has cancer. I'm scared she's not going to be okay. Not ever maybe."

A sob rose up my throat, but I forced it down. I took my mom's hand instead, squeezing it as I steadied myself.

"I'm really sorry to hear that . . . ?"

"Katie."

"I'm so sorry, Katie."

"I told her that I would find you, though. I thought maybe if you pray for her, she might get better. Or maybe . . . maybe you could give me something to take back to her? Like a bracelet or a glove or something? Just something that you've touched. Like a good luck charm to help save her."

"Katie, I . . ." I stopped, struggling with what to say. It felt morally wrong, deceitful to give her the hope that anything I could do would make any difference for her mom.

But at the same time, was it so awful to give someone hope? Wasn't hope sometimes all we needed to be stronger? To pass through something hard—to make it to the other side.

Maybe hope isn't always about the perfect ending. Hope is making the journey easier.

"Sure," I said, before I could change my mind. I slipped a thin silver band from my thumb, a random find from a Saturday thrifting with the girls at the local flea market.

The look of pure joy on Katie's face erased any regret I might have felt.

"Thank you, Mina," she said through happy, glistening tears. We hugged, and she ran off, anxious, it seemed, to get the ring to her mom as soon as possible.

"I don't even know her last name," I said, looking up at my mom as Katie disappeared down the sidewalk. "I'll never know if her mom gets better."

"You did the right thing, sweetie. You did what you could do." Mom sighed, tugging me gently toward the door. "It's out of our hands now."

"Everything looked great in the exam room today," Dr. Keller said, "perfectly normal and on schedule." I sat up straighter in my chair, trying to focus on what she was saying, but my thoughts were still with Katie. I considered calling my mom in from the waiting room, worried that I probably wouldn't remember anything about the visit without her listening in.

"One more week and your baby will be full-term, Mina. Strange to think about, isn't it? It feels like just a few weeks ago that you first came in here, so scared and confused. You hardly even seem like the same girl. Or the same woman, I should say."

I nodded, still only half listening.

"Mina?" Dr. Keller leaned over her desk to stare at me straight on. "What's going on? I guess that's a silly question, though. I'm sure it's been an interesting month, with everything that's been happening after that video of yours."

"Interesting," I echoed, staring back at her. I smiled. "Interesting is probably the best word for it."

When Jesse's video went out to the news circuit, it was like a brilliant, blinding comet had burst from the roof of my house—fanning out its shimmering trail across the country, around the world. News stations played clips during prime-time broadcasts, the whole video could be found everywhere online, and people—well, people certainly watched. People were engrossed. The Virgin Mina website and online network was stronger and more active than ever, and the page was quickly becoming less of a trashy high school tabloid and more of a streamlined public forum for critics of all ages. I had my detractors, yes, the cynics, the disbelievers, and the angry zealots. People were still calling my house, still shoving notes in my locker, in our mailbox. People were still posting cruel accusations and compromising pictures that had been taken of me in private, unsuspecting moments. Even some of the more bored, indifferent kids at school had started getting angry with me now. Not because they cared about why or how I'd gotten pregnant, but because—as I'd heard one stranger put it while ranting to friends at her locker—I'd become a "total media whore who would do anything to stay in the spotlight."

But . . .

There were other sorts of outspoken people surfacing, too, people who were speaking out not against me, but against those who were pointing their fingers and publicly flagellating me. They saw me as a human being who deserved privacy and the right to live my own life. And there were also people like Katie. People of all different ages, religions, and nationalities who could accept the unexplainable, open their minds to new possibilities. They were people who wanted hope. People who *needed* hope.

And I, somehow, had become their source.

"You've heard," I said, "that I have 'followers' now, I'm sure. I saw one of them on my way in, actually. That's why I've been so . . . distracted."

She nodded, and I kept going, suddenly needing to talk.

"Some days I don't know who I'm more scared of, Dr. Keller: the people who hate me or the people who claim to worship me. I got a letter the other day from a Muslim woman in Indonesia. Written in Arabic, so we had to take it to the police to translate. A woman in *Indonesia* knows about me. And she hates me, too, according to the letter. Told me all about how this is not 'the Day of Resurrection,' and I'll pay the price for all my lies in the afterlife. It was nothing I hadn't heard before, but still . . . she lives across the world. It's absurd to even think about her knowing about my life, let alone *caring* about it."

"That's so scary and so upsetting, Mina," Dr. Keller said, reaching over the desk to hold my hands in hers. "I can't begin to imagine how you feel when you read something like that."

"It sounds crazy, but I'm almost unfazed by people like her now. But these others, the ones who seem to worship me . . . Sometimes I'm terrified, Dr. Keller. I've been getting all these strange letters and e-mails—begging for locks of my hair, my clothing, anything I've touched. They all seem so desperate—so obsessed. Obsessed. With *me*. It's entirely surreal. I worry that some of them will do whatever it takes to feel close to me. To feel saved by me, blessed somehow. Which is ridiculous. I'm still only me, Dr. Keller. Only Mina. How can I save anyone? I'm just fighting to save myself."

We sat in silence, the ticking of the clock above her desk the only sound in the room. She still held my hands tightly, which left the tears dripping down her cheeks unstopped.

"Dr. Keller," I said, eager to make the moment feel

lighter, easier again. "Dr. Keller . . . I'm sure this probably isn't orthodox, and if you're not comfortable with it or you're busy, I completely understand, no pressure at all. But my mom's having a little baby shower for me this Saturday, and I'd love it if you came. It's nothing big, just a few friends and family, and of course you don't have to bring me anything. Any gifts, I mean. It would just be nice to have you there. But like I said . . ."

"Mina," she said, laughing as she let go of my hands. "You're right. It's not traditional for me to go to patients' baby showers. But I want to be there. And I think for you, Mina Dietrich, I can make an exception." She lowered her head and lifted her brows, shifting her eyes left to right. "Just don't tell on me, okay?"

"Secret's safe." I grinned at her as I grabbed at the edge of the desk to haul myself up from the chair. "Wow. It'll be amazing to actually have any kind of balance again. I feel like a fat, clumsy penguin, waddling instead of walking. I could accidentally tip and roll over at any second."

"Patience, Mina. Soon enough you'll be carrying that round bump in your arms instead."

I closed my eyes for a second and let myself really picture it—my newborn, wrapped in blankets and nestled in my arms. I could almost feel him or her, the warm weight pressing against my chest, the sweet, milky smell of baby filling my nose. "Soon enough." I sighed, turning to wave

as I reached for the door handle. "Noon on Saturday, then?"

"Noon on Saturday."

I hadn't wanted a shower and had adamantly insisted against one, in fact. But my mom was determined, and she made a valid point, tacky as it may have sounded: I needed whatever donations I could get. And so it was settled. I would be having a baby shower. It was a small crowd, anyway, just my aunt Vera and Lucy, Hannah and her mom, Dr. Keller, Pastor Lewis's wife, and a few of my mom's closest friends and coworkers who had supported her throughout the whole ordeal—regardless of what they actually believed or didn't believe about my explanation. They were all at least polite to me, and that was enough.

I was nervous, though, despite the small guest list, and I posed and squinted in front of the mirror for a solid half hour, changing back and forth between three different maternity dresses my mom had bought for the occasion. I wanted to look casual but capable, mature but pretty in that glowing soon-to-be-mom kind of way. I finally settled on a dark green sweater dress with an empire waist that seemed to be just the right balance of subtle and showy—classy but still proud of the gigantic bump I couldn't have hidden even if I'd wanted to.

I was still contemplating myself in the mirror when I heard a knock at the front door. I figured it was Aunt Vera, coming over early to help my mom set out the food and finish with any last-minute decorations. I didn't pay much attention to the quiet voices down below, at least not until I heard footsteps on the stairs.

They stopped just beyond my door, and whoever it was stayed there, still and silent, hesitating. I could hear myself breathing, could almost believe that I heard them breathing, too, from across the closed door. My heart started racing, which was ridiculous, admittedly, because it was probably just my aunt, maybe Hannah, even, just coming up to say hello.

I stepped back from the mirror and yanked at the knob, freezing when I saw the face, the eyes, staring back at me. I couldn't breathe. Couldn't use my lungs, my lips.

"Mina," Izzy said. My name sounded so familiar on her lips—so normal and natural and wonderful.

"What are you doing here?" I was surprised that I did still have lips after all, and a mouth and a throat and vocal cords that functioned. One by one, piece by piece, my body started coming back to me, and I could actually feel what was happening—feel all the confused and angry and bizarrely happy sensations humming through me.

"Can we talk?" Her voice was quiet, almost shy. I studied her face, trying to relearn all the intricate details I'd missed for so long, and was surprised to see the dark circles under her red, sleepy-looking eyes.

"You want to talk now?" I took a deep breath and pressed my hands to my belly to center myself. "Today's my baby shower, Izzy. Not now. I can't argue with you now."

"I'm not here to argue, Mina. I'm really not, I promise."

"Then why are you here?" I was proud of how strong I sounded. A few months ago I would have already been fighting back tears, but Dr. Keller had been right—I *had* changed. I'd learned to be tough, to stand up for myself and what I believed in. I'd learned that the people who couldn't accept us didn't deserve my tears.

Izzy stepped farther into the room and closed the door before I could move to stop her.

"I'm here to say that I'm sorry, Meen."

I was *Meen* again, not even Mina. As if nothing had changed, and we hadn't spent nearly the last six months without each other.

"I'm sorry for so many things, I don't even know where to begin. I'm sorry that I didn't stick by you from day one like Hannah did. You wouldn't lie, not to us, unless you had a really good reason to, and I should have respected that. I should have just been there for you and figured the rest out as we went along. The fact that I abandoned you when you were going through something like this makes me feel like the absolute shittiest friend ever. You deserved so much more than that. And I realize I can never make up for it. I can never go back and support you through the last six months. But I can help you now. I can help you every day after, because I want to be in your life again, Meen. I *need* to be in your life." Her shoulders started shaking, and she buried her head in her hands.

I felt stuck to the floor, like I couldn't run to her side even if I wanted to. And I wasn't sure if I wanted to. Not yet. Not that easily.

She put up her hand, wiping at her dripping eyes with the other. "I'm not done yet. That's just part one." She laughed, but the sound turned into more of a twisting, broken sob that knocked away at my already weakening defenses.

"I know you saw me on New Year's Eve with Nate, and I haven't been able to forgive myself since. I have no excuse for what I did—it was disgusting and unacceptable of me, and my only explanation is that he was really all I had at the beginning, after I first lost you and Han. Or after I first walked away from you and Han, I see now. But he was the only person I could talk to at the beginning, before everyone else knew. And once everyone did know, he was still the only one that I wanted to talk to about all of it. Do you think it was easy for me to watch Kyle Baker and all his pathetic followers treat you like that? I couldn't stand to hear what people were saying about you, and for the record, neither could Nate. When he first found out that Arielle had started the website—"

"Arielle?" I interrupted, not knowing if I wanted to laugh or cry at the revelation. "Arielle Fowler? She's the evil mastermind behind the Virgin Mina website?"

Izzy bit down on her lip, her eyes flickering away from me. "I'm sorry. I thought you would have heard about that by now. Or guessed, at least. Nate was furious at her, which is ironic since we all knew she probably did it just to make you look even worse in his eyes, like that would somehow make him more likely to pick her. But that certainly backfired. Maybe being a malicious bitch attracts someone like Kyle Baker, but Nate's too good for that shit." She sighed. "He did love you, Mina. And he's not a bad guy, despite everything." She paused, those last words hanging in the air between us. "Anyway, so Arielle started the website, but a lot of their crowd had a hand in it after a while. It wasn't just her. I heard that Sara Fritz helped her with a lot of the tech work, too. I guess she and her mom aren't so different after all. Or maybe Sara just didn't know how to say no to a popular girl who was giving her any kind of attention."

I nodded, feeling strangely indifferent about finally knowing who was responsible. It wasn't as if I was surprised, and it wasn't as if it mattered. Not really. This was never just about one person turning on me. It was much, much bigger than that. Arielle was one tiny piece of the problem.

And Sara—I just felt bad for Sara. I remembered the panicked look in her eyes that day she had bumped into me. Growing up with a mom like Tana, she probably didn't know how to be anything but obedient.

"Nate was really struggling, Mina, and once he started seeing you and Jesse together, and everyone kept beating him down saying that he was a pushover for not stepping up and doing anything about it . . . well, it pushed him over the edge. It pushed *us* over the edge, I guess. I went over to his house that day after the fight with Jesse to talk him through some things, and . . . and it just happened. It never meant anything, not to either of us, I don't think. It just made us feel less sad somehow about not having you anymore. I know this sounds odd, but it filled at least a tiny piece of the hole that you'd left in our lives. It's over now, though, whatever it was. I ended it right after New Year's. Right after I saw you."

She looked back up at me, her dark eyes pleading.

"So why now, Iz?" I asked. "What's changed?"

Izzy shook her head, tears still running down her cheeks. I could count on one hand the number of times I'd seen Izzy cry—a broken leg in the middle of a soccer field, and a stick to the head in a fierce game of field hockey. This fragile and exhausted-looking Izzy breaking down on my bed was completely new to me.

"I watch the video every night, you know. Every night,

Meen. And every time I watch it, I end up sobbing, for you, for your family. For me, because I ran away from all of it and I've been afraid that you'd never let me back in, especially not after New Year's. I knew all along how hard it must be for you, but I was convinced that it was just as hard for me, too, to go through senior year without you and Han. But then I saw Jesse's video, and I felt like such a selfish, stupid child. I hadn't ever really thought about how hard it was for you, how different life was not just for you but for Gracie and your parents . . . I've wanted to apologize every day, Mina. I just didn't know how. I was hurt, too, you know, after everything you accused me of that day on my porch. That was some pretty cold stuff you said, and it took me time to move past it all. To realize you said it because you were angry and not because you really meant it. Or at least I hope you didn't." She took a shaky breath and exhaled, struggling to compose herself.

I looked down, my stomach tight with shame as I replayed through everything I'd said on that terrible morning. "I should never have said those things, Iz. They were ugly and mean and untrue. It just . . . it made me feel better to take you down with me. And I feel completely awful admitting that to you. I feel awful admitting that to *me*, too."

"It's behind us," she said, reaching out to lift my chin up, forcing our eyes to meet. I saw the truth there, saw that it *was* behind us, just like that. "When Hannah e-mailed me about the baby shower this week, I was shocked to see a message from her, and even more shocked when I read it. But I guess she still had hope for me. Hope for all of us. So . . . here I am. Thank God your mom actually let me in the door. Not that I would expect anything less from Mrs. D. She's been pretty amazing through all this, huh? They all have, except maybe your dad at the beginning. But it seems like he came to his senses, long before I did, anyway."

I couldn't stop myself from smiling at that. "They have been pretty amazing. And so has Hannah. And Jesse. But that's a long story for another time."

"I was dying to know more about him," she said, grinning back at me. "He seems like a really great guy, Meen. Not that Nate wasn't great for you, at least in his great Nate way, but Jesse . . . Jesse seems pretty special, at least from what I've seen. And trust me, that's more than a month of watching his eloquent speech every night, so I know what I'm talking about."

"Yeah, Jesse is definitely *special*," I said, a happy glow at just the thought of him beaming down on me, warming me from the inside out—until I remembered all the ways I'd hurt him, all the words I could never undo. But Izzy being right here, right now, gave me faith that even the most brutal, bone-deep wounds could be healed, that the scars they left could strengthen us rather than tear us apart. "It's funny, you know, how, before all this happened, I would have bet everything that Nate and I would be together forever. *Forever.*" I laughed, the absurd permanence of the word sounding so silly and useless to me now.

"But when it came down to it, when I *really* needed him to trust me, he couldn't do it. My promises weren't enough for him. But Jesse—Jesse barely knew me at all, and he still had faith in me. Jesse took a chance. He was willing to believe in the impossible. And Nate will never be able to do that. It's not his fault, really, that he couldn't trust me. He's wired to only see the things that he can explain, the proven, the rational, the expected. And maybe that's how I used to be, too. But that's not my world anymore. My world is a whole lot more gray than that. And I'm okay with it. I kind of like the gray better."

"I want to live in that gray world with you," Izzy said quietly, her face so solemn and serious, she suddenly looked like a much older, wiser Isabelle.

With that I could feel every last block Izzy and I had built between us falling away. I felt lighter than I had in months, as if there was nothing, no one pressing me down. Before I could analyze that feeling, second-guess whether I was letting go too fast, forgiving too hastily, I floated over to my bed and wrapped my arms around her. She squealed as she pressed up against my belly, cupping her hands around my baby for the first time.

"Really, I just couldn't stand the idea that Hannah would be the godmother over me. I've always expected the co-godmother role, like an avant-garde lesbian godmother couple."

We both lost it over that, collapsing on my bed in hysterical giggles.

"So can I join in on the party, ladies?"

I jumped to see Hannah leaning against the doorframe, a massive smile nearly splitting her face across the middle.

"Thanks, Hannah, for inviting this wench to my party," I said, lazily hitting Izzy over the head with my pillow. "You can escort her out now, please."

"Even I'm impressed by how well I worked my magic," Hannah said, hopping up onto the bed and wriggling in between us. "This feels right, doesn't it?"

"It doesn't feel too awful, I suppose," Izzy said, propping herself on her elbow as she smiled over at us.

"As long as you brought a ridiculously nice present, I guess I'm okay with you being here." I reached across Hannah and grabbed Izzy by the shoulder, pulling the three of us together in a tight huddle. "Promise me that this won't ever happen again. Promise me that whatever absolutely crazy and absurd things happen in our lives, we don't run away from one another. And we don't *let* any of us run away, either. Each of us could have tried harder."

We all reached our pinkies out and squeezed them in a knot, our sacred, unspoken oath.

"Well, then, now that we have that cleared up, I do believe there's a baby shower happening downstairs for you, Mina," Hannah said, hopping up from the bed. "Dr. Keller and Mrs. Lewis are here already. They're waiting for the guest of honor to make her appearance."

"Ugh. My hair looks like shit." I pushed myself up and tried frantically to smooth down the frizz.

"You're pregnant. Your hair's allowed to look like shit," Izzy said.

"Man, how I've missed your brilliant humor."

"Get used to it, Mama. You're going to be hearing it for the rest of your life."

I could feel my dad hovering throughout the shower, a static buzz in the background that I couldn't ignore. I was surprised that he was there at all, really, and not tinkering out in the garage or huddled up in his room with the door closed tight and some sort of sports news on the TV. He looked painfully anxious, as if he was just waiting for the shower to end and the ladies to leave. I couldn't shut him out of my peripheral—couldn't stop wondering what it was that had him so worked up. But I was in the middle of a circle of women, oohing and ahing over fuzzy onesies and miniature stuffed animals, and any sort of momentary escape was impossible.

As soon as the last present was opened, I excused myself for the bathroom and ducked into the hallway, hoping that my dad would still be poking around in the kitchen where I'd last seen him. He was there, luckily, standing by the large bay window with his back to me as I walked into the room.

"Dad?" I asked quietly, to avoid startling him. "What's wrong? You seem so tense."

He turned to me, his face gray against the dark blue of his sweater. My stomach swelled with dread. "What is it? What's happening?"

"I've been following things online, Mina, and there's been a sort of leak today about some plans that people have. Angry people. People who can't accept that you're sticking by your story. I think they're making plans to all come together, to meet in Green Hill maybe, some kind of crazy protest mob. The details are a little hazy online, but I think it's happening soon. More than a few people are referencing the *plan*. I don't like it, Mina. I don't want these people anywhere near you. Anywhere near our family."

"Can you . . ." I choked, the words constricting in my throat. "Can you call the police?"

"Of course I can call the police," he grunted. "And I

will, but they've been pretty damn useless so far. Driving a few rounds during the night to make sure everything's looking normal, but other than that, what have they done?"

Police weren't the only ones patrolling at night, keeping watch over our house—I'd heard my dad shuffling and creaking around downstairs off and on for the past few weeks, and I'd seen the dark circles under his eyes, the new flecks of silver in his hair. The fear was taking its toll on all of us, but it was hitting him the hardest. He wanted to be our protector. He *needed* to be.

"People still call," he said. "People still write. They're a crew of small town cops up against an enemy they can't begin to compete with, and an enemy they may even agree with." He looked apologetic about that last part, but kept going. "We need to find out as much as we can on our own first. We need to find out what we're really up against before we can decide on anything else. But we're not going to sit around and do nothing, goddamn it. We're not just going to let them win."

"What's going on?"

I turned to see Izzy and Hannah standing in the doorway.

"Who's not going to win what?" Izzy asked, her eyes shifting from me to my dad.

"My dad thinks there's going to be some sort of protest. An organized event in Green Hill, maybe."

Hannah gasped, her eyes widening with alarm. Izzy reached an arm around her shoulders to steady her.

"So what are we going to do?" she asked. "What's the plan?"

"I . . . I don't know. I have to think about it," I said, dropping into a kitchen chair. "I guess I shouldn't be completely surprised that this is happening. I mean, really, it's only been building up to this, right? The more pregnant I am, the closer I get to having this baby, the more the tension is rising, and they couldn't possibly just let it all go. Not now, not after they've put this much attention on me for the last few months."

"I don't think it can just be you versus them," Hannah said, her voice shaky, barely above a whisper. "Or even us versus them. I don't think we can stop them from meeting, not if they're not technically doing anything illegal. But maybe we can help bring out other voices, too, the people who have been supporting you, especially since the video went out. The people who believe you—the people who would be outraged that this, this . . . this *hate group* . . . is taking it so far. What if they came, too? What if they all came?"

Izzy whistled and sagged against the doorframe. "That sounds like an epic battle, Han. A little too explosive, maybe."

"Maybe, but maybe an explosion is what we need to

blow everyone else away. I mean, it can't keep going on like this, can it? Something has to be done. And if we can't stop them from coming, the least we can do is make sure it's a balanced fight, right?"

"Jesus, Han, you've certainly changed in six months."

"It's been a long six months, Izzy." Hannah sighed. Izzy's cheeks flamed, and she looked down at the tiled floor.

"I don't know, Han, it does sound a little risky." I looked up at my dad, waiting for his vote.

"She might be right," he said, turning back to stare out the front window. "If we can't stop them, we do the best we can to show that we're not alone. It will at least make me feel like you're less vulnerable if there are other people standing in front of you. It's either that . . . It's that, Mina, or we take you away from here. You leave Green Hill and hide out, at least until everything cools off. Protecting you and the baby is my first priority."

It wasn't as if this idea were new to me—it was exactly what I had promised myself I'd do if necessary on that dark, gloomy car ride back from Long Beach Island. And I had thought about it the very first time Gracie told me that she was scared for our safety. But now that I was getting so close to the end, now that Izzy was back, I wasn't ready to let go of my life here. I wasn't ready to surrender.

"No," I said, shaking my head. "That seems like giving in

to them. Everyone will be fine, no matter who comes and who doesn't come. The worst they can do is hold signs and scream names at me, and trust me, there's nothing I haven't heard before."

My dad dropped his fist against the wooden table, banging a few times without saying a word. Knocking on wood. The action, so subconscious and immediate, made me shiver. I usually laughed when he did that, an old family joke, since none of us were actually superstitious enough to believe in jinxes. But no one laughed this time. I was actually thankful he had done it. Just in case.

I needed anything—any kind of luck or good fortune I could get.

Anything that would keep me and my baby safe.

chapter nineteen

Once word of the official meeting was leaked, none of the details were hard to come by. One of my more fanatical critics had rented out the Green Hill Firehouse for the meeting, and since there wasn't anything technically illegal about the protest, the powers that be at the firehouse couldn't stop it from happening. Or maybe they didn't want to stop it in the first place, since they very well might have been at home painting their own anti-Mina signs and T-shirts.

And as it turned out, when word spread and the media picked up on the event, I didn't have to do much to rally my supporters. They were outraged enough as it was, and once a leader seemed to emerge, the voice of Team Mina—a feisty fiftysomething woman named Stella from Philly with a background in social advocacy—it was clear that they would be coming to the meeting, too.

"We're going to be there for you, Mina," Stella had

said to me on the phone a few days after the shower. "Don't you worry about that for a minute." I'd reached out to her after she'd first spoken up online about the protest. I was thankful, but even more, I was curious. Curious about how a stranger could care this much about my cause, about protecting me from "injustice."

"It's not right what those people are doing to you, and it's about time they realize how far they've overstepped." She'd paused then and took a deep breath that I could hear rattle against the phone. "Look, Mina, truthfully, I'm not sure what I believe about all this, but that part doesn't matter to me. I believe in your right to privacy. And there are plenty of people who *do* believe you. Good and honest people who have more faith in this world than I may have. But I have faith in the fact that it's the right thing to do, standing up for you. Faith is all different things to all different people. Faith is trust. And I feel the trust in my bones, Mina. You can't always explain feelings like this. You just do. You just act."

I'd hung up feeling stronger than ever. But more nervous than ever, too.

I couldn't let Stella down. I couldn't let any of these people down.

The big day—Saturday, February 16—arrived sooner than I would have liked, but time was moving strangely in general, too fast and too slow all at once. I was officially full-term, just three weeks left before March 7, though really it could happen at any time now—a crazy idea that made my heart race and my palms sweat every time I thought about it. And I couldn't *stop* thinking about it. I was ready for the baby to be out, ready to have my body back, ready to not feel so tired and achy and stretched to the absolute limit. But I was also *not* ready at all—not ready to put my mothering skills to the test, not ready to see how the media would react once there was an actual child, breathing, crying, laughing. Existing.

We had decided not to go anywhere near the firehouse, of course, but the local news and possibly even national outlets would be covering the event and airing it live, so we wouldn't miss any of the action. Two police officers were stationed in a car in our driveway, just in case any stragglers made a pit stop here on their way to the main event. I still couldn't really comprehend the purpose of physically meeting—why the online forum wasn't enough of a space to bash me. What more was there to say? Why could they not just move on and get back to the business of living their own lives? The time and the effort they funneled into this, it never ceased to amaze and horrify me—their single-minded, long-term dedication to this *cause*.

Hannah and Izzy, Jesse, my parents, were all there in the living room with me, hunched in front of the TV, waiting for any news updates to come in. Gracie was staying over at Aunt Vera's and was strictly forbidden from following any of the coverage. My parents had thought it would be too much for her, and they had stuck to their decision, no matter how many times she had begged them to change their minds. As much as I wanted her calming presence, my parents were right. She'd already grown up too fast in the last six months.

I was glad Jesse had come, though. He hadn't set foot inside of our house since first showing us the footage, though he still insisted on driving me to and from school. He sat with us at lunch, too, but his mind seemed to spend most of the period somewhere else entirely, that distracted, distant look back in his eyes. In the tense moments we found ourselves alone together, in the car or between classes, I had made a few awkward attempts to apologize for New Year's. But he always cut me off, changed the subject, or cranked the stereo louder. I gave up then on trying for forgiveness. I didn't deserve it, for one, and maybe it was easier for him to hold on to his grudge. Maybe it was helping both of us to let go gradually, to make the inevitable ending less abrupt.

Because the truth was, once the baby was born—once things settled down and my world felt at least a little bit safer again—his obligation as my guardian could end, any promise to Iris more than fulfilled. He would go off to college, and I'd still be here, in Green Hill. Jesse didn't owe me anything. He certainly wasn't duty bound to me for life.

But he was here today, and I was thankful for that much.

At exactly noon the live coverage started, and my stomach burned at the image on the screen: hundreds of people squeezed into the firehouse, and from what I could see, bursting out the door and into the parking lot. I could only hope that some of them at least were Stella's supporters, because the thought that every single one of those people on the screen was against me—it was inconceivable. T-shirts, banners, posters with my name on it, bright and bold, were broadcasting their messages of hate and anger. I could hear chants, too, rippling under the loud hum of voices echoing in the large, brick-lined hall. I had read hundreds, maybe thousands of messages online, but none of that had prepared me for this—a living, breathing mass of people, actual faces to go with the names, the slurs, the threats. My enemies were no longer black-and-white words and thumbnail photos on my computer screen or hollow voices on the other end of the phone line. They were there, together and unified, just a few streets away.

"I just don't get it." Hannah sighed. "I don't understand what they really want to get out of this. Like, what does yelling and bitching about you all in one room together really accomplish?"

"Unless there's more to it than we know," my dad said quietly. The thought gave me chills, and I leaned closer into Hannah to warm myself.

"So you think there's an ulterior motive to meeting today?" Jesse asked, the first time he'd really spoken up all day.

"I just get the sense that there's something bigger. Why else come all the way to Green Hill? It just doesn't add up." My dad frowned at the TV and reached for the remote to turn up the volume as the reporter came on-screen.

"We're told that a speech will be starting momentarily, to be given by longtime Green Hill resident Tana Fritz."

I sighed out loud, shaking my head in bewilderment. Another strike from the Fritzes. The petition—which must have failed, seeing as Green Hill High still hadn't booted me—the website, now Tana, heading up a protest. Taking it upon herself to be the voice of the town, the public defender of morality and ethics. But she, like her daughter, had never once in all these months reached out to me directly—never once tried to fill in the other half of the story. Her own life must be very sad and very pathetic if she could spend so much energy trying to tear mine down.

"That woman," my mom muttered, squinting at the screen. "I swear, she thinks she's the damn mayor of this town."

We sat in silence while the reporter walked outside of

the firehouse to show us the parking lot, which was even more crowded than I could have imagined—a rowdy line of people winding around the side of the building, others bundled up and crammed in lawn chairs set outside of their cars. One man actually seemed to have some sort of electric grill propped up on the bed of his truck, a handwritten sign on it advertising two-dollar hot dogs and sausage sandwiches. It was surreal, completely surreal, like some sort of bizarre tailgate leading up to the big event, only there was no epic sports game or performer set to hit the stage. They were there for me—to attack me or to support me. I did, thankfully, see some pro-Mina banners hovering on the outskirts of the main line. Some of them had shown up at least, driving who knows how many miles just to make sure their voices were heard, too.

We were shifted back into the main room, which Tana was now presiding over, standing behind a makeshift raised podium in the front. She had on a crisp tweed pantsuit and pearls, and I'd have bet money that she'd gone to the salon for a blowout in honor of the big day, with her brassy gold hair so flawlessly bobbed around her chin.

"We are here in this town today"—she looked around the room, hands raised in welcoming—"for one reason. We are here because of Mina Dietrich—because of the lies and the slander of our religions, the abomination of our sacred beliefs that has persisted for months now.

Despite our different backgrounds, our different faiths, and our different scriptures, we are here because our morals and our ethics align. We are here because together we are stronger—together we can help to put an end to the lies. Together we can succeed in cleansing this town, our nation, the world. Mina Dietrich must come to understand that her lies must end, especially as we continue to watch others fall blindly into her deception, the increasing number of supporters who are even here amongst us today. They have deceived themselves into honoring this false idol, making a mockery of the truths of our religions that we hold so dear.

"We have gathered here to extend our request. We ask that Mina Dietrich publicly admit that this child was not conceived from some higher power. We ask that she back down from her claims and remove herself from the public eye, before any more innocent followers are ruined along her path. And, furthermore, we ask that she give this child up for adoption, place this innocent baby in the hands of more capable, rational parents who can give him or her a better life. The thought of this baby in the arms of such a young, unstable mother chills me." Tana shuddered and slammed her fist against the podium. "I call to the authorities to recognize this, to mandate the removal of the child immediately after birth if Mina Dietrich refuses on her own accord. We cannot stand idle. We cannot close our eyes and our ears to the madness happening around us.

"And now . . . we march. We march to Mina's house and we make our requests known. We will stand proud, united, and determined for as long as necessary to achieve our victory." Anxious murmurs hissed across the banquet room, punctuated by enthusiastic whistles and catcalls.

Our living room, however, was silent except for the ticking of the grandfather clock and the sound of our own heavy breathing. No matter how many breaths I took, I couldn't get enough air into my lungs, and pinpricks of black seemed to float in and out of my vision. I blinked, trying to recall everything that I'd just heard.

Tana, the protesters, coming to my house.

My dad was out on the porch yelling at the police officers before I'd even realized he'd left the living room, and he sounded more upset—more scared—than I'd ever heard him in my life.

"What now?" I whispered. "We just wait? How are what, all five maybe, of the Green Hill cops going to handle them?"

I should have left town, should have taken my dad's advice more seriously. My baby was in danger now. We all were.

"They're not going to come inside, Mina. We're fine as long as we stay here," my mom said, though her voice sounded even flimsier than mine. "The cops will get it sorted, I'm sure. These people can't just camp out on our lawn forever."

"I don't want them here at all," I said, trying to ignore the frantic pounding of my heart against my rib cage. "I don't want them anywhere near me and the baby."

"Damn it!" my dad erupted, slamming the front door behind him and stomping back into the living room. "Damn them, damn all of them!"

The next five, ten, fifteen minutes passed in slow motion, the pause between each tick of the clock seeming to stretch longer than the one before it. The live stream had stopped abruptly amid the chaos of the crowd's mass exodus, and an infomercial was airing instead. The reporter had apologized, explaining that they'd be back on the scene as soon as they'd relocated to the next destination. Hopewell Lane, our home.

Two more cop cars had pulled into the driveway, and the officers were powwowing with speakerphones in hand out front. My dad and Izzy checked all the locks before standing watch, my dad by the bay window in the kitchen and Izzy peeking out the glass windows framing our front door. The rest of them seemed to subconsciously circle in on me tight like a cocoon, as if their presence was enough to keep me safe and untouched.

But then I heard it, we all did—the sound of voices

yelling in unison in the distance, the roar growing louder and louder until Izzy screamed, "They're here!" and we all stared, dazed, down the hallway that led to the door.

"They're in our driveway!" my dad yelled from the kitchen. "They're standing on our goddamn property! Why aren't the cops bombing them with tear gas?"

I stood up without deciding to move, my curiosity yanking me toward the front of the house. I had to watch them for myself, because the idea of not seeing the enemy, not knowing their exact moves as they made them, was even scarier than whatever image was waiting for me outside.

I stepped behind Izzy, and she shifted to make room for me in front of the glass panes, wrapping her arm around my waist as we watched together. Tana Fritz was leading the procession, megaphone to her lips as she repeated the same line, over and over, the words crashing against me harder and angrier each time: "Give up the truth and give up the baby, give up the truth and give up the baby, give up . . ."

Jesse and Hannah leaned in behind us. We stayed like that, as close to the glass as we dared to get, clumped into a quiet huddle for what felt like hours but must have been just minutes. There were two clear camps, two groups that edged closer and closer toward an invisible central barrier: the protesters, with their anti-Mina signs and sentiments filling the driveway and overflowing into the field that ran along the edge of Hopewell Lane, and the supporters, who were even bolder in their movements, pressing up above the driveway and into our actual yard, forming a sort of defensive line between me and my enemies. The cops were scattered and patrolling on all sides, yelling into megaphones and waving the mob off, but no one seemed to be obeying. There was too much power in their numbers.

I spotted Stella as she pushed farther toward where the protesters stood, her OPEN HEARTS, OPEN MINDS FOR MINA sign flapping high in her outstretched arms above her head. Her dark braided hair, threaded with strands of glowing copper, was loose around her face, and she looked fierce as she fought to scream over the megaphones. In a move that happened so fast I nearly missed it with a blink, Stella was on top of Tana as they both tumbled to the ground.

After a split second of stunned amazement on both sides, the two crowds merged, our front yard suddenly a clashing of two armies, poster sticks flailing, arms held up over faces in defense.

I flinched at the sound of a shrill, grating whimper before I realized that it was coming out of my own throat. I grabbed my belly, swallowing the urge to be sick all over the foyer floor.

"I can't," I whispered, resting my palm against the

cool glass. "I can't let people hurt each other over me. I can't just stand here and watch this."

Before anyone could stop me—before I could stop myself—I twisted the lock and flung the door open, hurtling myself down the front step and onto the porch.

"Stop!" I screamed, my one voice nothing against the howling of the warring mobs. "Stop!" I tried again. "Just *stop*!"

One person noticed me, and then another, until word of my appearance snaked its way through the crowd. Fists and feet froze midfight, and faces tilted toward me, alone on the porch in my baggy maternity sweatshirt and plaid flannel pajama pants.

"Stop!" I yelled again, this time with all eyes on me. "Stop fighting over me. Go back to your own lives and let me live mine. I never asked for this. I never asked for your opinions. Let God—or some other higher power—do the judging here. You have no right to ask anything of me."

"Mina, get back in here," my dad called from behind me, his voice shrill and panicked. But before I could turn back to him, I watched as the crowd surged forward—my supporters first, excitedly chanting my name, and the anti-Mina protesters chasing close behind them.

There was a large man leading the pack, tall and broad, his silvery hair long and gnarled around the shoulders of his ratty black leather jacket. He was on the steps, and then the porch, and others were right behind him, reaching out toward me, touching my belly, yelling my name. Soon there were more people, more and more, and somehow I fell down—no, I was pushed—my back slamming against the wooden boards below me, and I looked up and saw faces, so many faces . . .

Iris, that was Iris just above me, fighting back that man who was two or three times her size. She looked so strong, so furious.

And then in a blurry whirl of skin and lips and teeth and hands, clawing hands, everything stopped.

Everything disappeared.

I heard a faint rustling, a crisp, familiar sound that I tried to place. My eyes were still closed, but everything around me seemed bright, too bright, white and sharp and hot against my eyelids. I focused on the ground beneath me instead, hard and solid, with uneven grooves that pressed into my back. A breeze laced with pine and damp earth swept over me, and I knew. The tree house. I was in the tree house. But I was warm, and it was February, and none of it made any sense. How was I in the tree house?

I willed my eyes open, clenching my fists as I put all my energy into that one tiny movement. Light spilled in and I squinted, tears pricking from the brightness.

"I'm here, Mina." A soft voice floated above me. "I'm here with you." I tilted my head and saw a hazy form, a silhouette darkened by the sunlight pouring in from behind.

"I'm sorry that it all went so far, Mina. I'm sorry that you faced that kind of danger. I should have helped sooner. I know that now." She sighed as she stepped forward, the details of her face filling in.

"Iris," I whispered. My hand reached out, needing to touch her, to feel her skin beneath my fingers. She knelt down next to me, resting her warm palm—her wonderfully real, solid palm—on my forehead.

"I had hoped that I wouldn't have to step in, Mina. That there was enough good in this world to protect you without our help. I wanted to believe that. But it's obvious now that the world needs you and this baby more than we had even realized."

"But why me, Iris? Why me? What can *I* do? I'm no one. I'm nothing." I wanted to scream, wanted to cry, but I didn't have the energy for either.

She smiled at me as she reached to clasp my hand in hers.

"Why *not* you, Mina? That's the right question. Because you are so much more than nothing. You are so much more than you realize. No matter how scared you felt, or how alone, or how angry, you always chose this baby. Even before you could admit it to yourself, you *believed* in this baby. There are very few people who could have been capable of that. You possess so much more strength and resolve than you give yourself credit for." She paused for a breath and squeezed my hand even more tightly. "Remember that *you* are special, too, Mina—you have never been just a simple carrier. You are very much an essential part of all this. Your life matters, too."

I breathed in her words, letting them fill every dark, empty place where I had hidden away any of my lingering doubts. I valued this baby, of course I did—but I valued myself, too, and I deserved my own happiness. College, a career, goals for my future. And love. I deserved to let myself be in love. And that didn't make me selfish or flawed or destined to be a bad mom. It just made me human. It made me whole and full and alive.

I let the relief linger for another brief moment, a shimmering golden bubble floating within the grasp of my fingertips. But I needed to focus now—there were still so many questions, so much more I needed Iris to tell me before she left again.

"But what now, Iris? What do I do now?" I closed my eyes, the weight of so much emotion pressing down against me.

"You wait, Mina. You just take care of yourself and this precious baby for now. The time will come. You'll know when it does."

Her voice was fading now, her hand seeming to melt away from my own.

"Have faith, Mina—in this child, but also in *yourself.* You must always have faith. Because faith . . . faith is what makes our lives worth living."

chapter twenty

When I opened my eyes again, I was staring at a tile ceiling, a strip of fluorescent lights beaming down on me. I turned my head, desperate, searching for Iris, until the details of the room clicked into place—the counter crowded with swabs and cotton balls, the collection of brown medicine bottles and shiny metal instruments, the slick crinkle of paper on the exam table beneath me.

"Mina?"

Dr. Keller appeared, hovering over me, her eyes lit up with relief.

"You're awake, thank God." She reached a hand out, pressing her cool, smooth skin against my cheek. "You've been in and out for almost an hour now. Do you remember what happened?"

I shut my eyes and reached back toward Iris, the intense light that I could still feel, burning, radiating inside of me. She *had* been real. She had to have been real. I squeezed my hands into balls, fighting against the sudden emptiness I felt without her standing next to me.

But I realized as I squeezed that there was something in my right palm, the hand Iris had touched just seconds before. I released my fingers slowly and glanced down, trying not to draw Dr. Keller's attention.

It was a leaf. A bright green maple leaf.

Which was impossible, because it was February, and all the maple leaves had long ago fallen to the ground, shriveled into broken flecks of brown and black under the winter's snow.

But there it was, in my hand.

I had been in the tree house, warm and sunny.

I had seen Iris.

I wrapped my fingers back around the leaf. It was my secret, at least for now.

Strength swelled through me, filling every last piece of me with reassurances. Or maybe, it was as Iris had said—not just strength, but *faith*. A laugh and a sob both hit me at once, a hysterical choking sound that made Dr. Keller reach out for me in a panic.

"Oh no, Mina," Dr. Keller said, squeezing my shoulder. "I should have said right away. The baby is fine. I've checked the heartbeat, and everything is fine. Your baby is safe and strong, and so are you."

I'd known the baby would be fine, of course. Iris

would have told me otherwise. But I was still overcome with relief to hear the words from Dr. Keller's mouth, to know without a doubt that my baby was still here with me, that we were fighting—and winning—together. Any other answer wouldn't have made sense to me. I couldn't begin to imagine my world without this baby anymore, what my life would look like without his or her fragile little spirit growing inside of me, making me a better and more whole person, making my life deeper and richer and *happier*—a kind of happy I wouldn't have understood before Iris stepped into my world and changed everything.

But there were still roadblocks to cross, questions to answer, before I could start feeling too content.

"What's happening?" I asked, trying to push myself up to sit. "How did I get here? Where is everyone else?"

"Your parents and your friends are in the waiting room, and will all be enormously relieved to know you're awake. From what I hear, your dad and Jesse managed to carry you back inside, and your friend Izzy drove her Jeep through the crowd and pulled around to the back of the house to pick you up. Most people were clearing out as soon as you went down, though. For as threatening and determined as they may have tried to sound, I suspect most of them hadn't planned on actual violence. But then again, most violence isn't planned, is it? The heat of the moment is a powerful force."

She leaned down to lightly kiss my forehead. "You've been unconscious since you got here, but your vitals have been fine. No signs of premature labor. I was about to take you to the hospital, though, if you'd been unconscious much longer. You had us worried. It was like you didn't want to wake up."

"No," I said, my lips curling into a small smile. "I think I just wasn't ready." Not until after Iris was finished with me.

"Mina."

The door opened, and my mom peered in, her eyes red and swollen. "We thought we heard voices. Oh, thank God, you're okay. We were so scared. So scared." She rushed over to me, sweeping Dr. Keller aside as she lifted me up into her arms. My dad came in after her, but Hannah, Izzy, and Jesse trailed behind, waiting at the door.

"Come on, guys," I said, waving them in. "You're family, too. Don't be so silly."

For the next few minutes we were all a tangle of arms and hair and tears, until finally, after everyone had been adequately squeezed and comforted, we were quiet again—thinking about what would come next. What *should* come next.

Dr. Keller coughed and edged her way to the center of the room.

"I want to propose something," she said, her eyes fixed on me. "As far as anyone else knows, you were ambushed by a crowd and knocked unconscious, rushed away for medical assistance. No one else but the people in this room right now know that the baby is fine. What I'm suggesting, what might be easier for you, Mina, for everyone—is that we keep this our secret. We tell the rest of the world that you lost the baby. That you're leaving town to recover and mourn after everything that's happened. And then you escape. You go somewhere, find a safe place to hide out, at least for now. Have this baby in peace. Figure out the rest of the plan one day at a time. People can speculate as much as they like, but according to the record—according to what I'm prepared to tell the staff here and the press and whoever else asks—there is no baby, not anymore. I'll worry about the details. Let everyone who was involved in the protest today think that the blood is partially on their hands. It's the least of what they deserve."

This wasn't a new suggestion, the idea of leaving, disappearing with the baby and starting over somewhere new. It was what I should have done straight after the shower, right when I'd first learned of the protest. But as I heard it all now, the details arranged out loud, each of Dr. Keller's words rained down on me like hot, biting pellets. A distant possibility had instantly become reality. The whole proposition was so sudden . . . but maybe so perfect, too— so much harder and somehow maybe so much simpler than anything else I'd already considered on my own.

"I . . ." I started and stopped, still too taken aback with the abruptness of it all. I tried to let the suggestion settle, to see if the parts all actually fit into a rational whole. Was it possible? Could I—could we—really pull this off? The idea that no one would have to know, that I could disappear, raise my baby in peace until . . . until when? Until Iris came back for us? Or forever?

"But what if I could never be Mina Dietrich again?" I asked, not able to look anyone in the eyes. My skin was hot and clammy, and I tugged at the neck of my sweatshirt for cooler air. "I can't ever really come back, can I? People—some people, at least—will always remember. Green Hill will always remember. I'll have to spend the rest of my life with a new identity."

I could never go home.

Or at least, not if I kept the baby. And giving the baby up, giving my little miracle away to strangers—that had never been an option, and it still wasn't.

I would miss my family. I would miss Izzy and Hannah. And *Jesse*. I would miss Jesse. I'd miss all the things I hated most about Green Hill, too, all the annoying little small-town quirks—the way that everybody knew who everybody was and everybody knew everybody's business.

I would miss Mina, the girl I'd been, the girl I'd known, for the last eighteen years.

Because without my family, without Green Hill, without my past . . . who would I be?

"What do you think?" I asked, lifting my head up to face all of them. "All of you, I want to hear what you think I should do."

My dad cleared his throat and we all turned to stare at him, waiting. "I think it's the only idea that makes sense right now. We all saw how crazy people can be when religion is in question, when basic beliefs are threatened. Maybe we'll come up with a better solution down the road, but for now . . . I think we get you out of Green Hill. I think we get you away from everyone."

"But how will we disguise her? Where will she go that no one will recognize her?" my mom asked, her eyes darting between me and my dad. "Who will go with her?" Her skin looked suddenly so sallow to me, so lined with stress, and I realized with absolute certainty that something had to change—that I couldn't keep putting all of them through this kind of anxiety.

"I have family in New York City," Jesse said quietly. "Brooklyn. An aunt and an uncle whose kids have all moved out. Mina could stay there, at least for a little while, until she can find a place of her own. New York seems like a good place to disappear, no?"

"Oh, I don't know," my mom said, biting her lip as she wrapped her hands protectively around my wrist. "Mina, alone in the city, and I can't ask your family to take her in like that..."

"I would go, too," Jesse said. "I was already planning on living with them this fall. When school started. I'll just move in a little earlier than expected."

My head snapped up in his direction. But just as quickly he looked down at his feet, leaving me alone with the dizzying rush of the possibility of it—of me and Jesse, together, running away to New York City to start a new life.

"You can visit, of course," he continued, "though I have a feeling people would try following you, at least at the beginning. I don't think Mina will have to do much—a different hairstyle, maybe, and a different name—but other than that, she'll just be another pregnant woman in New York. Another young single mom. My aunt homeschooled my cousins, so she can help us finish out school that way, and I can do odd jobs for now—work at a restaurant, apply for film crews. And then once Mina has the baby, well... we can figure the rest out then."

I couldn't fight the feeling that this wasn't the first time Jesse had thought through his suggestion—it seemed too polished, too logical for him to have come up with it on the spot. Had he been thinking about this exact setup that day on the beach in LBI, talking about the future? Maybe if things had gone differently from there, if I hadn't said what I did on New Year's Eve... would we have had this conversation sooner? Before things had gone so far?

I would never know. But I could accept the offer now. I could walk into this new era, start my new life—and I wouldn't have to be alone.

"I think it makes sense," I said, before anyone else could challenge me with a list of reasons for why it couldn't possibly work.

"I agree," my dad said, clapping a hand on Jesse's shoulder.

"Me, too," Izzy said. "But I'll miss you. At least it's only two hours away . . . I can visit. We can all visit."

"And if I go to NYU . . ." Hannah trailed off, leaning in to hug me.

My eyes drifted from face to face, and in each expression I saw the same mix of fear and hope and acceptance that I felt pulsing through me, growing thicker and heavier with every breath. Maybe the plan was rushed, maybe flaws would snag us somewhere along the way, but this was the best we had. This was the only way forward I could see.

"Well, then," I said, my gaze stopping on Jesse, my cheeks burning when I found his warm brown eyes finally meeting mine. "I guess we're going to New York City."

Jesse's uncle Carl volunteered to drive us up to his sister's home in Brooklyn as soon as we could be packed and ready to go. We left in the middle of the night, the back of

―――― Immaculate ――――

Carl's van filled with my new crib and stroller and all the presents from the shower. My parents had wanted to come up, too, but we decided it was for the best that they lie low, and keep the reporters and any lingering detractors or followers guessing about when and how I had left. Dr. Keller had executed her role in the whole scheme perfectly—in the interview that was looping over television and the Internet, she played the part of the devastated, infuriated doctor so well that even I could almost believe she was telling the truth: "A baby has been killed. A young woman is heartbroken, destroyed. Robbed of her child's existence. Because of senseless violence and ignorant hatred. I hope those responsible acknowledge their blame in this. I hope the country—the world—has learned a valuable lesson about the media's power of destruction."

I had planned to stay awake for the drive, desperate to memorize every last detail of this monumental life journey. But instead I fell asleep before we were even out of Pennsylvania, my head propped too comfortably against Jesse's shoulder. I didn't open my eyes again until I heard the sound of Frank Sinatra's "New York, New York" blaring from the radio as we drove through the Holland Tunnel. Carl was grinning at me in the rearview mirror, bopping his head along to the beat—to the lyrics about leaving behind small-town blues, heading into the big city for a brand-new start.

"Jesse's song request for our grand entry. Welcome to

New York, kid," he sang out over the lyrics, rolling down his window to let in a blast of frosty winter air.

We pulled out of the fluorescently lit tunnel and into the city streets, the sky pinkish-gray as the first trace of morning sunlight fought to rise above the towering skyline. For the rest of the ride across lower Manhattan, I stared wide-eyed out the window, my nose practically smearing against the glass. I had only been to New York a few times growing up, and always for typically touristy reasons—the Met, a Broadway play, the Statue of Liberty. But now I looked out at it from a new perspective, amazed by how many delis there were, how many coffee shops and pizza places and Chinese takeout restaurants we passed, dozens on every block.

There were people everywhere, but they weren't the Times Square tourists who were still asleep in their hotel rooms, hours away from starting on the day's itinerary. They were New Yorkers, *real* New Yorkers—heads ducked against the early morning cold, walking so briskly and with so much purpose that I could barely catch a glimpse of them as they streamed along the sidewalks.

I found Jesse's hand on the seat next to mine and squeezed it in my palm.

This wasn't anything like Green Hill. This was an entirely different world.

By the time we crossed the bridge into Brooklyn, the

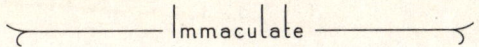

fresh orange sun shining along the East River, I knew that I would be okay.

I knew that this could be home.

I stuck to my plan of having a home birth, though the home itself was very different from the house on Hopewell Lane that I'd pictured. But Jesse's aunt and uncle, Maria and Tony Russo, had made me feel as if I belonged in their homey, well-worn brownstone from the minute I arrived. They cooked all my meals and refused to let me lift a finger toward housework no matter how much I insisted, and they were always adding to the growing collection of diapers and bottles and wipes to prepare for the baby's arrival. So I spent my days instead studying with Jesse under Maria's instruction, determined to get through as much material as possible before the baby arrived. My senior year might have been very different from the one I'd imagined for myself for so long, but I would still have a diploma at the end, and I would still have options, open doors, for my future. I wouldn't be Green Hill High's valedictorian, but I had achieved so much more than just a string of perfect scores.

When my mind couldn't absorb any more equations or theorems or definitions, I busied myself with knitting, another subject Maria was well versed in, and I'd already finished my first pair of nearly identifiable baby socks. Knitting kept me sane, distracted me from thoughts of the world beyond our brownstone. The television news was rarely on, and I used the Internet strictly for studying—no Virgin Mina site updates, no social media—but from the bits and scraps that I did see, I could tell that I was no longer a major story. The anchors had moved on—all hoping to wipe away any unpleasant reminders of their guilt as quickly as possible.

But not everyone was forgetting and forgiving themselves so quickly. According to my parents, the town of Green Hill in particular was attempting to absolve itself with an onslaught of casseroles and flower displays and fruit baskets. Sympathy cards were flooding our mailbox from across the globe, more and more each day—so many that the post office was making a separate trip to our house every afternoon with an overfilled sack of paper apologies. Someday maybe I would open them. But I wasn't ready for any pardons. Not yet. Not until my baby was safely, finally in my arms.

I felt the first contractions two weeks after the day we arrived, a week before my official due date. Dr. Keller and my parents and Gracie were all packed in the van and on the road within minutes of my call, and were somehow, miraculously, knocking on the door almost a half hour before we expected them.

Immaculate

My mom and Dr. Keller never left my side during the next fourteen hours of painkiller-free labor, rubbing cool cloths along my forehead, counting my breaths, letting me claw against their arms as I did my best not to scream, terrified that neighbors would alert the cops if they heard.

I felt as if I were being pulled apart, inside out, and in my most delusional flashes of pain, I was tormented with the fear that this was to be my ultimate punishment—that I was becoming unmade and undone, nothing more than a heap of broken, bloody pieces. But in the darkest moments, I imagined Iris's voice in my ear—or was she really there somehow, inside my head?—whispering encouragement, telling me that I'd be fine, that it would all be over soon.

Just when I thought that I couldn't take a second more, that my body and mind couldn't possibly go through any more torture, I heard the cry. A long, earsplitting wail that was without a doubt the most beautiful noise I'd ever experienced. I pushed again with Dr. Keller's command, harder, pulling together every last bit of energy I could find.

And then I felt the baby, *my baby*, slip out of me. I heard Dr. Keller and my mom shrieking and crying with joy, and I watched from the corner of my tired, tired eyes as they cleaned a tiny face, a tiny body.

And then there the baby was—there *she* was, my little

girl—so pink and wrinkly and perfect, wrapped in a soft yellow blanket and resting in my arms.

I had just said my weepy, grateful good-byes to Dr. Keller and my family, all of whom had spent the last two days since the baby was born alternatingly cooing, crying—happy, relieved, amazed tears—and waiting on both of us hand and foot. My parents had promised to visit again as soon as possible, hopefully with Hannah and Izzy the next time, but it still hurt to let them go. It was only now sinking in that I wouldn't be going back home with them.

I would never be going back home.

After they'd driven away, I shut myself up in my room, just me and my baby. It was the first time we'd been alone together, no grandparent or aunt or doting doctor hovering at our side. I was propped up in my bed, staring down at her precious face—staring, though I had certainly memorized every piece of her by now, every last wrinkle and freckle and adorable fluff of dark brown hair. I saw myself there, but I saw details that I couldn't identify, too, like a canvas that I'd started painting, but someone else had finished. She had my full lips and my round nose, and my wide eyes, eyes that were already bursting with curiosity and intelligence. But where my eyes were blue, hers were green. A piercing, emerald green, a green that you couldn't look away from once they'd caught you in their grip.

A green that I could never, would never forget.

She was mesmerizing, my still unnamed gorgeous baby girl—unnamed because nothing seemed right enough, perfect enough to capture everything that she was and everything that she could be. I was waiting for some sign, some bright flash of inspiration. I was also waiting for Iris to come back, though I had the sinking feeling that I wouldn't see her again for a while. Not until I really needed her.

The time will come, she'd said. *You'll know when it does.*

The words still gave me chills.

But I wanted more than that. I wanted to know what I was up against.

I wanted to know if my little girl would be obviously, glaringly *special*, and not just special in the way that most parents probably saw their own child. Would she be *too* different from other kids? Would other people see it, feel it somehow, a shimmer, a prickle, without understanding what it could possibly mean? Who she could possibly *be*? I hoped not, for her sake. I hoped not, with a dread and a conviction that I'd never felt before I'd held her in my arms. I wanted her to fit in, to be like every other kid. I wanted her to blend in with the rest of the world. Because what would happen to her if the truth came out? If people had fixated so fiercely on me—so much hate from some, so much adoration from others—I couldn't help but think it would be even worse for her. Much worse.

But—and this thought scraped at me, gnawed and bit and tugged no matter how hard I tried to keep it shackled down—why would she be here *at all* if her life would be a secret? There was a reason for this. Iris had made that much clear. And I doubted that the reason involved her living an ordinary, invisible kind of life.

I still hadn't told Jesse about that final moment with Iris, or about the leaf, which was now safely pressed between the pages of *Anne of Green Gables*, stowed in my purse for the journey to Brooklyn. There'd been too much else to think about since, but I would. I would tell him everything. I needed him to know, needed him to process, analyze, and hypothesize alongside of me. But we had time, surely? Time before my baby needed to be anything but a baby?

A knock on the door interrupted my thoughts. I took a deep breath, sweeping all the worries and unanswered questions back into their dark corner. My fingers trailed along the charm bracelet on my wrist, the birthday present from Gracie that I never took off, and I willed myself to remember that they were still there—that they were always still there, just a call or a two-hour drive away.

"Come in."

The door opened, and Jesse peeked in before stepping

into the room, carrying a tray with two steaming mugs and a plate of delicious-smelling chocolate chip cookies.

"I know you probably wanted to just be alone right now, but Maria baked these fresh for you," he said, a nervous smile on his lips. "She thought it would be the best cure for homesickness."

"She's so amazing," I said, patting the crumpled sheets on the bed next to me. He put the tray down on the nightstand and settled in beside me, reaching out to stroke the baby's dark and feathery hair. "And so are you." My cheeks flamed, but I kept going. "You're beyond amazing, really. I still can't believe everything you're sacrificing for me. I think I could spend the rest of my life thanking you and it still wouldn't be anywhere close to enough."

"There was no other choice, Mina," he said, his voice steady, so matter-of-fact as he turned his face to look me in the eyes. "You need a safe place for you and the baby. And I . . . well, I need you. I wasn't going to let you run away from me, too. Not a chance."

He reached out, his hand soft and gentle as he found my fingers and laced his around mine.

"It's not going to be easy," I said, though it was difficult to think properly with the sensation of his thumb rubbing circles on my palm. "It might never be easy."

Jesse leaned in closer, and I shut my eyes as his lips met mine. It was a very different kiss from that first eager, thrilling touch on my birthday or the desperate, pleading demand of New Year's Eve. This kiss was slow and sweet and steady. There was no rush, no urgency, because this kiss was a beginning. A promise.

After a few minutes we broke apart.

"I told you that night at Frankie's, out on the stoop. I want a little crazy in my life. Remember? And besides that, I made a promise to Iris . . ." He paused, his eyes burning into mine. "I saw her, Mina. At the protest. Only for a second or so, right when you went down. Maybe I imagined it, but she looked so real. So completely real. It's crazy, but I felt like she was looking out for you."

"It's not crazy," I said, feeling instantly lighter and more hopeful than I had in a very long time. "Not crazy at all."

I could tell that he wanted to ask more, but he didn't know where to start. "Iris . . ." He said, shaking his head.

"Iris," I repeated, the name a delicate, warming hum on my lips. "Has a nice ring to it, doesn't it?"

I smiled, raising my baby up to look straight into her perfect green eyes.

"Iris?" I looked at her and I knew. "Yes. *Iris*."

This is the end, but this is also the beginning.

This is the story that I'll wait to tell you until life—

inevitably, I suspect—forces the truth to the surface. A secret that I hope to keep buried until you are old enough to ask and understand your own questions. Old enough to know that life is not always what you expect, that reality is not always as neat and orderly as it may seem—and that there aren't always answers, as much as we want them, as hard as we may try to seek them out.

This is the story of how you came to be, of falling in love, of starting down new paths.

This is the story of a miracle.

Acknowledgments

Even before I worked in publishing, I would always start a book by flipping through to the last page—not to take a peek at the ending (never!), but to read the acknowledgments first. I was curious about whom an author would thank, and how they would do so. Because a book is never born from just one person. It is shaped by so many hands—before, while, after the actual writing takes place. And now, better than ever, I appreciate just how true that really is. I am *incredibly* blessed to be surrounded by so much love, so much inspiration, and so much talent every single day of my life.

Jill Grinberg—my agent, my boss, my guide, my friend. I am eternally grateful that my path brought me to you and to JGLM. Thank you for believing in me as a writer and as an agent—and for always encouraging me to be both. Signing with you and your brilliant arsenal of authors was the day I first considered myself to be a *writer*.

Katelyn Detweiler

Cheryl Pientka—my cheerleader from day one, there's no one else I'd rather have championing my baby all around the globe. Thank you for the endless pep talks and the endless insights. I am so glad that you're always just a shout across the office away.

Leila Sales—I feel tremendously lucky to have not just an exceptionally talented editor at my side, but an exceptionally talented writer to boot. You have a way of talking to the voices inside my head and making much more sense of them than I ever could. Thank you for being my Book Whisperer, and for making *Immaculate* everything that it is today. So glad we got that coffee.

To the entire Viking team—I am honored to be a part of your list. Thank you to each and every one of you for working your special magic. I know how much time and energy and passion goes into every single book, and I respect and value your efforts beyond measure.

Leslie York and Sarah Barley, my publishing wing girls—your wise words and your cheers from the sidelines helped transform a questionable rough draft into a living, breathing, viable creation. I will always be supremely grateful for your role in crafting Mina's story.

Thank you to my OB/GYN experts, Dr. Anne d'Avenas and Dr. Molly McStravick, for making sure that I kept as much fact in the fiction as possible.

Thank you to the authors whom I'm lucky enough to

work with firsthand—you motivate me every day to be a better writer.

Thank you to the amazing teachers along the way who convinced me that making a career out of reading and writing wasn't just a silly pipe dream, and that I only had to keep reaching. Mr. Leskusky, Mr. Quatrani, Mr. McCaig—you made all the difference.

Thank you to Laura, Ashleigh, and Therese, my beautiful roommates who read and reread and let me hole away on Friday nights and sunny Saturdays. Thank you for keeping me sane—for being my home and my family in this crazy, magical city.

So many, many thanks to my childhood muses, my Hannahs and my Izzies, my lifelines who will always tie my heart back to Hoppenville. Melissa, Sarah and Amy, Kathy, Jenny, Betty, Christine Ellen, Mindy. You are part of my forever story. And thank you as well to the rest of my amazing early readers—Rob, Prinky, Rachel, Katie, Charlie. You are all the best friends and the best fans a girl could ask for.

Thank you to my family—the full clan of Detweilers and Noels—for encouraging my nuttiness over the years, and for always making me feel loved and supported (even during the more obnoxious phases). You are the ground beneath my feet.

Thank you to my dearest big brother Peter—I may

have scrapped Mina's brother from the story, but you are still here, on every single page. You are the co-author of my childhood. And Lauren—I feel lucky every day that life handed me a sister like you. (Your vast and inimitable expertise of YA is just a bonus, of course.)

Dad and Mom—it's impossible to adequately express my appreciation when it comes to you two. There is such a never-ending flow of gratitude for the hope, reason, and inspiration you gift me with each and every day. Thank you, Denny, for always reminding me that it's not what happens to us in life, but how we deal with what happens. Because this book is all about "dealing" with a quite unexpected happening, and how someone—how Mina—becomes better and braver because of that ultimate test of character. And Carebear, thank you for that moment all of those years ago, when I turned to you in the old van and asked yet another of my many obnoxious hypothetical questions to fill the time: *Would you believe me if I said I was a pregnant virgin?* You looked at me and smiled—and then you said *yes*. Your answer made me realize that this story was possible, that there is so much trust and hope and faith in this world, if we could only just keep our hearts and minds open wide.

Thank you, lastly, to all of the readers. To everyone who gives this story a chance, who pushes themselves to

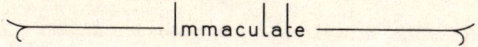

wonder—and maybe even believe—outside of the black and white lines. Thank you to those who dare to venture into the gray.

Thank you, because truly, you are *my* miracle.

Peter and Lauren Detweiler

Katelyn Detweiler (www.katelyndetweiler.com) was born and raised in Pennsylvania—in a small town much like Mina's—living in a lovely centuries-old farmhouse surrounded by fields and woods. After graduating from Penn State University, she made the move to New York City, where she is a literary agent representing books for all ages and across all genres. Katelyn currently lives, works, and writes in Brooklyn. Follow her @katedetweiler.